JOSEPH CONRAD lived a life that was as fantastic as any of his fiction. Born in Poland, December 3, 1857, he died in England on August 3, 1924. This native of an inland country spent his youth at sea, and although relatively ignorant of the English language until the age of twenty, he ultimately became one of the greatest of English novelists and stylists. Conrad's parents were aristocrats, ardent patriots who died when he was a child as a result of their revolutionary activities. He went to sea at sixteen, taught himself English, and after diligent study, gradually worked his way up until he passed his master's examination and was given command of merchant ships in the Orient and on the Congo. At the age of thirty-two he decided to try his hand at writing, left the sea, married and became the father of two sons. Although his work won the admiration of critics, sales were small, and debts and poor health plagued Conrad for many years. He was a nervous, introverted, gloomy man, for whom writing was an agony, but he was rich in friends who appreciated his genius, among them Henry James, Stephen Crane and Ford Madox Ford. Although the ocean and the mysterious lands that border it are the settings for his books, the truth of human experience is his theme, depicted with vigor, rhythm and passionate contemplation of reality. Among his most famous works are: *Heart of Darkness, Lord Jim, Nostromo,* and *The Secret Agent* (all available in Signet Classic editions).

CHANCE

by Joseph Conrad

With an Introduction by Alfred Kazin

A SIGNET CLASSIC

TO
SIR HUGH CLIFFORD, K.C.M.G.
WHOSE STEADFAST FRIENDSHIP
IS RESPONSIBLE FOR THE
EXISTENCE OF THESE PAGES

SIGNET CLASSIC
Published by the Penguin Group
Penguin Books USA Inc., 375 Hudson Street,
New York, New York 10014, U.S.A.
Penguin Books Ltd, 27 Wrights Lane,
London W8 5TZ, England
Penguin Books Australia Ltd, Ringwood,
Victoria, Australia
Penguin Books Canada Ltd, 10 Alcorn Avenue,
Toronto, Ontario, Canada M4V 3B2
Penguin Books (N.Z.) Ltd, 182–190 Wairau Road,
Auckland 10, New Zealand

Penguin Books Ltd, Registered Offices:
Harmondsworth, Middlesex, England

Published by Signet Classic, an imprint of New American Library,
a division of Penguin Books USA Inc.

First Signet Classic Printing, March, 1992
10 9 8 7 6 5 4 3 2 1

Introduction copyright © Alfred Kazin, 1992
All rights reserved

 REGISTERED TRADEMARK—MARCA REGISTRADA

Library of Congress Catalog Card Number: 91–66247

Printed in the United States of America

BOOKS ARE AVAILABLE AT QUANTITY DISCOUNTS WHEN USED TO PRO-
MOTE PRODUCTS OR SERVICES. FOR INFORMATION PLEASE WRITE TO
PREMIUM MARKETING DIVISION, PENGUIN BOOKS USA INC., 375 HUDSON
STREET, NEW YORK, NEW YORK 10014.

Contents

Part II. The Knight

Introduction to Chance

In 1914, the celebrated novelist and always busy critic Henry James, discussing some new novels in the *Times Literary Supplement*, had some astonished things to say about *Chance*, the latest production of his friend Joseph Conrad. Since the novel was an unexpected commercial success, something the older man had not experienced for years, James could not restrain himself from peevishly noting that "we are in the presence of something really of the strangest, a general and diffused lapse of authenticity which an inordinate number of readers . . . have not only condoned but have emphatically commended."

James seemed more than a little stumped by the most obvious technical feature of the book: the fact that it is "told" by one narrator after another, with all of them being quoted by some chief narrator, "I," who remains anonymous. And all this to tell the story of the swindler de Barral, who goes to jail abandoning his daughter to a succession of predatory people: the Fynes who take her in; the sea captain, Anthony, who persuades her to elope; and the mate, Powell, who gives us information lacking to the dominant narrator, Marlow. With so many leads, sooner or later we get to know everything. Nothing is finally withheld, but it takes some time to get the whole picture. The story is constantly rewoven rather than merely added to in order to give us the full effect of what part "chance" plays in human affairs.

Chance lives up to its title philosophically, in addition to being a story of the unexpected things in life that come together fortuitously, magically—sooner or later—to create harmony where none was expected. Conrad employed so many narrators because all his experience had convinced him that this is a world where anything can happen. Where all to the solitary sailor is silence and blackness, as on a vast sea at night, a single human being telling his story and passing it on to another is the only constant in human affairs we can hold on to and depend on.

Conrad had an exile's bitter self-dependence in a treacherous world. As everybody knows, he was a Pole, born in 1857 in territory under Russian rule. His real name was Jósef Teodor Konrad Nalecz Korzeniowski. He lost both parents in the struggle for Polish independence. After many adventures, he entered the British merchant service as an ordinary seaman, eventually attaining a master's certificate and British citizenship. He left the sea in 1894, and published his first novel, *Almayer's Folly*, in 1895. Long before his death in 1924, Conrad was recognized not only as one of the great English novelists, but as a uniquely adventurous, independent, and resolute mind, who by an amazing act of will had incorporated his arduous life experience into a language and literature not his own.

Why did Conrad choose so complex a narrative scheme for *Chance*—one voice within another relaying the story, with the principal voice belonging to the retired mariner Marlow? Conrad, one of the inventors of the twentieth-century novel, understood that a narrative need not pretend to tell itself, that it could be rooted directly in individual consciousness, as life itself is. After all, every story in life is told by someone in particular, and is modified, enlarged, transformed by another. So here the story keeps shifting under the pressure of different narrators. Each new voice imparts a new tone and depth of experience to the story—becomes a character itself.

All this gives an effect to the novel of perspective on perspective, of anything-may-happen-here. *Chance* is not one of those tight, minimalist, austerely stylized works of fiction in which you are aware of the writer's dominating wish to create something faultless in every line. The book certainly wanders a lot, and is of course meant to repeat itself with each new "provider" adding to the story. But one should not assume that Conrad rigged all this up to show what a clever innovator he could be. The Conrad scholar Frederick R. Karl has written that Conrad felt "all stories had already been told, and what remained to the serious writer was the freshness of his vision, not the novelty of his material." No novelist thinks all the stories have been told, for what he always starts from is his own story as a base from which to observe the world.

So one must regard *Chance* as fundamentally a story of the distance and silence between people, the ambiguity at the heart of the simplest event, the endless knots and tangles that have to be cleared up. We live, Conrad seems to be saying, in a world as inscrutable, infinite, and measureless as the sea, a world in which people turn up suddenly, meet, and disappear as quickly—without any overmastering reason. So the task of the storyteller in this strange drama under heaven is to make definite marks, to get as close to the situation as possible by the intensity of his vision. The key to Conrad's art is not just the multiple perspectives created by one narrator after another, but the focusing on anything immediate to the sight. Conrad is one of the most intensely visual writers who ever lived. When he gets hold of a scene, even the merest item to be described, he seems to stare and stare it into being. The effect is hypnotic.

The pace of *Chance* is leisurely to a fault, but the plot is actually very tight. It is only when we get to the end of the book that we realize why it began with Powell and his accidentally becoming second mate on the *Ferndale*. At the end, it is Powell on shipboard who discovers that the swindler de Barral,—who has just been released from prison and has been given every possible help and comfort by his son-in-law, Anthony, the ship's master—is trying to poison Anthony. De Barral does not want anyone to supplant him in his relation with his daughter, Flora, not even the chivalrous captain. Captain Anthony has proved to be the one selfless friend the "waif" Flora has had since she was fifteen, when her insanely self-centered father was imprisoned after creating a national scandal by swindling thousands of people.

De Barral is the kind of character, as mysterious to himself as he is to everyone else, that only a master novelist can devise—and handle. Although his financial schemes prove him to be a swindler on a grand scale, he can never realize that he has done anything wrong and is always whining for "more time" to set things right.

Never does he seem to grasp the situation in which he has left his daughter. Flora, alone and defenseless, becomes dangerously depressed. She is open to every kind of "protection" and exploitation. Frederick Karl has rightly suggested that in Flora's situation, Conrad was reliving the painful solitude of his early life. As exile, as sailor, Conrad came to know the deepest solitude. Solitude is such a central feature of Conrad's makeup, his innate sense of things, that one can see why he was drawn to the story of Flora. In the end, Flora turns out to be less passive and hopeless than she has been up to her marriage. It is her abjectness for the greater part of the novel that enables Conrad to surround her with people who are out to use her.

Conrad calls Flora a "damsel" waiting, as in a fairy tale or medieval chronicle, for a "knight" to deliver her. There is nothing romantic about the schemes different people have for remaking or possessing or cheating her. Early on, there is a governess who discovers that Flora has none of the vast sums she might have expected from her father and abandons her after brutally abusing her for being penniless. There is a totally philistine relative who grudgingly takes Flora in, is indifferent to the humiliation she suffers in his household, and is always pompously ready to take her back after she repeatedly escapes. There is a horrid experience in Germany. Poor Flora! But her most decisive experience is with the Fynes, a married couple whose designs on her are subtler than those of the others because they are so excessively "protective."

We get to see the Fynes in greater detail than other characters because of the closeness with which they are portrayed for us by the principal "inside" narrator, Marlow. Marlow is someone we know from *Lord Jim, Youth,* and *Heart of Darkness.* He is someone we do not so much see as hear as he leans back in company with his pipe and a glass, talking, talking, commenting, putting everything in place from the point of view of a sardonically reflective mariner who seems to have retired not only from the sea but from the usual pieties and conventions. Who is Marlow, what is he, that Conrad allows him such free range to say what he thinks about *anything?* You might call him Conrad's secret agent, the voice of pure intelligence without human ties. When

Freud said that the intelligence is weak but persistent, he could have been thinking of Marlow, who is always around, misses nothing and, understandably, compares himself to a bird perched in a tree.

The Fynes have taken the desperately unhappy Flora into their country cottage. Flora, dazedly walking about with her dog one morning, stops at the edge of a quarry as if making up her mind to throw herself in. Marlow fortunately sees her, and intervenes, only to have her say, "I don't see why I shouldn't be as reckless as I please." If this scene had been written in the style of the "omniscient author," giving us the story as if no one was on the spot but the invisible author, we would miss the complex consideration Marlow gives to Flora's possibly intended suicide. In fact, Flora kept herself from jumping because she was afraid the dog would jump with her. But Marlow, studying the girl in this breathless moment, urges playfully "the distress of the poor Fynes in case of accident, if nothing else." There would be a coroner's inquest; people would think that "unhappy love" had driven her to suicide. "She retorted that, once one was dead, what horrid people thought of one did not matter. It was said with infinite contempt; but something like a suppressed quaver in the voice made me look at her again . . . She looked unhappy. And—I don't know how to say it—well—it suited her."

Marlow, who cheerfully admits to being suspicious of women (God knows where the old sailor learned to know any), makes us see Mrs. Fyne as something more than the anxious protectress of Flora. Her husband is a civil servant of such rigid and dutiful instincts that his subservience to his wife, his immovable solemnity of manner, all laughable to Marlow, suggests the tyranny of her real nature. Her positive confinement of Flora even gives us a hint—we don't have to accept this from a misogynist!— that Mrs. Fyne's vociferous feminism may conceal sexual designs on "poor" Flora.

Imagine her outrage, then, when her very own brother, Captain Anthony, down on a visit, manages in the briefest time to persuade Flora to elope. This is pure comedy, for Mrs. Fyne does not quickly understand, as we do, that on Flora's part this is not a love match, but her only way of providing for her father on his imminent release from prison. She is an unhappy "damsel" all right, and the "knight" who has fortuitously appeared on the scene cares for her as a "knight" should. But Flora, bound to the father who has nearly wrecked her young life, cares only about getting de Barral onto her husband's ship.

Poor Captain Anthony, respectful of his wife's complicated feelings, nobly gives up his conjugal rights. This does not exactly please his wife, who is used to being rejected. Fortunately, de Barral brings things to a head by trying to poison Captain Anthony, so desperate is he still to possess his daughter exclusively. It is the young second mate, Powell, who discovers this attempt. In the end, as things turn out by chance, it is Powell who may be nearest to Flora's heart. The book ends, as it began, in a fairly indeterminate manner. All things are possible, but Flora has certainly come to the end of her ordeal.

Henry James said that *Chance* "places Mr. Conrad alone as the votary of the way to do a thing that shall make it undergo most doing." This has become the most famous thing ever said about the book, and is funny enough when you think of how much "doing" James gave to his late productions, even to the hopelessly involved style in which he expressed his impatience with this novel. In fact, *Chance* is more relaxed, and in many ways more cheerful and ironic than James's own work.

Conrad was not at his most concentrated here; he seems to have been casting about in many directions, reusing remembrances and episodes from books he had let go. In the end, *Chance* is many things at once—and even genial in a temper new to a writer who as a matter of course always saw the terror in human affairs, the sense of being forever on the edge of life. In the end, I confess, the book means less to me than Conrad himself—Conrad's eye, Conrad's attentiveness to the very look of things, the hungry grasp that made him say in the famous preface to *The Nigger Of The Narcissus:* "My task which I am trying to achieve is, by the power of the written word, to make you hear, to make you feel—it is, above all, to make you *see!* That—and no more—and it is everything! If I succeed, you shall find there . . . perhaps, also that glimpse of truth for which you have forgotten to ask."

—Alfred Kazin

Part I

THE DAMSEL

Those that hold that all things are governed by Fortune had not erred, had they not persisted there.
—Sir Thomas Browne

CHAPTER ONE

Young Powell and His Chance

I believe he had seen us out of the window coming off to dine in the dinghy of a fourteen-ton yawl belonging to Marlow, my host and skipper. We helped the boy we had with us to haul the boat up on the landing-stage before we went up to the river-side inn, where we found our new acquaintance eating his dinner in dignified loneliness at the head of a long table, white and inhospitable like a snow bank.

The red tint of his clear-cut face with trim short black whiskers under a cap of curly iron-grey hair was the only warm spot in the dinginess of that room cooled by the cheerless tablecloth. We knew him already by sight as the owner of a little five-ton cutter, which he sailed alone apparently, a fellow yachtsman in the unpretending band of fanatics who cruise at the mouth of the Thames. But the first time he addressed the waiter sharply as "steward" we knew him at once for a sailor as well as a yachtsman.

Presently he had occasion to reprove that same waiter for the slovenly manner in which the dinner was served. He did it with considerable energy and then turned to us.

"If we at sea," he declared, "went about our work as people ashore high and low go about theirs we should never make a living. No one would employ us. And moreover no ship navigated and sailed in the happy-go-lucky manner people conduct their business on shore would ever arrive into port."

Since he had retired from the sea he had been astonished to discover that the educated people were not much better than the others. No one seemed to take any proper pride in his work: from plumbers who were simply thieves to, say, newspaper men (he seemed to think them a specially intellectual class) who never by any chance gave a correct version of the simplest affair. This universal inefficiency of what he called "the shore gang" he ascribed in general to the want of responsibility and to a sense of security.

"They see," he went on, "that no matter what they do this tight little island won't turn turtle with them or spring a leak and go to the bottom with their wives and children."

From this point the conversation took a special turn relating exclusively to sea-life. On that subject he got quickly in touch with Marlow who in his time had followed the sea. They kept up a lively exchange of reminiscences while I listened. They agreed that the happiest time in their lives was as youngsters in good ships with no care in the world but not to lose a watch below when at sea and not a moment's time in going ashore after work hours when in harbour. They agreed also as to the proudest moment they had known in that calling which is never embraced on rational and practical grounds, because of the glamour of its romantic associations. It was the moment when they had passed successfully their first examination and left the seamanship Examiner with the little precious slip of blue paper in their hands.

"That day I wouldn't have called the Queen my cousin," declared our new acquaintance enthusiastically.

At that time the Marine Board examinations took place at the St. Katherine's Dock House on Tower Hill and he informed us that he had a special affection for the view of that historic locality, with the Gardens to the left, the front of the Mint to the right, the miserable tumble-down little houses farther away, a cabstand, boot-blacks squatting on the edge of the pavement and a pair of big policemen gazing with an air of superiority at the doors of the Black Horse public-house across the road. This was the part of the world, he said, his eyes first took notice of, on the finest day of his life. He had emerged from the main entrance of St. Katherine's Dock House a full-fledged second mate after the hottest time of his life with Captain R——, the most dreaded of the three seamanship Examiners who at the time were responsible for the merchant service officers qualifying in the Port of London.

"We all who were preparing to pass," he said, "used to shake in our shoes at the idea of going before him. He kept me for an hour and a half in the torture chamber and behaved as though he hated me. He kept his eyes shaded with one of his hands. Suddenly he let it drop saying, 'You will do!' Before I realized what he meant he was pushing the blue slip across the table. I jumped up as if my chair had caught fire.

" 'Thank you, sir,' says I, grabbing the paper.

" 'Good morning, good luck to you,' he growls at me.

"The old doorkeeper fussed out of the cloak-room with my hat. They always do. But he looked very hard at me before he ventured to ask in a sort of timid whisper: 'Got through all right, sir?' For all answer I dropped a half-crown into his soft broad palm. 'Well,' says he with a sudden grin from ear to ear, 'I never knew him keep any of you gentlemen so long. He failed two second mates this morning before your turn came. Less than twenty minutes each: that's about his usual time.'

"I found myself downstairs without being aware of the steps as if I had floated down the staircase. The finest day in my life. The day you get your first command is nothing to it. For one thing a man is not so young then and for another with us, you know, there is nothing much more to expect. Yes, the finest day of one's life, no doubt, but then it is just a day and no more. What comes after is about the most unpleasant time for a youngster, the trying to get an officer's berth with nothing much to show but a brand-new certificate. It is surprising how useless you find that piece of ass's skin that you have been putting yourself in such a state about. It didn't strike me at the time that a Board of Trade certificate

does not make an officer, not by a long, long way. But
the skippers of the ships I was haunting with demands
for a job knew that very well. I don't wonder at them
now, and I don't blame them either. But this 'trying to
get a ship' is pretty hard on a youngster all the
same. . . ."

He went on then to tell us how tired he was and how
discouraged by this lesson of disillusion following swiftly
upon the finest day of his life. He told us how he went
the round of all the ship-owners' offices in the City where
some junior clerk would furnish him with printed forms
of application which he took home to fill up in the evening. He used to run out just before midnight to post
them in the nearest pillar-box. And that was all that ever
came of it. In his own words: he might just as well have
dropped them all properly addressed and stamped into
the sewer grating.

Then one day, as he was wending his weary way to
the docks, he met a friend and former shipmate a little
older than himself outside the Fenchurch Street Railway
Station.

He craved for sympathy but his friend had just "got a
ship" that very morning and was hurrying home in a state
of outward joy and inward uneasiness usual to a sailor
who after many days of waiting suddenly gets a berth.
This friend had the time to condole with him but briefly.
He must be moving. Then as he was running off, over
his shoulder as it were, he suggested: "Why don't you
go and speak to Mr. Powell in the Shipping Office?" Our
friend objected that he did not know Mr. Powell from
Adam. And the other already pretty near round the corner shouted back advice: "Go to the private door of the
Shipping Office and walk right up to him. His desk is by
the window. Go up boldly and say I sent you."

Our new acquaintance looking from one to the other
of us declared: "Upon my word, I had grown so desperate that I'd have gone boldly up to the devil himself on
the mere hint that he had a second mate's job to give
away."

It was at this point that interrupting his flow of talk to
light his pipe but holding us with his eye he inquired
whether we had known Powell. Marlow with a slight rem-

iniscent smile murmured that he "remembered him very well."

Then there was a pause. Our new acquaintance had become involved in a vexatious difficulty with his pipe which had suddenly betrayed his trust and disappointed his anticipation of self-indulgence. To keep the ball rolling I asked Marlow if this Powell was remarkable in any way.

"He was not exactly remarkable," Marlow answered with his usual nonchalance. "In a general way it's very difficult for one to become remarkable. People won't take sufficient notice of one, don't you know. I remember Powell so well simply because as one of the Shipping Masters in the Port of London he dispatched me to sea on several long stages of my sailor's pilgrimage. He resembled Socrates. I mean he resembled him genuinely: that is in the face. A philosophical mind is but an accident. He reproduced exactly the familiar bust of the immortal sage, if you will imagine the bust with a high top hat riding far on the back of the head and a black coat over the shoulders. As I never saw him except from the other side of the long official counter bearing the five writing-desks of the five Shipping Masters, Mr. Powell has remained a bust to me."

Our new acquaintance advanced now from the mantelpiece with his pipe in good working order.

"What was the most remarkable about Powell," he enunciated dogmatically with his head in a cloud of smoke, "is that he should have had just that name. You see, my name happens to be Powell too."

It was clear that this intelligence was not imparted to us for social purposes. It required no acknowledgment. We continued to gaze at him with expectant eyes.

He gave himself up to the vigorous enjoyment of his pipe for a silent minute or two. Then picking up the thread of his story he told us how he had started hot foot for Tower Hill. He had not been that way since the day of his examination—the finest day of his life—the day of his overweening pride. It was very different now. He would not have called the Queen his cousin, still, but this time it was from a sense of profound abasement. He didn't think himself good enough for anybody's kinship. He envied the purple-nosed old cab-drivers on the stand,

the boot-black boys at the edge of the pavement, the two
large bobbies pacing slowly along the Tower Gardens
railings in the consciousness of their infallible might, and
the bright scarlet sentries walking smartly to and fro
before the Mint. He envied them their places in the
scheme of world's labour. And he envied also the miserable, sallow, thin-faced loafers blinking their obscene eyes
and rubbing their greasy shoulders against the doorjambs
of the Black Horse pub, because they were too far gone
to feel their degradation.

I must render the man the justice that he conveyed
very well to us the sense of his youthful hopelessness
surprised at not finding its place in the sun and no recognition of its right to live.

He went up the outer steps of St. Katherine's Dock
House, the very steps from which he had some six weeks
before surveyed the cabstand, the buildings, the policemen, the boot-blacks, the paint, gilt, and plateglass of
the Black Horse, with the eye of a Conqueror. At the
time he had been at the bottom of his heart surprised
that all this had not greeted him with songs and incense,
but now (he made no secret of it) he made his entry in
a slinking fashion past the doorkeeper's glass box. "I
hadn't any half-crowns to spare for tips," he remarked
grimly. The man, however, ran out after him asking:
"What do you require?" but with a grateful glance up at
the first floor in remembrance of Captain R——'s examination room (how easy and delightful all that had been)
he bolted down a flight leading to the basement and
found himself in a place of dusk and mystery and many
doors. He had been afraid of being stopped by some rule
of no admittance. However he was not pursued.

The basement of St. Katherine's Dock House is vast
in extent and confusing in its plan. Pale shafts of light
slant from above into the gloom of its chilly passages.
Powell wandered up and down there like an early Christian refugee in the catacombs; but what little faith he
had in the success of his enterprise was oozing out at his
finger-tips. At a dark turn under a gas bracket whose
flame was half turned down his self-confidence abandoned him altogether.

"I stood there to think a little," he said. "A foolish
thing to do because of course I got scared. What could

you expect? It takes some nerve to tackle a stranger with a request for a favour. I wished my namesake Powell had been the devil himself. I felt somehow it would have been an easier job. You see, I never believed in the devil enough to be scared of him; but a man can make himself very unpleasant. I looked at a lot of doors, all shut tight, with a growing conviction that I would never have the pluck to open one of them. Thinking's no good for one's nerve. I concluded I would give up the whole business. But I didn't give up in the end, and I'll tell you what stopped me. It was the recollection of that confounded doorkeeper who had called after me. I felt sure the fellow would be on the look out at the head of the stairs. If he asked me what I had been after, as he had the right to do, I wouldn't know what to answer that wouldn't make me look silly if no worse. I got very hot. There was no chance of slinking out of this business.

"I had lost my bearings somehow down there. Of the many doors of various sizes, right and left, a good few had glazed lights above; some, however, must have led merely into lumber rooms or such like, because when I brought myself to try one or two I was disconcerted to find that they were locked. I stood there irresolute and uneasy like a baffled thief. The confounded basement was as still as a grave and I became aware of my heart-beats. Very uncomfortable sensation. Never happened to me before or since. A bigger door to the left of me, with a large brass handle, looked as if it might lead into the Shipping Office. I tried it, setting my teeth. 'Here goes!'

"It came open quite easily. And lo! the place it opened into was hardly any bigger than a cupboard. Anyhow it wasn't more than ten feet by twelve; and as I in a way expected to see the big shadowy cellar-like extent of the Shipping Office where I had been once or twice before, I was extremely startled. A gas bracket hung from the middle of the ceiling over a dark, shabby writing-desk covered with a litter of yellowish dusty documents. Under the flame of the single burner which made the place ablaze with light, a plump, little man was writing hard, his nose very near the desk. His head was perfectly bald and about the same drab tint as the papers. He appeared pretty dusty too.

"I didn't notice whether there were any cobwebs on

him, but I shouldn't wonder if there were because he looked as though he had been imprisoned for years in that little hole. The way he dropped his pen and sat blinking my way upset me very much. And his dungeon was hot and musty; it smelt of gas and mushrooms, and seemed to be somewhere 120 feet below the ground. Solid, heavy stacks of paper filled all the corners halfway up to the ceiling. And when the thought flashed upon me that these were the premises of the Marine Board and that this fellow must be connected in some way with ships and sailors and the sea, my astonishment took my breath away. One couldn't imagine why the Marine Board should keep that bald, fat creature slaving down there. For some reason or other I felt sorry and ashamed to have found him out in his wretched captivity. I asked gently and sorrowfully: 'The Shipping Office, please.'

"He piped up in a contemptuous squeaky voice which made me start: 'Not here. Try the passage on the other side. Street side. This is the Dock side. You've lost your way . . .'

"He spoke in such a spiteful tone that I thought he was going to round off with the words: 'You fool' . . . and perhaps he meant to. But what he finished sharply with was: 'Shut the door quietly after you.'

"And I did shut it quietly—you bet. Quick and quiet. The indomitable spirit of that chap impressed me. I wonder sometimes whether he has succeeded in writing himself into liberty and a pension at last, or had to go out of his gas-lighted grave straight into that other dark one where nobody would want to intrude. My humanity was pleased to discover he had so much kick left in him, but I was not comforted in the least. It occurred to me that if Mr. Powell had the same sort of temper. . . . However, I didn't give myself time to think and scuttled across the space at the foot of the stairs into the passage where I'd been told to try. And I tried the first door I came to, right away, without any hanging back, because coming loudly from the hall above an amazed and scandalized voice wanted to know what sort of game I was up to down there. 'Don't you know there's no admittance that way?' it roared. But if there was anything more I shut it out of my hearing by means of a door marked *Private* on the outside. It let me into a six-feet-wide strip between a long counter and the wall, taken off a spacious, vaulted room with a grated window and a glazed door giving daylight to the farther end. The first thing I saw right in front of me were three middle-aged men having a sort of romp together round about another fellow with a thin, long neck and sloping shoulders who stood up at a desk writing on a large sheet of paper and taking no notice except that he grinned quietly to himself. They turned very sour at once when they saw me. I heard one of them mutter: 'Hullo! What have we here?'

" 'I want to see Mr. Powell, please,' I said, very civil but firm; I would let nothing scare me away now. This was the Shipping Office right enough. It was after 3 o'clock and the business seemed over for the day with them. The long-necked fellow went on with his writing steadily. I observed that he was no longer grinning. The three others tossed their heads all together towards the far end of the room where a fifth man had been looking on at their antics from a high stool. I walked up to him boldly as if he had been the devil himself. With one foot raised up and resting on the cross-bar of his seat he never stopped swinging the other which was well clear of the stone floor. He had unbuttoned the top of his waistcoat and he wore his tall hat very far at the back of his head. He had a full unwrinkled face and such clear-shining eyes that his grey beard looked quite false on him, stuck on for a disguise. You said just now he resembled Socrates—didn't you? I don't know about that. This Socrates was a wise man, I believe?"

"He was," assented Marlow. "And a true friend of youth. He lectured them in a peculiarly exasperating manner. It was a way he had."

"Then give me Powell every time," declared our new acquaintance sturdily. "He didn't lecture me in any way. Not he. He said: 'How do you do?' quite kindly to my mumble. Then says he looking very hard at me: 'I don't think I know you—do I?'

" 'No, sir,' I said, and down went my heart sliding into my boots, just as the time had come to summon up all my cheek. There's nothing meaner in the world than a piece of impudence that isn't carried off well. For fear of appearing shamefaced I started about it so free and easy as almost to frighten myself. He listened for a while looking at my face with surprise and curiosity and then held up his hand. I was glad enough to shut up, I can tell you.

" 'Well, you are a cool hand,' says he. 'And that friend of yours too. He pestered me coming here every day for a fortnight till a captain I'm acquainted with was good enough to give him a berth. And no sooner he's provided for than he turns you on. You youngsters don't seem to mind whom you get into trouble.'

"It was my turn now to stare with surprise and curiosity. He hadn't been talking loud, but he lowered his voice still more.

" 'Don't you know it's illegal?'

"I wondered what he was driving at till I remembered that procuring a berth for a sailor is a penal offence under the Act. That clause was directed of course against the swindling practices of the boarding-house crimps. It had never struck me it would apply to everybody alike no matter what the motive, because I believed then that people on shore did their work with care and foresight.

"I was confounded at the idea, but Mr. Powell made me soon see that an Act of Parliament hasn't any sense of its own. It has only the sense that's put into it; and that's precious little sometimes. He didn't mind helping a young man to a ship now and then, he said, but if we kept on coming constantly it would soon get about that he was doing it for money.

" 'A pretty thing that would be: the Senior Shipping Master of the Port of London hauled up in a police court and fined fifty pounds,' says he. 'I've another four years to serve to get my pension. It could be made to look very black against me and don't you make any mistake about it,' he says.

"And all the time with one knee well up he went on swinging his other leg like a boy on a gate and looking at me very straight with his shining eyes. I was confounded I tell you. It made me sick to hear him imply that somebody would make a report against him.

" 'Oh!' I asked shocked, 'who would think of such a scurvy trick, sir?' I was half disgusted with him for having the mere notion of it.

" 'Who?' says he, speaking very low. 'Anybody. One of the office messengers maybe. I've risen to be the

Senior of this office and we are all very good friends here, but don't you think that my colleague that sits next to me wouldn't like to go up to this desk by the window four years in advance of the regulation time? Or even one year for that matter. It's human nature.'

"I could not help turning my head. The three fellows who had been skylarking when I came in were now talking together very soberly, and the long-necked chap was going on with his writing still. He seemed to me the most dangerous of the lot. I saw him sideface and his lips were set very tight. I had never looked at mankind in that light before. When one's young human nature shocks one. But what startled me most was to see the door I had come through open slowly and give passage to a head in a uniform cap with a Board of Trade badge. It was that blamed old doorkeeper from the hall. He had run me to earth and meant to dig me out too. He walked up the office smirking craftily, cap in hand.

" 'What is it, Symons?' asked Mr. Powell.

" 'I was only wondering where this 'ere gentleman 'ad gone to, sir. He slipped past me upstairs, sir.'

"I felt mighty uncomfortable.

" 'That's all right, Symons. I know the gentleman,' says Mr. Powell as serious as a judge.

" 'Very well, sir. Of course, sir. I saw the gentleman running races all by 'isself down 'ere, so I . . .'

" 'It's all right, I tell you,' Mr. Powell cut him short with a wave of his hand; and, as the old fraud walked off at last, he raised his eyes to me. I did not know what to do: stay there, or clear out, or say that I was sorry.

" 'Let's see,' says he, 'what did you tell me your name was?'

"Now, observe, I hadn't given him my name at all and his question embarrassed me a bit. Somehow or other it didn't seem proper for me to fling his own name at him as it were. So I merely pulled out my new certificate from my pocket and put it into his hand unfolded, so that he could read *Charles Powell* written very plain on the parchment.

"He dropped his eyes on to it and after a while laid it quietly on the desk by his side. I didn't know whether he meant to make any remark on this coincidence. Before he had time to say anything the glass door came open with a bang and a tall, active man rushed in with great strides. His face looked very red below his high silk hat. You could see at once he was the skipper of a big ship.

"Mr. Powell, after telling me in an undertone to wait a little, addressed him in a friendly way.

" 'I've been expecting you in every moment to fetch away your Articles, Captain. Here they are all ready for you.' And turning to a pile of agreements lying at his elbow he took up the topmost of them. From where I stood I could read the words: 'Ship *Ferndale*' written in a large round hand on the first page.

" 'No, Mr. Powell, they aren't ready, worse luck,' says that skipper. 'I've got to ask you to strike out my second officer.' He seemed excited and bothered. He explained that his second mate had been working on board all the morning. At one o'clock he went out to get a bit of dinner and didn't turn up at two as he ought to have done. Instead there came a messenger from the hospital with a note signed by a doctor. Collar bone and one arm broken. Let himself be knocked down by a pair horse van while crossing the road outside the dock gate, as if he had neither eyes nor ears. And the ship ready to leave the dock at six o'clock to-morrow morning!

"Mr. Powell dipped his pen and began to turn the leaves of the agreement over. 'We must then take his name off,' he says in a kind of unconcerned sing-song.

" 'What am I to do?' burst out the skipper. 'This office closes at four o'clock. I can't find a man in half an hour.'

" 'This office closes at four,' repeats Mr. Powell glancing up and down the pages and touching up a letter here and there with perfect indifference.

" 'Even if I managed to lay hold some time to-day of a man ready to go at such short notice I couldn't ship him regularly here—could I?'

"Mr. Powell was busy drawing his pen through the entries relating to that unlucky second mate and making a note in the margin.

" 'You could sign him on yourself on board,' says he without looking up. 'But I don't think you'll find easily an officer for such a pier-head jump.'

"Upon this the fine-looking skipper gave signs of distress. The ship mustn't miss the next morning's tide. He had to take on board forty tons of dynamite and a hundred and twenty tons of gunpowder at a place down the river before proceeding to sea. It was all arranged for next day. There would be no end of fuss and complications if the ship didn't turn up in time. . . . I couldn't help hearing all this, while wishing him to take himself off, because I wanted to know why Mr. Powell had told me to wait. After what he had been saying there didn't seem any object in my hanging about. If I had had my certificate in my pocket I would have tried to slip away quietly; but Mr. Powell had turned about into the same position I found him in at first and was again swinging his leg. My certificate open on the desk was under his left elbow and I couldn't very well go up and jerk it away.

" 'I don't know,' says he carelessly, addressing the helpless captain but looking fixedly at me with an expression as if I hadn't been there. 'I don't know whether I ought to tell you that I know of a disengaged second mate at hand.'

" 'Do you mean you've got him here?' shouts the other, looking all over the empty public part of the office as if he were ready to fling himself bodily upon anything resembling a second mate. He had been so full of his difficulty that I verily believe he had never noticed me. Or perhaps seeing me inside he may have thought I was some understrapper belonging to the place. But when Mr. Powell nodded in my direction he became very quiet and gave me a long stare. Then he stooped to Mr. Powell's ear—I suppose he imagined he was whispering, but I heard him well enough.

" 'Looks very respectable.'

" 'Certainly,' says the Shipping Master, quite calm and staring all the time at me. 'His name's Powell.'

" 'Oh, I see!' says the skipper, as if struck all of a heap. 'But is he ready to join at once?'

"I had a sort of vision of my lodgings—in the North of London, too, beyond Dalston, away to the devil— and all my gear scattered about, and my empty sea-chest somewhere in an outhouse the good people I was staying with had at the end of their sooty strip of garden. I heard the Shipping Master say in the coolest sort of way, " 'He'll sleep on board to-night.'

" 'He had better,' says the Captain of the *Ferndale* very businesslike, as if the whole thing were settled. I can't say I was dumb for joy as you may suppose. It wasn't exactly that. I was more by way of being out of breath with the quickness of it. It didn't seem possible that this was happening to me. But the skipper, after he had talked for a while with Mr. Powell, too low for me to hear, became visibly perplexed.

"I suppose he had heard I was freshly passed and without experience as an officer, because he turned about and looked me over as if I had been exposed for sale.

" 'He's young,' he mutters. 'Looks smart, though. . . . You're smart and willing (this to me very sudden and loud) and all that, aren't you?'

"I just managed to open and shut my mouth, no more, being taken unawares. But it was enough for him. He made as if I had deafened him with protestations of my smartness and willingness.

" 'Of course, of course. All right.' And then turning to the Shipping Master who sat there swinging his leg, he said that he certainly couldn't go to sea without a second officer. I stood by as if all these things were happening to some other chap whom I was seeing through with it. Mr. Powell stared at me with those shining eyes of his. But that bothered skipper turns upon me again as though he wanted to snap my head off.

" 'You aren't too big to be told how to do things—are you? You've a lot to learn yet though you mayn't think so.'

"I had half a mind to save my dignity by telling him that if it was my seamanship he was alluding to I wanted him to understand that a fellow who had survived being turned inside out for an hour and a half by Captain R—— was equal to any demand his old ship was likely to make on his competence. However he didn't give me a chance to make that sort of fool of myself, because before I could open my mouth he had gone round on another tack and was addressing himself affably to Mr. Powell, who swinging his leg never took his eyes off me.

" 'I'll take your young friend willingly, Mr. Powell. If you let him sign on as second mate at once I'll take the Articles away with me now.'

"It suddenly dawned upon me that the innocent skipper of the *Ferndale* had taken it for granted that I was a relative of the Shipping Master! I was quite astonished at this discovery, though indeed the mistake was natural enough under the circumstances. What I ought to have admired was the reticence with which this misunderstanding had been established and acted upon. But I was too stupid then to admire anything. All my anxiety was that this should be cleared up. I was ass enough to wonder exceedingly at Mr. Powell failing to notice the misapprehension. I saw a slight twitch come and go on his face; but instead of setting right that mistake the Shipping Master swung round on his stool and addressed me as 'Charles.' He did. And I detected him taking a hasty squint at my certificate just before, because clearly till he did so he was not sure of my Christian name. 'Now then, come round in front of the desk, Charles,' says he in a loud voice.

"Charles! At first, I declare to you, it didn't seem possible that he was addressing himself to me. I even looked round for that Charles, but there was nobody behind me except the thin-necked chap still hard at his writing, and the other three Shipping Masters who were changing their coats and reaching for their hats, making ready to go home. It was the industrious thin-necked man who without laying down his pen lifted with his left hand a flap near his desk and said kindly: 'Pass this way.'

"I walked through in a trance, faced Mr. Powell, from whom I learned that we were bound to Port Elizabeth first, and signed my name on the Articles of the ship *Ferndale* as second mate—the voyage not to exceed two years.

" 'You won't fail to join—eh?' says the captain anxiously. 'It would cause no end of trouble and expense if you did. You've got a good six hours to get your gear together, and then you'll have time to snatch a sleep on board before the crew joins in the morning.'

"It was easy enough for him to talk of getting ready in six hours for a voyage that was not to exceed two years. He hadn't to do that trick himself, and with his sea-chest locked up in an outhouse the key of which had been mislaid for a week as I remembered. But neither was I much concerned. The idea that I was absolutely going to sea at six o'clock next morning hadn't got quite into my head yet. It had been too sudden.

"Mr. Powell, slipping the Articles into a long envelope, spoke up with a sort of cold half-laugh without looking at either of us.

" 'Mind you don't disgrace the name, Charles.'

"And the skipper chimes in very kindly—

" 'He'll do well enough, I dare say. I'll look after him a bit.'

"Upon this he grabs the Articles, says something about trying to run in for a minute to see that poor devil in the hospital, and off he goes with his heavy swinging step after telling me sternly, 'Don't you go like that poor fellow and get yourself run over by a cart as if you hadn't either eyes or ears.'

" 'Mr. Powell,' says I timidly (there was by then only the thin-necked man left in the office with us, and he was already by the door, standing on one leg to turn the bottom of his trousers up before going away). 'Mr. Powell,' says I, 'I believe the captain of the *Ferndale* was thinking all the time that I was a relation of yours.'

"I was rather concerned about the propriety of it, you know, but Mr. Powell didn't seem to be in the least.

" 'Did he?' says he. 'That's funny, because it seems to me too that I've been a sort of good uncle to several of you young fellows lately. Don't you think so yourself? However, if you don't like it you may put him right— when you get out to sea.' At this I felt a bit queer. Mr. Powell had rendered me a very good service:—because it's a fact that with us merchant sailors the first voyage as officer is the real start in life. He had given me no less than that. I told him warmly that he had done more for me that day than all my relations put together ever did.

" 'Oh, no, no,' says he. 'I guess it's that shipment of explosives waiting down the river which has done most for you. Forty tons of dynamite have been your best friend to-day, young man.'

"That was true too, perhaps. Anyway I saw clearly enough that I had nothing to thank myself for. But as I tried to thank him he checked my stammering.

" 'Don't be in a hurry to thank me,' says he. 'The voyage isn't finished yet.' "

Our new acquaintance paused, then added meditatively: "Queer man. As if it made any difference. Queer man."

"It's certainly unwise to admit any sort of responsibility for our actions, whose consequences we are never able to foresee," remarked Marlow by way of assent.

"The consequence of his action was that I got a ship," said the other. "That could not do much harm," he added with a laugh which argued a probably unconscious contempt of general ideas.

But Marlow was not put off. He was patient and reflective. He had been at sea many years, and I verily believe he liked sea-life because upon the whole it is favourable to reflection. I am speaking of the now nearly vanished sea-life under sail. To those who may be surprised at the statement I will point out that this life secured for the mind of him who embraced it the inestimable advantages of solitude and silence. Marlow had the habit of pursuing general ideas in a peculiar manner, between jest and earnest.

"Oh, I wouldn't suggest," he said, "that your namesake, Mr. Powell, the Shipping Master, had done you much harm. Such was hardly his intention. And even if it had been he would not have had the power. He was but a man, and the incapacity to achieve anything distinctly good or evil is inherent in our earthly condition. Mediocrity is our mark. And perhaps it's just as well, since, for the most part, we cannot be certain of the effect of our actions."

"I don't know about the effect," the other stood up to Marlow manfully. "What effect did you expect anyhow? I tell you he did something uncommonly kind."

"He did what he could," Marlow retorted gently, "and on his own showing that was not a very great deal. I cannot help thinking that there was some malice in the way he seized the opportunity to serve you. He managed to make you uncomfortable. You wanted to go to sea, but he jumped at the chance of accommodating your desire with a vengeance. I am inclined to think your cheek alarmed him. And this was an excellent occasion to suppress you altogether. For if you accepted he was relieved of you with every appearance of humanity, and if you made objections (after requesting his assistance, mind you) it was open to him to drop you as a sort of impostor. You might have had to decline that berth for some very valid reason. From sheer necessity perhaps. The notice was too uncommonly short. But under the circumstances you'd have covered yourself with ignominy."

Our new friend knocked the ashes out of his pipe.

"Quite a mistake," he said. "I am not of the declining sort, though I'll admit it was something like telling a man that you would like a bath, and in consequence being instantly knocked overboard to sink or swim with your clothes on. However, I didn't feel as if I were in deep water at first. I left the Shipping Office quietly and for a time strolled along the street as easy as if I had a week before me to fit myself out. But by and by I reflected that the notice was even shorter than it looked. The afternoon was well advanced; I had some things to get, a lot of small matters to attend to, one or two persons to see. One of them was an aunt of mine, my only relation, who quarrelled with poor father as long as he lived about some silly matter that had neither right nor wrong to it. She left her money to me when she died. I used always to go and see her for decency's sake. I had so much to do before night that I didn't know where to begin. I felt inclined to sit down on the kerb and hold my head in my hands. It was as if an engine had been started going under my skull. Finally I sat down in the first cab that came along and it was a hard matter to keep on sitting there, I can tell you, while we rolled up and down the streets, pulling up here and there, the parcels accumulating round me and the engine in my head gathering more way every minute. The composure of the people on the pavements was provoking to a degree, and as to the people in shops, they were benumbed, more than half frozen—imbecile. Funny how it affects you to be in a peculiar state of mind: everybody that does not act up to your excitement seems so confoundedly unfriendly. And my state of mind, what with the hurry, the worry and a growing exultation, was peculiar enough. That engine in my head went round at its top speed hour after hour till at about eleven at night it let up on me suddenly at the entrance to the Dock before large iron gates in a dead wall."

*   *   *

These gates were closed and locked. The cabby, after shooting his things off the roof of his machine into young Powell's arms, drove away, leaving him alone with his sea-chest, a sail cloth bag and a few parcels on the pavement about his feet. It was a dark, narrow thoroughfare, he told us. A mean row of houses on the other side looked empty: there wasn't the smallest gleam of light in them. The white-hot glare of a gin palace a good way off made the intervening piece of the street pitch black. Some human shapes appearing mysteriously, as if they had sprung up from the dark ground, shunned the edge of the faint light thrown down by the gateway lamps. These figures were wary in their movements and perfectly silent of foot, like beasts of prey slinking about a camp fire. Powell gathered up his belongings and hovered over them like a hen over her brood. A gruffly insinuating voice said—

"Let's carry your things in, Capt'in! I've got my pal 'ere."

He was a tall, bony, grey-haired ruffian with a bulldog jaw, in a torn cotton shirt and moleskin trousers. The shadow of his hobnailed boots was enormous and coffinlike. His pal, who didn't come up much higher than his elbow, stepping forward, exhibited a pale face with a long drooping nose and no chin to speak of. He seemed to have just scrambled out of a dust-bin in a tam-o'-shanter cap and a tattered soldier's coat much too long for him. Being so deadly white, he looked like a horrible dirty invalid in a ragged dressing-gown. The coat flapped open in front and the rest of his apparel consisted of one brace which crossed his naked, bony chest, and a pair of trousers. He blinked rapidly as if dazed by the faint light, while his patron, the old bandit, glowered at young Powell from under his beetling brow:

"Say the word, Capt'in. The bobby'll let us in all right. 'E knows both of us."

"I didn't answer him," continued Mr. Powell. "I was listening to footsteps on the other side of the gate, echoing between the walls of the warehouses as if in an uninhabited town of very high buildings dark from basement to roof. You could never have guessed that within a stone's throw there was an open sheet of water and big ships lying afloat. The few gas lamps showing up a bit of brickwork here and there appeared in the blackness like penny dips in a range of cellars—and the solitary footsteps came on, tramp, tramp. A dock policeman strode into the light on the other side of the gate, very broadchested and stern.

" 'Hallo! What's up here?'

"He was really surprised, but after some palaver he let me in together with the two loafers carrying my luggage. He grumbled at them, however, and slammed the gate violently with a loud clang. I was startled to discover how many night prowlers had collected in the darkness of the street in such a short time and without my being aware of it. Directly we were through they came surging against the bars, silent, like a mob of ugly spectres. But suddenly, up the street somewhere, perhaps near that public-house, a row started as if Bedlam had broken loose: shouts, yells, an awful shrill shriek—and at that noise all these heads vanished from behind the bars.

" 'Look at this,' marvelled the constable. 'It's a wonder to me they didn't make off with your things while you were waiting.'

" 'I would have taken good care of that,' I said defiantly. But the constable wasn't impressed.

" 'Much you would have done. The bag going off round one dark corner; the chest round another. Would you have run two ways at once? And anyhow you'd have been tripped up and jumped upon before you had run three yards. I tell you you've had a most extraordinary chance that there wasn't one of them regular boys about to-night, in the High Street, to twig your loaded cab go by. Ted here is honest. . . . You are on the honest lay, Ted, ain't you?'

" 'Always was, orficer,' said the big ruffian with feeling. The other frail creature seemed dumb and only hopped about with the edge of its soldier coat touching the ground.

" 'Oh yes, I dare say,' said the constable. 'Now then, forward, march. . . . He's that because he ain't game for the other thing,' he confided to me. 'He hasn't got the nerve for it. However, I ain't going to lose sight of them two till they go out through the gate. That little chap's a devil. He's got the nerve for anything, only he hasn't got the muscle. Well! Well! You've had a chance to get in with a whole skin and with all your things.'

"I was incredulous a little. It seemed impossible that after getting ready with so much hurry and inconvenience I should have lost my chance of a start in life from such a cause. I asked—

" 'Does that sort of thing happen often so near the dock gates?'

" 'Often! No! Of course not often. But it ain't often either that a man comes along with a cabload of things to join a ship at this time of night. I've been in the dock police thirteen years and haven't seen it done once.'

"Meantime we followed my sea-chest which was being carried down a sort of deep narrow lane, separating two high warehouses, between honest Ted and his little devil of a pal who had to keep up a trot to the other's stride. The skirt of his soldier's coat floating behind him nearly swept the ground so that he seemed to be running on castors. At the corner of the gloomy passage a rigged jib boom with a dolphin-striker ending in an arrow-head stuck out of the night close to a cast-iron lamp-post. It was the quay-side. They set down their load in the light and honest Ted asked hoarsely—

" 'Where's your ship, guv'nor?'

"I didn't know. The constable was interested at my ignorance.

" 'Don't know where your ship is?' he asked with curiosity. 'And you the second officer! Haven't you been working on board of her?'

"I couldn't explain that the only work connected with my appointment was the work of chance. I told him briefly that I didn't know her at all. At this he remarked—

" 'So I see. Here she is, right before you. That's her.'

"At once the head-gear in the gas light inspired me with interest and respect; the spars were big, the chains and ropes stout, and the whole thing looked powerful and trustworthy. Barely touched by the light, her bows rose faintly alongside the narrow strip of the quay; the rest of her was a black smudge in the darkness. Here I was face to face with my start in life. We walked in a body a few steps on a greasy pavement between her side and the towering wall of a warehouse and I hit my shins cruelly against the end of the gangway. The constable

hailed her quietly in a bass undertone, '*Ferndale* there!'
A feeble and dismal sound, something in the nature of
a buzzing groan, answered from behind the bulwarks.

"I distinguished vaguely an irregular round knob, of
wood, perhaps, resting on the rail. It did not move in
the least; but as another broken-down buzz like a still
fainter echo of the first dismal sound proceeded from it
I concluded it must be the head of the shipkeeper. The
stalwart constable jeered in a mock-official manner.

" 'Second officer coming to join. Move yourself a bit.'

"The truth of the statement touched me in the pit of
the stomach (you know that's the spot where emotion
gets home on a man), for it was borne upon me that
really and truly I was nothing but a second officer of a
ship just like any other second officer to that constable.
I was moved by this solid evidence of my new dignity.
Only his tone offended me. Nevertheless I gave him the
tip he was looking for. Thereupon he lost all interest in
me, humorous or otherwise, and walked away driving
sternly before him the honest Ted, who went off grum-
bling to himself like a hungry ogre, and his horrible dumb
little pal in the soldier's coat, who, from first to last,
never emitted the slightest sound.

"It was very dark on the quarter-deck of the *Ferndale*
between the deep bulwarks overshadowed by the break
of the poop and frowned upon by the front of the warehouse. I plumped down on to my chest near the after
hatch as if my legs had been jerked from under me. I felt
suddenly very tired and languid. The shipkeeper, whom I
could hardly make out, hung over the capstan in a fit of
weak, pitiful coughing. He gasped out very low, 'Oh!
dear! Oh! dear!' and struggled for breath so long that I
got up, alarmed and irresolute.

" 'I've been took like this since last Christmas twelve-
month. It ain't nothing.'

"He seemed a hundred years old at least. I never saw
him properly, because he was gone ashore and out of
sight when I came on deck in the morning; but he gave
me the notion of the feeblest creature that ever breathed.
His voice was thin like the buzzing of a mosquito. As it
would have been cruel to demand assistance from such
a shadowy wreck, I went to work myself, dragging my
chest along a pitch-black passage under the poopdeck,

while he sighed and moaned around me as if my exertions were more than his weakness could stand. At last, as I banged pretty heavily against the bulkheads, he warned me in his faint breathless wheeze to be more careful.

" 'What's the matter?' I asked rather roughly, not relishing to be admonished by this forlorn broken-down ghost.

" 'Nothing! Nothing, sir,' he protested so hastily that he lost his poor breath again and I felt sorry for him. 'Only the captain and his missus are sleeping on board. She's a lady that mustn't be disturbed. They came about half-past eight, and we had a permit to have lights in the cabin till ten to-night.'

"This struck me as a considerable piece of news. I had never been in a ship where the captain had his wife with him. I'd heard fellows say that captains' wives could work a lot of mischief on board ship if they happened to take a dislike to any one; especially the new wives if young and pretty. The old and experienced wives, on the other hand, fancied they knew more about the ship than the skipper himself and had an eye like a hawk's for what went on. They were like an extra chief mate of a particularly sharp and unfeeling sort who made his report in the evening. The best of them were a nuisance. In the general opinion a skipper with his wife on board was more difficult to please; but whether to show off his authority before an admiring female, or from loving anxiety for her safety, or simply from irritation at her presence— nobody I ever heard on the subject could tell for certain.

"After I had bundled in my things somehow I struck a match and had a dazzling glimpse of my berth; then I pitched the roll of my bedding into the bunk, but took no trouble to spread it out. I wasn't sleepy now, neither was I tired. And the thought that I was done with the earth for many many months to come made me feel very quiet and self-contained as it were. Sailors will understand what I mean."

Marlow nodded. "It is a strictly professional feeling," he commented. "But other professions or trades know nothing of it. It is only this calling whose primary appeal lies in the suggestion of restless adventure which holds out that deep sensation to those who embrace it. It is difficult to define, I admit."

"I should call it the peace of the sea," said Mr. Charles Powell in an earnest tone, but looking at us as though he expected to be met by a laugh of derision and were half prepared to salve his reputation for common sense by joining in it. But neither of us laughed at Mr. Charles Powell, in whose start in life we had been called to take a part. He was lucky in his audience.

"A very good name," said Marlow looking at him approvingly. "A sailor finds a deep feeling of security in the exercise of his calling. The exacting life of the sea has this advantage over the life of the earth, that its claims are simple and cannot be evaded."

"Gospel truth," assented Mr. Powell. "No! they cannot be evaded."

That an excellent understanding should have established itself between my old friend and our new acquaintance was remarkable enough. For they were exactly dissimilar—one individuality projecting itself in length and the other in breadth, which is already a sufficient ground for irreconcilable difference. Marlow, who was lanky, loose, quietly composed in varied shades of brown, robbed of every vestige of gloss, had a narrow, veiled glance, the neutral bearing and the secret irritability which go together with a predisposition to congestion of the liver. The other compact, broad and sturdy of limb, seemed extremely full of sound organs functioning vigorously all the time in order to keep up the brilliance of his colouring, the light curl of his coal-black hair and the lustre of his eyes, which asserted themselves roundly in an open, manly face. Between two such organisms one would not have expected to find the slightest temperamental accord. But I have observed that profane men living in ships, like the holy men gathered together in monasteries, develop traits of profound resemblance. This must be because the service of the sea and the service of a temple are both detached from the vanities and errors of a world which follows no severe rule. The men of the sea understand each other very well in their view of earthly things, for simplicity is a good counsellor and isolation not a bad educator. A turn of mind composed of innocence and scepticism is common to them all, with the addition of an unexpected insight into motives, as of disinterested lookers-on at a game. Mr. Powell took me aside to say—

"I like the things he says."

"You understand each other pretty well," I observed.

"I know his sort," said Powell, going to the window to look at his cutter still riding to the flood. "He's the sort that's always chasing some notion or other round and round his head just for the fun of the thing."

"Keeps them in good condition," I said.

"Lively enough I dare say," he admitted.

"Would you like better a man who let his notions lie curled up?"

"That I wouldn't," answered our new acquaintance. Clearly he was not difficult to get on with. "I like him, very well," he continued, "though it isn't easy to make him out. He seems to be up to a thing or two. What's he doing?"

I informed him that our friend Marlow had retired from the sea in a sort of half-hearted fashion some years ago.

Mr. Powell's comment was: "Fancied had enough of it?"

"Fancied's the very word to use in this connection," I observed, remembering the subtly provisional character of Marlow's long sojourn amongst us. From year to year he dwelt on land as a bird rests on the branch of a tree, so tense with the power of brusque flight into its true element that it is incomprehensible why it should sit still minute after minute. The sea is the sailor's true element, and Marlow, lingering on shore, was to me an object of incredulous commiseration like a bird, which, secretly, should have lost its faith in the high virtue of flying.

CHAPTER TWO

The Fynes and the Girl-Friend

We were on our feet in the room by then, and Marlow, brown and deliberate, approached the window where Mr. Powell and I had retired.

"What was the name of your chance again?" he asked. Mr. Powell stared for a moment.

"Oh! The *Ferndale*. A Liverpool ship. Composite built."

"*Ferndale*," repeated Marlow thoughtfully. "*Ferndale*."

"Know her?"

"Our friend," I said, "knows something of every ship. He seems to have gone about the seas prying into things considerably."

Marlow smiled.

"I've seen her, at least once."

"The finest sea-boat ever launched," declared Mr. Powell sturdily. "Without exception."

"She looked a stout, comfortable ship," assented Marlow. "Uncommonly comfortable. Not very fast tho'."

"She was fast enough for any reasonable man—when I was in her," growled Mr. Powell with his back to us.

"Any ship is that—for a reasonable man," generalized Marlow in a conciliatory tone. "A sailor isn't a globe-trotter."

"No," muttered Mr. Powell.

"Time's nothing to him," advanced Marlow.

"I don't suppose it's much," said Mr. Powell. "All the same, a quick passage is a feather in a man's cap."

"True. But that ornament is for the use of the master only. And, by the by, what was his name?"

"The master of the *Ferndale*? Anthony. Captain Anthony."

"Just so. Quite right," approved Marlow thoughtfully. Our new acquaintance looked over his shoulder.

"What do you mean? Why is it more right than if it had been Brown?"

"He has known him, probably," I explained. "Marlow here appears to know something of every soul that ever went afloat in a sailor's body."

Mr. Powell seemed wonderfully amenable to verbal suggestions, for looking again out of the window, he muttered: "He was a good soul."

This clearly referred to Captain Anthony of the *Ferndale*. Marlow addressed his protest to me.

"I did not know him. I really didn't. He was a good soul. That's nothing very much out of the way—is it? And I didn't even know that much of him. All I knew of him was an accident called Fyne."

At this Mr. Powell, who evidently could be rebellious, too, turned his back squarely on the window.

"What on earth do you mean?" he asked. "An—accident—called Fyne," he repeated, separating the words with emphasis.

Marlow was not disconcerted.

"I don't mean accident in the sense of a mishap. Not in the least. Fyne was a good little man in the Civil Service. By accident I mean that which happens blindly and without intelligent design. That's generally the way a brother-in-law happens into a man's life."

Marlow's tone being apologetic and our new acquaintance having again turned to the window, I took it upon myself to say—

"You are justified. There is very little intelligent design in the majority of marriages; but they are none the worse for that. Intelligence leads people astray as far as passion sometimes. I know you are not a cynic."

Marlow smiled his retrospective smile, which was kind

as though he bore no grudge against people he used to know.

"Little Fyne's marriage was quite successful. There was no design at all in it. Fyne, you must know, was an enthusiastic pedestrian. He spent his holidays tramping all over our native land. His tastes were simple. He put infinite conviction and perseverance into his holidays. At the proper season you would meet in the fields Fyne, a serious-faced, broad-chested, little man, with a shabby knapsack on his back, making for some church steeple. He had a horror of roads. He wrote once a little book called 'Tramp's Itinerary,' and was recognized as an authority on the footpaths of England. So one year, in his favourite over-the-fields, back-way fashion he entered a pretty Surrey village where he met Miss Anthony. Pure accident, you see. They came to an understanding, across some stile, most likely. Little Fyne held very solemn views as to the destiny of women on this earth, the nature of our sublunary love, the obligations of this transient life, and so on. He probably disclosed them to his future wife. Miss Anthony's views of life were very decided, too, but in a different way. I don't know the story of their wooing. I imagine it was carried on clandestinely and, I am certain, with portentous gravity, at the back of copses, behind hedges. . . ."

"Why was it carried on clandestinely?" I inquired.

"Because of the lady's father. He was a savage sentimentalist who had his own decided views of his paternal prerogatives. He was a terror; but the only evidence of imaginative faculty about Fyne was his pride in his wife's parentage. It stimulated his ingenuity, too. Difficult—is it not?—to introduce one's wife's maiden name into general conversation. But my simple Fyne made use of Captain Anthony for that purpose, or else I would never even have heard of the man. 'My wife's sailor-brother' was the phrase. He trotted out the sailor-brother in a pretty wide range of subjects: Indian and colonial affairs, matters of trade, talk of travels, of seaside holidays and so on. Once I remember 'My wife's sailor-brother Captain Anthony' being produced in connection with nothing less recondite than a sunset. And little Fyne never failed to add: 'The son of Carleon Anthony, the poet—you know.' He used to lower his voice for that statement, and people were impressed, or pretended to be."

The late Carleon Anthony, the poet, sang in his time of the domestic and social amenities of our age with a most felicitous versification, his object being, in his own words, "to glorify the result of six thousand years' evolution towards the refinement of thought, manners, and feelings." Why he fixed the term at six thousand years I don't know. His poems read like sentimental novels told in verse of a really superior quality. You felt as if you were being taken out for a delightful country drive by a charming lady in a pony carriage. But in his domestic life that same Carleon Anthony showed traces of the primitive cave-dweller's temperament. He was a massive, implacable man with a handsome face, arbitrary and exacting with his dependents, but marvellously suave in his manner to admiring strangers. These contrasted displays must have been particularly exasperating to his long-suffering family. After his second wife's death his boy, whom he persisted by a mere whim in educating at home, ran away in conventional style and, as if disgusted with the amenities of civilization, threw himself, figuratively speaking, into the sea. The daughter (the elder of the two children), either from compassion or because women are naturally more enduring, remained in bondage to the poet for several years, till she too seized a chance of escape by throwing herself into the arms, the muscular arms, of the pedestrian Fyne. This was either great luck or great sagacity. A civil servant is, I should imagine, the last human being in the world to preserve those traits of the cave-dweller from which she was fleeing. Her father would never consent to see her after the marriage. Such unforgiving selfishness is difficult to understand unless as a perverse sort of refinement. There were also doubts as to Carleon Anthony's complete sanity for some considerable time before he died.

Most of the above I elicited from Marlow, for all I knew of Carleon Anthony was his unexciting but fascinating verse. Marlow assured me that the Fyne marriage was perfectly successful and even happy, in an earnest, unplayful fashion, being blessed besides by three healthy, active, self-reliant children, all girls. They were all pedestrians, too. Even the youngest would wander away for miles if not restrained. Mrs. Fyne had a ruddy out-of-doors complexion and wore blouses with a starched front like a man's shirt, a stand-up collar and a long necktie. Marlow had made their acquaintance one summer in the country, where they were accustomed to take a cottage for the holidays. . . .

At this point we were interrupted by Mr. Powell, who declared that he must leave us. The tide was on the turn, he announced, coming away from the window abruptly. He wanted to be on board his cutter before she swung, and of course he would sleep on board. Never slept away from the cutter while on a cruise. He was gone in a moment, unceremoniously, but giving us no offence and leaving behind an impression as though we had known him for a long time. The ingenuous way he had told us of his start in life had something to do with putting him on that footing with us. I gave no thought to seeing him again. Marlow expressed a confident hope of coming across him before long.

"He cruises about the mouth of the river all the summer. He will be easy to find any week-end," he remarked, ringing the bell so that we might settle up with the waiter.

Later on I asked Marlow why he wished to cultivate this chance acquaintance. He confessed apologetically that it was the commonest sort of curiosity. I flatter myself that I understand all sorts of curiosity. Curiosity about daily facts, about daily things, about daily men. It is the most respectable faculty of the human mind—in fact, I cannot conceive the uses of an incurious mind. It would be like a chamber perpetually locked up. But in this particular case Mr. Powell seemed to have given us already a complete insight into his personality such as it was; a personality capable of perception and with a feeling for the vagaries of fate, but essentially simple in itself.

Marlow agreed with me so far. He explained, however, that his curiosity was not excited by Mr. Powell exclusively. It originated a good way further back in the fact of his accidental acquaintance with the Fynes in the country. This chance meeting with a man who had sailed with Captain Anthony had revived it. It had revived it to some purpose, to such purpose that to me too was given the knowledge of its origin and of its nature. It was given to me in several stages, at intervals which are not indicated here. On this first occasion I remarked to Marlow with some surprise: "But, if I remember rightly, you said you didn't know Captain Anthony."

"No. I never saw the man. It's years ago now, but I seem to hear solemn little Fyne's deep voice announcing the approaching visit of his wife's brother, 'the son of the poet, you know.' He had just arrived in London from a long voyage, and, directly his occupations permitted, was coming down to stay with his relatives for a few weeks. No doubt we two should find many things to talk about by ourselves in reference to our common calling, added little Fyne portentously in his grave undertones, as if the Mercantile Marine were a secret society.

"You must understand that I cultivated the Fynes only in the country, in their holiday time. This was the third year. Of their existence in town I knew no more than may be inferred from analogy. I played chess with Fyne in the late afternoon, and sometimes came over to the cottage early enough to have tea with the whole family at a big round table. They sat about it, an unsmiling, sunburnt company of very few words indeed. Even the children were silent and as if contemptuous of each other and of their elders. Fyne muttered sometimes deep down in his chest some insignificant remark. Mrs. Fyne smiled mechanically (she had splendid teeth) while distributing tea and bread and butter. A something which was not coldness, nor yet indifference, but a sort of peculiar self-possession gave her the appearance of a very trustworthy, very capable and excellent governess; as if Fyne were a widower and the children not her own, but only entrusted to her calm, efficient, unemotional care. One expected her to address Fyne as Mr. When she called him John it surprised one like a shocking familiarity. The atmosphere of that holiday was—if I may put it so—brightly dull. Healthy faces, fair complexions, clear eyes, and never a frank smile in the whole lot, unless perhaps from a girl-friend.

"The girl-friend problem exercised me greatly. How and where the Fynes got all these pretty creatures to come and stay with them I can't imagine. I had at first the wild suspicion that they were obtained to amuse Fyne. But I soon discovered that he could hardly tell one from the other, though obviously their presence met with his solemn approval. These girls in fact came for Mrs. Fyne. They treated her with admiring deference. She answered to some need of theirs. They sat at her feet. They were like disciples. It was very curious. Of Fyne they took but scanty notice. As to myself, I was made to feel that I did not exist.

"After tea we would sit down to chess and then Fyne's everlasting gravity became faintly tinged by an attenuated gleam of something inward which resembled sly satisfaction. Of the divine frivolity of laughter he was only capable over a chessboard. Certain positions of the game struck him as humorous, which nothing else on earth could do. . . ."

"He used to beat you," I asserted with confidence.

"Yes. He used to beat me," Marlow owned up hastily.

So he and Fyne played two games after tea. The children romped together outside, gravely, unplayfully, as one would expect from Fyne's children, and Mrs. Fyne would be gone to the bottom of the garden with the girl-friend of the week. She always walked off directly after tea with her arm round the girl-friend's waist. Marlow said that there was only one girlfriend with whom he had conversed at all. It had happened quite unexpectedly, long after he had given up all hope of getting into touch with these reserved girl-friends.

One day he saw a woman walking about on the edge of a high quarry, which rose a sheer hundred feet, at least, from the road winding up the hill out of which it had been excavated. He shouted warningly to her from below where he happened to be passing. She was really in considerable danger. At the sound of his voice she started back and retreated out of his sight amongst some young Scotch firs growing near the very brink of the precipice.

"I sat down on a bank of grass," Marlow went on. "She had given me a turn. The hem of her skirt seemed to float over that awful sheer drop, she was so close to the edge. An absurd thing to do. A perfectly mad trick—for no conceivable object! I was reflecting on the foolhardiness of the average girl and remembering some other instances of the kind, when she came into view walking down the steep curve of the road. She had Mrs. Fyne's walking-stick and was escorted by the Fyne dog. Her dead white face struck me with astonishment, so that I forgot to raise my hat. I just sat and stared. The dog, a vivacious and amiable animal which for some inscrutable reason had bestowed his friendship on my unworthy self, rushed up the bank demonstratively and insinuated himself under my arm.

"The girl-friend (it was one of them) went past some way as though she had not seen me, then stopped and called the dog to her several times; but he only nestled closer to my side, and when I tried to push him away developed that remarkable power of internal resistance by which a dog makes himself practically immovable by anything short of a kick. She looked over her shoulder and her arched eyebrows frowned above her blanched face. It was almost a scowl. Then the expression changed. She looked unhappy. 'Come here!' she cried once more in an angry and distressed tone. I took off my hat at last, but the dog, hanging out his tongue with that cheerfully imbecile expression some dogs know so well how to put on when it suits their purpose, pretended to be deaf.

"She cried from the distance desperately.

" 'Perhaps you will take him to the cottage then. I can't wait.'

" 'I won't be responsible for that dog,' I protested, getting down the bank and advancing towards her. She looked very hurt, apparently by the desertion of the dog. 'But if you let me walk with you he will follow us all right,' I suggested.

"She moved on without answering me. The dog launched himself suddenly full speed down the road, receding from us in a small cloud of dust. It vanished in the distance, and presently we came up with him lying on the grass. He panted in the shade of the hedge with shining eyes, but pretended not to see us. We had not exchanged a word so far. The girl by my side gave him a scornful glance in passing.

" 'He offered to come with me,' she remarked bitterly.

" 'And then abandoned you!' I sympathized. 'It looks very unchivalrous. But that's merely his want of tact. I believe he meant to protest against your reckless proceedings. What made you come so near the edge of that quarry? The earth might have given way. Haven't you noticed a smashed fir tree at the bottom? Tumbled over only the other morning after a night's rain.'

" 'I don't see why I shouldn't be as reckless as I please.'

"I was nettled by her brusque manner of asserting her folly, and I told her that neither did I as far as that went, in a tone which almost suggested that she was welcome to break her neck for all I cared. This was considerably more than I meant, but I don't like rude girls. I had been introduced to her only the day before—at the round tea-table—and she had barely acknowledged the introduc-tion. I had not caught her name, but I had noticed her fine, arched eyebrows which, so the physiognomists say, are a sign of courage.

"I examined her appearance quietly. Her hair was nearly black, her eyes blue, deeply shaded by long dark eyelashes. She had a little colour now. She looked straight before her; the corner of her lip on my side drooped a little; her chin was fine, somewhat pointed. I went on to say that some regard for others should stand in the way of one's playing with danger. I urged playfully the distress of the poor Fynes in case of accident, if noth-ing else. I told her that she did not know the bucolic mind. Had she given occasion for a coroner's inquest the verdict would have been suicide, with the implication of unhappy love. They would never be able to understand that she had taken the trouble to climb over two post-and-rail fences only for the fun of being reckless. Indeed, even as I talked chaffingly, I was greatly struck myself by the fact. She retorted that, once one was dead, what horrid people thought of one did not matter. It was said with infinite contempt; but something like a suppressed quaver in the voice made me look at her again. I per-ceived then that her thick eyelashes were wet. This sur-prising discovery silenced me as you may guess. She looked unhappy. And—I don't know how to say it— well—it suited her. The clouded brow, the pained mouth, the vague fixed glance! A victim. And this characteristic aspect made her attractive; an individual touch—you know.

"The dog had run on ahead and now gazed at us by

the side of the Fynes' garden gate in a tense attitude and wagging his stumpy tail very, very slowly, with an air of concentrated attention. The girl-friend of the Fynes bolted violently through the aforesaid gate and into the cottage, leaving me on the road—astounded.

"A couple of hours afterwards I returned to the cottage for chess as usual. I saw neither the girl nor Mrs. Fyne then. We had our two games and on parting I warned Fyne that I was called to town on business and might be away for some time. He regretted it very much. His brother-in-law was expected next day but he didn't know whether he was a chess-player. Captain Anthony ('the son of the poet—you know') was of a retiring disposition, shy with strangers, unused to society, and very much devoted to his calling, Fyne explained. All the time they had been married he could be induced only once before to come and stay with them for a few days. He had had a rather unhappy boyhood; and it made him a silent man. But no doubt, concluded Fyne, as if dealing portentously with a mystery, we two sailors should find much to say to one another.

"This point was never settled. I was detained in town from week to week till it seemed hardly worth while to go back. But as I had kept on my rooms in the farmhouse I concluded to go down again for a few days.

"It was late, deep dusk, when I got out at our little country station. My eyes fell on the unmistakable broad back and the muscular legs in cycling stockings of little Fyne. He passed along the carriages rapidly towards the rear of the train, which presently pulled out and left him solitary at the end of the rustic platform. When he came back to where I waited I perceived that he was much perturbed, so perturbed as to forget the convention of the usual greetings. He only exclaimed Oh! on recognizing me, and stopped irresolute. When I asked him if he had been expecting somebody by that train he didn't seem to know. He stammered disconnectedly. I looked hard at him. To all appearances he was perfectly sober; moreover, to suspect Fyne of a lapse from the proprieties high or low, great or small, was absurd. He was also a too serious and deliberate person to go mad suddenly. But as he seemed to have forgotten that he had a tongue in his head I concluded I would leave him to his mystery.

To my surprise he followed me out of the station and kept by my side, though I did not encourage him. I did not, however, repulse his attempts at conversation. He was no longer expecting me, he said. He had given me up. The weather had been uniformly fine—and so on. I gathered also that the son of the poet had curtailed his stay somewhat and had gone back to his ship the day before.

"That information touched me but little. Believing in heredity in moderation, I knew well how sea-life fashions a man outwardly and stamps his soul with the mark of a certain prosaic fitness—because a sailor is not an adventurer. I expressed no regret at missing Captain Anthony, and we proceeded in silence till, on approaching the holiday cottage, Fyne suddenly and unexpectedly broke it by the hurried declaration that he would go on with me a little farther.

" 'Go with you to your door,' he mumbled, and started forward to the little gate where the shadowy figure of Mrs. Fyne hovered, clearly on the look out for him. She was alone. The children must have been already in bed, and I saw no attending girl-friend shadow near her vague but unmistakable form, half-lost in the obscurity of the little garden.

"I heard Fyne exclaim 'Nothing,' and then Mrs. Fyne's well-trained, responsible voice uttered the words, 'It's what I have said,' with incisive equanimity. By that time I had passed on, raising my hat. Almost at once Fyne caught me up and slowed down to my strolling gait which must have been infinitely irksome to his high pedestrian faculties. I am sure that all his muscular person must have suffered from awful physical boredom; but he did not attempt to charm it away by conversation. He preserved a portentous and dreary silence. And I was bored too. Suddenly I perceived the menace of even worse boredom. Yes! He was so silent because he had something to tell me.

"I became extremely frightened. But man, reckless animal, is so made that in him curiosity, the paltriest curiosity, will overcome all terrors, every disgust, and even despair itself. To my laconic invitation to come in for a drink he answered by a deep, gravely accented: 'Thanks, I will,' as though it were a response in church.

His face as seen in the lamplight gave me no clue to the character of the impending communication; as indeed from the nature of things it couldn't do, its normal expression being already that of the utmost possible seriousness. It was perfect and immovable; and for a certainty if he had something excruciatingly funny to tell me it would be all the same.

"He gazed at me earnestly and delivered himself of some weighty remarks on Mrs. Fyne's desire to befriend, counsel, and guide young girls of all sorts on the path of life. It was a voluntary mission. He approved his wife's action and also her views and principles in general.

"All this with a solemn countenance and in deep measured tones. Yet somehow I got an irresistible conviction that he was exasperated by something in particular. In the unworthy hope of being amused by the misfortunes of a fellow-creature I asked him point-blank what was wrong now.

"What was wrong was that a girl-friend was missing. She had been missing precisely since six o'clock that morning. The woman who did the work of the cottage saw her going out at that hour, for a walk. The pedestrian Fyne's ideas of a walk were extensive, but the girl did not turn up for lunch, nor yet for tea, nor yet for dinner. She had not turned up by footpath, road or rail. He had been reluctant to make inquiries. It would have set all the village talking. The Fynes had expected her to reappear every moment, till the shades of the night and the silence of slumber had stolen gradually over the wide and peaceful rural landscape commanded by the cottage.

"After telling me that much, Fyne sat helpless in unconclusive agony. Going to bed was out of the question—neither could any steps be taken just then. What to do with himself he did not know!

"I asked him if this was the same young lady I saw a day or two before I went to town? He really could not remember. Was she a girl with dark hair and blue eyes? I asked further. He really couldn't tell what colour her eyes were. He was very unobservant except as to the peculiarities of footpaths, on which he was an authority.

"I thought with amazement and some admiration that Mrs. Fyne's young disciples were to her husband's gravity no more than evanescent shadows. However, with but little hesitation Fyne ventured to affirm that—yes, her hair was of some dark shade.

" 'We had a good deal to do with that girl first and last,' he explained solemnly; then getting up as if moved by a spring, he snatched his cap off the table. 'She may be back in the cottage,' he cried in his bass voice. I followed him out on the road.

"It was one of those dewy, clear, starry nights, oppressing our spirit, crushing our pride, by the brilliant evidence of the awful loneliness, of the hopeless obscure insignificance of our globe lost in the splendid revelation of a glittering, soulless universe. I hate such skies. Daylight is friendly to man toiling under a sun which warms his heart; and cloudy soft nights are more kindly to our littleness. I nearly ran back again to my lighted parlour; Fyne fussing in a knickerbocker suit before the hosts of heaven, on a shadowy earth, about a transient, phantom-like girl, seemed too ridiculous to associate with. On the other hand there was something fascinating in the very absurdity. He cut along in his best pedestrian style and I found myself let in for a spell of severe exercise at eleven o'clock at night.

"In the distance over the fields and trees smudging and blotching the vast obscurity, one lighted window of the cottage with the blind up was like a bright beacon kept alight to guide the lost wanderer. Inside, at the table bearing the lamp, we saw Mrs. Fyne sitting with folded arms and not a hair of her head out of place. She looked exactly like a governess who had put the children to bed; and her manner to me was just the neutral manner of a governess. To her husband, too, for that matter.

"Fyne told her that I was fully informed. Not a muscle of her ruddy, smooth, handsome face moved. She had schooled herself into that sort of thing. Having seen two successive wives of the delicate poet chivied and worried into their graves, she had adopted that cool, detached manner to meet her gifted father's outbreaks of selfish temper. It had now become a second nature. I suppose she was always like that; even in the very hour of elopement with Fyne. That transaction when one remembered it in her presence acquired a quaintly marvellous aspect to one's imagination. But somehow her self-possession matched very well little Fyne's invariable solemnity.

"I was rather sorry for him. Wasn't he worried! The agony of solemnity. At the same time I was amused. I didn't take a gloomy view of that 'vanishing girl' trick. Somehow I couldn't. But I said nothing. None of us said anything. We sat about that big round table as if assembled for a conference and looked at each other in a sort of fatuous consternation. I would have ended by laughing outright if I had not been saved from that impropriety by poor Fyne becoming preposterous.

"He began with grave anguish to talk of going to the police in the morning, of printing descriptive bills, of setting people to drag the ponds for miles around. It was extremely gruesome. I murmured something about communicating with the young lady's relatives. It seemed to me a very natural suggestion; but Fyne and his wife exchanged such a significant glance that I felt as though I had made a tactless remark.

"But I really wanted to help poor Fyne; and as I could see that, manlike, he suffered from the present inability to act, the passive waiting, I said: 'Nothing of this can be done till tomorrow. But as you have given me an insight into the nature of your thoughts I can tell you what may be done at once. We may go and look at the bottom of the old quarry which is on the level of the road, about a mile from here.'

"The couple made big eyes at this, and then I told them of my meeting with the girl. You may be surprised, but I assure you I had not perceived this aspect of it till that very moment. It was like a startling revelation; the past throwing a sinister light on the future. Fyne opened his mouth gravely and as gravely shut it. Nothing more. Mrs. Fyne said, 'You had better go,' with an air as if her self-possession had been pricked with a pin in some secret place.

"And I—you know how stupid I can be at times—I perceived with dismay for the first time that by pandering to Fyne's morbid fancies I had let myself in for some more severe exercise. And wasn't I sorry I spoke! You know how I hate walking—at least on solid, rural earth; for I can walk a ship's deck a whole foggy night through, if necessary, and think little of it. There is some satisfaction too in playing the vagabond in the streets of a big town till the sky pales above the ridges of the roofs. I have done that repeatedly for pleasure—of a sort. But to tramp the slumbering country-side in the dark is for me a wearisome nightmare of exertion.

"With perfect detachment Mrs. Fyne watched me go out after her husband. That woman was flint.

"The fresh night had a smell of soil, of turned-up sods like a grave—an association particularly odious to a sailor by its idea of confinement and narrowness; yes, even when he has given up the hope of being buried at sea; about the last hope a sailor gives up consciously after he has been, as it does happen, decoyed by some chance into the toils of the land. A strong grave-like sniff. The ditch by the side of the road must have been freshly dug in front of the cottage.

"Once clear of the garden Fyne gathered way like a racing cutter. What was a mile to him—or twenty miles? You think he might have gone shrinkingly on such an errand. But not a bit of it. The force of pedestrian genius, I suppose. I raced by his side in a mood of profound self-derision, and infinitely vexed with that minx. Because dead or alive, I thought of her as a minx. . . ."

I smiled incredulously at Marlow's ferocity; but Marlow, pausing with a whimsically retrospective air, never flinched.

"Yes, yes. Even dead. And now you are shocked. You see, you are such a chivalrous masculine beggar. But there is enough of the woman in my nature to free my judgment of women from glamorous reticency. And then, why should I upset myself? A woman is not necessarily either a doll or an angel to me. She is a human being, very much like myself. And I have come across too many dead souls lying, so to speak, at the foot of high unscalable places for a merely possible dead body at the bottom of a quarry to strike my sincerity dumb.

"The cliff-like face of the quarry looked forbiddingly impressive. I will admit that Fyne and I hung back for a moment before we made a plunge off the road into the bushes growing in a broad space at the foot of the towering limestone wall. These bushes were heavy with dew. There were also concealed mudholes in there. We crept and tumbled and felt about with our hands along the ground. We got wet, scratched, and plastered with mire all over our nether garments. Fyne fell suddenly into a strange cavity—probably a disused lime-kiln. His voice uplifted in grave distress sounded more than usually rich, solemn and profound. This was the comic relief of an absurdly dramatic situation. While hauling him out I permitted myself to laugh aloud at last. Fyne, of course, didn't.

"I need not tell you that we found nothing after a most conscientious search. Fyne even pushed his way into a decaying shed half-buried in dew-soaked vegetation. He struck matches, several of them too, as if to make absolutely sure that the vanished girl-friend of his wife was not hiding there. The short flares illuminated his grave, immovable countenance, while I let myself go completely and laughed in peals.

"I asked him if he really and truly supposed that any sane girl would go and hide in that shed; and if so, why?

"Disdainful of my mirth, he merely muttered his basso-profundo thankfulness that we had not found her anywhere about there. Having grown extremely sensitive (an effect of irritation) to the tonalities, I may say, of this affair, I felt that it was only an imperfect, reserved thankfulness, with one eye still on the possibilities of the several ponds in the neighbourhood. And I remember I snorted, I positively snorted, at that poor Fyne.

"What really jarred upon me was the rate of his walking. Differences in politics, in ethics, and even in aesthetics need not arouse angry antagonism. One's opinion may change; one's tastes may alter—in fact they do. One's very conception of virtue is at the mercy of some felicitous temptation which may be sprung on one any day. All these things are perpetually on the swing. But a temperamental difference, temperament being immutable, is the parent of hate. That's why religious quarrels are the fiercest of all. My temperament, in matters pertaining to solid land, is the temperament of leisurely movement, of deliberate gait. And there was that little Fyne pounding along the road in a most offensive manner: a man wedded to thick-soled, laced boots; whereas my temperament demands thin shoes of the lightest kind. Of course there could never have been question of friendship between us; but under the provocation of having to keep up with his pace I began to dislike him actively. I begged sarcastically to know whether he could tell me if we were engaged in a farce or in a tragedy. I wanted to regulate my feelings which, I told him, were in an unbecoming state of confusion.

"But Fyne was as impervious to sarcasm as a turtle. He tramped on, and all he did was to ejaculate twice out of his deep chest, vaguely, doubtfully—

" 'I am afraid. . . . I am afraid! . . .'

"This was tragic. The thump of his boots was the only sound in a shadowy world. I kept by his side with a comparatively ghostly, silent tread. By a strange illusion the road appeared to run up against a lot of low stars at no very great distance, but as we advanced new stretches of whitey-brown ribbon seemed to come up from under the black ground. I observed, as we went by, the lamp in my parlour in the farm-house still burning. But I did not leave Fyne to run in and put it out. The impetus of his pedestrian excellence carried me past in his wake before I could make up my mind.

" 'Tell me, Fyne,' I cried, 'you don't think the girl was mad—do you?'

"He answered nothing. Soon the lighted beacon-like window of the cottage came into view. Then Fyne uttered a solemn 'Certainly not,' with profound assurance. But immediately after he added a 'Very highly strung young person indeed,' which unsettled me again. Was it a tragedy?

" 'Nobody ever got up at six o'clock in the morning to commit suicide,' I declared crustily. 'It's unheard of! This is a farce.'

"As a matter of fact it was neither farce nor tragedy.

"Coming up to the cottage we had a view of Mrs. Fyne inside, still sitting in the strong light at the round table with folded arms. It looked as though she had not moved her very head by as much as an inch since we went away. She was amazing in a sort of unsubtle way; crudely amazing—I thought. Why crudely? I don't know. Perhaps because I saw her then in a crude light. I mean this materially—in the light of an unshaded lamp. Our mental conclusions depend so much on momentary physical sensations—don't they? If the lamp had been shaded I should perhaps have gone home after expressing politely my concern at the Fynes' unpleasant predicament.

"Losing a girl-friend in that manner is unpleasant. It is also mysterious. So mysterious that a certain mystery attaches to the people to whom such a thing does happen. Moreover, I had never really understood the Fynes; he with his solemnity which extended to the very eating of bread and butter; she with that air of detachment and resolution in breasting the commonplace current of their unexciting life, in which the cutting of bread and butter appeared to me, by a long way, the most dangerous episode. Sometimes I amused myself by supposing that to their minds this world of ours must be wearing a perfectly overwhelming aspect and that their heads contained respectively awfully serious and extremely desperate thoughts—and trying to imagine what an exciting time they must be having of it in the inscrutable depths of their being. My efforts had invested them with a sort of profundity.

"But when Fyne and I got back into the room, then in the searching, domestic glare of the lamp, inimical to the play of fancy, I saw these two stripped of every vesture it had amused me to put on them for fun. Queer enough they were. Is there a human being that isn't that—more or less secretly? But whatever their secret, it was manifest to me that it was neither subtle nor profound. They were a good, stupid, earnest couple and very much bothered. They were that—with the usual unshaded crudity of average people. There was nothing in them that the lamplight might not touch without the slightest risk of indiscretion.

"Directly we had entered the room Fyne announced the result by saying 'Nothing' in the same tone as at the gate on his return from the railway station. And as then Mrs. Fyne uttered an incisive 'It's what I've said,' which might have been the veriest echo of her words in the garden. We three looked at each other as if on the brink of a disclosure. I don't know whether she was vexed at my presence. It could hardly be called intrusion—could it? Little Fyne began it. It had to go on. We stood before her, plastered with the same mud (Fyne was a sight!), scratched by the same brambles, conscious of the same experience. Yes. Before her. And she looked at us with folded arms, with an extraordinary fullness of assumed responsibility. I addressed her.

" 'You don't believe in an accident, Mrs. Fyne, do you?'

"She shook her head in curt negation, while, caked in mud and inexpressibly serious-faced, Fyne seemed to be backing her up with all the weight of his solemn presence. Nothing more absurd could be conceived. It was delicious. And I went on in deferential accents: 'Am I to understand then that you entertain the theory of suicide?'

"I don't know that I am liable to fits of delirium, but by a sudden and alarming aberration while waiting for her answer I became mentally aware of three trained dogs dancing on their hind legs. I don't know why. Perhaps because of the pervading solemnity. There's nothing more solemn on earth than a dance of trained dogs.

" 'She has chosen to disappear. That's all.'

"In these words Mrs. Fyne answered me. The aggressive tone was too much for my endurance. In an instant I found myself out of the dance and down on all-fours so to speak, with liberty to bark and bite.

" 'The devil she has,' I cried. 'Has chosen to. . . . Like this, all at once, anyhow, regardless . . . I've had the privilege of meeting that reckless and brusque young lady, and I must say that with her air of an angry victim . . .'

" 'Precisely,' Mrs. Fyne said very unexpectedly like a steel trap going off. I stared at her. How provoking she was! So I went on to finish my tirade. 'She struck me at first sight as the most wrong-headed inconsiderate girl that I ever . . .'

" 'Why should a girl be more considerate than any one else? More than any man, for instance?' inquired Mrs. Fyne with a still greater assertion of responsibility in her bearing.

"Of course I exclaimed at this, not very loudly it is true, but forcibly. Were, then, the feelings of friends, relations, and even of strangers, to be disregarded? I asked Mrs. Fyne if she did not think it was a sort of duty to show elementary consideration, not only for the natural feelings, but even for the prejudices of one's fellow-creatures.

"Her answer knocked me over.

" 'Not for a woman.'

"Just like that. I confess that I went down flat. And while in that collapsed state I learned the true nature of

Mrs. Fyne's feminist doctrine. It was not political, it was not social. It was a knock-me-down doctrine—a practical individualistic doctrine. You would not thank me for expounding it to you at large. Indeed I think that she herself did not enlighten me fully. There must have been things not fit for a man to hear. But shortly, and as far as my bewilderment allowed me to grasp its naïve atrociousness, it was something like this: that no consideration, no delicacy, no tenderness, no scruples should stand in the way of a woman (who by the mere fact of her sex was the predestined victim of conditions created by men's selfish passions, their vices and their abominable tyranny) from taking the shortest cut towards securing for herself the easiest possible existence. She had even the right to go out of existence without considering any one's feelings or convenience, since some women's existences were made impossible by the short-sighted baseness of men.

"I looked at her, sitting before the lamp at one o'clock in the morning, with her mature, smooth-cheeked face of masculine shape robbed of its freshness by fatigue; at her eyes dimmed by this senseless vigil. I looked also at Fyne; the mud was drying on him; he was obviously tired. The weariness of solemnity. But he preserved an unflinching, endorsing gravity of expression. Endorsing it all as became a good, convinced husband.

" 'Oh! I see,' I said. 'No consideration. . . . Well, I hope you like it.'

"They amused me beyond the wildest imaginings of which I was capable. After the first shock, you understand, I recovered very quickly. The order of the world was safe enough. He was a civil servant and she his good and faithful wife. But when it comes to dealing with human beings anything, anything may be expected. So even my astonishment did not last very long. How far she developed and illustrated that conscienceless and austere doctrine to the girl-friends, who were mere transient shadows to her husband, I could not tell. Any length I supposed. And he looked on, acquiesced, approved, just for that very reason—because these pretty girls were but shadows to him. O! Most Virtuous Fyne! He cast his eyes down. He didn't like it. But I eyed him with hidden

animosity, for he had got me to run after him under
somewhat false pretences.

"Mrs. Fyne had only smiled at me very expressively,
very self-confidently. 'Oh, I quite understand that you
accept the fullest responsibility,' I said. 'I am the only
ridiculous person in this—this—I don't know how to call
it—performance. However, I've nothing more to do
here, so I'll say good-night—or good morning, for it must
be past one.'

"But before departing, in common decency, I offered
to take any wires they might write. My lodgings were
nearer the post office than the cottage and I would send
them off the first thing in the morning. I supposed they
would wish to communicate, if only as to the disposal of
the luggage, with the young lady's relatives . . .

"Fyne, he looked rather downcast by then, thanked
me and declined.

" 'There is really no one,' he said, very grave.

" 'No one,' I exclaimed.

" 'Practically,' said curt Mrs. Fyne.

"And my curiosity was aroused again.

" 'Ah! I see. An orphan.'

"Mrs. Fyne looked away, weary and sombre, and Fyne
said 'Yes' impulsively, and then qualified the affirmative
by the quaint statement: 'To a certain extent.'

"I became conscious of a languid, exhausted embarrassment, bowed to Mrs. Fyne, and went out of the cottage to be confronted outside its door by the bespangled,
cruel revelation of the Immensity of the Universe. The
night was not sufficiently advanced for the stars to have
paled; and the earth seemed to me more profoundly
asleep—perhaps because I was alone now. Not having
Fyne with me to set the pace, I let myself drift, rather
than walk, in the direction of the farm-house. To drift is
the only reposeful sort of motion (ask any ship if it isn't)
and therefore consistent with thoughtfulness. And I pon-
dered: How can one be an orphan 'to a certain extent'?

"No amount of solemnity could make such a statement
other than bizarre. What a strange condition to be in.
Very likely one of the parents only was dead? But no; it
couldn't be, since Fyne had said just before that 'there
was really no one' to communicate with. No one! And
then remembering Mrs. Fyne's snappy 'Practically,' my

thoughts fastened upon that lady as a more tangible object of speculation.

"I wondered—and wondering, I doubted—whether she really understood herself the theory she had propounded to me. Everything may be said—indeed ought to be said—providing we know how to say it. She probably did not. She was not intelligent enough for that. She had no knowledge of the world. She had got hold of words as a child might get hold of some poisonous pills and play with them for 'dear, tiny little marbles.' No! The domestic-slave daughter of Carleon Anthony and the little Fyne of the Civil Service (that flower of civilization) were not intelligent people. They were commonplace, earnest, without smiles and without guile. But he had his solemnities and she had her reveries, her lurid, violent, crude reveries. And I thought with some sadness that all these revolts and indignations, all these protests, revulsions of feeling, pangs of suffering and of rage, expressed but the uneasiness of sensual beings trying for their share in the joys of form, colour, sensations—the only riches of our world of senses. A poet may be a simple being, but he is bound to be various and full of wiles, ingenious and irritable. I reflected on the variety of ways the ingenuity of the late bard of civilization would be able to invent for the tormenting of his dependents. Poets not being generally foresighted in practical affairs, no vision of consequences would restrain him. Yes. The Fynes were excellent people, but Mrs. Fyne wasn't the daughter of a domestic tyrant for nothing. There were no limits to her revolt. But they were excellent people. It was clear that they must have been extremely good to that girl whose position in the world seemed somewhat difficult, with her face of a victim, her obvious lack of resignation and the bizarre status of orphan 'to a certain extent.'

"Such were my thoughts, but in truth I soon ceased to trouble about all these people. I found that my lamp had gone out, leaving behind an awful smell. I fled from it up the stairs and went to bed in the dark. My slumbers— I suppose the one good in pedestrian exercise, confound it, is that it helps our natural callousness—my slumbers were deep, dreamless and refreshing.

"My appetite at breakfast was not affected by my ignorance of the facts, motives, events and conclusions. I think that to understand everything is not good for the intellect. A well-stocked intelligence weakens the impulse to action; an overstocked one leads gently to idiocy. But Mrs. Fyne's individualist woman-doctrine, naïvely unscrupulous, flitted through my mind. The salad of unprincipled notions she put into these girl-friends' heads! Good innocent creature, worthy wife, excellent mother (of the strict governess type), she was as guileless of consequences as any determinist philosopher ever was.

"As to honour—you know—it's a very fine mediæval inheritance which women never got hold of. It wasn't theirs. Since it may be laid as a general principle that women always get what they want, we must suppose they didn't want it. In addition they are devoid of decency. I mean masculine decency. Cautiousness too is foreign to them—the heavy reasonable cautiousness which is our glory. And if they had it they would make of it a thing of passion, so that its own mother—I mean the mother of cautiousness—wouldn't recognize it. Prudence with them is a matter of thrill like the rest of sublunary contrivances. 'Sensation at any cost,' is their secret device. All the virtues are not enough for them; they want also all the crimes for their own. And why? Because in such completeness there is power—the kind of thrill they love most. . . ."

"Do you expect me to agree with all this?" I interrupted.

"No, it isn't necessary," said Marlow feeling the check to his eloquence, but with a great effort at amiability. "You need not even understand it. I continue: with such disposition, what prevents women—to use the phrase an old boatswain of my acquaintance applied descriptively to his captain—what prevents them from 'coming on deck and playing hell with the ship' generally, is that something in them precise and mysterious, acting both as restraint and as inspiration; their femininity, in short, which they think they can get rid of by trying hard, but can't, and never will. Therefore we may conclude that, for all their enterprises, the world is and remains safe enough. Feeling, in my character of a lover of peace, soothed by that conclusion, I prepared myself to enjoy a fine day.

"And it was a fine day; a delicious day, with the horror of the Infinite veiled by the splendid tent of blue; a day innocently bright like a child with a washed face, fresh like an innocent young girl, suave in welcoming one's respects like—like a Roman prelate. I love such days. They are perfection for remaining indoors. And I enjoyed it temperamentally in a chair, my feet up on the sill of the open window, a book in my hands and the murmured harmonies of wind and sun in my heart making an accompaniment to the rhythms of my author. Then looking up from the page I saw outside a pair of grey eyes thatched by ragged yellowy-white eyebrows gazing at me solemnly over the toes of my slippers. There was a grave, furrowed brow surmounting that portentous gaze, a brown tweed cap set far back on the perspiring head.

" 'Come inside,' I cried as heartily as my sinking heart would permit.

"After a short but severe scuffle with his dog at the outer door, Fyne entered. I treated him without ceremony and only waved my hand towards a chair. Even before he sat down he gasped out—

" 'We've heard—midday post.'

"Gasped out! The grave, immovable Fyne of the Civil Service gasped! This was enough, you'll admit, to cause me to put my feet to the ground swiftly. That fellow was always making me do things in subtle discord with my meditative temperament. No wonder that I had but a qualified liking for him. I said with just a suspicion of jeering tone—

" 'Of course. I told you last night on the road that it was a farce we were engaged in.'

"He made the little parlour resound to its foundations with a note of anger positively sepulchral in its depth of tone. 'Farce be hanged! She has bolted with my wife's brother, Captain Anthony.' This outburst was followed by complete subsidence. He faltered miserably as he added from force of habit: 'The son of the poet, you know.'

"A silence fell. Fyne's several expressions were so many examples of varied consistency. This was the discomfiture of solemnity. My interest of course was revived.

" 'But hold on,' I said. 'They didn't go together. Is it a suspicion or does she actually say that. . . .'

" 'She has gone after him,' stated Fyne in comminatory tones. 'By previous arrangement. She confesses that much.'

"He added that it was very shocking. I asked him whether he should have preferred them going off together; and on what ground he based that preference. This was sheer fun for me in regard of the fact that Fyne's too was a runaway match, which even got into the papers in its time, because the late indignant poet had no discretion and sought to avenge this outrage publicly in some absurd way before a bewigged judge. The dejected gesture of little Fyne's hand disarmed my mocking mood. But I could not help expressing my surprise that Mrs. Fyne had not detected at once what was brewing. Women were supposed to have an unerring eye.

"He told me that his wife had been very much engaged in a certain work. I had always wondered how she occupied her time. It was in writing. Like her husband, she too published a little book. It had nothing to do with pedestrianism. It was a sort of handbook for women with grievances (and all women had them), a sort of compendious theory and practice of feminine free morality. It made you laugh at its transparent simplicity. But that authorship was revealed to me much later. I didn't of course ask Fyne what work his wife was engaged on; but I marvelled to myself at her complete ignorance of the world, of her own sex, and of the other kind of sinners. Yet, where could she have got any experience? Her father had kept her strictly cloistered. Marriage with Fyne was certainly a change, but only to another kind of claustration. You may tell me that the ordinary powers of observation ought to have been enough. Why, yes! But, then, as she had set up for a guide and teacher, there was nothing surprising for me in the discovery that she was blind. That's quite in order. She was a profoundly innocent person; only it would not have been proper to tell her husband so.

CHAPTER THREE

Thrift—and the Child

"But there was nothing improper in my observing to Fyne that, last night, Mrs. Fyne seemed to have some idea where that enterprising young lady had gone to. Fyne shook his head. No; his wife had been by no means so certain as she had pretended to be. She merely had her reasons to think, to hope, that the girl might have taken a room somewhere in London, had buried herself in town—in readiness or perhaps in horror of the approaching day——

"He ceased and sat solemnly dejected, in a brown study. 'What day?' I asked at last; but he did not hear me apparently. He diffused such portentous gloom into the atmosphere that I lost patience with him.

" 'What on earth are you so dismal about?' I cried, being genuinely surprised and puzzled. 'One would think the girl was a state prisoner under your care.'

"And suddenly I became still more surprised at myself, at the way I had somehow taken for granted things which did appear queer when one thought them out.

" 'But why this secrecy? Why did they elope—if it is an elopement? Was the girl afraid of your wife? And your brother-in-law? What on earth possessed him to make a clandestine match of it? Was he afraid of your wife too?'

"Fyne made an effort to rouse himself.

" 'Of course my brother-in-law, Captain Anthony, the son of . . .' He checked himself as if trying to break a bad habit. 'He would be persuaded by her. We have been most friendly to the girl!'

" 'She struck me as a foolish and inconsiderate little person. But why should you and your wife take to heart so strongly mere folly—or even a want of consideration?'

" 'It's the most unscrupulous action,' declared Fyne weightily—and sighed.

" 'I suppose she is poor,' I observed after a short silence. 'But after all . . .'

" 'You don't know who she is.' Fyne had regained his average solemnity.

"I confessed that I had not caught her name when his wife had introduced us to each other. 'It was something beginning with an S—wasn't it?' And then with the utmost coolness Fyne remarked that it did not matter. The name was not her name.

" 'Do you mean to say that you made a young lady known to me under a false name?' I asked, with the amused feeling that the days of wonders and portents had not passed away yet. That the eminently serious Fyne should do such an exceptional thing was simply staggering. With a more hasty enunciation than usual little Fyne was sure that I would not demand an apology for this irregularity if I knew what her real name was. A sort of warmth crept into his deep tone.

" 'We have tried to befriend that girl in every way. She is the daughter and only child of de Barral.'

"Evidently he expected to produce a sensation; but I merely returned his intense, awaiting gaze. For a time we stared at each other. Conscious of being reprehensibly dense I groped in the darkness of my mind: De Barral, de Barral—and all at once noise and light burst on me as if a window of my memory had been suddenly flung open on a street in the City. De Barral! But could it be the same? Surely not!

" 'The financier?' I suggested half incredulous.

" 'Yes,' said Fyne; and in this instance his native

solemnity of tone seemed to be strangely appropriate, 'The convict.' "

Marlow looked at me, significantly, and remarked in an explanatory tone—

"One somehow never thought of de Barral as having any children, or any other home than the offices of the 'Orb'; or any other existence, associations or interests than financial. I see you remember the crash . . ."

"I was away in the Indian Seas at the time," I said. "But of course——"

"Of course," Marlow struck in. "All the world . . . You may wonder at my slowness in recognizing the name. But you know that my memory is merely a mauso- leum of proper names. In de Barral's case, it got put away in my mausoleum in company with so many names of his own creation that really he had to throw off a monstrous heap of grisly bones before he stood before me at the call of the wizard Fyne. The fellow had a pretty fancy in names: the 'Orb' Deposit Bank, the 'Sceptre' Mutual Aid Society, the 'Thrift and Independence' Asso- ciation. Yes, a very pretty taste in names; and nothing else besides—absolutely nothing—no other merit. Well, yes. He had another name, but that's pure luck—his own name of de Barral which he did not invent. I don't think that a mere Jones or Brown could have fished out from the depths of the Incredible such a colossal manifestation of human folly as that man did. But it may be that I am underestimating the alacrity of human folly in rising to the bait. No doubt I am. The greed of that absurd mon- ster is incalculable, unfathomable, inconceivable. The career of de Barral demonstrates that it will rise to a naked hook. He didn't lure it with a fairy tale. He hadn't enough imagination for it . . ."

"Was he a foreigner?" I asked. "It's clearly a French name. I suppose it *was* his name?"

"Oh, he didn't invent it. He was born to it, in Bethnal Green, as it came out during the proceedings. He was in the habit of alluding to his Scotch connections. But every great man has done that. The mother, I believe, was Scotch, right enough. The father, de Barral, whatever his origins, retired from the Customs Service (tide-waiter I think), and started lending money in a very, very small way in the East End to people connected with the docks, stevedores, minor barge-owners, ship-chandlers, tally clerks, all sorts of very small fry. He made his living at it. He was a very decent man, I believe. He had enough influence to place his only son as junior clerk in the account department of one of the Dock Companies. 'Now, my boy,' he said to him, 'I've given you a fine start.' But de Barral didn't start. He stuck. He gave perfect satisfaction. At the end of three years he got a small rise of salary and went out courting in the evenings. He went courting the daughter of an old sea-captain who was a church-warden of his parish and lived in an old badly preserved Georgian house with a garden: one of these houses standing in a reduced bit of 'grounds' that you discover in a labyrinth of the most sordid streets, exactly alike and composed of six-roomed hutches.

"Some of them were the vicarages of slum parishes. The old sailor had got hold of one cheap, and de Barral got hold of his daughter—which was a good bargain for him. The old sailor was very good to the young couple and very fond of their little girl. Mrs. de Barral was an equable, unassuming woman, at that time with a fund of simple gaiety, and with no ambitions; but, womanlike, she longed for change and for something interesting to happen now and then. It was she who encouraged de Barral to accept the offer of a post in the West-End branch of a great bank. It appears he shrank from such a great adventure for a long time. At last his wife's arguments prevailed. Later she used to say: 'It's the only time he ever listened to me; and I wonder now if it hadn't been better for me to die before I ever made him go into that bank.'

"You may be surprised at my knowledge of these details. Well, I had them ultimately from Mrs. Fyne. Mrs. Fyne, while yet Miss Anthony, in her days of bondage, knew Mrs. de Barral in her days of exile. Mrs. de Barral was living then in a big stone mansion with mullioned windows in a large damp park, called the Priory, adjoining the village where the refined poet had built himself a house.

"These were the days of de Barral's success. He had bought the place without ever seeing it and had packed off his wife and child at once there to take possession. He did not know what to do with them in London. He himself had a suite of rooms in an hotel. He gave there dinner parties followed by cards in the evening. He had developed the gambling passion—or else a mere card mania—but at any rate he played heavily, for relaxation, with a lot of dubious hangers on.

"Meantime Mrs. de Barral, expecting him every day, lived at the Priory, with a carriage and pair, a governess for the child and many servants. The village people would see her through the railings wandering under the trees with her little girl, lost in her strange surroundings. Nobody ever came near her. And there she died as some faithful and delicate animals die—from neglect, absolutely from neglect, rather unexpectedly and without any fuss. The village was sorry for her because, though obviously worried about something, she was good to the poor and was always ready for a chat with any of the humble folks. Of course they knew that she wasn't a lady—not what you would call a real lady. And even her acquaintance with Miss Anthony was only a cottage-door, a village-street acquaintance. Carleon Anthony was a tremendous aristocrat (his father had been a 'restoring' architect), and his daughter was not allowed to associate with any one but the county young ladies. Nevertheless, in defiance of the poet's wrathful concern for undefiled refinement, there were some quiet, melancholy strolls to and fro in the great avenue of chestnuts leading to the park-gate, during which Mrs. de Barral came to call Miss Anthony 'my dear'—and even 'my poor dear.' The lonely soul had no one to talk to but that not very happy girl. The governess despised her. The housekeeper was distant in her manner. Moreover Mrs. de Barral was no foolish gossiping woman. But she made some confidences to Miss Anthony. Such wealth was a terrific thing to have thrust upon one, she affirmed. Once she went so far as to confess that she was dying with anxiety. Mr. de Barral (so she referred to him) had been an excellent husband and an exemplary father, but 'you see, my dear, I have had a great experience of him. I am sure he won't know what to do with all that money people are giving to him to take care of for them. He's as likely as not to do something rash. When he comes here I must have a good long serious talk with him, like the talks we often used to have together in the good old times of our life.' And then one day a cry of anguish was wrung from her: 'My dear, he will never come here, he will never, never come!'

"She was wrong. He came to the funeral, was extremely cut up, and holding the child tightly by the hand wept bitterly at the side of the grave. Miss Anthony, at the cost of a whole week of sneers and abuse from the poet, saw it all with her own eyes. De Barral clung to the child like a drowning man. He managed, though, to catch the half-past five fast train, travelling to town alone in a reserved compartment, with all the blinds down . . ."

"Leaving the child?" I said interrogatively.

"Yes. Leaving . . . He shirked the problem. He was born that way. He had no idea what to do with her or for that matter with anything or anybody including himself. He bolted back to his suite of rooms in the hotel. He was the most helpless . . . She might have been left in the Priory to the end of time had not the high-toned governess threatened to send in her resignation. She didn't care for the child a bit, and the lonely, gloomy Priory had got on her nerves. She wasn't going to put up with such a life and, having just come out of some ducal family, she bullied de Barral in a very lofty fashion. To pacify her he took a splendidly furnished house in the most expensive part of Brighton for them, and now and then ran down for a week-end, with a trunk full of exquisite sweets and with his hat full of money. The governess spent it for him in extra ducal style. She was nearly forty and harboured a secret taste for patronizing young men of sorts—of a certain sort. But of that Mrs. Fyne of course had no personal knowledge then; she told me, however, that even in the Priory days she had suspected her of being an artificial, heartless, vulgar-minded woman with the lowest possible ideals. But de Barral did not know it. He literally did not know anything . . ."

"But tell me, Marlow," I interrupted, "how do you account for this opinion? He must have been a personality in a sense—in some one sense surely. You don't work the greatest material havoc of a decade at least, in a commercial community, without having something in you."

Marlow shook his head.

"He was a mere sign, a portent. There was nothing in

him. Just about that time the word Thrift was to the fore.
You know the power of words. We pass through periods
dominated by this or that word—it may be development,
or it may be competition, or education, or purity, or
efficiency, or even sanctity. It is the word of the time.
Well, just then it was the word Thrift which was out in
the streets walking arm in arm with righteousness, the
inseparable companion and backer up of all such national
catch-words, looking everybody in the eye as it were.
The very drabs of the pavement, poor things, didn't
escape the fascination. . . . However! . . . Well, the
greatest portion of the press was screeching in all possible
tones, like a confounded company of parrots instructed
by some devil with a taste for practical jokes, that the
financier de Barral was helping the great moral evolution
of our character towards the newly discovered virtue of
Thrift. He was helping it by all these great establishments
of his, which made the moral merits of Thrift manifest
to the most callous hearts, simply by promising to pay
ten per cent. interest on all deposits. And you didn't
want necessarily to belong to the well-to-do classes in
order to participate in the advantages of virtue. If you
had but a spare sixpence in the world and went and gave
it to de Barral it was Thrift! It's quite likely that he
himself believed it. He must have. It's inconceivable that
he alone should stand out against the infatuation of the
whole world. He couldn't tell . . ."

"You did see him then?" I said with some curiosity.

"I did. Strange, isn't it? It was only once, in the days
of his glory or splendour. No! Neither of these words
will fit his success. There was never any glory or splendour about that figure. Well, let us say in the days when
he was, according to the majority of the daily press, a
financial force working for the improvement of the character of the people. I'll tell you how it came about.

"At that time I used to know a podgy, wealthy, bald
little man having chambers in the Albany; a financier,
too, in his way, carrying out transactions of an intimate
nature and of no moral character; mostly with young men
of birth and expectations—though I dare say he didn't
withhold his ministrations from elderly plebeians either.
He was a true democrat; he would have done business
(a sharp kind of business) with the devil himself. Every-

thing was fly that came into his web. He received the applicants in an alert, jovial fashion which was quite surprising. It gave relief without giving too much confidence, which was just as well perhaps. His business was transacted in an apartment furnished like a drawing-room, the walls hung with several brown, heavily framed, oil paintings. I don't know if they were good, but they were big, and with their elaborate, tarnished gilt-frames had a melancholy dignity. The man himself sat at an inlaid writing-table which looked like a rare piece from a museum of art; his chair had a high, oval, carved back, upholstered in faded tapestry; and these objects made of the costly black Havana cigar, which he rolled incessantly from the middle to the left corner of his mouth and back again, an inexpressibly cheap and nasty object. I had to see him several times in the interest of a poor devil so unlucky that he didn't even have a more competent friend than myself to speak for him at a very difficult time in his life.

"I don't know at what hour my private financier began his day, but he used to give one appointments at unheard of times: such as a quarter to eight in the morning, for instance. On arriving one found him busy at that marvellous writing-table, looking very fresh, exhaling a faint fragrance of scented soap and with the cigar already well alight. You may believe that I entered on my mission with many unpleasant forebodings; but there was in that fat, admirably washed, little man such a profound contempt for mankind that it amounted to a species of good nature; which, unlike the milk of genuine kindness, was never in danger of turning sour. Then, once, during a pause in business, while we were waiting for the production of a document for which he had sent (perhaps to the cellar?) I happened to remark, glancing round the room, that I had never seen so many fine things assembled together out of a collection. Whether this was unconscious diplomacy on my part, or not, I shouldn't like to say—but the remark was true enough, and it pleased him extremely. 'It *is* a collection,' he said emphatically. 'Only I live right in it, which most collectors don't. But I see that you know what you are looking at. Not many people who come here on business do. Stable fittings are more in their way.'

"I don't know whether my appreciation helped to advance my friend's business, but at any rate it helped our intercourse. He treated me with a shade of familiarity as one of the initiated.

"The last time I called on him to conclude the transaction we were interrupted by a person, something like a cross between a bookmaker and a private secretary, who, entering through a door which was not the anteroom door, walked up and stooped to whisper into his ear.

" 'Eh? Who, did you say?'

"The nondescript person stooped and whispered again, adding a little louder: 'Says he won't detain you a moment.'

"My little man glanced at me, said 'Ah! Well,' irresolutely. I got up from my chair and offered to come again later. He looked whimsically alarmed. 'No, no. It's bad enough to lose my money, but I don't want to waste any more of my time over your friend. We must be done with this to-day. Just go and have a look at that *garniture de cheminée* yonder. There's another, something like it, in the castle of Laeken, but mine's much superior in design.'

"I moved accordingly to the other side of that big room. The *garniture* was very fine. But while pretending to examine it I watched my man going forward to meet a tall visitor, who said, 'I thought you would be disengaged so early. It's only a word or two'—and after a whispered confabulation of no more than a minute, reconduct him to the door and shake hands ceremoniously. 'Not at all, not at all. Very pleased to be of use. You can depend absolutely on my information'—'Oh thank you, thank you. I just looked in.' 'Certainly, quite right. Any time. . . . Good morning.'

"I had a good look at the visitor while they were exchanging these civilities. He was clad in black. He wore a flat, broad, black satin tie in which was stuck a large cameo pin; and a small turn-down collar. His hair, discoloured and silky, curled slightly over his ears. His cheeks were hairless and round, and apparently soft. He carried himself stiffly, walked with small steps and spoke in a gentle, inward voice. Perhaps from contrast with the magnificent polish of the room and the neatness of its owner, he struck me as indigent, and, if not exactly humble, then much subdued by evil fortune.

"I wondered greatly at my fat little financier's civility to that dubious personage when he asked me, as we resumed our respective seats, whether I knew who it was that had just gone out. On my shaking my head negatively he smiled queerly, said 'De Barral,' and enjoyed my surprise. Then becoming grave: 'That's a deep fellow, if you like. We all know where he started from and where he got to; but nobody knows what he means to do.' He became thoughtful for a moment and added as if speaking to himself, 'I wonder what his game is.'

"And, you know, there was no game, no game of any sort, or shape, or kind. It came out plainly at the trial. As I've told you before, he was a clerk in a bank, like thousands of others. He got that berth as a second start in life and there he stuck again, giving perfect satisfaction. Then one day as though a supernatural voice had whispered into his ear or some invisible fly had stung him, he put on his hat, went out into the street and began advertising. That's absolutely all that there was to it. He caught in the street the word of the time and harnessed it to his preposterous chariot.

"One remembers his first modest advertisements headed with the magic word Thrift, Thrift, Thrift, thrice repeated; promising ten per cent. on all deposits and giving the address of the Thrift and Independence Aid Association in Vauxhall Bridge Road. Apparently nothing more was necessary. He didn't even explain what he meant to do with the money he asked the public to pour into his lap. Of course he meant to lend it out at high rates of interest. He did so—but he did it without system, plan, foresight or judgment. And as he frittered away the sums that flowed in, he advertised for more—and got it. During a period of general business prosperity he set up The Orb Bank and The Sceptre Trust, simply, it seems, for advertising purposes. They were mere names. He was totally unable to organize anything, to promote any sort of enterprise if it were only for the purpose of juggling with the shares. At that time he could have had for the asking any number of Dukes, retired Generals, active M.P.'s, ex-ambassadors and so on as Directors to sit at the wildest boards of his invention. But he never

tried. He had no real imagination. All he could do was
to publish more advertisements and open more branch
offices of the Thrift and Independence, of The Orb, of
The Sceptre, for the receipt of deposits; first in this town,
then in that town, north and south—everywhere where
he could find suitable premises at a moderate rent. For
this was the great characteristic of the management.
Modesty, moderation, simplicity. Neither The Orb nor
The Sceptre nor yet their parent the Thrift and Independence had built for themselves the usual palaces. For
this abstention they were praised in silly public prints as
illustrating in their management the principle of Thrift
for which they were founded. The fact is that de Barral
simply didn't think of it. Of course he had soon moved
from Vauxhall Bridge Road. He knew enough for that.
What he got hold of next was an old, enormous, rat-
infested brick house in a small street off the Strand.
Strangers were taken in front of the meanest possible,
begrimed, yellowy, flat brick wall, with two rows of
unadorned window-holes one above the other, and were
exhorted with bated breath to behold and admire the simplicity of the head-quarters of the great financial force of
the day. The word THRIFT perched right up on the roof
in giant gilt letters, and two enormous shield-like brass-
plates curved round the corners on each side of the doorway were the only shining spots in de Barral's business
outfit. Nobody knew what operations were carried on
inside except this—that if you walked in and tendered
your money over the counter it would be calmly taken
from you by somebody who would give you a printed
receipt. That and no more. It appears that such knowledge is irresistible. People went in and tendered; and
once it was taken from their hands their money was more
irretrievably gone from them than if they had thrown it
into the sea. This then, and nothing else, was being carried on in there . . ."

"Come, Marlow," I said, "you exaggerate surely—if
only by your way of putting things. It's too startling."

"I exaggerate!" he defended himself. "My way of putting things! My dear fellow, I have merely stripped the
rags of business verbiage and financial jargon off my
statements. And you are startled! I am giving you the
naked truth. It's true too that nothing lays itself open to

the charge of exaggeration more than the language of naked truth. What comes with a shock is admitted with difficulty. But what will you say to the end of his career! It began with the Orb Deposit Bank. Under the name of that institution de Barral, with the frantic obstinacy of an unimaginative man, had been financing an Indian prince who was prosecuting a claim for immense sums of money against the government. It was an enormous number of scores of lakhs—a miserable remnant of his ancestors' treasures—that sort of thing. And it was all authentic enough. There was a real prince; and the claim too was sufficiently real—only unfortunately it was not a valid claim. So the prince lost his case on the last appeal, and the beginning of de Barral's end became manifest to the public in the shape of a half-sheet of note-paper wafered by the four corners on the closed door of The Orb offices, notifying that payment was stopped at that establishment.

"Its consort The Sceptre collapsed within the week. I won't say in American parlance that suddenly the bottom fell out of the whole of de Barral concerns. There never had been any bottom to it. It was like the cask of the Danaides into which the public had been pleased to pour its deposits. That they were gone was clear; and the bankruptcy proceedings which followed were like a sinister farce, bursts of laughter in a setting of mute anguish—that of the depositors; hundreds of thousands of them. The laughter was irresistible; the accompaniment of the bankrupt's public examination.

"I don't know if it was from utter lack of all imagination or from the possession in undue proportion of a particular kind of it, or from both—and the three alternatives are possible—but it was discovered that this man who had been raised to such a height by the credulity of the public was himself more gullible than any of his depositors. He had been the prey of all sorts of swindlers, adventurers, visionaries, and even lunatics. Wrapping himself up in deep and imbecile secrecy he had gone in for the most fantastic schemes: a harbour and docks on the coast of Patagonia, quarries in Labrador—such-like speculations. Fisheries to feed a canning factory on the banks of the Amazon was one of them. A principality to be bought in Madagascar was another. As the grotesque details of these incredible transactions came out, one by one, ripples of laughter ran over the closely packed court—each one a little louder than the other. The audience ended by fairly roaring under the cumulative effect of absurdity. The Registrar laughed, the barristers laughed, the reporters laughed, the serried ranks of the miserable depositors watching anxiously every word laughed like one man. They laughed hysterically—the poor wretches—on the verge of tears.

"There was only one person who remained unmoved. It was de Barral himself. He preserved his serene, gentle expression, I am told (for I have not witnessed those scenes myself), and looked around at the people with an air of placid sufficiency which was the first hint to the world of the man's overweening, unmeasurable conceit, hidden hitherto under a diffident manner. It could be seen too in his dogged assertion that if he had been given enough time and a lot more money everything would have come right. And there were some people (yes, amongst his very victims) who more than half believed him, even after the criminal prosecution which soon followed. When placed in the dock he lost his steadiness as if some sustaining illusion had gone to pieces within him suddenly. He ceased to be himself in manner completely, and even in disposition, in so far that his faded neutral eyes matching his discoloured hair so well were discovered then to be capable of expressing a sort of underhand hate. He was at first defiant, then insolent, then broke down and burst into tears; but it might have been from rage. Then he calmed down, returned to his soft manner of speech and to that unassuming quiet bearing which had been usual with him even in his greatest days. But it seemed as though in this moment of change he had at last perceived what a power he had been; for he remarked to one of the prosecuting counsel who had assumed a lofty moral tone in questioning him, that— yes, he had gambled—he liked cards. But that only a year ago a host of smart people would have been only too pleased to take a hand at cards with him. Yes— he went on—some of the very people who were there accommodated with seats on the bench; and turning upon the counsel, 'You yourself as well,' he cried. He could have had half the town at his rooms to fawn upon him

if he had cared for that sort of thing. 'Why, now I think
of it, it took me most of my time to keep people, just
of your sort, off me,' he ended with a good-humoured,
quite unobtrusive, contempt, as though the fact had
dawned upon him for the first time.

"This was the moment, the only moment, when he had
perhaps all the audience in Court with him, in a hush of
dreary silence. And then the dreary proceedings were
resumed. For all the outside excitement it was the most
dreary of all celebrated trials. The bankruptcy proceedings had exhausted all the laughter there was in it. Only
the fact of widespread ruin remained, and the resentment
of a mass of people for having been fooled by means too
simple to save their self-respect from a deep wound
which the cleverness of a consummate scoundrel would
not have inflicted. A shamefaced amazement attended
these proceedings in which de Barral was not being
exposed alone. For himself his only cry was: Time! Time!
Time would have set everything right. In time some of
these speculations of his were certain to have succeeded.
Sometimes, I am told, his appearance was ecstatic, his
motionless pale eyes seemed to be gazing down the vista
of future ages. Time—and of course, more money. 'Ah!
If only you had left me alone for a couple of years more,'
he cried once in accents of passionate belief. 'The money
was coming in all right.' The deposits you understand—
the savings of Thrift. Oh yes they had been coming in to
the very last moment. And he regretted them. He had
arrived to regard them as his own by a sort of mystical
persuasion. And yet it was a perfectly true cry, when he
turned once more on the counsel who was beginning a
question with the words 'You have had all these immense
sums . . .' with the indignant retort, *What* have I had
out of them?'

"It was perfectly true. He had had nothing out of
them—nothing of the prestigious or the desirable things
of the earth, craved for by predatory natures. He had
gratified no tastes, had known no luxury; he had built
no gorgeous palaces, had formed no splendid galleries
out of these 'immense sums.' He had not even a home.
He had gone into these rooms in an hotel and had stuck
there for years, giving no doubt perfect satisfaction to
the management. They had twice raised his rent to show,

I suppose, their high sense of his distinguished patronage. He had bought for himself out of all the wealth streaming through his fingers neither adulation nor love, neither splendour nor comfort. There was something perfect in his consistent mediocrity. His very vanity seemed to miss the gratification of even the mere show of power. In the days when he was most fully in the public eye the invincible obscurity of his origins clung to him like a shadowy garment. He had handled millions without ever enjoying anything of what is counted as precious in the community of men, because he had neither the brutality of temperament nor the fineness of mind to make him desire them with the will power of a masterful adventurer . . ."

"You seem to have studied the man," I observed.

"Studied," repeated Marlow thoughtfully. "No! Not studied. I had no opportunities. You know that I saw him only on that one occasion I told you of. But it may be that a glimpse and no more is the proper way of seeing an individuality; and de Barral was that, in virtue of his very deficiencies, for they made of him something quite unlike one's preconceived ideas. I have not studied de Barral, but that is how I understand him so far as he could be understood through the din of the crash; the wailing and gnashing of teeth, the newspaper contents bills: 'The Thrift Frauds. Cross-examination of the accused. Extra special'—blazing fiercely; the charitable appeals for the victims, the grave tones of the dailies rumbling with compassion as if they were the national bowels. All this lasted a whole week of industrious sittings. A pressman whom I knew told me, 'He's an idiot'; which was possible. Before that I overheard once somebody declaring that he had a criminal type of face; which I knew was untrue. The sentence was pronounced by artificial light in a stifling poisonous atmosphere. Something edifying was said by the judge weightily, about the retribution overtaking the perpetrator of 'the most heartless frauds on an unprecedented scale.' I don't understand these things much, but it appears that he had juggled with accounts, cooked balance sheets, had gathered in deposits months after he ought to have known himself to be hopelessly insolvent, and done enough of other things, highly reprehensible in the eyes of the law, to earn for himself seven years' penal servitude. The sentence making its way outside met with a good reception. A small mob composed mainly of people who themselves did not look particularly clever and scrupulous, leavened by a slight sprinkling of genuine pickpockets, amused itself by cheering in the most penetrating, abominable cold drizzle that I remember. I happened to be passing there on my way from the East End where I had spent my day about the Docks with an old chum who was looking after the fitting out of a new ship. I am always eager, when allowed, to call on a new ship. They interest me like charming young persons.

"I got mixed up in that crowd seething with an animosity as senseless as things of the street always are, and it was while I was laboriously making my way out of it that the pressman of whom I spoke was jostled against me. He did me the justice to be surprised. 'What? You here! The last person in the world . . . If I had known I could have got you inside. Plenty of room. Interest been over for the last three days. Got seven years. Well, I am glad.'

"'Why are you glad? Because he's got seven years?' I asked, greatly incommoded by the pressure of a hulking fellow who was remarking to some of his equally oppressive friends that the 'beggar ought to have been pole-axed.' I don't know whether he had ever confided his savings to de Barral, but if so, judging from his appearance, they must have been the proceeds of some successful burglary. The pressman by my side said 'No' to my question. He was glad because it was all over. He had suffered from the heat and the bad air of the court. The clammy, raw chill of the streets seemed to affect his liver instantly. He became contemptuous and irritable, and plied his elbows viciously, making way for himself and me.

"A dull affair this. All such cases were dull. No really dramatic moments. The book-keeping of The Orb and all the rest of them was certainly a burlesque revelation, but the public did not care for revelations of that kind. Dull dog that de Barral—he grumbled. He could not or would not take the trouble to characterize for me the appearance of that man now officially a criminal (we had gone across the road for a drink), but told me with a sourly derisive snigger that, after the sentence had been pronounced the fellow clung to the dock long enough to make a sort of protest. 'You haven't given me time. If I had been given time I would have ended by being made a peer like some of them.' And he had permitted himself his very first and last gesture in all these days, raising a hard-clenched fist above his head.

"The pressman disapproved of that manifestation. It was not his business to understand it. Is it ever the business of any pressman to understand anything? I guess not. It would lead him too far away from the actualities which are the daily bread of the public mind. He probably thought the display worth very little from a picturesque point of view; the weak voice, the colourless personality as incapable of an attitude as a bed-post, the very fatuity of the clenched hand so ineffectual at that time and place—no, it wasn't worth much. And then, for him, an accomplished craftsman in his trade, thinking was distinctly 'bad business.' His business was to write a readable account. But I, who had nothing to write, permitted myself to use my mind as we sat before our still untouched glasses. And the disclosure which so often rewards a moment of detachment from mere visual impressions gave me a thrill very much approaching a shudder. I seemed to understand that, with the shock of the agonies and perplexities of his trial, the imagination of that man, whose moods, notions, and motives wore frequently an air of grotesque mystery—that his imagination had been at last roused into activity. And this was awful. Just try to enter into the feelings of a man whose imagination wakes up at the very moment he is about to enter the tomb. . . .

"You must not think," went on Marlow after a pause, "that on that morning with Fyne I went consciously in my mind over all this, let us call it information; no, better say, this fund of knowledge which I had, or rather which existed, in me in regard to de Barral. Information is something one goes out to seek and puts away when found as you might do a piece of lead: ponderous, useful, dull, unvibrating. Whereas knowledge comes to one, this sort of knowledge, a chance acquisition preserving in its repose a fine resonant quality. . . . But as such distinctions touch upon the transcendental I shall spare you the pain of listening to them. There are limits to my cruelty.

No! I didn't reckon up carefully in my mind all this I
have been telling you. How could I have done so, with
Fyne in the room? He sat perfectly still, statuesque in
homely fashion, after having delivered himself of his
effective assent: 'Yes. The convict,' and I, far from
indulging in a reminiscent excursion into the past,
remained sufficiently in the present to muse in a vague,
absent-minded way on the respectable proportions and
on the (upon the whole) comely shape of his pedestrian's
calves, for he had thrown one leg over his knee, carelessly, to conceal the trouble of his mind by an air of
ease. But all the same the knowledge was in me, the
awakened resonance of which I spoke just now. I said
wondering, rather irrationally—

" 'And so de Barral had a wife and child! That girl's
his daughter. And how . . .'

"Fyne, interrupted me by stating again earnestly, as
though it were something not easy to believe, that his
wife and himself had tried to befriend the girl in every
way—indeed they had! I did not doubt him for a
moment, of course, but my wonder at this was more
rational. At that hour of the morning, you mustn't forget,
I knew nothing as yet of Mrs. Fyne's contact (it was hardly
more) with de Barral's wife and child during their exile at
the Priory, in the culminating days of that man's fame.

"Fyne, who had come over, it was clear, solely to talk
to me on that subject, gave me the first hint of this initial,
merely out of doors, connection. 'The girl was quite a
child then,' he continued. 'Later on she was removed out
of Mrs. Fyne's reach in charge of a governess—a very
unsatisfactory person,' he explained. His wife had then—
h'm—met him; and on her marriage she lost sight of the
child completely. But after the birth of Polly (Polly was
the third Fyne girl) she did not get on very well, and
went to Brighton for some months to recover her
strength—and there, one day in the street, the child (she
wore her hair down her back still) recognized her outside
a shop and rushed, actually rushed, into Mrs. Fyne's
arms. Rather touching this. And so, disregarding the cold
impertinence of that . . . h'm . . . governess, his wife
naturally responded.

"He was solemnly fragmentary. I broke in with the
observation that it must have been before the crash.

"Fyne nodded with deepened gravity, stating in his bass tone—

" 'Just before,' and indulged himself with a weighty period of solemn silence.

"De Barral, he resumed suddenly, was not coming to Brighton for week-ends regularly, then. Must have been conscious already of the approaching disaster. Mrs. Fyne avoided being drawn into making his acquaintance, and this suited the views of the governess person, very jealous of any outside influence. But in any case it would not have been an easy matter. Extraordinary, stiff-backed, thin figure all in black, the observed of all, while walking hand-in-hand with the girl; apparently shy, but—and here Fyne came very near showing something like insight—probably nursing under a diffident manner a considerable amount of secret arrogance. Mrs. Fyne pitied Flora de Barral's fate long before the catastrophe. Most unfortunate guidance. Very unsatisfactory surroundings. The girl was known in the streets, was stared at in public places as if she had been a sort of princess, but she was kept, with a very ominous consistency, from making any acquaintances—though of course there were many people no doubt who would have been more than willing to—h'm—make themselves agreeable to Miss de Barral. But this did not enter into the plans of the governess, an intriguing person hatching a most sinister plot under her air of distant, fashionable exclusiveness. Good little Fyne's eyes bulged with solemn horror as he revealed to me, in agitated speech, his wife's more than suspicions, at the time, of that Mrs., Mrs. What's-her-name's perfidious conduct. She actually seemed to have—Mrs. Fyne asserted—formed a plot already to marry eventually her charge to an impecunious relation of her own—a young man with furtive eyes and something impudent in his manner, whom that woman called her nephew, and whom she was always having down to stay with her.

" 'And perhaps not her nephew. No relation at all'—Fyne emitted with a convulsive effort this, the most awful part of the suspicions Mrs. Fyne used to impart to him piecemeal when he came down to spend his weekends gravely with her and the children. The Fynes, in their good-natured concern for the unlucky child of the man busied in stirring casually so many millions, spent the

moments of their weekly reunion in wondering earnestly
what could be done to defeat the most wicked of conspiracies, trying to invent some tactful line of conduct in such
extraordinary circumstances. I could see them, simple
and scrupulous, worrying honestly about that unprotected big girl while looking at their own little girls playing on the seashore. Fyne assured me that his wife's rest
was disturbed by the great problem of interference.

" 'It was very acute of Mrs. Fyne to spot such a deep
game,' I said, wondering to myself where her acuteness
had gone to now, to let her be taken unawares by a game
so much simpler and played to the end under her very
nose. But then, at that time, when her nightly rest was
disturbed by the dread of the fate preparing for de Barral's unprotected child, she was not engaged in writing a
compendious and ruthless handbook on the theory and
practice of life, for the use of women with a grievance.
She could as yet, before the task of evolving the philoso-
phy of rebellious action had affected her intuitive sharp-
ness, perceive things which were, I suspect, moderately
plain. For I am inclined to believe that the woman whom
chance had put in command of Flora de Barral's destiny
took no very subtle pains to conceal her game. She was
conscious of being a complete master of the situation,
having once for all established her ascendancy over de
Barral. She had taken all her measures against outside
observation of her conduct; and I could not help smiling
at the thought what a ghastly nuisance the serious, innocent Fynes must have been to her. How exasperated she
must have been by that couple falling into Brighton as
completely unforeseen as a bolt from the blue—if not so
prompt. How she must have hated them!

"But I conclude she would have carried out whatever
plan she might have formed. I can imagine de Barral
accustomed for years to defer to her wishes and, either
through arrogance, or shyness, or simply because of his
unimaginative stupidity, remaining outside the social
pale, knowing no one but some card-playing cronies; I
can picture him to myself terrified at the prospect of
having the care of a marriageable girl thrust on his hands,
forcing on him a complete change of habits and the
necessity of another kind of existence which he would
not even have known how to begin. It is evident to me

that Mrs. What's-her-name would have had her atrocious way with very little trouble even if the excellent Fynes had been able to do something. She would simply have bullied de Barral in a lofty style. There's nothing more subservient than an arrogant man when his arrogance has once been broken in some particular instance.

"However there was no time and no necessity for any one to do anything. The situation itself vanished in the financial crash as a building vanishes in an earthquake—here one moment and gone the next with only an ill omened, slight, preliminary rumble. Well, to say 'in a moment' is an exaggeration perhaps; but that everything was over in just twenty-four hours is an exact statement. Fyne was able to tell me all about it; and the phrase that would depict the nature of the change best is: an instant and complete destitution. I don't understand these matters very well, but from Fyne's narrative it seemed as if the creditors or the depositors, or the competent authorities, had got hold in the twinkling of an eye of everything de Barral possessed in the world, down to his watch and chain, the money in his trousers' pocket, his spare suits of clothes, and I suppose the cameo pin out of his black satin cravat. Everything! I believe he gave up the very wedding ring of his late wife. The gloomy Priory with its damp park and a couple of farms had been made over to Mrs. de Barral; but when she died (without making a will) it reverted to him, I imagine. They got that of course; but it was a mere crumb in a Sahara of starvation, a drop in the thirsty ocean. I dare say that not a single soul in the world got the comfort of as much as a recovered threepenny bit out of the estate. Then, less than crumbs, less than drops, there were to be grabbed, the lease of the big Brighton house, the furniture therein, the carriage and pair, the girl's riding-horse, her costly trinkets; down to the heavily gold-mounted collar of her pedigree St. Bernard. The dog too went: the most noble-looking item in the beggarly assets.

"What however went first of all, or rather vanished, was nothing in the nature of an asset. It was that plotting governess with the trick of a 'perfect lady' manner (severely conventional) and the soul of a remorseless brigand. When a woman takes to any sort of unlawful man-trade, there's nothing to beat her in the way of

thoroughness. It's true that you will find people who'll
tell you that this terrific virulence in breaking through
all established things is altogether the fault of men. Such
people will ask you with a clever air why the servile wars
were always the most fierce, desperate and atrocious of
all wars. And you may make such answer as you can—
even the eminently feminine one, if you choose, so typi-
cal of the women's literal mind, 'I don't see what this
has to do with it!' How many arguments have been
knocked over (I won't say knocked down) by these few
words! For if we men try to put the spaciousness of all
experiences into our reasoning and would fain put the
Infinite itself into our love, it isn't, as some writer has
remarked, 'It isn't women's doing.' Oh, no. They don't
care for these things. That sort of aspiration is not
much in their way; and it shall be a funny world, the
world of their arranging, where the Irrelevant would fan-
tastically step in to take the place of the sober humdrum
Imaginative. . . ."

I raised my hand to stop my friend Marlow.

"Do you really believe what you have said?" I asked,
meaning no offence, because with Marlow one never
could be sure.

"Only on certain days of the year," said Marlow with
a malicious smile. "To-day I have been simply trying to
be spacious and I perceive I've managed to hurt your
susceptibilities which are consecrated to women. When
you sit alone and silent you are defending in your mind
the poor women from attacks which cannot possibly
touch them. I wonder *what* can touch them? But to
soothe your uneasiness I will point out again that an
Irrelevant world would be very amusing, if the women
would take care to make it as charming as they alone
can, by preserving for us certain well-known, well-
established, I'll almost say hackneyed, illusions, without
which the average male creature cannot get on. And that
condition is very important. For there is nothing more
provoking than the Irrelevant when it has ceased to
amuse and charm; and then the danger would be of the
subjugated masculinity in its exasperation, making some
brusque, unguarded movement and accidentally putting
its elbow through the fine tissue of the world of which I
speak. And that would be fatal to it. For nothing looks

more irretrievably deplorable than fine tissue which has been damaged. The women themselves would be the first to become disgusted with their own creation.

"There was something of women's highly practical sanity and also of their irrelevancy in the conduct of Miss de Barral's amazing governess. It appeared from Fyne's narrative that the day before the first rumble of the cataclysm the questionable young man arrived unexpectedly in Brighton to stay with his 'Aunt.' To all outward appearance everything was going on normally; the fellow went out riding with the girl in the afternoon as he often used to do—a sight which never failed to fill Mrs. Fyne with indignation. Fyne himself was down there with his family for a whole week and was called to the window to behold the iniquity in its progress and to share in his wife's feelings. There was not even a groom with them. And Mrs. Fyne's distress was so strong at this glimpse of the unlucky girl, all unconscious of her danger riding smilingly by, that Fyne began to consider seriously whether it wasn't their plain duty to interfere at all risks—simply by writing a letter to de Barral. He said to his wife with a solemnity I can easily imagine, 'You ought to undertake that task, my dear. You have known his wife after all. That's something at any rate.' On the other hand the fear of exposing Mrs. Fyne to some nasty rebuff worried him exceedingly. Mrs. Fyne on her side gave way to despondency. Success seemed impossible. Here was a woman for more than five years in charge of the girl and apparently enjoying the complete confidence of the father. What, that would be effective, could one say, without proofs, without . . . This Mr. de Barral must be, Mrs. Fyne pronounced, either a very stupid or a downright bad man, to neglect his child so.

"You will notice that perhaps because of Fyne's solemn view of our transient life and Mrs. Fyne's natural capacity for responsibility, it had never occurred to them that the simplest way out of the difficulty was to do nothing and dismiss the matter as no concern of theirs. Which in a strict worldly sense it certainly was not. But they spent, Fyne told me, a most disturbed afternoon, considering the ways and means of dealing with the danger hanging over the head of the girl out for a ride (and no doubt enjoying herself) with an abominable scamp.

CHAPTER FOUR

The Governess

"And the best of it was that the danger was all over already. There was no danger any more. The supposed nephew's appearance had a purpose. He had come, full, full to trembling—with the bigness of his news. There must have been rumours already as to the shaky position of the de Barrals' concerns; but only amongst those in the very inmost know. No rumour or echo of rumour had reached the profane in the West End—let alone in the guileless marine suburb of Hove. The Fynes had no suspicion; the governess, playing with cold, distinguished exclusiveness the part of mother to the fabulously wealthy Miss de Barral, had no suspicion; the masters of music, of drawing, of dancing to Miss de Barral, had no idea; the minds of her medical man, of her dentist, of the servants in the house, of the tradesmen proud of having the name of de Barral on their books, were in a state of absolute serenity. Thus, that fellow, who had unexpectedly received a most alarming straight tip from somebody in the City, arrived in Brighton, at about lunchtime, with something very much in the nature of a deadly bomb in his possession. But he knew better than to throw it on the public pavement. He ate his lunch impenetrably sitting opposite Flora de Barral, and then, on some excuse closeted himself with the woman whom little Fyne's charity described (with a slight hesitation of speech however) as his 'Aunt.'

"What they said to each other in private we can imagine. She came out of her own sitting-room with red spots on her cheek-bones, which having provoked a question from her 'beloved' charge, were accounted for by a curt 'I have a headache coming on.' But we may be certain that the talk being over she must have said to that young blackguard: 'You had better take her out for a ride as usual.' We have proof positive of this in Fyne and Mrs. Fyne observing them mount at the door and pass under the windows of their sitting-room, talking together, and the poor girl all smiles; because she enjoyed in all innocence the company of Charley. She made no secret of it whatever to Mrs. Fyne; in fact, she had confided to her, long before, that she liked him very much: a confidence which had filled Mrs. Fyne with desolation and that sense of powerless anguish which is experienced in certain kinds of nightmare. For how could she warn the girl? She did venture to tell her once that she didn't like Mr. Charley. Miss de Barral heard her with astonishment. How was it possible not to like Charley? Afterwards with naïve loyalty she told Mrs. Fyne that, immensely as she was fond of her, she could not hear a word against Charley—the wonderful Charley.

"The daughter of de Barral probably enjoyed her jolly ride with the jolly Charley (infinitely more jolly than going out with a stupid old riding-master) very much indeed, because the Fynes saw them coming back at a later hour than usual. In fact it was getting nearly dark. On dismounting, helped off by the delightful Charley, she patted the neck of her horse and went up the steps. Her last ride. She was then within a few days of her sixteenth birthday, a slight figure in a riding-habit, rather shorter than the average height for her age, in a black bowler hat from under which her fine rippling dark hair cut square at the ends was hanging well down her back. The delightful Charley mounted again to take the two horses round to the mews. Mrs. Fyne remaining at the window saw the house door close on Miss de Barral returning from her last ride.

"And meantime what had the governess (out of a nobleman's family) so judiciously selected (a lady, and connected with well-known county people as she said) to direct the studies, guard the health, form the mind, polish the manners, and generally play the perfect mother to that luckless child—what had she been doing? Well, having got rid of her charge by the most natural device possible, which proved her practical sense, she started packing her belongings, an act which showed her clear view of the situation. She had worked methodically, rapidly, and well, emptying the drawers, clearing the tables in her special apartment, with something silently passionate in her thoroughness; taking everything belonging to her and some things of less unquestionable ownership, a jewelled penholder, an ivory and gold paper knife (the house was full of common, costly objects), some chased silver boxes presented by de Barral, and other trifles; but the photograph of Flora de Barral, with the loving inscription, which stood on her writing-desk, of the most modern and expensive style, in a silver-gilt frame, she neglected to take. Having accidentally, in the course of the operations, knocked it off on the floor, she let it lie there after a downward glance. Thus it, or the frame at least, became, I suppose, part of the assets in the de Barral bankruptcy.

"At dinner that evening the child found her company dull and brusque. It was uncommonly slow. She could get nothing from her governess but monosyllables, and the jolly Charley actually snubbed the various cheery openings of his 'little chum'—as he used to call her at times—but not at that time. No doubt the couple were nervous and preoccupied. For all this we have evidence, and for the fact that Flora being offended with the delightful nephew of her profoundly respected governess sulked through the rest of the evening and was glad to retire early. Mrs., Mrs.—I've really forgotten her name— the governess, invited her nephew to her sitting-room, mentioning aloud that it was to talk over some family matters. This was meant for Flora to hear, and she heard it—without the slightest interest. In fact there was nothing sufficiently unusual in such an invitation to arouse in her mind even a passing wonder. She went bored to bed, and being tired with her long ride slept soundly all night.

Her last sleep, I won't say of innocence—that word would not render my exact meaning, because it has a special meaning of its own—but I will say: of that ignorance, or better still, of that unconsciousness of the world's ways, the unconsciousness of danger, of pain, of humiliation, of bitterness, of falsehood. An unconsciousness which in the case of other beings like herself is removed by a gradual process of experience and information, often only partial at that, with saving reserves, softening doubts, veiling theories. Her unconsciousness of the evil which lives in the secret thoughts and therefore in the open acts of mankind, whenever it happens that evil thought meets evil courage; her unconsciousness was to be broken into with profane violence, with desecrating circumstances like a temple violated by a mad, vengeful impiety. Yes, that very young girl, almost no more than a child—this was what was going to happen to her. And if you ask me how, wherefore, for what reason? I will answer you: Why, by chance! By the merest chance, as things do happen, lucky and unlucky, terrible or tender, important or unimportant; and even things which are neither, things so completely neutral in character that you would wonder why they do happen at all if you didn't know that they, too, carry in their insignificance the seeds of further incalculable chances.

"Of course, all the chances were that de Barral should have fallen upon a perfectly harmless, naïve, usual, inefficient specimen of respectable governess for his daughter; or on a commonplace silly adventuress who would have tried, say, to marry him or work some other sort of common mischief in a small way. Or again he might have chanced on a model of all the virtues, or the repository of all knowledge, or anything equally harmless, conventional, and middle class. All calculations were in his favour; but, chance being incalculable, he fell upon an individuality whom it is much easier to define by opprobrious names than to classify in a calm and scientific spirit—but an individuality certainly, and a temperament as well. Rare? No. There is a certain amount of what I would politely call unscrupulousness in all of us. Think for instance of the excellent Mrs. Fyne, who herself, and in the bosom of her family, resembled a governess of a conventional type. Only, her mental excesses were theo-

retical, hedged in by so much humane feeling and conventional reserves, that they amounted to no more than
mere libertinage of thought; whereas the other woman,
the governess of Flora de Barral, was, as you may have
noticed, severely practical—terribly practical. No! Hers
was not a rare temperament, except in its fierce resentment of repression; a feeling which like genius or lunacy
is apt to drive people into sudden irrelevancy. Hers was
feminine irrelevancy. A male genius, a male ruffian, or
even a male lunatic, would not have behaved exactly as
she did behave. There is a softness in masculine nature,
even the most brutal, which acts as a check.

"While the girl slept those two, the woman of forty,
an age in itself terrible, and that hopeless young 'wrong
'un' of twenty-three (also well connected I believe), had
some sort of subdued row in the cleared rooms: ward-
robes open, drawers half pulled out and empty, trunks
locked and strapped, furniture in idle disarray, and not
so much as a single scrap of paper left behind on the
tables. The maid, whom the governess and the pupil
shared between them, after finishing with Flora, came to
the door as usual, but was not admitted. She heard the
two voices in dispute before she knocked, and then being
sent away retreated at once—the only person in the
house convinced at that time that there was 'something
up.'

"Dark and, so to speak, inscrutable spaces being met
with in life, there must be such places in any statement
dealing with life. In what I am telling you of now—an
episode of one of my humdrum holidays in the green
country, recalled quite naturally after all the years by our
meeting a man who has been a blue-water sailor—this
evening confabulation is a dark, inscrutable spot. And
we may conjecture what we like. I have no difficulty in
imagining that the woman—of forty, and the chief of the
enterprise—must have raged at large. And perhaps the
other did not rage enough. Youth feels deeply it is true,
but it has not the same vivid sense of lost opportunities.
It believes in the absolute reality of time. And then, in
that abominable scamp no very genuine feeling about
anything could exist—not even about the hazards of his
own unclean existence. A sneering half-laugh with some
such remark as: 'We are properly sold and no mistake'

would have been enough to make trouble in that way. And then another sneer, 'Waste time enough over it too,' followed perhaps by the bitter retort from the other party, 'You seemed to like it well enough though, playing the fool with that chit of a girl.' Something of that sort. Don't you see it—eh? . . .'"

Marlow looked at me with his dark penetrating glance. I was struck by the absolute verisimilitude of this suggestion. But we were always tilting at each other. I saw an opening and pushed my uncandid thrust.

"You have a ghastly imagination," I said with a cheerfully sceptical smile.

"Well, and if I have," he returned unabashed. "But let me remind you that this situation came to me unasked. I am like a puzzle-headed chief-mate we had once in the dear old *Samarcand* when I was a youngster. The fellow went gravely about trying to 'account to himself'—his favourite expression—for a lot of things no one would care to bother one's head about. He was an old idiot, but he was also an accomplished practical seaman. I was quite a boy and he impressed me. I must have caught the disposition from him."

"Well—go on with your accounting then," I said, assuming an air of resignation.

"That's just it." Marlow fell into his stride at once. "That's just it. Mere disappointed cupidity cannot account for the proceedings of the next morning; proceedings which I shall not describe to you—but which I shall tell you of presently, not as a matter of conjecture but of actual fact. Meantime returning to that evening altercation in deadened tones within the private apartment of Miss de Barral's governess, what if I were to tell you that disappointment had most likely made them touchy with each other, but that perhaps the secret of his careless, railing behaviour, was in the thought, springing up within him with an emphatic oath of relief, 'Now there's nothing to prevent me from breaking away from that old woman.' And that the secret of her envenomed rage, not against this miserable and attractive wretch, but against fate, accident and the whole course of human life, concentrating its venom on de Barral and including the innocent girl herself, was in the thought, in the fear crying within her, 'Now I have nothing to hold him with. . . .' "

I couldn't refuse Marlow the tribute of a prolonged whistle. "Phew! So you suppose that . . ."

He waved his hand impatiently.

"I don't suppose. It was so. And anyhow why shouldn't you accept the supposition. Do you look upon governesses as creatures above suspicion or necessarily of moral perfection? I suppose their hearts would not stand looking into much better than other people's. Why shouldn't a governess have passions, all the passions, even that of libertinage, and even ungovernable passions; yet suppressed by the very same means which keep the rest of us in order: early training—necessity—circumstances—fear of consequences; till there comes an age, a time when the restraint of years becomes intolerable—and infatuation irresistible? . . ."

"But if infatuation—quite possible I admit," I argued, "how do you account for the nature of the conspiracy?"

"You expect a cogency of conduct not usual in women," said Marlow. "The subterfuges of a menaced passion are not to be fathomed. You think it is going on the way it looks, whereas it is capable, for its own ends, of walking backwards into a precipice.

"When one once acknowledges that she was not a common woman, then all this is easily understood. She was abominable, but she was not common. She had suffered in her life not from its constant inferiority but from constant self-repression. A common woman finding herself placed in a commanding position might have formed the design to become the second Mrs. de Barral. Which would have been impracticable. De Barral would not have known what to do with a wife. But even if by some impossible chance he had made advances, this governess would have repulsed him with scorn. She had treated him always as an inferior being with an assured, distant politeness. In her composed, schooled manner she despised and disliked both father and daughter exceedingly. I have a notion that she had always disliked intensely all her charges including the two ducal (if they were ducal) little girls with whom she had dazzled de Barral. What an odious, ungratified existence it must have been for a woman as avid of all the sensuous emotions which life can give as most of her betters!

"She had seen her youth vanish, her freshness disappear, her hopes die, and now she felt her flaming middle-age slipping away from her. No wonder that with her admirably dressed, abundant hair, thickly sprinkled with white threads and adding to her elegant aspect the piquant distinction of a powdered coiffure—no wonder, I say, that she clung desperately to her last infatuation for that graceless young scamp, even to the extent of hatching for him that amazing plot. He was not so far gone in degradation as to make him utterly impossible for such an attempt. She hoped to keep him straight with that enormous bribe. She was clearly a woman uncommon enough to live without illusions—which, of course, does not mean that she was reasonable. She had said to herself, perhaps with a fury of self-contempt, 'In a few years I shall be too old for anybody. Meantime I shall have him—and I shall hold him by throwing to him the money of that ordinary, silly little girl of no account.' Well, it was a desperate expedient—but she thought it worth while. And besides there is hardly a woman in the world, no matter how hard, depraved or frantic, in whom something of the maternal instinct does not survive, unconsumed like a salamander, in the fires of the most abandoned passion. Yes, there might have been that sentiment for him too. There *was* no doubt. So I say again: No wonder! No wonder that she raged at everything—and perhaps even at him, with contradictory reproaches: for regretting the girl, a little fool who would never in her life be worth anybody's attention, and for taking the disaster itself with a cynical levity in which she perceived a flavour of revolt.

"And so the altercation in the night went on, over the irremediable. He arguing, 'What's the hurry? Why clear out like this?' perhaps a little sorry for the girl and as usual without a penny in his pocket, appreciating the comfortable quarters, wishing to linger on as long as possible in the shameless enjoyment of this already doomed luxury. There was really no hurry for a few days. Always time enough to vanish. And, with that, a touch of masculine softness, a sort of regard for appearances surviving his degradation: 'You might behave decently at the last, Eliza.' But there was no softness in the sallow face under the gala effect of powdered hair, its formal calmness gone, the dark-ringed eyes glaring at him with a sort of hunger. 'No! No! If it is as you say, then not a day, not an hour, not a moment.' She stuck to it, very determined that there should be no more of that boy and girl philandering since the object of it was gone; angry with herself for having suffered from it so much in the past, furious at its having been all in vain.

"But she was reasonable enough not to quarrel with him finally. What was the good? She found means to placate him. The only means. As long as there was some money to be got she had hold of him. 'Now go away. We shall do no good by any more of this sort of talk. I want to be alone for a bit.' He went away, sulkily acquiescent. There was a room always kept ready for him on the same floor, at the farther end of a short thickly carpeted passage.

"How she passed the night, this woman, with no illusions to help her through the hours which must have been sleepless, I shouldn't like to say. It ended at last; and this strange victim of the de Barral failure, whose name would never be known to the Official Receiver, came down to breakfast, impenetrable in her everyday perfection. From the very first, somehow, she had accepted the fatal news for true. All her life she had never believed in her luck, with that pessimism of the passionate who at bottom feel themselves to be the outcasts of a morally restrained universe. But this did not make it any easier, on opening the morning paper feverishly, to see the thing confirmed. Oh, yes! It was there. The Orb had suspended payment—the first growl of the storm faint as yet, but to the initiated the forerunner of a deluge. As an item of news it was not indecently displayed. It was not displayed at all in a sense. The serious paper, the only one of the great dailies which had always maintained an attitude of reserve towards the de Barral group of banks, had its 'manner.' Yes! a modest item of news! But there was also, on another page, a special financial article in a hostile tone beginning with the words, 'We have always feared,' and a guarded, half-column leader, opening with the phrase: 'It is a deplorable sign of the times,' what was, in effect, an austere, general rebuke to the absurd infatuations of the investing public. She glanced through these articles, a line here and a line there—no more was necessary to catch beyond

doubt the murmur of the oncoming flood. Several slight-
ing references by name to de Barral revived her animosity against the man, suddenly, as by the effect of
unforeseen moral support. The miserable wretch! . . .

"—You understand," Marlow interrupted the current
of his narrative, "that in order to be consecutive in my
relation of this affair I am telling you at once the details
which I heard from Mrs. Fyne later in the day, as well
as what little Fyne imparted to me with his usual solemnity during that morning call. As you may easily guess,
the Fynes, in their apartments, had read the news at the
same time, and, as a matter of fact, in the same august
and highly moral newspaper, as the governess in the luxurious mansion a few doors down on the opposite side
of the street. But they read them with different feelings.
They were thunderstruck. Fyne had to explain the full
purport of the intelligence to Mrs. Fyne whose first cry
was that of relief. Then that poor child would be safe
from these designing, horrid people. Mrs. Fyne did not
know what it might mean to be suddenly reduced from
riches to absolute penury. Fyne with his masculine imagination was less inclined to rejoice extravagantly at the
girl's escape from the moral dangers which had been
menacing her defenceless existence. It was a confoundedly big price to pay. What an unfortunate little thing
she was! 'We might be able to do something to comfort
that poor child, at any rate for the time she is here,' said
Mrs. Fyne. She felt under a sort of moral obligation not
to be indifferent. But no comfort for any one could be
got by rushing out into the street at this early hour; and
so, following the advice of Fyne not to act hastily, they
both sat down at the window and stared feelingly at the
great house, awful to their eyes in its stolid, prosperous,
expensive respectability, with ruin absolutely standing at
the door.

By that time, or very soon after, all Brighton had the
information and formed a more or less just appreciation
of its gravity. The butler in Miss de Barral's big house
had seen the news, perhaps earlier than anybody within
a mile of the Parade, in the course of his morning duties,
of which one was to dry the freshly delivered paper
before the fire—an occasion to glance at it which no

intelligent man could have neglected. He communicated to the rest of the household his vaguely forcible impression that something had gone d——bly wrong with the affairs of 'her father in London.'

"This brought an atmosphere of constraint through the house, which Flora de Barral coming down somewhat later than usual could not help noticing in her own way. Everybody seemed to stare so stupidly somehow; she feared a dull day.

"In the dining-room the governess in her place, a newspaper half-concealed under the cloth on her lap, after a few words exchanged with lips that seemed hardly to move, remaining motionless, her eyes fixed before her in an enduring silence; and presently Charley coming in to whom she did not even give a glance. He hardly said good morning, though he had a half-hearted try to smile at the girl, and sitting opposite her with his eyes on his plate and slight quivers passing along the line of his clean-shaven jaw, he too had nothing to say. It was dull, horribly dull to begin one's day like this; but she knew what it was. These never-ending family affairs! It was not for the first time that she had suffered from their depressing after-effects on these two. It was a shame that the delightful Charley should be made dull by these stupid talks, and it was perfectly stupid of him to let himself be upset like this by his aunt.

"When after a period of still, as if calculating, immobility, her governess got up abruptly and went out with the paper in her hand, almost immediately afterwards followed by Charley who left his breakfast half eaten, the girl was positively relieved. They would have it out that morning whatever it was, and be themselves again in the afternoon. At least Charley would be. To the moods of her governess she did not attach so much importance.

"For the first time that morning the Fynes saw the front door of the awful house open and the objectionable young man issue forth, his rascality visible to their prejudiced eyes in his very bowler hat and in the smart cut of his short fawn overcoat. He walked away rapidly like a man hurrying to catch a train, glancing from side to side as though he were carrying something off. Could he be departing for good? Undoubtedly, undoubtedly! But

Mrs. Fyne's fervent 'thank goodness' turned out to be a bit, as the Americans—some Americans—say 'previous.' In a very short time the odious fellow appeared again, strolling, absolutely strolling back, his hat now tilted a little on one side, with an air of leisure and satisfaction. Mrs. Fyne groaned not only in the spirit, at this sight, but in the flesh, audibly; and asked her husband what it might mean. Fyne naturally couldn't say. Mrs. Fyne believed that there was something horrid in progress and meantime the object of her detestation had gone up the steps and had knocked at the door which at once opened to admit him.

"He had been only as far as the bank.

"His reason for leaving his breakfast unfinished to run after Miss de Barral's governess, was to speak to her in reference to that very errand possessing the utmost possible importance in his eyes. He shrugged his shoulders at the nervousness of her eyes and hand, at the half-strangled whisper, 'I had to go out. I could hardly contain myself.' That was her affair. He was, with a young man's squeamishness, rather sick of her ferocity. He did not understand it. Men do not accumulate hate against each other in tiny amounts, treasuring every pinch carefully till it grows at last into a monstrous and explosive hoard. He had run out after her to remind her of the balance at the bank. What about lifting that money without wasting any more time? She had promised him to leave nothing behind.

"An account opened in her name for the expenses of the establishment in Brighton had been fed by de Barral with deferential lavishness. The governess crossed the wide hall into a little room at the side where she sat down to write the cheque, which he hastened out to go and cash as if it were stolen or a forgery. As observed by the Fynes, his uneasy appearance on leaving the house arose from the fact that his first trouble having been caused by a cheque of doubtful authenticity, the possession of a document of the sort made him unreasonably uncomfortable till it was safely cashed. And after all you know it was stealing of an indirect sort; for the money was de Barral's money if the account was in the name of the accomplished lady. At any rate the cheque was cashed. On getting hold of the notes and gold he recov-

ered his jaunty bearing, it being well known that with
certain natures the presence of money (even stolen) in
the pocket acts as a tonic, or at least as a stimulant. He
cocked his hat a little on one side as though he had had
a drink or two—which indeed he might have had in reality, to celebrate the occasion.

"The governess had been waiting for his return in the
hall, disregarding the side-glances of the butler as he went
in and out of the dining-room clearing away the breakfast
things. It was she, herself, who had opened the door so
promptly. 'It's all right,' he said touching his breast-
pocket; and she did not dare, the miserable wretch without illusions, she did not dare ask him to hand it over.
They looked at each other in silence. He nodded significantly: 'Where is she now?' and she whispered, 'Gone
into the drawing-room. Want to see her again?' with an
archly black look which he acknowledged by a muttered,
surly: 'I am damned if I do. Well, as you want to bolt
like this, why don't we go now?'

"She set her lips with cruel obstinacy and shook her
head. She had her idea, her completed plan. At that
moment the Fynes, still at the window and watching like
a pair of private detectives, saw a man with a long grey
beard and a jovial face go up the steps helping himself
with a thick stick, and knock at the door. Who could he
be?

"He was one of Miss de Barral's masters. She had
lately taken up painting in water-colours, having read in
a high-class woman's weekly paper that a great many
princesses of the European royal houses were cultivating
that art. This was the water-colour morning; and the
teacher, a veteran of many exhibitions, of a venerable
and jovial aspect, had turned up with his usual punctual-
ity. He was no great reader of morning papers, and even
had he seen the news it is very likely he would not have
understood its real purport. At any rate he turned up,
as the governess expected him to do, and the Fynes saw
him pass through the fateful door.

"He bowed cordially to the lady in charge of Miss de
Barral's education, whom he saw in the hall engaged in
conversation with a very good-looking but somewhat
raffish young gentleman. She turned to him graciously:
'Flora is already waiting for you in the drawing-room.'

"The cultivation of the art said to be patronized by princesses was pursued in the drawing-room from considerations of the right kind of light. The governess preceded the master up the stairs and into the room where Miss de Barral was found arrayed in a holland pinafore (also of the right kind for the pursuit of the art) and smilingly expectant. The water-colour lesson enlivened by the jocular conversation of the kindly, humorous old man was always great fun; and she felt she would be compensated for the tiresome beginning of the day.

"Her governess generally was present at the lesson; but on this occasion she only sat down till the master and pupil had gone to work in earnest, and then as though she had suddenly remembered some order to give, rose quietly and went out of the room.

"Once outside, the servants summoned by the passing maid without a bell being rung, and quick, quick, let all this luggage be taken down into the hall, and let one of you call a cab. She stood outside the drawing-room door on the landing, looking at each piece, trunk, leather cases, portmanteaux, being carried past her, her brows knitted and her aspect so sombre and absorbed that it took some little time for the butler to muster courage enough to speak to her. But he reflected that he was a free-born Briton and had his rights. He spoke straight to the point, but in the usual respectful manner.

" 'Beg your pardon, ma'am—but are you going away for good?'

"He was startled by her tone. Its unexpected, unladylike harshness fell on his trained ear with the disagreeable effect of a false note. 'Yes. I am going away. And the best thing for all of you is to go away too, as soon as you like. You can go now, to-day, this moment. You had your wages paid you only last week. The longer you stay the greater your loss. But I have nothing to do with it now. You are the servants of Mr. de Barral—you know.'

"The butler was astounded by the manner of this advice, and as his eyes wandered to the drawing-room door the governess extended her arm as if to bar the way. 'Nobody goes in there.' And that was said still in another tone, such a tone that all trace of the trained respectfulness vanished from the butler's bearing. He stared at her with a frank wondering gaze. 'Not till I am gone,' she added, and there was such an expression on her face that the man was daunted by the mystery of it. He shrugged his shoulders slightly and without another word went down the stairs on his way to the basement, brushing in the hall past Mr. Charles, who hat on head and both hands rammed deep into his overcoat pockets paced up and down as though on sentry duty there.

"The ladies' maid was the only servant upstairs, hovering in the passage on the first floor, curious and as if fascinated by the woman who stood there guarding the door. Being beckoned closer imperiously and asked by the governess to bring out of the now empty rooms the hat and veil, the only objects besides the furniture still to be found there, she did so in silence but inwardly fluttered. And while waiting uneasily with the veil, before that woman who, without moving a step away from the drawing-room door, was pinning with careless haste her hat on her head, she heard within a sudden burst of laughter from Miss de Barral enjoying the fun of the water-colour lesson given her for the last time by the cheery old man.

"Mr. and Mrs. Fyne ambushed at their window—a most incredible occupation for people of their kind—saw with renewed anxiety a cab come to the door and watched some luggage being carried out and put on its roof. The butler appeared for a moment, then went in again. What did it mean? Was Flora going to be taken to her father; or were these people, that woman and her horrible nephew, about to carry her off somewhere? Fyne couldn't tell. He doubted the last, Flora having now, he judged, no value, either positive or speculative. Though no great reader of character, he did not credit the governess with humane intentions. He confessed to me naïvely that he was excited as if watching some action on the stage. Then the thought struck him that the girl might have had some money settled on her, be possessed of some means, of some little fortune of her own and therefore—

"He imparted this theory to his wife who shared fully his consternation. 'I can't believe the child will go away without running in to say good-bye to us,' she murmured. 'We must find out! I shall ask her.' But at that very moment the cab rolled away, empty inside, and the door of the house which had been standing slightly ajar till then was pushed to.

"They remained silent staring at it till Mrs. Fyne whispered doubtfully, 'I really think I must go over.' Fyne didn't answer for a while (his is a reflective mind, you know), and then as if Mrs. Fyne's whispers had an occult power over that door it opened wide again and the white-bearded man issued, astonishingly active in his movements, using his stick almost like a leaping-pole to get down the steps; and hobbled away briskly along the pavement. Naturally the Fynes were too far off to make out the expression of his face. But it would not have helped them very much to a guess at the conditions inside the house. The expression was humorously puzzled—nothing more.

"For, at the end of his lesson, seizing his trusty stick and coming out with his habitual vivacity, he very nearly cannoned just outside the drawing-room door into the back of Miss de Barral's governess. He stopped himself in time and she turned round swiftly. It was embarrassing; he apologized; but her face was not startled; it was not aware of him; it wore a singular expression of resolution. A very singular expression which, as it were, detained him for a moment. In order to cover his embarrassment, he made some inane remark on the weather, upon which, instead of returning another inane remark according to the tacit rules of the game, she only gave him a smile of unfathomable meaning. Nothing could have been more singular. The good-looking young gentleman of questionable appearance took not the slightest notice of him in the hall. No servant was to be seen. He let himself out, pulling the door to behind him with a crash as, in a manner, he was forced to do to get it shut at all.

"When the echo of it had died away the woman on the landing leaned over the banister and called out bitterly to the man below, 'Don't you want to come up and say good-bye?' He had an impatient movement of the shoulders and went on pacing to and fro as though he had not heard. But suddenly he checked himself, stood still for a moment, then with a gloomy face and without taking his hands out of his pockets ran smartly up the stairs.

Already facing the door, she turned her head for a whispered taunt: 'Come! Confess you were dying to see her stupid little face once more'—to which he disdained to answer.

"Flora de Barral, still seated before the table at which she had been working on her sketch, raised her head at the noise of the opening door. The invading manner of their entrance gave her the sense of something she had never seen before. She knew them well. She knew the woman better than she knew her father. There had been between them an intimacy of relation as great as it can possibly be without the final closeness of affection. The delightful Charley walked in, with his eyes fixed on the back of her governess, whose raised veil hid her forehead like a brown band above the black line of the eyebrows. The girl was astounded and alarmed by the altogether unknown expression in the woman's face. The stress of passion often discloses an aspect of the personality completely ignored till then by its closest intimates. There was something like an emanation of evil from her eyes and from the face of the other, who, exactly behind her and overtopping her by half a head, kept his eyelids lowered in a sinister fashion—which in the poor girl reached, stirred, set free that faculty of unreasoning explosive terror lying locked up at the bottom of all human hearts and of the hearts of animals as well. With suddenly enlarged pupils and a movement as instinctive almost as the bounding of a startled fawn, she jumped up and found herself in the middle of the big room, exclaiming at those amazing and familiar strangers.

" 'What do you want?'

"You will note that she cried: What do you want? Not: What has happened? She told Mrs. Fyne that she had received suddenly the feeling of being personally attacked. And that must have been very terrifying. The woman before her had been the wisdom, the authority, the protection of life, security embodied and visible and undisputed.

"You may imagine then the force of the shock in the intuitive perception not merely of danger, for she did not know what was alarming her, but in the sense of the security being gone. And not only security. I don't know how to explain it clearly. Look! Even a small child lives, plays and suffers in terms of its conception of its own

existence. Imagine, if you can, a fact coming in suddenly
with a force capable of shattering that very conception
itself. It was only because of the girl being still so much
of a child that she escaped mental destruction; that, in
other words, she got over it. Could one conceive of her
more mature, while still as ignorant as she was, one must
conclude that she would have become an idiot on the
spot—long before the end of that experience. Luckily,
people, whether mature or not mature (and who really
is ever mature?), are for the most part quite incapable
of understanding what is happening to them: a merciful
provision of nature to preserve an average amount of
sanity for working purposes in this world. . . ."

"But we, my dear Marlow, have the inestimable
advantage of understanding what is happening to others," I struck in. "Or at least some of us seem to. Is that
too a provision of nature? And what is it for? Is it that
we may amuse ourselves gossiping about each other's
affairs? You, for instance, seem——"

"I don't know what I seem," Marlow silenced me,
"and surely life must be amused somehow. It would be
still a very respectable provision if it were only for that
end. But from that same provision of understanding,
there springs in us compassion, charity, indignation, the
sense of solidarity; and in minds of any largeness an inclination to that indulgence which is next to affection. I
don't mean to say that I am inclined to an indulgent view
of the precious couple which broke upon an unsuspecting
girl. They came marching in (it's the very expression she
used later on to Mrs. Fyne), but at her cry they stopped.
It must have been startling enough to them. It was like
having the mask torn off when you don't expect it. The
man stopped for good; he didn't offer to move a step
farther. But, though the governess had come in there for
the very purpose of taking the mask off for the first time
in her life, she seemed to look upon the frightened cry
as a fresh provocation. 'What are you screaming for, you
little fool?' she said advancing alone close to the girl who
was affected exactly as if she had seen Medusa's head with
serpentine locks set mysteriously on the shoulders
of that familiar person, in that brown dress, under that
hat she knew so well. It made her lose all her hold on
reality. She told Mrs. Fyne: 'I didn't know where I was.

I didn't even know that I was frightened. If she had told me it was a joke I would have laughed. If she had told me to put on my hat and go out with her I would have put on my hat and gone out with her and never said a single word; I should have been convinced I had been mad for a minute or so, and I would have worried myself to death rather than breathe a hint of it to her or any one. But the wretch put her face close to mine and I could not move. Directly I had looked into her eyes I felt grown on to the carpet.'

"It was years afterwards that she used to talk like this to Mrs. Fyne—and to Mrs. Fyne alone. Nobody else ever heard the story from her lips. But it was never forgotten. It was always felt; it remained like a mark on her soul, a sort of mystic wound, to be contemplated, to be meditated over. And she said further to Mrs. Fyne, in the course of many confidences provoked by that contemplation, that, as long as that woman called her names, it was almost soothing, it was in a manner reassuring. Her imagination had, like her body, gone off in a wild bound to meet the unknown; and then to hear after all something which more in its tone than in its substance was mere venomous abuse, had steadied the inward flutter of all her being.

" 'She called me a little fool more times than I can remember. I! A fool! Why, Mrs. Fyne! I do assure you I had never yet thought at all; never of anything in the world, till then. I just went on living. And one can't be a fool without one has at least tried to think. But what had I ever to think about?'

"And no doubt," commented Marlow, "her life had been a mere life of sensations—the response to which can neither be foolish nor wise. It can only be temperamental; and I believe that she was of a generally happy disposition, a child of the average kind. Even when she was asked violently whether she imagined that there was anything in her, apart from her money, to induce any intelligent person to take any sort of interest in her existence, she only caught her breath in one dry sob and said nothing, made no other sound, made no movement. When she was viciously assured that she was in heart, mind, manner and appearance an utterly common and insipid creature, she listened without indignation, without anger. She stood, a frail and passive vessel into which the other went on pouring all the accumulated dislike for all her pupils, her scorn of all her employers (the ducal one included), the accumulated resentment, the infinite hatred of all these unrelieved years of—I won't say hypocrisy. The practice of hypocrisy is a relief in itself, a secret triumph of the vilest sort, no doubt, but still a way of getting even with the common morality from which some of us appear to suffer so much. No! I will say the years, the passionate, bitter years, of restraint, the iron, admirably mannered restraint at every moment, in a never-failing correctness of speech, glances, movements, smiles, gestures, establishing for her a high reputation, an impressive record of success in her sphere. It had been like living half strangled for years.

"And all this torture for nothing, in the end! What looked at last like a possible prize (oh, without illusions! but still a prize) broken in her hands, fallen in the dust, the bitter dust, of disappointment, she revelled in the miserable revenge—pretty safe too—only regretting the unworthiness of the girlish figure which stood for so much she had longed to be able to spit venom at, if only once, in perfect liberty. The presence of the young man at her back increased both her satisfaction and her rage. But the very violence of the attack seemed to defeat its end by rendering the representative victim as it were insensible. The cause of this outrage naturally escaping the girl's imagination, her attitude was in effect that of dense, hopeless stupidity. And it is a fact that the worst shocks of life are often received without outcries, without gestures, without a flow of tears and the convulsions of sobbing. The insatiable governess missed these signs exceedingly. This pitiful stolidity was only a fresh provocation. Yet the poor girl was deadly pale.

" 'I was cold,' she used to explain to Mrs. Fyne. 'I had had time to get terrified. She had pushed her face so near mine and her teeth looked as though she wanted to bite me. Her eyes seemed to have become quite dry, hard and small in a lot of horrible wrinkles. I was too afraid of her to shudder, too afraid of her to put my fingers to my ears. I didn't know what I expected her to call me next, but when she told me I was no better than a beggar—that there would be no more masters, no more servants, no more horses for me—I said to myself: Is that all? I should have laughed if I hadn't been too afraid of her to make the least little sound.'

"It seemed that poor Flora had to know all the possible phases of that sort of anguish, beginning with instinctive panic, through the bewildered stage, the frozen stage and the stage of blanched apprehension, down to the instinctive prudence of extreme terror—the stillness of the mouse. But when she heard herself called the child of a cheat and a swindler, the very monstrous unexpectedness of this caused in her a revulsion towards letting herself go. She screamed out suddenly, 'You mustn't speak like this of papa!'

"The effort of it uprooted her from that spot where her little feet seemed dug deep into the thick luxurious carpet, and she retreated backwards to a distant part of the room, hearing herself repeat, 'You mustn't, you mustn't,' as if it were somebody else screaming. She came to a chair and dropped into it. Thereupon the somebody else ceased screaming and she lolled, exhausted, sightless, in a silent room, indifferent to everything and without a single thought in her head.

"The next few seconds seemed to last for ever so long; a black abyss of time separating what was past and gone from the reappearance of the governess and the reawakening of fear. And that woman was forcing the words through her set teeth: 'You say I mustn't, I mustn't. All the world will be speaking of him like this to-morrow. They will say it, and they'll print it. You shall hear it and you shall read it—and then you will know whose daughter you are.'

"Her face lighted up with an atrocious satisfaction. 'He's nothing but a thief,' she cried, 'this father of yours. As to you I have never been deceived in you for a moment. I have been growing more and more sick of you for years. You are a vulgar, silly nonentity, and you shall go back to where you belong, whatever low place you have sprung from, and beg your bread—that is if anybody's charity will have anything to do with you, which I doubt——'

"She would have gone on regardless of the enormous eyes, of the open mouth of the girl who sat up suddenly with the wild staring expression of being choked by invisible fingers on her throat, and yet horribly pale. The effect on her constitution was so profound, Mrs. Fyne told me, that she who as a child had a rather pretty delicate colouring, showed a white bloodless face for a couple of years afterwards, and remained always liable at the slightest emotion to an extraordinary ghost-like whiteness. The end came in the abomination of desolation of the poor child's miserable cry for help: 'Charley! Charley!' coming from her throat in hidden gasping efforts. Her enlarged eyes had discovered him where he stood motionless and dumb.

"He started from his immobility, a hand withdrawn brusquely from the pocket of his overcoat, strode up to the woman, seized her by the arm from behind, saying in a rough commanding tone: 'Come away, Eliza.' In an instant the child saw them close together and remote, near the door, gone through the door, which she neither heard nor saw being opened or shut. But it was shut. Oh yes, it was shut. Her slow unseeing glance wandered all over the room. For some time longer she remained leaning forward, collecting her strength, doubting if she would be able to stand. She stood up at last. Everything about her spun round in an oppressive silence. She remembered perfectly—as she told Mrs. Fyne—that clinging to the arm of the chair she called out twice 'Papa! Papa!' At the thought that he was far away in London everything about her became quite still. Then, frightened suddenly by the solitude of that empty room, she rushed out of it blindly.

"With that fatal diffidence in well-doing inherent in the present condition of humanity, the Fynes continued to watch at their window. 'It's always so difficult to know what to do for the best,' Fyne assured me. It is. Good intentions stand in their own way so much. Whereas if you want to do harm to any one you needn't hesitate. You have only to go on. No one will reproach you with your mistakes or call you a confounded, clumsy meddler. The Fynes watched the door, the closed street door inimical somehow to their benevolent thoughts, the face of the house cruelly impenetrable. The unchanged daily aspect of inanimate things is so impressive that Fyne went back into the room for a moment, picked up the

paper again, and ran his eyes over the item of news. No
doubt of it. It looked very bad. He came back to the
window and Mrs. Fyne. Tired out as she was she sat
there resolute and ready for responsibility. But she had
no suggestion to offer. People do fear a rebuff wonderfully, and all her audacity was in her thoughts. She
shrank from the incomparably insolent manner of the
governess. Fyne stood by her side, as in those old-
fashioned photographs of married couples where you see
a husband with his hand on the back of his wife's chair.
And they were about as efficient as an old photograph,
and as still, till Mrs. Fyne started slightly. The street
door had swung open, and, bursting out, appeared the
odious young man, his hat (Mrs. Fyne observed) tilted
forward over his eyes. After him the governess slipped
through, turning round at once to shut the door behind
her with care. Meantime the man went down the white
steps and strode along the pavement, his hands rammed
deep into the pockets of his fawn overcoat. The woman,
that woman of composed movements, of deliberate superior manner, took a little run to catch up with him, and
directly she had caught up with him tried to introduce
her hand under his arm. Mrs. Fyne saw the brusque half
turn of the fellow's body as one avoids an importunate
contact, defeating her attempt rudely. She did not try
again but kept pace with his stride, and Mrs. Fyne
watched them, walking independently, turn the corner of
the street side by side, disappear for ever.

"The Fynes looked at each other eloquently, doubtfully. What do you think of this? Then with common
accord turned their eyes back to the street door, closed,
massive, dark; the great, clear brass knocker shining in
a quiet slant of sunshine cut by a diagonal line of heavy
shade filling the farther end of the street. Could the girl
be already gone? Sent away to her father? Had she any
relations? Nobody but de Barral himself ever came to
see her, Mrs. Fyne remembered; and she had the instan-
taneous, profound, maternal perception of the child's
loneliness—and a girl too! It was irresistible. And,
besides, the departure of the governess was not without
its encouraging influence. 'I am going over at once to
find out,' she declared resolutely but still staring across
the street. Her intention was arrested by the sight of that

awful, sombrely glistening door, swinging back suddenly on the yawning darkness of the hall, out of which literally flew, right out on the pavement, almost without touching the white steps, a little figure swathed in a holland pinafore up to the chin, its hair streaming back from its head, darting past a lamp-post, past the red pillarbox. . . . 'Here,' cried Mrs. Fyne; 'she's coming here! Run John! Run!'

"Fyne bounded out of the room. This is his own word. Bounded! He assured me with intensified solemnity that he bounded; and the sight of the short and muscular Fyne bounding gravely about the circumscribed passages and staircases of a small, private hotel, would have been worth any amount of money to a person greedy of memorable impressions. But as I looked at him, the desire of laughter at my very lips, I asked myself: how many men could be found ready to compromise their cherished gravity for the sake of the unimportant child of a ruined financier with an ugly, black cloud already wreathing his head? I didn't laugh at little Fyne. I encouraged him: 'You did!—very good. . . . Well?'

"His main thought was to save the child from some unpleasant interference. There was a porter downstairs, page boys; some people going away with their trunks in the passage; a railway omnibus at the door, whitebreasted waiters dodging about the entrance.

"He was in time. He was at the door before she reached it in her blind course. She did not recognize him; perhaps she did not see him. He caught her by the arm as she ran past and, very sensibly, without trying to check her, simply darted in with her and up the stairs, causing no end of consternation amongst the people in his way. They scattered. What might have been their thoughts at the spectacle of a middle-aged man abducting headlong into the upper regions of a respectable hotel a terrified young girl obviously under age, I don't know. And Fyne (he told me so) did not care for what people might think. All he wanted was to reach his wife before the girl collapsed. For a time she ran with him, but at the last flight of stairs he had to seize and half drag, half carry her to his wife. Mrs. Fyne waited at the door with her quite unmoved physiognomy and her readiness to confront any sort of responsibility, which already characterized her,

long before she became a ruthless theorist. Relieved, his
mission accomplished, Fyne closed hastily the door of the
sitting-room.

"But before long both Fynes became frightened. After
a period of immobility in the arms of Mrs. Fyne, the girl,
who had not said a word, tore herself out from that
slightly rigid embrace. She struggled dumbly between
them, they did not know why, soundless and ghastly, till
she sank exhausted on a couch. Luckily the children were
out with the two nurses. The hotel housemaid helped
Mrs. Fyne to put Flora de Barral to bed. She was as if
gone speechless and insane. She lay on her back, her
face white like a piece of paper, her dark eyes staring at
the ceiling, her awful immobility broken by sudden shivering fits with a loud chattering of teeth in the shadowy
silence of the room, the blinds pulled down, Mrs. Fyne
sitting by patiently, her arms folded, yet inwardly moved
by the riddle of that distress of which she could not guess
the word, and saying to herself: 'That child is too emotional—much too emotional to be ever really sound!' As
if any one not made of stone could be perfectly sound in
this world. And then how sound? In what sense—to resist
what? Force or corruption? And even in the best armour
of steel there are joints a treacherous stroke can always
find if chance gives the opportunity.

"General considerations never had the power to trouble Mrs. Fyne much. The girl not being in a state to be
questioned, she waited by the bedside. Fyne had crossed
over to the house, his scruples overcome by his anxiety
to discover what really had happened. He did not have
to lift the knocker; the door stood open on the inside
gloom of the hall; he walked into it and saw no one
about, the servants having assembled for a fatuous consultation in the basement. Fyne's uplifted bass voice startled them down there, the butler coming up, staring and
in his shirt sleeves, very suspicious at first, and then, on
Fyne's explanation that he was the husband of a lady who
had called several times at the house—Miss de Barral's
mother's friend—becoming humanely concerned and communicative, in a man to man tone, but preserving his
trained high-class servant's voice: 'Oh bless you, sir, no!
She does not mean to come back. She told me so her-

self'—he assured Fyne with a faint shade of contempt creeping into his tone.

"As regards their young lady nobody downstairs had any idea that she had run out of the house. He dared say they all would have been willing to do their very best for her, for the time being; but since she was now with her mother's friends . . .

"He fidgeted. He murmured that all this was very unexpected. He wanted to know what he had better do with letters or telegraphs which might arrive in the course of the day.

" 'Letters addressed to Miss de Barral, you had better bring over to my hotel over there,' said Fyne beginning to feel extremely worried about the future. The man said, 'Yes, sir,' adding, 'and if a letter comes addressed to Mrs. . . .'

"Fyne stopped him by a gesture. 'I don't know. . . . Anything you like.'

" 'Very well, sir.'

"The butler did not shut the street door after Fyne, but remained on the doorstep for a while, looking up and down the street in the spirit of independent expectation like a man who is again his own master. Mrs. Fyne hearing her husband return came out of the room where the girl was lying in bed. 'No change,' she whispered; and Fyne could only make a hopeless sign of ignorance as to what all this meant and how it would end.

"He feared future complications—naturally: a man of limited means, in a public position, his time not his own. Yes. He owned to me in the parlour of my farmhouse that he had been very much concerned then at the possible consequences. But as he was making this artless confession I said to myself that, whatever consequences and complications he might have imagined, the complication from which he was suffering now could never, never have presented itself to his mind. Slow but sure (for I conceive that the Book of Destiny has been written up from the beginning to the last page) it had been coming up for something like six years—and now it had come. The complication was there! I looked at his unshaken solemnity with the amused pity we give the victim of a funny if somewhat ill-natured practical joke.

" 'Oh hang it,' he exclaimed—in no logical connection

with what he had been relating to me. Nevertheless the exclamation was intelligible enough.

"However at first there were, he admitted, no untoward complications, no embarrassing consequences. To a telegram in guarded terms dispatched to de Barral no answer was received for more than twenty-four hours. This certainly caused the Fynes some anxiety. When the answer arrived late on the evening of next day it was in the shape of an elderly man. An unexpected sort of man. Fyne explained to me with precision that he evidently belonged to what is most respectable in the lower middle classes. He was calm and slow in his speech. He was wearing a frock-coat, had grey whiskers meeting under his chin, and declared on entering that Mr. de Barral was his cousin. He hastened to add that he had not seen his cousin for many years, while he looked on Fyne (who received him alone) with so much distrust that Fyne felt hurt (the person actually refusing at first the chair offered to him) and retorted tartly that he, for his part, had *never* seen Mr. de Barral, in his life, and that, since the visitor did not want to sit down, he, Fyne, begged him to state his business as shortly as possible. The man in black sat down then with a faint superior smile.

"He had come for the girl. His cousin had asked him in a note delivered by a messenger to go to Brighton at once and take 'his girl' over from a gentleman named Fyne and give her houseroom for a time in his family. And there he was. His business had not allowed him to come sooner. His business was the manufacture on a large scale of card-board boxes. He had two grown-up girls of his own. He had consulted his wife and so that was all right. The girl would get a welcome in his home. His home most likely was not what she had been used to, but, etc., etc.

"All the time Fyne felt subtly in that man's manner a derisive disapproval of everything that was not lower middle class, a profound respect for money, a mean sort of contempt for speculators that fail, and a conceited satisfaction with his own respectable vulgarity.

"With Mrs. Fyne the manner of the obscure cousin of de Barral was but little less offensive. He looked at her rather slyly, but her cold, decided demeanour impressed him. Mrs. Fyne on her side was simply appalled by the personage, but did not show it outwardly. Not even when the man remarked with false simplicity that Florrie—her name was Florrie wasn't it?—would probably miss at first all her grand friends. And when he was informed that the girl was in bed, not feeling well at all, he showed an unsympathetic alarm. She wasn't an invalid, was she? No. What was the matter with her then?

"An extreme distaste for that respectable member of society was depicted in Fyne's face even as he was telling me of him after all these years. He was a specimen of precisely the class of which people like the Fynes have the least experience; and I imagine he jarred on them painfully. He possessed all the civic virtues in their very meanest form, and the finishing touch was given by a low sort of consciousness he manifested of possessing them. His industry was exemplary. He wished to catch the earliest possible train next morning. It seems that for seven and twenty years he had never missed being seated on his office-stool at the factory punctually at ten o'clock every day. He listened to Mrs. Fyne's objections with undisguised impatience. Why couldn't Florrie get up and have her breakfast at eight like other people? In his house the breakfast was at eight sharp. Mrs. Fyne's polite stoicism overcame him at last. He had come down at a very great personal inconvenience, he assured her with displeasure, but he gave up the early train.

"The good Fynes didn't dare to look at each other before this unforeseen but perfectly authorized guardian, the same thought springing up in their minds: Poor girl! Poor girl! If the women of the family were like this too! . . . And of course they would be. Poor girl! But what could they have done even if they had been prepared to raise objections? The person in the frock-coat had the father's note; he had shown it to Fyne. Just a request to take care of the girl—as her nearest relative—without any explanation or a single allusion to the financial catastrophe, its tone strangely detached and in its very silence on the point giving occasion to think that the writer was not uneasy as to the child's future. Probably it was that very idea which had set the cousin so readily in motion. Men had come before out of commercial crashes with estates in the country and a comfortable income, if not for themselves then for their wives. And if a wife could be made comfortable by a little dexterous management then why not a daughter? Yes. This possibility might have been discussed in the person's household and judged worth acting upon.

"The man actually hinted broadly that such was his belief, and in face of Fyne's guarded replies gave him to understand that he was not the dupe of such reticences. Obviously he looked upon the Fynes as being disappointed because the girl was taken away from them. They, by a diplomatic sacrifice in the interests of poor Flora, had asked the man to dinner. He accepted ungraciously, remarking that he was not used to late hours. He had generally a bit of supper about half-past eight or nine. However . . .

"He gazed contemptuously round the prettily decorated dining-room. He wrinkled his nose in a puzzled way at the dishes offered to him by the waiter but refused none, devouring the food with a great appetite and drinking ('swilling' Fyne called it) gallons of ginger beer, which was procured for him (in stone bottles) at his request. The difficulty of keeping up a conversation with that being exhausted Mrs. Fyne herself, who had come to the table armed with adamantine resolution. The only memorable thing he said was when, in a pause of gorging himself 'with these French dishes,' he deliberately let his eyes roam over the little tables occupied by parties of diners, and remarked that his wife did for a moment think of coming down with him, but that he was glad she didn't do so. 'She wouldn't have been at all happy seeing all this alcohol about. Not at all happy,' he declared weightily.

" 'You must have had a charming evening,' I said to Fyne, 'if I may judge from the way you have kept the memory green.'

" 'Delightful,' he growled with, positively, a flash of anger at the recollection, but lapsed back into his solemnity at once. After we had been silent for a while I asked whether the man took away the girl next day.

"Fyne said that he did; in the afternoon, in a fly, with a few clothes the maid had got together and brought across from the big house. Fyne only saw Flora again ten minutes before they left for the railway station, in the Fynes' sitting-room at the hotel. It was a most painful ten minutes for the Fynes. The respectable citizen addressed Miss de Barral as 'Florrie' and 'my dear,' remarking to her that she was not very big, 'there's not much of you, my dear,' in a familiarly disparaging tone. Then turning to Mrs. Fyne, and quite loud, 'She's very white in the face. Why's that?' To this Mrs. Fyne made no reply. She had put the girl's hair up that morning with her own hands. It changed her very much, observed Fyne. He, naturally, played a subordinate, merely approving part. All he could do for Miss de Barral personally was to go downstairs and put her into the fly himself, while Miss de Barral's nearest relation, having been shouldered out of the way, stood by, with an umbrella and a little black bag, watching this proceeding with grim amusement, as it seemed. It was difficult to guess what the girl thought or what she felt. She no longer looked a child. She whispered to Fyne a faint 'Thank you' from the fly, and he said to her in very distinct tones and while still holding her hand: 'Pray don't forget to write fully to my wife in a day or two, Miss de Barral.' Then Fyne stepped back and the cousin climbed into the fly muttering quite audibly: 'I don't think you'll be troubled much with her in the future'; without however looking at Fyne on whom he did not even bestow a nod. The fly drove away.

CHAPTER FIVE

The Tea-Party

" 'Amiable personality,' I observed, seeing Fyne on the point of falling into a brown study. But I could not help adding with meaning: 'He hadn't the gift of prophecy though.'

"Fyne got up suddenly with a muttered 'No, evidently not.' He was gloomy, hesitating. I supposed that he would not wish to play chess that afternoon. This would dispense me from leaving my rooms on a day much too fine to be wasted in walking exercise. And I was disappointed when picking up his cap he intimated to me his hope of seeing me at the cottage about four o'clock—as usual.

" 'It wouldn't be as usual.' I put a particular stress on that remark. He admitted, after a short reflection, that it would not be. No. Not as usual. In fact it was his wife who hoped, rather, for my presence. She had formed a very favourable opinion of my practical sagacity.

"This was the first I ever heard of it. I had never suspected that Mrs. Fyne had taken the trouble to distinguish in me the signs of sagacity or folly. The few words we had exchanged last night in the excitement—or the bother—of the girl's disappearance, were the first moderately significant words which had ever passed between us. I had felt myself always to be in Mrs. Fyne's view her husband's chess-player and nothing else—a convenience—almost an implement.

" 'I am highly flattered,' I said. 'I have always heard that there are no limits to feminine intuition; and now I am half inclined to believe it is so. But still I fail to see in what way my sagacity, practical or otherwise, can be of any service to Mrs. Fyne. One man's sagacity is very much like any other man's sagacity. And with you at hand——'

"Fyne, manifestly not attending to what I was saying, directed straight at me his worried solemn eyes and struck in: 'Yes, yes. Very likely. But you will come—won't you?'

"I had made up my mind that no Fyne of either sex would make me walk three miles (there and back to their cottage) on this fine day. If the Fynes had been an average sociable couple one knows only because leisure must be got through somehow, I would have made short work of that special invitation. But they were not that. Their undeniable humanity had to be acknowledged. At the same time I wanted to have my own way. So I proposed that I should be allowed the pleasure of offering them a cup of tea at my rooms.

"A short reflective pause—and Fyne accepted eagerly in his own and his wife's name. A moment after I heard the click of the gate-latch and then in an ecstasy of barking from his demonstrative dog his serious head went past my window on the other side of the hedge, its troubled gaze fixed forward, and the mind inside obviously employed in earnest speculation of an intricate nature. One at least of his wife's girl-friends had become more than a mere shadow for him. I surmised however that it was not of the girl-friend but of his wife that Fyne was thinking. He was an excellent husband.

"I prepared myself for the afternoon's hospitalities, calling in the farmer's wife and reviewing with her the resources of the house and the village. She was a helpful woman. But the resources of my sagacity I did not review. Except in the gross material sense of the afternoon tea I made no preparations for Mrs. Fyne.

"It was impossible for me to make any such preparations. I could not tell what sort of sustenance she would look for from my sagacity. And as to taking stock of the wares of my mind, no one, I imagine, is anxious to do that sort of thing if it can be avoided. A vaguely grandiose state of mental self-confidence is much too agreeable to be disturbed recklessly by such a delicate investigation. Perhaps if I had had a helpful woman at my elbow, a dear, flattering, acute, devoted woman. . . . There are in life moments when one positively regrets not being married. No! I don't exaggerate. I have said—moments, not years or even days. Moments. The farmer's wife obviously could not be asked to assist. She could not have been expected to possess the necessary insight, and I doubt whether she would have known how to be flattering enough. She was being helpful in her own way, with an extraordinary black bonnet on her head, a good mile off by that time, trying to discover in the village shops a piece of eatable cake. The pluck of women! The optimism of the dear creatures!

"And she managed to find something which looked eatable. That's all I know as I had no opportunity to observe the more intimate effects of that comestible. I myself never eat cake, and Mrs. Fyne, when she arrived punctually, brought with her no appetite for cake. She had no appetite for anything. But she had a thirst—the sign of deep, of tormenting emotion. Yes, it was emotion, not the brilliant sunshine—more brilliant than warm as is the way of our discreet self-repressed, distinguished, insular sun, which would not turn a real lady scarlet— not on any account. Mrs. Fyne looked even cool. She wore a white skirt and coat; a white hat with a large brim reposed on her smoothly arranged hair. The coat was cut something like an army mess-jacket and the style suited her. I dare say there are many youthful subalterns, and not the worst-looking too, who resemble Mrs. Fyne in the type of face, in the sunburnt complexion, down to that something alert in bearing. But not many would have had that aspect breathing a readiness to assume any responsibility under Heaven. This is the sort of courage which ripens late in life, and of course Mrs. Fyne was of mature years for all her unwrinkled face.

"She looked round the room, told me positively that I

was very comfortable there; to which I assented, humbly, acknowledging my undeserved good fortune.

" 'Why undeserved?' she wanted to know.

" 'I engaged these rooms by letter without asking any questions. It might have been an abominable hole,' I explained to her. 'I always do things like that. I don't like to be bothered. This is no great proof of sagacity— is it? Sagacious people, I believe, like to exercise that faculty. I have heard that they can't even help showing it in the veriest trifles. It must be very delightful. But I know nothing of it. I think that I have no sagacity—no practical sagacity.'

"Fyne made an inarticulate bass murmur of protest. I asked after the children whom I had not seen yet since my return from town. They had been very well. They were always well. Both Fyne and Mrs. Fyne spoke of the rude health of their children as if it were a result of moral excellence; in a peculiar tone which seemed to imply some contempt for people whose children were liable to be unwell at times. One almost felt inclined to apologize for the inquiry. And this annoyed me; unreasonably, I admit, because the assumption of superior merit is not a very exceptional weakness. Anxious to make myself disagreeable by way of retaliation, I observed in accents of interested civility that the dear girls must have been wondering at the sudden disappearance of their mother's young friend. Had they been putting any awkward questions about Miss Smith? Wasn't it as Miss Smith that Miss de Barral had been introduced to me?

"Mrs. Fyne, staring fixedly but also colouring deeper under her tan, told me that the children had never liked Flora very much. She hadn't the high spirits which endear grown-ups to healthy children, Mrs. Fyne explained unflinchingly. Flora had been staying at the cottage several times before. Mrs. Fyne assured me that she often found it very difficult to have her in the house.

" 'But what else could we do?' she exclaimed.

"That little cry of distress, quite genuine in its inexpressiveness, altered my feeling towards Mrs. Fyne. It would have been so easy to have done nothing and to have thought no more about it. My liking for her began while she was trying to tell me of the night she spent by the girl's bedside, the night before her departure with her unprepossessing relative. That Mrs. Fyne found means to comfort the child I doubt very much. She had not the genius for the task of undoing that which the hate of an infuriated woman had planned so well.

"You will tell me perhaps that children's impressions are not durable. That's true enough. But here, child is only a manner of speaking. The girl was within a few days of her sixteenth birthday; she was old enough to be matured by the shock. The very effort she had to make in conveying the impression to Mrs. Fyne, in remembering the details, in finding adequate words—or any words at all—was in itself a terribly enlightening, an ageing process. She had talked a long time, uninterrupted by Mrs. Fyne, childlike enough in her wonder and pain, pausing now and then to interject the pitiful query: 'It was cruel of her. Wasn't it cruel, Mrs. Fyne?'

"For Charley she found excuses. He at any rate had not said anything while he had looked very gloomy and miserable. He couldn't have taken part against his aunt— could he? But after all he did, when she called upon him, take 'that cruel woman away.' He had dragged her out by the arm. She had seen that plainly. She remembered it. That was it! The woman was mad. 'Oh! Mrs. Fyne, don't tell me she wasn't mad. If you had only seen her face . . .'

"But Mrs. Fyne was unflinching in her idea that as much truth as could be told was due in the way of kindness to the girl, whose fate she feared would be to live exposed to the hardest realities of unprivileged existences. She explained to her that there were in the world evil-minded, selfish people. Unscrupulous people. . . . These two persons had been after her father's money. The best thing she could do was to forget all about them.

"'After papa's money? I don't understand,' poor Flora de Barral had murmured, and lay still as if trying to think it out in the silence and shadows of the room where only a night-light was burning. Then she had a long shivering fit while holding tight the hand of Mrs. Fyne whose patient immobility by the bedside of that brutally murdered childhood did infinite honour to her humanity. That vigil must have been the more trying because I could see very well that at no time did she think the victim particularly charming or sympathetic. It was a manifestation of pure compassion, of compassion in itself, so to speak, not many women would have been capable of displaying with that unflinching steadiness. The shivering fit over, the girl's next words in an outburst of sobs were, 'Oh! Mrs. Fyne, am I really such a horrid thing as she has made me out to be?'

" 'No, no!' protested Mrs. Fyne. 'It is your former governess who is horrid and odious. She is a vile woman. I cannot tell you that she was mad, but I think she must have been beside herself with rage and full of evil thoughts. You must try not to think of these abominations, my dear child.'

"They were not fit for any one to think of much, Mrs. Fyne commented to me in a curt positive tone. All that had been very trying. The girl was like a creature struggling under a net.

" 'But how can I forget? she called my father a cheat and a swindler! Do tell me, Mrs. Fyne, that it isn't true. It can't be true. How can it be true?'

"She sat up in bed with a sudden wild motion as if to jump out and flee from the sound of the words which had just passed her own lips. Mrs. Fyne restrained her, soothed her, induced her at last to lay her head on her pillow again, assuring her all the time that nothing this woman had had the cruelty to say deserved to be taken to heart. The girl, exhausted, cried quietly for a time. It may be she had noticed something evasive in Mrs. Fyne's assurances. After a while, without stirring, she whispered brokenly—

" 'That awful woman told me that all the world would call papa these awful names. Is it possible? Is it possible?'

"Mrs. Fyne kept silent.

" 'Do say something to me, Mrs. Fyne,' the daughter of de Barral insisted in the same feeble whisper.

"Again Mrs. Fyne assured me that it had been very trying. Terribly trying. 'Yes, thanks, I will.' She leaned back in the chair with folded arms while I poured another cup of tea for her, and Fyne went out to pacify the dog which, tied up under the porch, had become suddenly very indignant at somebody having the audacity to walk along the lane. Mrs. Fyne stirred her tea for a long time, drank a little, put the cup down and said with that air of accepting all the consequences—

" 'Silence would have been unfair. I don't think it would have been kind either. I told her that she must be prepared for the world passing a very severe judgment on her father . . .'

"Wasn't it admirable?" cried Marlow, interrupting his narrative. "Admirable!" And as I looked dubiously at this unexpected enthusiasm he started justifying it after his own manner.

"I say admirable because it was so characteristic. It was perfect. Nothing short of genius could have found better. And this was nature! As they say of an artist's work: this was a perfect Fyne. Compassion—judicious-ness—something correctly measured. None of your dishev-elled sentiment. And right! You must confess that nothing could have been more right. I had a mind to shout 'Brava! Brava!' but I did not do that. I took a piece of cake and went out to bribe the Fyne dog into some sort of self-control. His sharp comical yapping was unbearable, like stabs through one's brain, and Fyne's deeply modulated remonstrances abashed the vivacious animal no more than the deep, patient murmur of the sea abashes a nigger minstrel on a popular beach. Fyne was beginning to swear at him in low, sepulchral tones when I appeared. The dog became at once wildly demon-strative, half strangling himself in his collar, his eyes and tongue hanging out in the excess of his incomprehensible affection for me. This was before he caught sight of the cake in my hand. A series of vertical springs high up in the air followed, and then, when he got the cake, he instantly lost his interest in everything else.

"Fyne was slightly vexed with me. As kind a master as any dog could wish to have, he yet did not approve of cake being given to dogs. The Fyne dog was supposed to lead a Spartan existence on a diet of repulsive biscuits with an occasional dry, hygienic bone thrown in. Fyne looked down gloomily at the appeased animal, I too looked at that fool-dog; and (you know how one's mem-ory gets suddenly stimulated) I was reminded visually, with an almost painful distinctness, of the ghostly white face of the girl I saw last accompanied by that dog—deserted by that dog. I almost heard her distressed voice as if on the verge of resentful tears calling to the dog, the unsympathetic dog. Perhaps she had not the power of evoking sympathy, that personal gift of direct appeal to the feelings. I said to Fyne, mistrusting the supine attitude of the dog:

" 'Why don't you let him come inside?'

"Oh dear no! He couldn't think of it! I might indeed have saved my breath, I knew it was one of the Fynes' rules of life, part of their solemnity and responsibility, one of those things that were part of their unassertive but ever-present superiority, that their dog must not be allowed in. It was most improper to intrude the dog into the houses of the people they were calling on—if it were only a careless bachelor in farmhouse lodgings and a personal friend of the dog. It was out of the question. But they would let him bark one's sanity away outside one's window. They were strangely consistent in their lack of imaginative sympathy. I didn't insist but simply led the way back to the parlour, hoping that no wayfarer would happen along the lane for the next hour or so to disturb the dog's composure.

"Mrs. Fyne, seated immovable before the table charged with plates, cups, jugs, a cold teapot, crumbs, and the general litter of the entertainment, turned her head towards us.

" 'You see, Mr. Marlow,' she said in an unexpectedly confidential tone: 'they are so utterly unsuited for each other.'

"At the moment I did not know how to apply this remark. I thought at first of Fyne and the dog. Then I adjusted it to the matter in hand which was neither more nor less than an elopement. Yes, by Jove! It was something very much like an elopement—with certain unusual characteristics of its own which made it in a sense equivocal. With amused wonder I remembered that my sagacity was requisitioned in such a connection. How unexpected! But we never know what tests our gifts may be put to. Sagacity dictated caution first of all. I believe caution to be the first duty of sagacity. Fyne sat down as if preparing himself to witness a joust, I thought.

" 'Do you think so, Mrs. Fyne?' I said sagaciously. 'Of course you are in a position . . .' I was continuing with caution when she struck out vivaciously for immediate assent.

" 'Obviously! Clearly! You yourself must admit . . .'

" 'But, Mrs. Fyne,' I remonstrated, 'you forget that I don't know your brother.'

"This argument which was not only sagacious but true, overwhelmingly true, unanswerably true, seemed to surprise her.

"I wondered why. I did not know enough of her brother for the remotest guess at what he might be like. I had never set eyes on the man. I didn't know him so completely that by contrast I seemed to have known Miss de Barral—whom I had seen twice (altogether about sixty minutes) and with whom I had exchanged about sixty words—from the cradle so to speak. And perhaps, I thought, looking down at Mrs. Fyne (I had remained standing), perhaps she thinks that this ought to be enough for a sagacious assent.

"She kept silent; and I, looking at her with polite expectation, went on addressing her mentally in a mood of familiar approval which would have astonished her had it been audible: 'You, my dear, at any rate are a sincere woman . . .'

"I call a woman sincere," Marlow began again after giving me a cigar and lighting one himself, "I call a woman sincere when she volunteers a statement resembling remotely in form what she really would like to say, what she really thinks ought to be said if it were not for the necessity to spare the stupid sensitiveness of men. The women's rougher, simpler, more upright judgment embraces the whole truth, which their tact, their mistrust of masculine idealism, ever prevents them from speaking in its entirety. And their tact is unerring. We could not stand women speaking the truth. We could not bear it. It would cause infinite misery and bring about most awful disturbances in this rather mediocre, but still idealistic fool's paradise in which each of us lives his own little life—the unit in the great sum of existence. And they know it. They are merciful. This generalization does not apply exactly to Mrs. Fyne's outburst of sincerity in a matter in which neither my affections nor my vanity was engaged. That's why, may be, she ventured so far. For a woman she chose to be as open as the day with me. There was not only the form but almost the whole substance of her thought in what she said. She believed she could risk it. She had reasoned somewhat in this way; there's a man, possessing a certain amount of sagacity . . ."

Marlow paused with a whimsical look at me. The last few words he had spoken with the cigar in his teeth. He took it out now by an ample movement of his arm and blew a thin cloud.

"You smile? It would have been more kind to spare my blushes. But as a matter of fact I need not blush. This is not vanity; it is analysis. We'll let sagacity stand. But we must also note what sagacity in this connection stands for. When you see this you shall see also that there was nothing in it to alarm my modesty. I don't think Mrs. Fyne credited me with the possession of wisdom tempered by common sense. And had I had the wisdom of the Seven Sages of Antiquity, she would not have been moved to confidence or admiration. The secret scorn of women for the capacity to consider judiciously and to express profoundly a meditated conclusion is unbounded. They have no use for these lofty exercises which they look upon as a sort of purely masculine game—game meaning a respectable occupation devised to kill time in this man-arranged life which must be got through somehow. What women's acuteness really respects are the inept 'ideas' and the sheep-like impulses by which our actions and opinions are determined in matters of real importance. For if women are not rational they are indeed acute. Even Mrs. Fyne was acute. The good woman was making up to her husband's chess-player simply because she had scented in him that small portion of 'femininity,' that drop of superior essence of which I am myself aware; which, I gratefully acknowledge, has saved me from one or two misadventures in my life either ridiculous or lamentable, I am not very certain which. It matters very little. Anyhow misadventures. Observe that I say 'femininity,' a privilege—not 'feminism,' an attitude. I am not a feminist. It was Fyne who on certain solemn grounds had adopted that mental attitude; but it was enough to glance at him sitting on one side, to see that he was purely masculine to his finger tips, masculine solidly, densely, amusingly,—hopelessly.

"I did glance at him. You don't get your sagacity recognized by a man's wife without feeling the propriety and even the need to glance at the man now and again.

So I glanced at him. Very masculine. So much so that 'hopelessly' was not the last word of it. He was helpless. He was bound and delivered by it. And if by the obscure promptings of my composite temperament I beheld him with malicious amusement, yet being in fact, by definition and especially from profound conviction, a man, I could not help sympathizing with him largely. Seeing him thus disarmed, so completely captive by the very nature of things, I was moved to speak to him kindly.

" 'Well. And what do you think of it?'

" 'I don't know. How's one to tell? But I say that the thing is done now and there's an end of it,' said the masculine creature as bluntly as his innate solemnity permitted.

"Mrs. Fyne moved a little in her chair. I turned to her and remarked gently that this was a charge, a criticism, which was often made. Some people always ask: What could he see in her? Others wonder what she could have seen in him? Expressions of unsuitability.

"She said with all the emphasis of her quietly folded arms:

" 'I know perfectly well what Flora has seen in my brother.'

"I bowed my head to the gust but pursued my point.

" 'And then the marriage in most cases turns out no worse than the average, to say the least of it.'

"Mrs. Fyne was disappointed by the optimistic turn of my sagacity. She rested her eyes on my face as though in doubt whether I had enough femininity in my composition to understand the case.

"I waited for her to speak. She seemed to be asking herself: Is it, after all, worth while to talk to that man? You understand how provoking this was. I looked in my mind for something appallingly stupid to say, with the object of distressing and teasing Mrs. Fyne. It is humiliating to confess a failure. One would think that a man of average intelligence could command stupidity at will. But it isn't so. I suppose it's a special gift or else the difficulty consists in being relevant. Discovering that I could find no really telling stupidity, I turned to the next best thing: a platitude. I advanced, in a common-sense tone, that, surely, in the matter of marriage a man had only himself to please.

"Mrs. Fyne received this without the flutter of an eyelid. Fyne's masculine breast, as might have been expected, was pierced by that old, regulation shaft. He grunted most feelingly. I turned to him with false simplicity. 'Don't you agree with me?'

" 'The very thing I've been telling my wife,' he exclaimed in his extra-manly bass. 'We have been discussing——'

"A discussion in the Fyne ménage! How portentous! Perhaps the very first difference they had ever had: Mrs. Fyne unflinching and ready for any responsibility, Fyne solemn and shrinking—the children in bed upstairs; and outside the dark fields, the shadowy contours of the land on the starry background of the universe, with the crude light of the open window like a beacon for the truant who would never come back now; a truant no longer but a downright fugitive. Yet a fugitive carrying off spoils. It was the flight of a raider—or a traitor? This affair of the purloined brother, as I had named it to myself, had a very puzzling physiognomy. The girl must have been desperate, I thought, hearing the grave voice of Fyne well enough but catching the sense of his words not at all, except the very last words which were:

" 'Of course, it's extremely distressing.'

"I looked at him inquisitively. What was distressing him? The purloining of the son of the poet-tyrant by the daughter of the financier-convict? Or only, if I may say so, the wind of their flight disturbing the solemn placidity of the Fynes' domestic atmosphere? My incertitude did not last long, for he added:

" 'Mrs. Fyne urges me to go to London at once.'

"One could guess at, almost see, his profound distaste for the journey, his distress at a difference of feeling with his wife. With his serious view of the sublunary comedy Fyne suffered from not being able to agree solemnly with her sentiment as he was accustomed to do, in recognition of having had his way in one supreme instance: when he made her elope with him—the most momentous step imaginable in a young lady's life. He had been really trying to acknowledge it by taking the rightness of her feeling for granted on every other occasion. It had become a sort of habit at last. And it is never pleasant to break a habit. The man was deeply troubled. I said: 'Really! To go to London!'

"He looked dumbly into my eyes. It was pathetic and funny. 'And you of course feel it would be useless,' I pursued.

"He evidently felt that, though he said nothing. He only went on blinking at me with a solemn and comical slowness. 'Unless it be to carry there the family's blessing,' I went on, indulging my chaffing humour steadily, in a rather sneaking fashion, for I dared not look at Mrs. Fyne, to my right. No sound or movement came from that direction. 'You think very naturally that to match mere good, sound reasons, against the passionate conclusions of love is a waste of intellect bordering on the absurd.'

"He looked surprised as if I had discovered something very clever. He, dear man, had thought of nothing at all. He simply knew that he did not want to go to London on that mission. Mere masculine delicacy. In a moment he became enthusiastic.

" 'Yes! Yes! Exactly. A man in love . . . You hear, my dear? Here you have an independent opinion——'

" 'Can anything be more hopeless,' I insisted to the fascinated little Fyne, 'than to pit reason against love? I must confess however that in this case when I think of that poor girl's sharp chin I wonder if . . .'

"My levity was too much for Mrs. Fyne. Still leaning back in her chair she exclaimed:

" 'Mr. Marlow!'

"As if mysteriously affected by her indignation the absurd Fyne dog began to bark in the porch. It might have been at a trespassing bumble-bee however. That animal was capable of any eccentricity. Fyne got up quickly and went out to him. I think he was glad to leave us alone to discuss that matter of his journey to London. A sort of anti-sentimental journey. He, too, apparently, had confidence in my sagacity. It was touching, this confidence. It was at any rate more genuine than the confidence his wife pretended to have in her husband's chess-player, of three successive holidays. Confidence be hanged! Sagacity—indeed! She had simply marched in without a shadow of misgiving to make me back her up. But she had delivered herself into my hands. . . ."

Interrupting his narrative Marlow addressed me in his tone between grim jest and grim earnest:

"Perhaps you didn't know that my character is upon the whole rather vindictive."

"No, I didn't know," I said with a grin. "That's rather unusual for a sailor. They always seemed to me the least vindictive body of men in the world."

"H'm! Simple souls," Marlow muttered moodily. "Want of opportunity. The world leaves them alone for the most part. For myself it's towards women that I feel vindictive mostly, in my small way. I admit that it is small. But then the occasions in themselves are not great. Mainly I resent that pretence of winding us round their dear little fingers, as of right. Not that the result ever amounts to much generally. There are so very few momentous opportunities. It is the assumption that each of us is a combination of a kid and an imbecile which I find provoking—in a small way; in a very small way. You needn't stare as though I were breathing fire and smoke out of my nostrils. I am not a women-devouring monster. I am not even what is technically called 'a brute.' I hope there's enough of a kid and an imbecile in me to answer the requirements of some really good woman eventually—some day . . . Some day. Why do you gasp? You don't suppose I should be afraid of getting married? That supposition would be offensive . . ."

"I wouldn't dream of offending you," I said.

"Very well. But meantime please remember that I was not married to Mrs. Fyne. That lady's little finger was none of my legal property. I had not run off with it. It was Fyne who had done that thing. Let him be wound round as much as his backbone could stand—or even more, for all I cared. His rushing away from the discussion on the transparent pretence of quieting the dog confirmed my notion of there being a considerable strain on his elasticity. I confronted Mrs. Fyne resolved not to assist her in her eminently feminine occupation of thrusting a stick in the spokes of another woman's wheel.

"She tried to preserve her calm-eyed superiority. She was familiar and Olympian, fenced in by the tea-table, that excellent symbol of domestic life in its lighter hour and its perfect security. In a few severely unadorned words she gave me to understand that she had ventured to hope for some really helpful suggestion from me. To this almost chiding declaration—because my vindictiveness seldom goes further than a bit of teasing—I said that I was really doing my best. And being a physiognomist . . .

" 'Being what?' she interrupted me.

" 'A physiognomist,' I repeated, raising my voice a little. 'A physiognomist, Mrs. Fyne. And on the principles of that science a pointed little chin is a sufficient ground for interference. You want to interfere—do you not?'

"Her eyes grew distinctly bigger. She had never been bantered before in her life. The late subtle poet's method of making himself unpleasant was merely savage and abusive. Fyne had been always solemnly subservient. What other men she knew I cannot tell, but I assume they must have been gentlemanly creatures. The girl-friends sat at her feet. How could she recognize my intention? She didn't know what to make of my tone.

" 'Are you serious in what you say?' she asked slowly. And it was touching. It was as if a very young, confiding girl had spoken. I felt myself relenting.

" 'No. I am not, Mrs. Fyne,' I said. 'I didn't know I was expected to be serious as well as sagacious. No. That science is farcical and therefore I am not serious. It's true that most sciences are farcical except those which teach us how to put things together.'

" 'The question is how to keep these two people apart,' she struck in. She had recovered. I admired the quickness of women's wit. Mental agility is a rare perfection. And aren't they agile! Aren't they—just! And tenacious! When they once get hold you may uproot the tree but you won't shake them off the branch. In fact the more you shake . . . But only look at the charm of contradictory perfections! No wonder men give in—generally. I won't say I was actually charmed by Mrs. Fyne. I was not delighted with her. What affected me was not what she displayed but something which she could not conceal. And that was emotion—nothing less. The form of her declaration was dry, almost peremptory—but not its tone. Her voice faltered just the least bit, she smiled faintly; and as we were looking straight at each other I observed that her eyes were glistening in a peculiar manner. She was distressed. And indeed that Mrs. Fyne should have appealed to me at all was in itself the evidence of her profound distress. 'By Jove she's desperate too,' I thought. This discovery was followed by a movement of instinctive shrinking from this unreasonable and unmasculine affair. They were all alike, with their supreme interest aroused only by fighting with each other about some man: a lover, a son, a brother.

" 'But do you think there's time yet to do anything?' I asked.

"She had an impatient movement of her shoulders without detaching herself from the back of the chair. Time! Of course! It was less than forty-eight hours since she had followed him to London. . . . I am no great clerk at those matters but I murmured vaguely an allusion to special licences. We couldn't tell what might have happened to-day already. But she knew better, scornfully. Nothing had happened.

" 'Nothing's likely to happen before next Friday week,— if then.'

"This was wonderfully precise. Then after a pause she added that she should never forgive herself if some effort were not made, an appeal.

" 'To your brother?' I asked.

" 'Yes. John ought to go to-morrow. Nine o'clock train.'

" 'So early as that!' I said. But I could not find it in my heart to pursue this discussion in a jocular tone. I submitted to her several obvious arguments, dictated apparently by common sense but in reality by my secret compassion. Mrs. Fyne brushed them aside, with the semi-conscious egoism of all safe, established existences. They had known each other so little. Just three weeks. And of that time, too short for the birth of any serious sentiment, the first week had to be deducted. They would hardly look at each other to begin with. Flora barely consented to acknowledge Captain Anthony's presence. Good morning—good-night—that was all—absolutely the whole extent of their intercourse. Captain Anthony was a silent man, completely unused to the society of girls of any sort and so shy in fact that he avoided raising his eyes to her face at the table. It was perfectly absurd. It was even inconvenient, embarrassing to her—Mrs. Fyne. After breakfast Flora would go off by herself for a long walk and Captain Anthony (Mrs. Fyne referred to him at times also as Roderick) joined the children. But he was actually too shy to get on terms with his own nieces.

"This would have sounded pathetic if I hadn't known the Fyne children who were at the same time solemn and malicious, and nursed a secret contempt for all the world. No one could get on terms with those fresh and comely young monsters! They just tolerated their parents and seemed to have a sort of mocking understanding among themselves against all outsiders, yet with no visible affection for each other. They had the habit of exchanging derisive glances which to a shy man must have been very trying. They thought their uncle no doubt a bore and perhaps an ass.

"I was not surprised to hear that very soon Anthony formed the habit of crossing the two neighbouring fields to seek the shade of a clump of elms at a good distance from the cottage. He lay on the grass and smoked his pipe all the morning. Mrs. Fyne wondered at her brother's indolent habits. He had asked for books, it is true, but there were but few in the cottage. He read them through in three days and then continued to lie contentedly on his back with no other companion but his pipe. Amazing indolence! The live-long morning, Mrs. Fyne, busy writing upstairs in the cottage, could see him out of the window. She had a very long sight, and these elms were grouped on a rise of the ground. His indolence was plainly exposed to her criticism on a gentle green slope. Mrs. Fyne wondered at it; she was disgusted too. But having just then 'commenced author,' as you know, she could not tear herself away from the fascinating novelty. She let him wallow in his vice. I imagine Captain Anthony must have had a rather pleasant time in a quiet way. It was, I remember, a hot dry summer, favourable to contemplative life out of doors. And Mrs. Fyne was scandalized. Women don't understand the force of a contemplative temperament. It simply shocks them. They feel instinctively that it is the one which escapes best the domination of feminine influences. The dear girls were exchanging jeering remarks about 'lazy uncle Roderick' openly, in her indulgent hearing. And it was so strange,

she told me, because as a boy he was anything but indolent. On the contrary. Always active.

"I remarked that a man of thirty-five was no longer a
boy. It was an obvious remark but she received it without
favour. She told me positively that the best, the nicest
men remained boys all their lives. She was disappointed
not to be able to detect anything boyish in her brother.
Very, very sorry. She had not seen him for fifteen years
or thereabouts, except on three or four occasions for a
few hours at a time. No. Not a trace of the boy he used
to be left in him.

"She fell silent for a moment and I mused idly on the
boyhood of little Fyne. I could not imagine what it might
have been like. His dominant trait was clearly the remnant of still earlier days, because I've never seen such
staring solemnity as Fyne's except in a very young baby.
But where was he all that time? Didn't he suffer contamination from the indolence of Captain Anthony? I inquired.
I was told that Mr. Fyne was very little at the cottage at
the time. Some colleague of his was convalescing after a
severe illness in a little seaside village in the neighbourhood and Fyne went off every morning by train to spend
the day with the elderly invalid who had no one to look
after him. It was a very praiseworthy excuse for neglect-
ing his brother-in-law, 'the son of the poet, you know,'
with whom he had nothing in common even in the
remotest degree. If Captain Anthony (Roderick) had
been a pedestrian it would have been sufficient; but he
was not. Still, in the afternoon, he went sometimes for
a slow casual stroll, by himself of course, the children
having definitely cold-shouldered him, and his only sister
being busy with that inflammatory book which was to
blaze upon the world a year or more afterwards. It seems
however that she was capable of detaching her eyes from
her task now and then, if only for a moment, because it
was from that garret fitted out for a study that one afternoon she observed her brother and Flora de Barral coming down the road side by side. They had met somewhere
accidentally (which of them crossed the other's path, as
the saying is, I don't know), and were returning to tea
together. She noticed that they appeared to be conversing without constraint.

" 'I had the simplicity to be pleased,' Mrs. Fyne commented with a dry little laugh. 'Pleased for both their sakes.' Captain Anthony shook off his indolence from that day forth, and accompanied Miss Flora frequently on her morning walks. Mrs. Fyne remained pleased. She could now forget them comfortably and give herself up to the delights of audacious thought and literary composition. Only a week before the blow fell she, happening to raise her eyes from the paper, saw two figures seated on the grass under the shade of the elms. She could make out the white blouse. There could be no mistake.

" 'I suppose they imagined themselves concealed by the hedge. They forgot no doubt I was working in the garret,' she said bitterly. 'Or perhaps they didn't care. They were right. I am rather a simple person . . .' She laughed again . . . 'I was incapable of suspecting such duplicity.'

" 'Duplicity is a strong word, Mrs. Fyne—isn't it?' I expostulated. 'And considering that Captain Anthony himself . . .'

" 'Oh well—perhaps,' she interrupted me. Her eyes which never strayed away from mine, her set features, her whole immovable figure, how well I knew those appearances of a person who has 'made up her mind.' A very hopeless condition that, specially in women. I mistrusted her concession so easily, so stonily made. She reflected a moment. 'Yes. I ought to have said—ingratitude, perhaps.'

"After having thus disengaged her brother and pushed the poor girl a little further off as it were—isn't women's cleverness perfectly diabolic when they are really put on their mettle? —after having done these things and also made me feel that I was no match for her, she went on scrupulously: 'One doesn't like to use that word either. The claim is very small. It's so little one could do for her. Still . . .'

" 'I dare say,' I exclaimed, throwing diplomacy to the winds. 'But really, Mrs. Fyne, it's impossible to dismiss your brother like this out of the business . . .'

" 'She threw herself at his head,' Mrs. Fyne uttered firmly.

" 'He had no business to put his head in the way, then,' I retorted with an angry laugh. I didn't restrain myself because her fixed stare seemed to express the purpose to daunt me. I was not afraid of her, but it occurred to me that I was within an ace of drifting into a downright quarrel with a lady and, besides, my guest. There was the cold teapot, the emptied cups, emblems of hospitality. It could not be. I cut short my angry laugh while Mrs. Fyne murmured with a slight movement of her shoulder, 'He! Poor man! Oh come . . .'

"By a great effort of will I found myself able to smile amiably, to speak with proper softness.

" 'My dear Mrs. Fyne, you forget that I don't know him—not even by sight. It's difficult to imagine a victim as passive as all that; but granting you the (I very nearly said: imbecility, but checked myself in time) innocence of Captain Anthony, don't you think now, frankly, that there is a little of your own fault in what has happened? You bring them together, you leave your brother to himself!'

"She sat up and leaning her elbow on the table sustained her head in her open palm, casting down her eyes. Compunction? It was indeed a very off-hand way of treating a brother come to stay for the first time in fifteen years. I suppose she discovered very soon that she had nothing in common with that sailor, that stranger, fashioned and marked by the sea of long voyages. In her strong-minded way she had scorned pretences, had gone to her writing which interested her immensely. A very praiseworthy thing, your sincere conduct,—if it didn't at times resemble brutality so much. But I don't think it was compunction. That sentiment is rare in women . . ."

"Is it?" I interrupted indignantly.

"You know more women than I do," retorted the unabashed Marlow. "You make it your business to know them—don't you? You go about a lot amongst all sorts of people. You are a tolerably honest observer. Well, just try to remember how many instances of compunction you have seen. I am ready to take your bare word for it. Compunction! Have you ever seen as much as its shadow? Have you ever? Just a shadow—a passing shadow! I tell you it is so rare that you may call it nonexistent. They are too passionate. Too pedantic. Too courageous with themselves—perhaps. No, I don't think for a moment that Mrs. Fyne felt the slightest compunction at her treatment of her sea-going brother. What *he* thought of it who can tell? It is possible that he wondered why he had been so insistently urged to come. It is possible that he wondered bitterly—or contemptuously—or humbly. And it may be that he was only surprised and bored. Had he been as sincere in his conduct as his only sister he would have probably taken himself off at the end of the second day. But perhaps he was afraid of appearing brutal. I am not far removed from the conviction that between the sincerities of his sister and of his dear nieces, Captain Anthony of the *Ferndale* must have had his loneliness brought home to his bosom for the first time of his life, at an age, thirty-five or thereabouts, when one is mature enough to feel the pang of such a discovery. Angry or simply sad but certainly disillusioned he wanders about and meets the girl one afternoon and under the sway of a strong feeling forgets his shyness. This is no supposition. It is a fact. There was such a meeting in which the shyness must have perished before we don't know what encouragement, or in the community of mood made apparent by some casual word. You remember that Mrs. Fyne saw them one afternoon coming back to the cottage together. Don't you think that I have hit on the psychology of the situation? . . ."

"Doubtless . . ." I began to ponder.

"I was very certain of my conclusions at the time," Marlow went on impatiently. "But don't think for a moment that Mrs. Fyne in her new attitude and toying thoughtfully with a teaspoon was about to surrender. She murmured:

" 'It's the last thing I should have thought could happen.'

" 'You didn't suppose they were romantic enough,' I suggested dryly.

"She let it pass and with great decision, but as if speaking to herself:

" 'Roderick really must be warned.'

"She didn't give me the time to ask of what precisely. She raised her head and addressed me.

" 'I am surprised and grieved more than I can tell you at Mr. Fyne's resistance. We have been always completely at one on every question. And that we should differ now on a point touching my brother so closely is a most painful surprise to me.' Her hand rattled the teaspoon brusquely by an involuntary movement. 'It is intolerable,' she added tempestuously—for Mrs. Fyne that is. I suppose she had nerves of her own like any other woman.

"Under the porch where Fyne had sought refuge with the dog there was silence. I took it for a proof of deep sagacity. I don't mean on the part of the dog. He was a confirmed fool.

"I said: 'You want absolutely to interfere . . . ?' Mrs. Fyne nodded just perceptibly . . . 'Well—for my part . . . but I don't really know how matters stand at the present time. You have had a letter from Miss de Barral. What does that letter say?'

" 'She asks for her valise to be sent to her town address,' Mrs. Fyne uttered reluctantly and stopped. I waited a bit—then exploded.

" 'Well! What's the matter? Where's the difficulty? Does your husband object to that? You don't mean to say that he wants you to appropriate the girl's clothes?'

" 'Mr. Marlow!'

" 'Well, but you talk of a painful difference of opinion with your husband, and then, when I ask for information on the point, you bring out a valise. And only a few moments ago you reproached me for not being serious. I wonder who is the serious person of us two now.'

"She smiled faintly and in a friendly tone, from which I concluded at once that she did not mean to show me the girl's letter, she said that undoubtedly the letter disclosed an understanding between Captain Anthony and Flora de Barral.

" 'What understanding?' I pressed her. 'An engagement is an understanding.'

" 'There is no engagement—not yet,' she said decisively. 'That letter, Mr. Marlow, is couched in very vague terms. That is why——'

"I interrupted her without ceremony.

" 'You still hope to interfere to some purpose. Isn't it so? Yes? But how should you have liked it if anybody had tried to interfere between you and Mr. Fyne at the time when *your* understanding with each other could still have been described in vague terms?'

"She had a genuine movement of astonished indignation. It was with the accent of perfect sincerity that she cried out at me: 'But it isn't at all the same thing! How can you!'

"Indeed how could I! The daughter of a poet and the daughter of a convict are not comparable in the consequences of their conduct if their necessity may wear at times a similar aspect. Amongst these consequences I could perceive undesirable cousins for these dear healthy girls, and such like, possible causes of embarrassment in the future.

" 'No! You can't be serious,' Mrs. Fyne's smouldering resentment broke out again. 'You haven't thought——'

" 'Oh yes, Mrs. Fyne! I have thought. I am still thinking. I am even trying to think like you.'

" 'Mr. Marlow,' she said earnestly. 'Believe me that I really am thinking of my brother, in all this . . .' I assured her that I quite believed she was. For there is no law of nature making it impossible to think of more than one person at a time. Then I said:

" 'She has told him all about herself of course.'

" 'All about her life,' assented Mrs. Fyne with an air, however, of making some mental reservation which I did not pause to investigate. 'Her life!' I repeated. 'That girl must have had a mighty bad time of it.'

" 'Horrible,' Mrs. Fyne admitted with a ready frankness very creditable under the circumstances, and a warmth of tone which made me look at her with a friendly eye. 'Horrible! No! You can't imagine the sort of vulgar people she became dependent on . . . You know her father never attempted to see her while he was still at large. After his arrest he instructed that relative of his—the odious person who took her away from Brighton—not to let his daughter come to the court during the trial. He refused to hold any communication with her whatever.'

"I remembered what Mrs. Fyne had told me before of the view she had years ago of de Barral clinging to the child at the side of his wife's grave and later on of these two walking hand in hand the observed of all eyes by the sea. Figures from Dickens—pregnant with pathos.

CHAPTER SIX

Flora

"'A very singular prohibition,' remarked Mrs. Fyne after a short silence. 'He seemed to love the child.'

"She was puzzled. But I surmised that it might have been the sullenness of a man unconscious of guilt and standing at bay to fight his 'persecutors,' as he called them; or else the fear of a softer emotion weakening his defiant attitude; perhaps, even, it was a self-denying ordinance, in order to spare the girl the sight of her father in the dock, accused of cheating, sentenced as a swindler—proving the possession of a certain moral delicacy.

"Mrs. Fyne didn't know what to think. She supposed it might have been mere callousness. But the people amongst whom the girl had fallen had positively not a grain of moral delicacy. Of that she was certain. Mrs. Fyne could not undertake to give me an idea of their abominable vulgarity. Flora used to tell her something of her life in that household, over there, down Limehouse way. It was incredible. It passed Mrs. Fyne's comprehension. It was a sort of moral savagery which she could not have thought possible.

"I, on the contrary, thought it very possible. I could

imagine easily how the poor girl must have been bewildered and hurt at her reception in that household—
envied for her past while delivered defenceless to the
tender mercies of people without any fineness either of
feeling or mind, unable to understand her misery, grossly
curious, mistaking her manner for disdain, her silent
shrinking for pride. The wife of the 'odious person' was
witless and fatuously conceited. Of the two girls of the
house one was pious and the other a romp; both were
coarse-minded—if they may be credited with any mind
at all. The rather numerous men of the family were dense
and grumpy, or dense and jocose. None in that grubbing
lot had enough humanity to leave her alone. At first she
was made much of, in an offensively patronizing manner.
The connection with the great de Barral gratified their
vanity even in the moment of the smash. They dragged
her to their place of worship, whatever it might have
been, where the congregation stared at her, and they
gave parties to other beings like themselves at which they
exhibited her with ignoble self-satisfaction. She did not
know how to defend herself from their importunities,
insolence and exigencies. She lived amongst them, a passive victim, quivering in every nerve, as if she were
flayed. After the trial her position became still worse.
On the least occasion and even on no occasions at all
she was scolded, or else taunted with her dependence.
The pious girl lectured her on her defects, the romping
girl teased her with contemptuous references to her
accomplishments, and was always trying to pick insensate
quarrels with her about some 'fellow' or other. The
mother backed up her girls invariably, adding her own
silly, wounding remarks. I must say they were probably
not aware of the ugliness of their conduct. They were
nasty amongst themselves as a matter of course; their
disputes were nauseating in origin, in manner, in the
spirit of mean selfishness. These women, too, seemed to
enjoy greatly any sort of row and were always ready to
combine together to make awful scenes to the luckless
girl on incredibly flimsy pretences. Thus Flora on one
occasion had been reduced to rage and despair, had her
most secret feelings lacerated, had obtained a view of
the utmost baseness to which common human nature can
descend—I won't say à propos de bottes as the French

would excellently put it, but literally *à propos* of some
mislaid cheap lace trimmings for a nightgown the romping one was making for herself. Yes, that was the origin
of one of the grossest scenes which, in their repetition,
must have had a deplorable effect on the unformed character of the most pitiful of de Barral's victims. I have it
from Mrs. Fyne. The girl turned up at the Fynes' house
at half-past nine on a cold, drizzly evening. She had
walked bareheaded, I believe, just as she ran out of the
house, from somewhere in Poplar to the neighbourhood
of Sloane Square—without stopping, without drawing
breath, if only for a sob.

" 'We were having some people to dinner,' said the
anxious sister of Captain Anthony.

"She had heard the front door bell and wondered what
it might mean. The parlourmaid managed to whisper to
her without attracting attention. The servants had been
frightened by the invasion of that wild girl in a muddy
skirt and with wisps of damp hair sticking to her pale
cheeks. But they had seen her before. This was not the
first occasion, nor yet the last.

"Directly she could slip away from her guests Mrs.
Fyne ran upstairs.

" 'I found her in the night nursery crouching on the
floor, her head resting on the cot of the youngest of my
girls. The eldest was sitting up in bed looking at her
across the room.'

"Only a nightlight was burning there. Mrs. Fyne raised
her up, took her over to Mr. Fyne's little dressing-room
on the other side of the landing, to a fire by which she
could dry herself, and left her there. She had to go back
to her guests.

"A most disagreeable surprise it must have been to the
Fynes. Afterwards they both went up and interviewed
the girl. She jumped up at their entrance. She had shaken
her damp hair loose; her eyes were dry—with the heat
of rage.

"I can imagine little Fyne solemnly sympathetic, solemnly listening, solemnly retreating to the marital bedroom. Mrs. Fyne pacified the girl, and, fortunately, there
was a bed which could be made up for her in the
dressing-room.

" 'But what could one do after all!' concluded Mrs. Fyne.

"And this stereotyped exclamation, expressing the difficulty of the problem and the readiness (at any rate) of good intentions, made me, as usual, feel more kindly towards her.

"Next morning, very early, long before Fyne had to start for his office, the 'odious personage' turned up, not exactly unexpected perhaps, but startling all the same, if only by the promptness of his action. From what Flora herself related to Mrs. Fyne, it seems that without being very perceptibly less 'odious' than his family he had in a rather mysterious fashion interposed his authority for the protection of the girl. 'Not that he cares,' explained Flora. 'I am sure he does not. I could not stand being liked by any of these people. If I thought he liked me I would drown myself rather than go back with him.'

"For of course he had come to take 'Florrie' home. The scene was the dining-room—breakfast interrupted, dishes growing cold, little Fyne's toast growing leathery, Fyne out of his chair with his back to the fire, the newspaper on the carpet, servants shut out, Mrs. Fyne rigid in her place with the girl sitting beside her—the 'odious person,' who had bustled in with hardly a greeting, looking from Fyne to Mrs. Fyne as though he were inwardly amused at something he knew of them; and then beginning ironically his discourse. He did not apologize for disturbing Fyne and his 'good lady' at breakfast, because he knew they did not want (with a nod at the girl) to have more of her than could be helped. He came the first possible moment because he had his business to attend to. He wasn't drawing a tip-top salary (this staring at Fyne) in a luxuriously furnished office. Not he. He had risen to be an employer of labour and was bound to give a good example.

"I believe the fellow was aware of, and enjoyed quietly, the consternation his presence brought to the bosom of Mr. and Mrs. Fyne. He turned briskly to the girl. Mrs. Fyne confessed to me that they had remained all three silent and inanimate. He turned to the girl: 'What's this game, Florrie? You had better give it up. If you expect me to run all over London looking for you every time you happen to have a tiff with your auntie and cousins you are mistaken. I can't afford it.'

"Tiff—was the sort of definition to take one's breath away, having regard to the fact that both the word convict and the word pauper had been used a moment before Flora de Barral ran away from the quarrel about the lace trimmings. Yes, these very words! So at least the girl had told Mrs. Fyne the evening before. The word tiff in connection with her tale had a peculiar savour, a paralysing effect. Nobody made a sound. The relative of de Barral proceeded uninterrupted to a display of magnanimity. 'Auntie told me to tell you she's sorry—there! And Amelia (the romping sister) shan't worry you again. I'll see to that. You ought to be satisfied. Remember your position.'

"Emboldened by the utter stillness pervading the room he addressed himself to Mrs. Fyne with stolid effrontery—

" 'What I say is that people should be good-natured. She can't stand being chaffed. She puts on her grand airs. She won't take a bit of a joke from people as good as herself anyway. We are a plain lot. We don't like it. And that's how trouble begins.'

"Insensible to the stony stare of three pairs of eyes, which, if the stories of our childhood as to the power of the human eye are true, ought to have been enough to daunt a tiger, that unabashed manufacturer from the East End fastened his fangs, figuratively speaking, into the poor girl and prepared to drag her away for a prey to his cubs of both sexes.

" 'Auntie has thought of sending you your hat and coat. I've got them outside in the cab.'

"Mrs. Fyne looked mechanically out of the window. A four-wheeler stood before the gate under the weeping sky. The driver in his conical cape and tarpaulin hat streamed with water. The drooping horse looked as though it had been fished out, half unconscious, from a pond. Mrs. Fyne found some relief in looking at that miserable sight, away from the room in which the voice of the amiable visitor resounded with a vulgar intonation exhorting the strayed sheep to return to the delightful fold. 'Come, Florrie, make a move. I can't wait on you all day here.'

"Mrs. Fyne heard all this without turning her head

away from the window. Fyne on the hearthrug had to listen and to look on too. I shall not try to form a surmise as to the real nature of the suspense. Their very goodness must have made it very anxious. The girl's hands were lying in her lap; her head was lowered as if in deep thought; and the other went on delivering a sort of homily. Ingratitude was condemned in it, the sinfulness of pride was pointed out—together with the proverbial fact that it 'goes before a fall.' There were also some sound remarks as to the danger of nonsensical notions and the disadvantages of a quick temper. It sets one's best friends against one. 'And if anybody ever wanted friends in the world it's you, my girl.' Even respect for parental authority was invoked. 'In the first hour of his trouble your father wrote to me to take care of you—don't forget it. Yes, to me, just a plain man, rather than to any of his fine West-End friends. You can't get over that. And a father's a father no matter what a mess he's got himself into. You ain't going to throw over your own father— are you?'

"It was difficult to say whether he was more absurd than cruel or more cruel than absurd. Mrs. Fyne, with the fine ear of a woman, seemed to detect a jeering intention in his meanly unctuous tone, something more vile than mere cruelty. She glanced quickly over her shoulder and saw the girl raise her two hands to her head, then let them fall again on her lap. Fyne in front of the fire was like the victim of an unholy spell—bereft of motion and speech but obviously in pain. It was a short pause of perfect silence, and then that 'odious creature' (he must have been really a remarkable individual in his way) struck out into sarcasm.

" 'Well? . . .' Again a silence. 'If you have fixed it up with the lady and gentleman present here for your board and lodging you had better say so. I don't want to interfere in a bargain I know nothing of. But I wonder how your father will take it when he comes out . . . or don't you expect him ever to come out?'

"At that moment, Mrs. Fyne told me she met the girl's eyes. There was that in them which made her shut her own. She also felt as though she would have liked to put her fingers in her ears. She restrained herself, however;

and the 'plain man' passed in his appalling versatility from sarcasm to veiled menace.

" 'You have—eh? Well and good. But before I go home let me ask you, my girl, to think if by any chance you throwing us over like this won't be rather bad for your father later on? Just think it over.'

"He looked at his victim with an air of cunning mystery. She jumped up so suddenly that he started back. Mrs. Fyne rose too, and even the spell was removed from her husband. But the girl dropped again into the chair and turned her head to look at Mrs. Fyne. This time it was no accidental meeting of fugitive glances. It was a deliberate communication. To my question as to its nature Mrs. Fyne said she did not know. 'Was it appealing?' I suggested. 'No,' she said. 'Was it frightened, angry, crushed, resigned?' 'No! No! Nothing of these.' But it had frightened her. She remembered it to this day. She had been ever since fancying she could detect the lingering reflection of that look in all the girl's glances. In the attentive, in the casual—even in the grateful glances—in the expression of the softest moods.

" 'Has she her soft moods, then?' I asked with interest.

"Mrs. Fyne, much moved by her recollections, heeded not my inquiry. All her mental energy was concentrated on the nature of that memorable glance. The general tradition of mankind teaches us that glances occupy a considerable place in the self-expression of women. Mrs. Fyne was trying honestly to give me some idea, as much perhaps to satisfy her own uneasiness as my curiosity. She was frowning in the effort as you see sometimes a child do (what is delightful in women is that they so often resemble intelligent children—I mean the crustiest, the sourest, the most battered of them do—at times). She was frowning, I say, and I was beginning to smile faintly at her when all at once she came out with something totally unexpected.

" 'It was horribly merry,' she said.

"I suppose she must have been satisfied by my sudden gravity because she looked at me in a friendly manner.

" 'Yes, Mrs. Fyne,' I said, smiling no longer. 'I see. It would have been horrible even on the stage.'

" 'Ah!' she interrupted me—and I really believe her change of attitude back to folded arms was meant to check a shudder. 'But it wasn't on the stage, and it was not with her lips that she laughed.'

" 'Yes. It must have been horrible,' I assented. 'And then she had to go away ultimately—I suppose. You didn't say anything?'

" 'No,' said Mrs. Fyne. 'I rang the bell and told one of the maids to go and bring the hat and coat out of the cab. And then we waited.'

"I don't think that there ever was such waiting, unless possibly in a jail at some moment or other on the morning of an execution. The servant appeared with the hat and coat, and then, still as on the morning of an execution, when the condemned, I believe, is offered a breakfast, Mrs. Fyne, anxious that the white-faced girl should swallow something warm (if she could) before leaving her house for an interminable drive through raw cold air in a damp four-wheeler—Mrs. Fyne broke the awful silence: 'You really must try to eat something,' in her best resolute manner. She turned to the 'odious person,' with the same determination. 'Perhaps you will sit down and have a cup of coffee, too.'

"The worthy 'employer of labour' sat down. He might have been awed by Mrs. Fyne's peremptory manner—for she did not think of conciliating him then. He sat down provisionally, like a man who finds himself much against his will in doubtful company. He accepted ungraciously the cup handed to him by Mrs. Fyne, took an unwilling sip or two and put it down as if there were some moral contamination in the coffee of these 'swells.' Between whiles he directed mysteriously inexpressive glances at little Fyne, who, I gather, had no breakfast that morning at all. Neither had the girl. She never moved her hands from her lap till her appointed guardian got up, leaving his cup half full.

" 'Well. If you don't mean to take advantage of this lady's kind offer I may just as well take you home at once. I want to begin my day—I do.'

"After a few more dumb, leaden-footed minutes while Flora was putting on her hat and jacket, the Fynes without moving, without saying anything, saw these two leave the room.

" 'She never looked back at us,' said Mrs. Fyne. 'She just followed him out. I've never had such a crushing impression of the miserable dependence of girls—of women. This was an extreme case. But a young man— any man—could have gone to break stones on the roads or something of that kind—or enlisted—or——'

"It was very true. Women can't go forth on the high roads and by-ways to pick up a living even when dignity, independence or existence itself are at stake. But what made me interrupt Mrs. Fyne's tirade was my profound surprise at the fact of that respectable citizen being so willing to keep in his home the poor girl for whom it seemed there was no place in the world. And not only willing but anxious. I couldn't credit him with generous impulses. For it seemed obvious to me from what I had learned that, to put it mildly, he was not an impulsive person.

" 'I confess that I can't understand his motive,' I exclaimed.

" 'This is exactly what John wondered at, at first,' said Mrs. Fyne. By that time an intimacy—if not exactly confidence—had sprung up between us which permitted her in this discussion to refer to her husband as John. 'You know he had not opened his lips all that time,' she pursued. 'I don't blame his restraint. On the contrary. What could he have said? I could see he was observing the man very thoughtfully.'

" 'And so, Mr. Fyne listened, observed and meditated,' I said. 'That's an excellent way of coming to a conclusion. And may I ask at what conclusion he had managed to arrive? On what ground did he cease to wonder at the inexplicable? For I can't admit humanity to be the explanation. It would be too monstrous.'

"It was nothing of the sort Mrs. Fyne assured me with some resentment, as though I had aspersed little Fyne's sanity. Fyne very sensibly had set himself the mental task of discovering the self-interest. I should not have thought him capable of so much cynicism. He said to himself that for people of that sort (religious fears or the vanity of righteousness put aside) money—not great wealth, but money, just a little money—is the measure of virtue, of expediency, of wisdom—of pretty well everything. But the girl was absolutely destitute. The father was in prison after the most terribly complete and disgraceful smash of modern times. And then it dawned upon Fyne that this

was just it. The great smash, in the great dust of vanishing millions! Was it possible that they all had vanished
to the last penny? Wasn't there, somewhere, something
palpable; some fragment of the fabric left?

" 'That's it,' had exclaimed Fyne, startling his wife by
this explosive unsealing of his lips less than half an hour
after the departure of de Barral's cousin with de Barral's
daughter. It was still in the dining-room, very near the
time for him to go forth affronting the elements in order
to put in another day's work in his country's service. All
he could say at the moment in elucidation of this break-
down from his usual placid solemnity was—

" 'The fellow imagines that de Barrel has got some
plunder put away somewhere.'

"This being the theory arrived at by Fyne, his comment on it was that a good many bankrupts had been
known to have taken such a precaution. It was possible in
de Barral's case. Fyne went so far in his display of cynical
pessimism as to say that it was extremely probable.

"He explained at length to Mrs. Fyne that de Barral
certainly did not take any one into his confidence. But
the beastly relative had made up his low mind that it was
so. He was selfish and pitiless in his stupidity, but he had
clearly conceived the notion of making a claim on de
Barral when de Barral came out of prison on the strength
of having 'looked after' (as he would have himself
expressed it) his daughter. He nursed his hopes, such as
they were, in secret, and it is to be supposed kept them
even from his wife.

"I could see it very well. That belief accounted for his
mysterious air while he interfered in favour of the girl.
He was the only protector she had. It was as though
Flora had been fated to be always surrounded by treachery and lies stifling every better impulse, every instinctive
aspiration of her soul to trust and to love. It would have
been enough to drive a fine nature into the madness of
universal suspicion—into any sort of madness. I don't
know how far a sense of humour will stand by one. To
the foot of the gallows, perhaps. But from my recollection of Flora de Barral I feared that she hadn't much
sense of humour. She had cried at the desertion of the
absurd Fyne dog. That animal was certainly free from
duplicity. He was frank and simple and ridiculous. The

indignation of the girl at his unhypocritical behaviour had been funny but not humorous.

"As you may imagine I was not very anxious to resume the discussion on the justice, expediency, effectiveness or what not, of Fyne's journey to London. It isn't that I was unfaithful to little Fyne out in the porch with the dog. (They kept amazingly quiet there. Could they have gone to sleep?) What I felt was that either my sagacity or my conscience would come out damaged from that campaign. And no man will willingly put himself in the way of moral damage. I did not want a war with Mrs. Fyne. I much preferred to hear something more of the girl. I said—

" 'And so she went away with that respectable ruffian.'

"Mrs. Fyne moved her shoulders slightly—'What else could she have done?' I agreed with her by another hopeless gesture. It isn't so easy for a girl like Flora de Barral to become a factory hand, a pathetic seamstress or even a barmaid. She wouldn't have known how to begin. She was the captive of the meanest conceivable fate. And she wasn't mean enough for it. It is to be remarked that a good many people are born curiously unfitted for the fate awaiting them on this earth. As I don't want you to think that I am unduly partial to the girl we shall say that she failed decidedly to endear herself to that simple, virtuous and, I believe, teetotal household. It's my conviction that an angel would have failed likewise. It's no use going into details; suffice it to state that before the year was out she was again at the Fynes' door.

"This time she was escorted by a stout youth. His large pale face wore a smile of inane cunning soured by annoyance. His clothes were new and the indescribable smartness of their cut, a *genre* which had never been obtruded on her notice before, astonished Mrs. Fyne, who came out into the hall with her hat on; for she was about to go out to hear a new pianist (a girl) in a friend's house. The youth addressing Mrs. Fyne easily begged her not to let 'that silly thing go back to us any more.' There had been, he said, nothing but 'ructions' at home about her for the last three weeks. Everybody in the family was heartily sick of quarrelling. His governor had charged him to bring her to this address and say that the lady and gentleman were quite welcome to all there was in it.

She hadn't enough sense to appreciate a plain, honest English home and she was better out of it.

"The young pimply-faced fellow was vexed by this job his governor had sprung on him. It was the cause of his missing an appointment for that afternoon with a certain young lady. The lady he was engaged to. But he meant to dash back and try for a sight of her that evening yet 'if he were to burst over it.' 'Good-bye, Florrie. Good luck to you—and I hope I'll never see your face again.'

"With that he ran out in lover-like haste leaving the hall-door wide open. Mrs. Fyne had not found a word to say. She had been too much taken aback even to gasp freely. But she had the presence of mind to grab the girl's arm just as she, too, was running out into the street—with the haste, I suppose, of despair and to keep I don't know what tragic tryst.

" 'You stopped her with your own hand, Mrs. Fyne,' I said. 'I presume she meant to get away. That girl is no comedian—if I am any judge.'

" 'Yes! I had to use some force to drag her in.'

"Mrs. Fyne had no difficulty in stating the truth. 'You see I was in the very act of letting myself out when these two appeared. So that, when that unpleasant young man ran off, I found myself alone with Flora. It was all I could do to hold her in the hall while I called to the servants to come and shut the door.'

"As is my habit, or my weakness, or my gift, I don't know which, I visualized the story for myself. I really can't help it. And the vision of Mrs. Fyne dressed for a rather special afternoon function, engaged in wrestling with a wild-eyed, white-faced girl, had a certain dramatic fascination.

" 'Really!' I murmured.

" 'Oh! There's no doubt that she struggled,' said Mrs. Fyne. She compressed her lips for a moment and then added: 'as to her being a comedian that's another question.'

"Mrs. Fyne had returned to her attitude of folded arms. I saw before me the daughter of the refined poet accepting life whole with its unavoidable conditions of which one of the first is the instinct of self-preservation and the egoism of every living creature. 'The fact remains nevertheless that you—yourself—have, in your own words, pulled her in,' I insisted in a jocular tone, with a serious intention.

" 'What was one to do?' exclaimed Mrs. Fyne with almost comic exasperation. 'Are you reproaching me with being too impulsive?'

"And she went on telling me that she was not that in the least. One of the recommendations she always insisted on (to the girl-friends, I imagine) was to be on guard against impulse. Always! But I had not been there to see the face of Flora at the time. If I had it would be haunting me to this day. Nobody unless made of iron would have allowed a human being with a face like that to rush out alone into the streets.

" 'And doesn't it haunt you, Mrs. Fyne?' I asked.

" 'No, not now,' she said implacably. 'Perhaps if I had let her go it might have done. . . . Don't conclude, though, that I think she was playing a comedy then, because after struggling at first she ended by remaining. She gave up very suddenly. She collapsed in our arms, mine and the maid's who came running up in response to my calls, and . . .'

" 'And the door was then shut,' I completed the phrase in my own way.

" 'Yes, the door was shut.' Mrs. Fyne lowered and raised her head slowly.

"I did not ask her for details. Of one thing I am certain and that is that Mrs. Fyne did not go out to the musical function that afternoon. She was no doubt considerably annoyed at missing the privilege of hearing privately an interesting young pianist (a girl) who, since, has become one of the recognized performers. Mrs. Fyne did not dare leave her house. As to the feelings of little Fyne when he came home from the office, via his club, just half an hour before dinner, I have no information. But I venture to affirm that in the main they were kindly, though it is quite possible that in the first moment of surprise he had to keep down a swear-word or two.

"The long and the short of it all is that next day the Fynes made up their minds to take into their confidence a certain wealthy old lady. With certain old ladies the passing years bring back a sort of mellowed youthfulness of feeling, an optimistic outlook, liking for novelty, readiness for experiment. The old lady was very much interested: 'Do let me see the poor thing!' She was accordingly allowed to see Flora de Barral in Mrs. Fyne's drawing-room on a day when there was no one else there, and she preached to her with charming, sympathetic authority: 'The only way to deal with our troubles, my dear child, is to forget them. You must forget yours. It's very simple. Look at me. I always forget mine. At your age one ought to be cheerful.'

"Later on when left alone with Mrs. Fyne she said to that lady: 'I do hope the child will manage to be cheerful. I can't have sad faces near me. At my age one needs cheerful companions.'

"And in this hope she carried off Flora de Barral to Bournemouth for the winter months in the quality of reader and companion. She had said to her with kindly jocularity: 'We shall have a good time together. I am not a grumpy old woman.' But on their return to London she sought Mrs. Fyne at once. She had discovered that Flora was not naturally cheerful. When she made efforts to be it was still worse. The old lady couldn't stand the strain of that. And then, to have the whole thing out, she could not bear to have for a companion any one who did not love her. She was certain that Flora did not love her. Why? She couldn't say. Moreover, she had caught the girl looking at her in a peculiar way at times. Oh no!—it was not an evil look—it was an unusual expression which one could not understand. And when one remembered that her father was in prison, shut up together with a lot of criminals and so on—it made one uncomfortable. If the child had only tried to forget her troubles! But she obviously was incapable or unwilling to do so. And that was somewhat perverse—wasn't it? Upon the whole, she thought it would be better perhaps——

"Mrs. Fyne assented hurriedly to the unspoken conclusion:

" 'Oh certainly! Certainly,' wondering to herself what was to be done with Flora next; but she was not very much surprised at the change in the old lady's view of Flora de Barral. She almost understood it.

"What came next was a German family, the continental acquaintances of the wife of one of Fyne's colleagues in the Home Office. Flora of the enigmatical glances was dispatched to them without much reflection. As it was not considered absolutely necessary to take them into full confidence, they neither expected the girl to be specially cheerful nor were they discomposed unduly by the indescribable quality of her glances. The German woman was quite ordinary; there were two boys to look after; they were ordinary, too, I presume; and Flora, I understand, was very attentive to them. If she taught them anything it must have been by inspiration alone, for she certainly knew nothing of teaching. But it was mostly 'conversation' which was demanded from her. Flora de Barral conversing with two small German boys, regularly, industriously, conscientiously in order to keep herself alive in the world which held for her the past we know and the future of an even more undesirable quality—seems to me a very fantastic combination. But I believe it was not so bad. She was being, she wrote, mercifully drugged by her task. She had learned to 'converse' all day long, mechanically, absently, as if in a trance. An uneasy trance it must have been! Her worst moments were when off duty—alone in the evening, shut up in her own little room, her dulled thoughts waking up slowly till she started into the full consciousness of her position, like a person waking up in contact with something venomous—a snake, for instance—experiencing a mad impulse to fling the thing away and run off screaming to hide somewhere.

"At this period of her existence Flora de Barral used to write to Mrs. Fyne, not regularly but fairly often. I don't know how long she would have gone on 'conversing' and, incidentally, helping to supervise the beautifully stocked linen closets of that well-to-do German household, if the man of it had not developed in the intervals of his avocations (he was a merchant and a thoroughly domesticated character) a psychological resemblance to the Bournemouth old lady. It appeared that he, too, wanted to be loved.

"He was not, however, of a conquering temperament—a kiss-snatching, door-bursting type of libertine. In the very act of straying from the path of virtue he remained a respectable merchant. It would have been perhaps better for Flora if he had been a mere brute. But he set about his sinister enterprise in a sentimental,

cautious, almost paternal manner; and thought he would
be safe with a pretty orphan. The girl for all her experience was still too innocent, and indeed not yet sufficiently aware of herself as a woman, to mistrust these
masked approaches. She did not see them, in fact. She
thought him sympathetic—the first expressively sympathetic person she had ever met. She was so innocent that
she could not understand the fury of the German woman.
For, as you may imagine, the wifely penetration was not
to be deceived for any great length of time—the more
so that the wife was older than the husband. The man
with the peculiar cowardice of respectability never said a
word in Flora's defence. He stood by and heard her
reviled in the most abusive terms, only nodding and
frowning vaguely from time to time. It will give you the
idea of the girl's innocence when I say that at first she
actually thought this storm of indignant reproaches was
caused by the discovery of her real name and her relation
to a convict. She had been sent out under an assumed
name—a highly recommended orphan of honourable parentage. Her distress, her burning cheeks, her endeavours
to express her regret for this deception were taken for a
confession of guilt. 'You attempted to bring dishonour
to my home,' the German woman screamed at her.

"Here's a misunderstanding for you! Flora de Barral,
who felt the shame but did not believe in the guilt of her
father, retorted fiercely, 'Nevertheless I am as honourable as you are.' And then the German woman nearly
went into a fit from rage. 'I shall have you thrown out
into the street.'

"Flora was not exactly thrown out into the street, I
believe, but she was bundled bag and baggage on board
a steamer for London. Did I tell you these people lived
in Hamburg? Well yes—sent to the docks late on a rainy
winter evening in charge of some sneering lackey or other
who behaved to her insolently and left her on deck burning with indignation, her hair half down, shaking with
excitement, and truth to say scared as near as possible
into hysterics. If it had not been for the stewardess who,
without asking questions, good soul, took charge of her
quietly in the ladies' saloon (luckily it was empty) it is
by no means certain she would ever have reached
England. I can't tell if a straw ever saved a drowning

man, but I know that a mere glance is enough to make despair pause. For in truth we who are creatures of impulse are not creatures of despair. Suicide, I suspect, is very often the outcome of mere mental weariness— not an act of savage energy but the final symptom of complete collapse. The quiet, matter-of-fact attentions of a ship's stewardess, who did not seem aware of other human agonies than seasickness, who talked of the prob- able weather of the passage—it would be a rough night, she thought—and who insisted in a professionally busy manner, 'Let me make you comfortable down below at once, miss,' as though she were thinking of nothing else but her tip—was enough to dissipate the shades of death gathering round the mortal weariness of bewildered thinking which makes the idea of non-existence welcome so often to the young. Flora de Barral did lie down, and it may be presumed she slept. At any rate she survived the voyage across the North Sea and told Mrs. Fyne all about it, concealing nothing and receiving no rebuke— for Mrs. Fyne's opinions had a large freedom in their pedantry. She held, I suppose, that a woman holds an absolute right—or possesses a perfect excuse—to escape in her own way from a man-mismanaged world.

"What is to be noted is that even in London, having had time to take a reflective view, poor Flora was far from being certain as to the true inwardness of her vio- lent dismissal. She felt the humiliation of it with an almost maddened resentment.

" 'And did you enlighten her on the point?' I ventured to ask.

"Mrs. Fyne moved her shoulders with a philosophical acceptance of all the necessities which ought not to be. Something had to be said, she murmured. She had told the girl enough to make her come to the right conclusion by herself.

" 'And she did?'

" 'Yes. Of course. She isn't a goose,' retorted Mrs. Fyne tartly.

" 'Then her education is completed,' I remarked with some bitterness. 'Don't you think she ought to be given a chance?'

"Mrs. Fyne understood my meaning.

" 'Not this one,' she snapped in a quite feminine way. 'It's all very well for you to plead, but I——'

" 'I do not plead. I simply asked. It seemed natural to ask what you thought.'

" 'It's what I feel that matters. And I can't help my feelings. You may guess,' she added in a softer tone, 'that my feelings are mostly concerned with my brother. We were very fond of each other. The difference of our ages was not very great. I suppose you know he is a little younger than I am. He was a sensitive boy. He had the habit of brooding. It is no use concealing from you that neither of us was happy at home. You have heard, no doubt. . . . Yes? Well, I was made still more unhappy and hurt—I don't mind telling you that. He made his way to some distant relations of our mother's people who I believe were not known to my father at all. I don't wish to judge their action.'

"I interrupted Mrs. Fyne here. I had heard. Fyne was not very communicative in general but he was proud of his father-in-law—'Carleon Anthony, the poet, you know.' Proud of his celebrity without approving of his character. It was on that account, I strongly suspect, that he seized with avidity upon the theory of poetical genius being allied to madness, which he got hold of in some idiotic book everybody was reading a few years ago. It struck him as being truth itself—illuminating like the sun. He adopted it devoutly. He bored me with it sometimes. Once, just to shut him up, I asked quietly if this theory which he regarded as so incontrovertible did not cause him some uneasiness about his wife and the dear girls? He transfixed me with a pitying stare and requested me in his deep solemn voice to remember the 'well-established fact' that genius was not transmissible.

"I said only 'Oh! Isn't it?' and he thought he had silenced me by an unanswerable argument. But he continued to talk of his glorious father-in-law, and it was in the course of that conversation that he told me how, when the Liverpool relations of the poet's late wife naturally addressed themselves to him in considerable concern, suggesting a friendly consultation as to the boy's future, the incensed (but always refined) poet wrote in answer a letter of mere polished *badinage* which offended mortally the Liverpool people. This witty outbreak of what was in fact mortification and rage appeared to them so heartless that they simply kept the boy. They let him go to sea not because he was in their way but because he begged hard to be allowed to go.

" 'Oh! You do know,' said Mrs. Fyne after a pause. 'Well—I felt myself very much abandoned. Then his choice of life—so extraordinary, so unfortunate, I may say. I was very much grieved. I should have liked him to have been distinguished—or at any rate to remain in the social sphere where we could have had common interests, acquaintances, thoughts. Don't think that I am estranged from him. But the precise truth is that I do not know him. I was most painfully affected when he was here by the difficulty of finding a single topic we could discuss together.'

"While Mrs. Fyne was talking of her brother I let my thoughts wander out of the room to little Fyne who by leaving me alone with his wife had, so to speak, entrusted his domestic peace to my honour.

" 'Well, then, Mrs. Fyne, does it not strike you that it would be reasonable under the circumstances to let your brother take care of himself?'

" 'And suppose I have grounds to think that he can't take care of himself in a given instance?' She hesitated in a funny, bashful manner which aroused my interest. Then: 'Sailors I believe are very susceptible,' she added with forced assurance.

"I burst into a laugh which only increased the coldness of her observing stare.

" 'They are. Immensely! Hopelessly! My dear Mrs. Fyne, you had better give it up! It only makes your husband miserable.'

" 'And I am quite miserable too. It is really our first difference. . . .'

" 'Regarding Miss de Barral?' I asked.

" 'Regarding everything. It's really intolerable that this girl should be the occasion. I think he really ought to give way.'

"She turned her chair round a little and picking up the book I had been reading in the morning began to turn the leaves absently.

"Her eyes being off me, I felt I could allow myself to leave the room. Its atmosphere had become hopeless for

little Fyne's domestic peace. You may smile. But to the
solemn all things are solemn. I had enough sagacity to
understand that.

"I slipped out into the porch. The dog was slumbering
at Fyne's feet. The muscular little man leaning on his
elbow and gazing over the fields presented a forlorn figure. He turned his head quickly, but seeing I was alone,
relapsed into his moody contemplation of the green
landscape.

"I said loudly and distinctly: 'I've come out to smoke
a cigarette,' and sat down near him on the little bench.
Then lowering my voice: 'Tolerance is an extremely difficult virtue,' I said. 'More difficult for some than heroism.
More difficult than compassion.'

"I avoided looking at him. I knew well enough that he
would not like this opening. General ideas were not to
his taste. He mistrusted them. I lighted a cigarette, not
that I wanted to smoke, but to give another moment to
the consideration of the advice—the diplomatic advice I
had made up my mind to bowl him over with. And I
continued in subdued tones:

" 'I have been led to make these remarks by what I
have discovered since you left us. I suspected from the
first. And now I am certain. What your wife cannot toler-
ate in this affair is Miss de Barral being what she is.'

"He made a movement, but I kept my eyes away from
him and went on steadily. 'That is—her being a woman.
I have some idea of Mrs. Fyne's mental attitude towards
society with its injustices, with its atrocious or ridiculous
conventions. As against them there is no audacity of
action your wife's mind refuses to sanction. The doctrine
which I imagine she stuffs into the pretty heads of your
girl-guests is almost vengeful. A sort of moral fire-and-
sword doctrine. How far the lesson is wise is not for me
to say. I don't permit myself to judge. I seem to see
her very delightful disciples singeing themselves with the
torches, and cutting their fingers with the swords of Mrs.
Fyne's furnishing.'

" 'My wife holds her opinions very seriously,' murmured Fyne suddenly.

" 'Yes. No doubt,' I assented in a low voice as before.
'But it is a mere intellectual exercise. What I see is that
in dealing with reality Mrs. Fyne ceases to be tolerant.

In other words, that she can't forgive Miss de Barral for being a woman and behaving like a woman. And yet this is not only reasonable and natural, but it is her only chance. A woman against the world has no resources but in herself. Her only means of action is to be what *she is*. You understand what I mean.'

"Fyne mumbled between his teeth that he understood. But he did not seem interested. What he expected of me was to extricate him from a difficult situation. I don't know how far credible this may sound, to less solemn married couples, but to remain at variance with his wife seemed to him a considerable incident. Almost a disaster.

" 'It looks as though I didn't care what happened to her brother,' he said. 'And after all if anything. . . .'

"I became a little impatient but without raising my tone: 'What thing?' I asked. 'The liability to get penal servitude is so far like genius that it isn't hereditary. And what else can be objected to the girl? All the energy of her deeper feelings, which she would use up vainly in the danger and fatigue of a struggle with society, may be turned into devoted attachment to the man who offers her a way of escape from what can be only a life of moral anguish. I don't mention the physical difficulties.'

"Glancing at Fyne out of the corner of one eye I discovered that he was attentive. He made the remark that I should have said all this to his wife. It was a sensible enough remark. But I had given Mrs. Fyne up. I asked him if his impression was that his wife meant to entrust him with a letter for her brother.

"No. He didn't think so. There were certain reasons which made Mrs. Fyne unwilling to commit her arguments to paper. Fyne was to be primed with them. But he had no doubt that if he persisted in his refusal she would make up her mind to write.

" 'She does not wish me to go unless with a full conviction that she is right,' said Fyne solemnly.

" 'She's very exacting,' I commented. And then I reflected that she was used to it. 'Would nothing else do for once?'

" 'You don't mean that I should give way—do you?' asked Fyne in a whisper of alarmed suspicion.

"As this was exactly what I meant, I let his fright sink

into him. He fidgeted. If the word may be used of so
solemn a personage, he wriggled. And when the horrid
suspicion had descended into his very heels, so to speak,
he became very still. He sat gazing stonily into space
bounded by the yellow, burnt-up slopes of the rising
ground a couple of miles away. The face of the down
showed the white scar of the quarry where not more than
sixteen hours before Fyne and I had been groping in the
dank with horrible apprehension of finding under our
hands the shattered body of a girl. For myself I had in
addition the memory of my meeting with her. She was
certainly walking very near the edge—courting a sinister
solution. But, now having by the most unexpected chance
come upon a man, she had found another way to escape
from the world. Such world as was open to her—without
shelter, without bread, without honour. The best she
could have found in it would have been a precarious dole
of pity diminishing as her years increased. The appeal of
the abandoned child Flora to the sympathies of the Fynes
had been irresistible. But now she had become a woman,
and Mrs. Fyne was presenting an implacable front to a
particularly feminine transaction. I may say triumphantly
feminine. It is true that Mrs. Fyne did not want women
to be women. Her theory was that they should turn themselves into unscrupulous sexless nuisances. An offended
theorist dwelt in her bosom somewhere. In what way she
expected Flora de Barral to set about saving herself from
a most miserable existence I can't conceive; but I verily
believe that she would have found it easier to forgive the
girl an actual crime; say the rifling of the Bournemouth
old lady's desk, for instance. And then—for Mrs. Fyne
was very much of a woman herself—her sense of proprie-
torship was very strong within her; and though she had
not much use for her brother, yet she did not like to see
him annexed by another woman. By a chit of a girl. And
such a girl, too. Nothing is truer than that, in this world,
the luckless have no right to their opportunities—as if
misfortune were a legal disqualification. Fyne's sentiments (as they naturally would be in a man) had more
stability. A good deal of his sympathy survived. Indeed
I heard him murmur 'Ghastly nuisance,' but I knew it
was of the integrity of his domestic accord that he was
thinking. With my eyes on the dog lying curled up in sleep

in the middle of the porch I suggested in a subdued impersonal tone: 'Yes. Why not let yourself be persuaded?'

"I never saw little Fyne less solemn. He hissed through his teeth in unexpectedly figurative style that it would take a lot to persuade him to 'push under the head of a poor devil of a girl quite sufficiently plucky'—and snorted. He was still gazing at the distant quarry, and I think he was affected by that sight. I assured him that I was far from advising him to do anything so cruel. I am convinced he had always doubted the soundness of my principles, because he turned on me swiftly as though he had been on the watch for a lapse from the straight path.

" 'Then what do you mean? That I should pretend!'

" 'No! What nonsense! It would he immoral. I may however tell you that if I had to make a choice I would rather do something immoral than something cruel. What I meant was that, not believing in the efficacy of the interference, the whole question is reduced to your consenting to do what your wife wishes you to do. That would be acting like a gentleman, surely. And acting unselfishly too, because I can very well understand how distasteful it may be to you. Generally speaking, an unselfish action is a moral action. I'll tell you what. I'll go with you.'

"He turned around and stared at me with surprise and suspicion. 'You would go with me?' he repeated.

" 'You don't understand,' I said, amused at the incredulous disgust of his tone. 'I must run up to town, tomorrow morning. Let us go together. You have a set of travelling chessmen.'

"His physiognomy, contracted by a variety of emotions, relaxed to a certain extent at the idea of a game. I told him that as I had business at the Docks he should have my company to the very ship.

" 'We shall beguile the way to the wilds of the East by improving conversation,' I encouraged him.

" 'My brother-in-law is staying at an hotel—the Eastern Hotel,' he said, becoming sombre again. 'I haven't the slightest idea where it is.'

" 'I know the place. I shall leave you at the door with the comfortable conviction that you are doing what's right since it pleases a lady and cannot do any harm to anybody whatever.'

" 'You think so? No harm to anybody?' he repeated doubtfully.

" 'I assure you it's not the slightest use,' I said with all possible emphasis which seemed only to increase the solemn discontent of his expression.

" 'But in order that my going should be a perfectly candid proceeding I must first convince my wife that it isn't the slightest use,' he objected portentously.

" 'Oh, you casuist!' I said. And I said nothing more because at that moment Mrs. Fyne stepped out into the porch. We rose together at her appearance. Her clear, colourless, unflinching glance enveloped us both critically. I sustained the chill smilingly, but Fyne stooped at once to release the dog. He was some time about it; then simultaneously with his recovery of upright position the animal passed at one bound from profoundest slumber into most tumultuous activity. Enveloped in the tornado of his inane scurryings and barkings I took Mrs. Fyne's hand extended to me woodenly and bowed over it with deference. She walked down the path without a word; Fyne had preceded her and was waiting by the open gate. They passed out and walked up the road surrounded by a low cloud of dust raised by the dog gyrating madly about their two figures progressing side by side with rectitude and propriety, and (I don't know why) looking to me as if they had annexed the whole country-side. Perhaps it was that they had impressed me somehow with the sense of their superiority. What superiority? Perhaps it consisted just in their limitations. It was obvious that neither of them had carried away a high opinion of me. But what affected me most was the indifference of the Fyne dog. He used to precipitate himself at full speed and with a frightful final upward spring upon my waistcoat, at least once at each of our meetings. He had neglected that ceremony this time notwithstanding my correct and even conventional conduct in offering him a cake; it seemed to me symbolic of my final separation from the Fyne household. And I remembered against him how on a certain day he had abandoned poor Flora de Barral—who was morbidly sensitive.

"I sat down in the porch and, maybe inspired by secret antagonism to the Fynes, I said to myself deliberately that Captain Anthony must be a fine fellow. Yet on the facts as I knew them he might have been a dangerous trifler or a downright scoundrel. He had made a miserable, hopeless girl follow him clandestinely to London. It is true that the girl had written since, only Mrs. Fyne had been remarkably vague as to the contents. They were unsatisfactory. They did not positively announce imminent nuptials as far as I could make it out from her rather mysterious hints. But then her inexperience might have led her astray. There was no fathoming the innocence of a woman like Mrs. Fyne who, venturing as far as possible in theory, would know nothing of the real aspect of things. It would have been comic if she were making all this fuss for nothing. But I rejected this suspicion for the honour of human nature.

"I imagined to myself Captain Anthony as simple and romantic. It was much more pleasant. Genius is not hereditary but temperament may be. And he was the son of a poet with an admirable gift of individualizing, of etherealizing the common-place; of making touching, delicate, fascinating the most hopeless conventions of the so-called, refined existence.

"What I could not understand was Mrs. Fyne's dog-in-the-manger attitude. Sentimentally she needed that brother of hers so little! What could it matter to her one way or another—setting aside common humanity which would suggest at least a neutral attitude? Unless indeed it was the blind working of the law that in our world of chances the luckless *must* be put in the wrong somehow.

"And musing thus on the general inclination of our instincts towards injustice I met unexpectedly, at the turn of the road, as it were, a shape of duplicity. It might have been unconscious on Mrs. Fyne's part, but her leading idea appeared to me to be not to keep, not to preserve her brother, but to get rid of him definitely. She did not hope to stop anything. She had too much sense for that. Almost any one out of an idiot asylum would have had enough sense for that. She wanted the protest to be made, emphatically, with Fyne's fullest concurrence in order to make all intercourse for the future impossible. Such an action would estrange the pair for ever from the Fynes! She understood her brother and the girl too. Happy together, they would never forgive that outspoken hostility—and should the marriage turn out badly. . . .

Well, it would be just the same. Neither of them would be likely to bring their troubles to such a good prophet of evil.

"Yes. That must have been her motive. The inspiration of a possibly unconscious Machiavellism! Either she was afraid of having a sister-in-law to look after during the husband's long absences; or dreaded the more or less distant eventuality of her brother being persuaded to leave the sea, the friendly refuge of his unhappy youth, and to settle on shore, bringing to her very door this undesirable, this embarrassing connexion. She wanted to be done with it—maybe simply from the fatigue of continuous effort in good or evil which, in the bulk of common mortals, accounts for so many surprising inconsistencies of conduct.

"I don't know that I had classed Mrs. Fyne, in my thoughts, amongst common mortals. She was too quietly sure of herself for that. But little Fyne, as I spied him next morning (out of the carriage window) speeding along the platform, looked very much like a common, flustered mortal who has made a very near thing of catching his train: the staring wild eyes, the tense and excited face, the distracted gait, all the common symptoms were there, rendered more impressive by his native solemnity which flapped about him like a disordered garment. Had he—I asked myself with interest—resisted his wife to the very last minute and then bolted up the road from the last conclusive argument, as though it had been a loaded gun suddenly produced? I opened the carriage door, and a vigorous porter shoved him in from behind just as the end of the rustic platform went gliding swiftly from under his feet. He was very much out of breath, and I waited with some curiosity for the moment he would recover his power of speech. That moment came. He said 'Good morning,' with a slight gasp, remained very still for another minute and then pulled out of his pocket the travelling chessboard, and holding it in his hand, directed at me a glance of inquiry.

" 'Yes. Certainly,' I said, very much disappointed.

CHAPTER SEVEN

On the Pavement

"Fyne was not willing to talk; but as I had been already let into the secret, the fair-minded little man recognized that I had some right to information if I insisted on it. And I did insist, after the third game. We were yet some way from the end of our Journey.

" 'Oh, if you want to know,' was his somewhat impatient opening. And then he talked rather volubly. First of all his wife had not given him to read the letter received from Flora (I had suspected him of having it in his pocket), but had told him all about the contents. It was not at all what it should have been even if the girl had wished to affirm her right to disregard the feelings of all the world. Her own had been trampled in the dirt out of all shape. Extraordinary thing to say—I would admit, for a young girl of her age. The whole tone of that letter was wrong, quite wrong. It was certainly not the product of a—say, of a well-balanced mind.

" 'If she were given some sort of footing in this world,' I said, 'if only no bigger than the palm of my hand, she would probably learn to keep a better balance.'

"Fyne ignored this little remark. His wife, he said, was not the sort of person to be addressed mockingly on a serious subject. There was an unpleasant strain of levity in that letter, extending even to the references to Captain Anthony himself. Such a disposition was enough, his wife had pointed out to him, to alarm one for the future, had all the circumstances of that preposterous project been as satisfactory as in fact they were not. Other parts of the letter seemed to have a challenging tone—as if daring them (the Fynes) to approve her conduct. And at the same time implying that she did not care, that it was for their own sakes that she hoped they would 'go against the world—the horrid world which had crushed poor papa.'

"Fyne called upon me to admit that this was pretty cool—considering. And there was another thing, too. It seems that for the last six months (she had been assisting two ladies who kept a kindergarten school in Bays-water—a mere pittance), Flora had insisted on devoting all her spare time to the study of the trial. She had been looking up files of old newspapers, and working herself up into a state of indignation with what she called the injustice and the hypocrisy of the prosecution. Her father, Fyne reminded me, had made some palpable hits in his answers in Court, and she had fastened on them triumphantly. She had reached the conclusion of her father's innocence, and had been brooding over it. Mrs. Fyne had pointed out to him the danger of this.

"The train ran into the station and Fyne, jumping out directly it came to a standstill, seemed glad to cut short the conversation. We walked in silence a little way, boarded a bus, then walked again. I don't suppose that since the days of his childhood, when surely he was taken to see the Tower, he had been once east of Temple Bar. He looked about him sullenly; and when I pointed out in the distance the rounded front of the Eastern Hotel at the bifurcation of two very broad, mean, shabby thor-oughfares, rising like a grey stucco tower above the lowly roofs of the dirty-yellow, two-storey houses, he only grunted disapprovingly.

" 'I wouldn't lay too much stress on what you have been telling me,' I observed quietly as we approached that unattractive building. 'No man will believe a girl who has just accepted his suit to be not well balanced,— you know.'

" 'Oh! Accepted his suit,' muttered Fyne, who seemed

to have been very thoroughly convinced indeed. 'It may have been the other way about.' And then he added: 'I am going through with it.'

"I said that this was very praiseworthy but that a certain moderation of statement . . . He waved his hand at me and mended his pace. I guessed that he was anxious to get his mission over as quickly as possible. He barely gave himself time to shake hands with me and made a rush at the narrow glass door with the words Hotel Entrance on it. It swung to behind his back with no more noise than the snap of a toothless jaw.

"The absurd temptation to remain and see what would come of it got over my better judgment. I hung about irresolute, wondering how long an embassy of that sort would take, and whether Fyne on coming out would consent to be communicative. I feared he would be shocked at finding me there, would consider my conduct incorrect, conceivably treat me with contempt. I walked off a few paces. Perhaps it would be possible to read something on Fyne's face as he came out; and, if necessary, I could always eclipse myself discreetly through the door of one of the bars. The ground floor of the Eastern Hotel was an unabashed pub, with plate-glass fronts, a display of brass rails, and divided into many compartments each having its own entrance.

"But of course all this was silly. The marriage, the love, the affairs of Captain Anthony were none of my business. I was on the point of moving down the street for good when my attention was attracted by a girl approaching the hotel entrance from the west. She was dressed very modestly in black. It was the white straw hat of a good form and trimmed with a bunch of pale roses which had caught my eye. The whole figure seemed familiar. Of course! Flora de Barral. She was making for the hotel, she was going in. And Fyne was with Captain Anthony! To meet him would not be pleasant for her. I wished to save her from the awkwardness, and as I hesitated what to do she looked up and our eyes happened to meet just as she was turning off the pavement into the hotel doorway. Instinctively I extended my arm. It was enough to make her stop. I suppose she had some faint notion that she had seen me before somewhere. She walked slowly forward, prudent and attentive, watching my faint smile.

" 'Excuse me,' I said directly she had approached me near enough. 'Perhaps you would like to know that Mr. Fyne is upstairs with Captain Anthony at this moment.'

"She uttered a faint 'Ah! Mr. Fyne!' I could read in her eyes that she had recognized me now. Her serious expression extinguished the imbecile grin of which I was conscious. I raised my hat. She responded with a slow inclination of the head while her luminous, mistrustful, maiden's glance seemed to whisper, 'What is this one doing here?'

" 'I came up to town with Fyne this morning,' I said in a businesslike tone. 'I have to see a friend in East India Dock. Fyne and I parted this moment at the door here. . . .' The girl regarded me with darkening eyes . . . 'Mrs. Fyne did not come with her husband,' I went on, then hesitated before that white face so still in the pearly shadow thrown down by the hat-brim. 'But she sent him,' I murmured by way of warning.

"Her eyelids fluttered slowly over the fixed stare. I imagine she was not much disconcerted by this development. 'I live a long way from here,' she whispered.

"I said perfunctorily, 'Do you?' And we remained gazing at each other. The uniform paleness of her complexion was not that of an anæmic girl. It had a transparent vitality and at that particular moment the faintest possible rosy tinge, the merest suspicion of colour; an equivalent, I suppose, in any other girl to blushing like a peony, while she told me that Captain Anthony had arranged to show her the ship that morning.

"It was easy to understand that she did not want to meet Fyne. And when I mentioned in a discreet murmur that he had come because of her letter she glanced at the hotel door quickly, and moved off a few steps to a position where she could watch the entrance without being seen. I followed her. At the junction of the two thoroughfares she stopped in the thin traffic of the broad pavement and turned to me with an air of challenge. 'And so you know.'

"I told her that I had not seen the letter. I had only heard of it. She was a little impatient. 'I mean all about me.'

"Yes. I knew all about her. The distress of Mr. and Mrs. Fyne—especially of Mrs. Fyne—was so great that they would have shared it with anybody almost—not belonging to their circle of friends. I happened to be at hand—that was all.

" 'You understand that I am not their friend. I am only a holiday acquaintance.'

" 'She was not very much upset?' queried Flora de Barral, meaning, of course, Mrs. Fyne. And I admitted that she was less so than her husband—and even less than myself. Mrs. Fyne was a very self-possessed person which nothing could startle out of her extreme theoretical position. She did not seem startled when Fyne and I proposed going to the quarry.

" 'You put that notion into their heads,' the girl said.

"I advanced that the notion was in their heads already. But it was much more vividly in my head since I had seen her up there with my own eyes, tempting Providence.

"She was looking at me with extreme attention, and murmured:

" 'Is that what you called it to them? Tempting. . . .'

" 'No. I told them that you were making up your mind and I came along just then. I told them that you were saved by me. My shout checked you . . .' She moved her head gently from right to left in negation. . . . 'No? Well, have it your own way.'

"I thought to myself: She has found another issue. She wants to forget now. And no wonder. She wants to persuade herself that she had never known such an ugly and poignant minute in her life. 'After all,' I conceded aloud, 'things are not always what they seem.'

"Her little head with its deep blue eyes, eyes of tenderness and anger under the black arch of fine eyebrows, was very still. The mouth looked very red in the white face peeping from under the veil, the little pointed chin had in its form something aggressive. Slight and even angular in her modest black dress she was an appealing and—yes—she was a desirable little figure.

"Her lips moved very fast asking me:

" 'And they believed you at once?'

" 'Yes, they believed me at once. Mrs. Fyne's word to us was "Go!" '

"A white gleam between the red lips was so short that

I remained uncertain whether it was a smile or a ferocious baring of little even teeth. The rest of the face
preserved its innocent, tense and enigmatical expression.
She spoke rapidly.

" 'No, it wasn't your shout. I had been there some
time before you saw me. And I was not there to tempt
Providence, as you call it. I went up there for—for what
you thought I was going to do. Yes. I climbed two fences.
I did not mean to leave anything to Providence. There
seem to be people for whom Providence can do nothing.
I suppose you are shocked to hear me talk like that?'

"I shook my head. I was not shocked. What had kept
her back all that time, till I appeared on the scene below,
she went on, was neither fear nor any other kind of hesitation. One reaches a point, she said with appalling
youthful simplicity, where nothing that concerns one
matters any longer. But something did keep her back. I
should have never guessed what it was. She herself confessed that it seemed absurd to say. It was the Fyne dog.

"Flora de Barral paused, looking at me with a peculiar
expression and then went on. You see, she imagined the
dog had become extremely attached to her. She took it
into her head that he might fall over or jump down after
her. She tried to drive him away. She spoke sternly to
him. It only made him more frisky. He barked and
jumped about her skirt in his usual, idiotic, high spirits.
He scampered away in circles between the pines charging
upon her and leaping as high as her waist. She commanded, 'Go away. Go home.' She even picked up from
the ground a bit of a broken branch and threw it at him.
At this his delight knew no bounds; his rushes became
faster, his yapping louder; he seemed to be having the
time of his life. She was convinced that the moment she
threw herself down he would spring over after her as if
it were part of the game. She was vexed almost to tears.
She was touched too. And when he stood still at some
distance as if suddenly rooted to the ground, wagging his
tail slowly and watching her intensely with his shining
eyes, another fear came to her. She imagined herself
gone and the creature sitting on the brink, its head
thrown up to the sky and howling for hours. This thought
was not to be borne. Then my shout reached her ears.

"She told me all this with simplicity. My voice had

destroyed her poise—the suicide poise of her mind. Every act of ours, the most criminal, the most mad presupposes a balance of thought, feeling and will, like a correct attitude for an effective stroke in a game. And I had destroyed it. She was no longer in proper form for the act. She was not very much annoyed. Next day would do. She would have to slip away without attracting the notice of the dog. She thought of the necessity almost tenderly. She came down the path carrying her despair with lucid calmness. But when she saw herself deserted by the dog, she had an impulse to turn round, go up again and be done with it. Not even that animal cared for her—in the end.

" 'I really did think that he was attached to me. What did he want to pretend for, like this? I thought nothing could hurt me any more. Oh yes. I would have gone up, but I felt suddenly so tired. So tired. And then you were there. I didn't know what you would do. You might have tried to follow me and I don't think I could run—not up hill—not then.'

"She had raised her white face a little, and it was queer to hear her say these things. At that time of the morning there are comparatively few people out in that part of the town. The broad interminable perspective of the East India Dock Road, the great perspective of drab brick walls, of grey pavement, of muddy roadway rumbling dismally with loaded carts and vans lost itself in the distance, imposing and shabby in its spacious meanness of aspect, in its immeasurable poverty of forms, of colouring, of life—under a harsh, unconcerned sky dried by the wind to a clear blue. It had been raining during the night. The sunshine itself seemed poor. From time to time a few bits of paper, a little dust and straw whirled past us on the broad, flat promontory of the pavement before the rounded front of the hotel.

"Flora de Barral was silent for a while. I said:

" 'And next day you thought better of it.'

"Again she raised her eyes to mine with that peculiar expression of informed innocence; and again her white cheeks took on the faintest tinge of pink—the merest shadow of a blush.

" 'Next day,' she uttered distinctly, 'I didn't think. I remembered. That was enough. I remembered what I should never have forgotten. Never. And Captain Anthony arrived at the cottage in the evening.'

" 'Ah yes. Captain Anthony,' I murmured. And she repeated also in a murmur, 'Yes! Captain Anthony.' The faint flush of warm life left her face. I subdued my voice still more and not looking at her: 'You found him sympathetic?' I ventured.

Her long dark lashes went down a little with an air of calculated discretion. At least so it seemed to me. And yet no one could say that I was inimical to that girl. But there you are! Explain it as you may, in this world the friendless, like the poor, are always a little suspect, as if honesty and delicacy were only possible to the privileged few.

" 'Why do you ask?' she said after a time, raising her eyes suddenly to mine in an effect of candour which on the same principle (of the disinherited not being to be trusted) might have been judged equivocal.

" 'If you mean what right I have . . .' She moved slightly a hand in a worn brown glove as much as to say she could not question any one's right against such an outcast as herself.

"I ought to have been moved perhaps; but I only noted the total absence of humility. . . . 'No right at all,' I continued, 'but just interest. Mrs. Fyne—it's too difficult to explain how it came about—has talked to me of you—well—extensively.'

"No doubt Mrs. Fyne had told me the truth, Flora said brusquely with an unexpected hoarseness of tone. This very dress she was wearing had been given her by Mrs. Fyne. Of course I looked at it. It could not have been a recent gift. Close-fitting and black, with heliotrope silk facings under a figured net, it looked far from new, just on this side of shabbiness; in fact, it accentuated the slightness of her figure, it went well in its suggestion of half mourning with the white face in which the unsmiling red lips alone seemed warm with the rich blood of life and passion.

"Little Fyne was staying up there an unconscionable time. Was he arguing, preaching, remonstrating? Had he discovered in himself a capacity and a taste for that sort of thing? Or was he perhaps, in an intense dislike for the job, beating about the bush and only puzzling Captain

Anthony, the providential man, who, if he expected the girl to appear at any moment, must have been on tenterhooks all the time, and beside himself with impatience to see the back of his brother-in-law? How was it that he had not got rid of Fyne long before in any case? I don't mean by actually throwing him out of the window, but in some other resolute manner.

"Surely Fyne had not impressed him. That Anthony was an impressionable man I could not doubt. The presence of the girl there on the pavement before me proved this up to the hilt—and, well, yes, touchingly enough.

"It so happened that in their wanderings to and fro our glances met. There was something comic in the whole situation, in the poor girl and myself waiting together on the broad pavement at a corner public-house for the issue of Fyne's ridiculous mission. But the comic when it is human becomes quickly painful. Yes, she was infinitely anxious. And I was asking myself whether this poignant tension of her suspense depended—to put it plainly—on hunger or love.

"The answer would have been of some interest to Captain Anthony. For my part, in the presence of a young girl I always become convinced that the dreams of sentiment—like the consoling mysteries of Faith—are invincible; that it is never, never reason which governs men and women.

"Yet what sentiment could there have been on her part? I remembered her tone only a moment since when she said: 'That evening Captain Anthony arrived at the cottage.' And considering, too, what the arrival of Captain Anthony meant in this connection, I wondered at the calmness with which she could mention that fact. He arrived at the cottage. In the evening. I knew that late train. He probably walked from the station. The evening would be well advanced. I could almost see a dark, indistinct figure opening the wicket gate of the garden. Where was she? Did she see him enter? Was she somewhere near by and did she hear without the slightest premonition his chance and fateful footsteps on the flagged path leading to the cottage door? In the shadow of the night made more cruelly sombre for her by the very shadow of death he must have appeared too strange, too remote, too unknown to impress himself on her thought as a living force—such a force as a man can bring to bear on a woman's destiny.

"She glanced towards the hotel door again; I followed suit and then our eyes met once more, this time intentionally. A tentative, uncertain intimacy was springing up between us two. She said simply: 'You are waiting for Mr. Fyne to come out; are you?'

"I admitted to her that I was waiting to see Mr. Fyne come out. That was all. I had nothing to say to him.

" 'I have said yesterday all I had to say to him,' I added meaningly. 'I have said it to them both, in fact. I have also heard all they had to say.'

" 'About me?' she murmured.

" 'Yes. The conversation was about you.'

" 'I wonder if they told you everything.'

"If she wondered I could do nothing else but wonder too. But I did not tell her that. I only smiled. The material point was that Captain Anthony should be told everything. But as to that I was very certan that the good sister would see to it. Was there anything more to disclose—some other misery, some other deception of which that girl had been a victim? It seemed hardly probable. It was not even easy to imagine. What struck me most was her—I suppose I must call it—composure. One could not tell whether she understood what she had done. One wondered. She was not so much unreadable as blank; and I did not know whether to admire her for it or dismiss her from my thoughts as a passive butt of ferocious misfortune.

"Looking back at the occasion when we first got on speaking terms on the road by the quarry, I had to admit that she presented some points of a problematic appearance. I don't know why I imagined Captain Anthony as the sort of man who would not be likely to take the initiative; not perhaps from indifference but from that peculiar timidity before women which often enough is found in conjunction with chivalrous instincts, with a great need for affection and great stability of feelings. Such men are easily moved. At the least encouragement they go forward with the eagerness, with the recklessness of starvation. This accounted for the suddenness of the affair. No! With all her inexperience this girl could not have found any great difficulty in her conquering enterprise. She must have begun it. And yet there she was, patient, almost unmoved, almost pitiful, waiting outside like a beggar, without a right to anything but compassion, for a promised dole.

"Every moment people were passing close by us singly, in twos and threes; the inhabitants of that end of the town where life goes on unadorned by grace or splendour; they passed us in their shabby garments, with sallow faces, haggard, anxious or weary, or simply without expression, in an unsmiling sombre stream not made up of lives but of mere unconsidered existences whose joys, struggles, thoughts, sorrows and their very hopes were miserable, glamourless, and of no account in the world. And when one thought of their reality to themselves one's heart became oppressed. But of all the individuals who passed by none appeared to me for the moment so pathetic in unconscious patience as the girl standing before me; none more difficult to understand. It is perhaps because I was thinking of things which I could not ask her about.

"In fact we had nothing to say to each other; but we two, strangers as we really were to each other, had dealt with the most intimate and final of subjects, the subject of death. It had created a sort of bond between us. It made our silence weighty and uneasy. I ought to have left her there and then; but, as I think I've told you before, the fact of having shouted her away from the edge of a precipice seemed somehow to have engaged my responsibility as to this other leap. And so we had still an intimate subject between us to lend more weight and more uneasiness to our silence. The subject of marriage. I used the word not so much in reference to the ceremony itself (I had no doubt of this, Captain Anthony being a decent fellow) or in view of the social institution in general, as to which I have no opinion, but in regard to the human relation. The first two views are not particularly interesting. The ceremony, I suppose, is adequate; the institution, I dare say, is useful or it would not have endured. But the human relation thus recognized is a mysterious thing in its origins, character and consequences. Unfortunately you can't buttonhole familiarly a young girl as you would a young fellow. I don't think that even another woman could really do it. She would not be trusted. There is not between women that fund of at least conditional loyalty which men may depend on in their dealings with each other. I believe that any woman would rather trust a man. The difficulty in such a delicate case was how to get on terms.

"So we held our peace in the odious uproar of that wide roadway thronged with heavy carts. Great vans carrying enormous piled-up loads advanced swaying like mountains. It was as if the whole world existed only for selling and buying and those who had nothing to do with the movement of merchandise were of no account.

" 'You must be tired,' I said. One had to say something if only to assert oneself against that wearisome, passionless and crushing uproar. She raised her eyes for a moment. No, she was not. Not very. She had not walked all the way. She came by train as far as Whitechapel Station and had only walked from there.

"She had had an ugly pilgrimage; but whether of love or necessity who could tell? And that precisely was what I should have liked to get at. This was not however a question to be asked point-blank, and I could not think of any effective circumlocution. It occurred to me too that she might conceivably know nothing of it herself— I mean by reflection. That young woman had been obviously considering death. She had gone the length of forming some conception of it. But as to its companion fatality—love, she, I was certain, had never reflected upon its meaning.

"With that man in the hotel, whom I did not know, and this girl standing before me in the street I felt that it was an exceptional case. He had broken away from his surroundings; she stood outside the pale. One aspect of conventions which people who declaim against them lose sight of is that conventions make both joy and suffering easier to bear in a becoming manner. But those two were outside all conventions. They would be as untrammelled in a sense as the first man and the first woman. The trouble was that I could not imagine anything about Flora de Barral and the brother of Mrs. Fyne. Or if you like, I could imagine *anything* which comes practically to the same thing. Darkness and chaos are first cousins. I should have liked to ask the girl for a word which would give my imagination its line. But how was one to venture so far? I can be rough sometimes but I am not naturally impertinent. I would have liked to ask her for instance: 'Do you know what you have done with yourself?' A question like that. Anyhow it was time for one of us to say something. A question it must be. And the question I asked was: 'So he's going to show you the ship?'

"She seemed glad I had spoken at last and glad of the opportunity to speak herself.

" 'Yes. He said he would—this morning. Did you say you did not know Captain Anthony?'

" 'No. I don't know him. Is he anything like his sister?'

"She looked startled and murmured 'Sister!' in a puzzled tone which astonished me. 'Oh! Mrs. Fyne,' she exclaimed, recollecting herself, and avoiding my eyes while I looked at her curiously.

"What an extraordinary detachment! And all the time the stream of shabby people was hastening by us, with the continuous dreary shuffling of weary footsteps on the flagstones. The sunshine falling on the grime of surfaces, on the poverty of tones and forms seemed of an inferior quality, its joy faded, its brilliance tarnished and dusty. I had to raise my voice in the dull vibrating noise of the roadway.

" 'You don't mean to say you have forgotten the connection?'

"She cried readily enough: 'I wasn't thinking.' And then, while I wondered what could have been the images occupying her brain at this time, she asked me: 'You didn't see my letter to Mrs. Fyne—did you?'

" 'No. I didn't,' I shouted. Just then the racket was distracting, a pair-horse trolly lightly loaded with loose rods of iron passing slowly very near us. 'I wasn't trusted so far.' And remembering Mrs. Fyne's hints that the girl was unbalanced, I added: 'Was it an unreserved confession you wrote?'

"She did not answer me for a time, and as I waited I thought that there's nothing like a confession to make one look mad; and that of all confessions a written one is the most detrimental all around. Never confess! Never, never! An untimely joke is a source of bitter regret always. Sometimes it may ruin a man; not because it is a joke, but because it is untimely. And a confession of whatever sort is always untimely. The one thing which makes it supportable for a while is curiosity. You smile? Ah, but it is so, or else people would be sent to the right-about at the second sentence. How many sympathetic souls can you reckon on in the world? One in ten, one in a hundred—in a thousand—in ten thousand? Ah! What a sell these confessions are! What a horrible sell! You seek sympathy, and all you get is the most evanescent sense of relief—if you get that much. For a confession, whatever it may be, stirs the secret depths of the hearer's character. Often depths that he himself is but dimly aware of. And so the righteous triumph secretly, the lucky are amused, the strong are disgusted, the weak either upset or irritated with you according to the measure of their sincerity with themselves. And all of them in their hearts brand you for either mad or impudent. . . ."

I had seldom seen Marlow so vehement, so pessimistic, so earnestly cynical before. I cut his declamation short by asking what answer Flora de Barral had given to his question. "Did the poor girl admit firing off her confidences at Mrs. Fyne—eight pages of close writing—that sort of thing?"

Marlow shook his head.

"She did not tell me. I accepted her silence as a kind of answer, and remarked that it would have been better if she had simply announced the fact to Mrs. Fyne at the cottage. 'Why didn't you do it?' I asked point-blank.

"She said: 'I am not a very plucky girl.' She looked up at me and added meaningly: 'And *you* know it. And you know why.'

"I must remark that she seemed to have become very subdued since our first meeting at the quarry. Almost a different person from the defiant, angry and despairing girl with quivering lips and resentful glances.

" 'I thought it was very sensible of you to get away from that sheer drop,' I said.

"She looked up with something of that old expression.

" 'That's not what I mean. I see you will have it that you saved my life. Nothing of the kind. I was concerned for that vile little beast of a dog. No! It was the idea of—of doing away with myself which was cowardly. That's what I meant by saying I am not a very plucky girl.'

" 'Oh!' I retorted airily. 'That little dog. He isn't really a bad little dog.' But she lowered her eyelids and went on:

" 'I was so miserable that I could think only of myself. This was mean. It was cruel too. And besides I had *not* given it up—not then.' "

Marlow changed his tone.

"I don't know much of the psychology of self-destruction. It's a sort of subject one has few opportunities to study closely. I knew a man once who came to my rooms one evening, and while smoking a cigar confessed to me moodily that he was trying to discover some graceful way of retiring out of existence. I didn't study his case, but I had a glimpse of him the other day at a cricket match, with some women, having a good time. That seems a fairly reasonable attitude. Considered as a sin, it is a case for repentance before the throne of a merciful God. But I imagine that Flora de Barral's religion under the care of the distinguished governess could have been nothing but outward formality. Remorse in the sense of gnawing shame and unavailing regret is only understandable to me when some wrong had been done to a fellow-creature.

"But why she, that girl who existed on sufferance, so to speak—why she should writhe inwardly with remorse because she had once thought of getting rid of a life which was nothing in every respect but a curse—*that* I could not understand. I thought it was very likely some obscure influence of common forms of speech, some traditional or inherited feeling—a vague notion that suicide is a legal crime; words of old moralists and preachers which remain in the air and help to form all the authorized moral conventions. Yes, I was surprised at her remorse. But lowering her glance unexpectedly till her dark eyelashes seemed to rest against her white cheeks she presented a perfectly demure aspect. It was so attractive that I could not help a faint smile. That Flora de Barral should ever, in any aspect, have the power to evoke a smile was the very last thing I should have believed. She went on after a slight hesitation:

" 'One day I started for there, for that place.'

"Look at the influence of a mere play of physiognomy! If you remember what we were talking about you will hardly believe that I caught myself grinning down at that demure little girl. I must say too that I felt more friendly to her at the moment than ever before.

" 'Oh, you did? To take that jump? You are a determined young person. Well, what happened that time?'

"An almost imperceptible alteration in her bearing; a slight droop of her head perhaps—a mere nothing—made her look more demure than ever.

" 'I had left the cottage,' she began a little hurriedly. 'I was walking along the road—you know, *the* road. I had made up my mind I was not coming back this time.'

"I won't deny that these words spoken from under the brim of her hat (oh yes, certainly, her head was down—she had put it down) gave me a thrill; for indeed I had never doubted her sincerity. It could never have been a make-believe despair.

" 'Yes,' I whispered. 'You were going along the road.'

" 'When . . .' Again she hesitated with an effect of innocent shyness worlds asunder from tragic issues; then glided on . . . 'When suddenly Captain Anthony came through a gate out of a field.'

"I coughed down the beginning of a most improper fit of laughter, and felt ashamed of myself. Her eyes raised for a moment seemed full of innocent suffering and unexpressed menace in the depths of the dilated pupils within the rings of sombre blue. It was—how shall I say it?—a night effect when you seem to see vague shapes and don't know what reality you may come upon at any time. Then she lowered her eyelids again, shutting all mysteriousness out of the situation except for the sobering memory of that glance, nightlike in the sunshine, expressively still in the brutal unrest of the street.

" 'So Captain Anthony joined you—did he?'

" 'He opened a field-gate and walked out on the road. He crossed to my side and went on with me. He had his pipe in his hand. He said: "Are you going far this morning?" '

"These words (I was watching her white face as she spoke) gave me a slight shudder. She remained demure, almost prim. And I remarked:

" 'You had been talking together before, of course.'

" 'Not more than twenty words altogether since he arrived,' she declared without emphasis. 'That day he had said, "Good morning" to me when we met at breakfast two hours before. And I said good morning to him. I did not see him afterwards till he came out on the road.'

"I thought to myself that this was not accidental. He had been observing her. I felt certain also that he had not been asking any questions of Mrs. Fyne.

" 'I wouldn't look at him,' said Flora de Barral. 'I had done with looking at people. He said to me: "My sister does not put herself out much for us. We had better keep each other company. I have read every book there is in that cottage." I walked on. He did not leave me. I thought he ought to. But he didn't. He didn't seem to notice that I would not talk to him.'

"She was now perfectly still. The wretched little parasol hung down against her dress from her joined hands. I was rigid with attention. It isn't every day that one culls such a volunteered tale on a girl's lips. The ugly street-noises swelling up for a moment covered the next few words she said. It was vexing. The next word I heard was 'worried.'

" 'It worried you to have him there, walking by your side?'

" 'Yes. Just that,' she went on with downcast eyes. There was something prettily comical in her attitude and her tone, while I pictured to myself a poor white-faced girl walking to her death with an unconscious man striding by her side. Unconscious? I don't know. First of all, I felt certain that this was no chance meeting. Something had happened before. Was he a man for a *coup-de-foudre*, the lightning stroke of love? I don't think so. That sort of susceptibility is luckily rare. A world of inflammable lovers of the Romeo and Juliet type would very soon end in barbarism and misery. But it is a fact that in every man (not in every woman) there lives a lover; a lover who is called out in all his potentialities often by the most insignificant little things—as long as they come at the psychological moment: the glimpse of a face at an unusual angle, an evanescent attitude, the curve of a cheek often looked at before, perhaps, but then, at the moment, charged with astonishing significance. These are great mysteries, of course. Magic signs.

"I don't know in what the sign consisted in this case.

It might have been her pallor (it wasn't pasty nor yet papery), that white face with eyes like blue gleams of fire and lips like red coals. In certain lights, in certain poises of head it suggested tragic sorrow. Or it might have been her wavy hair. Or even just that pointed chin stuck out a little, resentful and not particularly distinguished, doing away with the mysterious aloofness of her fragile presence. But any way at a given moment Anthony must have suddenly *seen* the girl. And then, that something had happened to him. Perhaps nothing more than the thought coming into his head that this was 'a possible woman.'

"Followed this waylaying! Its resolute character makes me think it was the chin's doing; that 'common mortal' touch which stands in such good stead to some women. Because men, I mean really masculine men, those whose generations have evolved an ideal woman, are often very timid. Who wouldn't be before the ideal? It's your sentimental trifler, who has just missed being nothing at all, who is enterprising, simply because it is easy to appear enterprising when one does not mean to put one's belief to the test.

"Well, whatever it was that encouraged him, Captain Anthony stuck to Flora de Barral in a manner which in a timid man might have been called heroic if it had not been so simple. Whether policy, diplomacy, simplicity, or just inspiration, he kept up his talk, rather deliberate, with very few pauses. Then suddenly as if recollecting himself:

" 'It's funny. I don't think you are annoyed with me for giving you my company unasked. But why don't you say something?'

"I asked Miss de Barral what answer she made to this query.

" 'I made no answer,' she said in that even, unemotional low voice which seemed to be her voice for delicate confidences. 'I walked on. He did not seem to mind. We came to the foot of the quarry where the road winds up hill, past the place where you were sitting by the roadside that day. I began to wonder what I should do. After we reached the top Captain Anthony said that he had not been for a walk with a lady for years and years—almost since he was a boy. We had then come to where I ought to have turned off and struck across a field. I thought of making a run of it. But he would have caught me up. I know he would; and, of course, he would not have allowed me. I couldn't give him the slip.'

" 'Why didn't you ask him to leave you?' I inquired curiously.

" 'He would not have taken any notice,' she went on steadily. 'And what could I have done then? I could not have started quarrelling with him—could I? I hadn't enough energy to get angry. I felt very tired suddenly. I just stumbled on straight along the road. Captain Anthony told me that the family—some relations of his mother—he used to know in Liverpool was broken up now, and he had never made any friends since. All gone their different ways. All the girls married. Nice girls they were and very friendly to him when he was but little more than a boy. He repeated: "Very nice, cheery, clever girls." I sat down on a bank against a hedge and began to cry.'

" 'You must have astonished him not a little,' I observed.

"Anthony, it seems, remained on the road looking down at her. He did not offer to approach her, neither did he make any other movement or gesture. Flora de Barral told me all this. She could see him through her tears, blurred to a mere shadow on the white road, and then again becoming more distinct, but always absolutely still and as if lost in thought before a strange phenomenon which demanded the closest possible attention.

"Flora learned later that he had never seen a woman cry; not in that way, at least. He was impressed and interested by the mysteriousness of the effect. She was very conscious of being looked at, but was not able to stop herself crying. In fact, she was not capable of any effort. Suddenly he advanced two steps, stooped, caught hold of her hands lying on her lap and pulled her up to her feet; she found herself standing close to him almost before she realized what he had done. Some people were coming briskly along the road and Captain Anthony muttered: 'You don't want to be stared at. What about that stile over there? Can we go back across the fields?'

"She snatched her hands out of his grasp (it seems he had omitted to let them go), marched away from him

and got over the stile. It was a big field sprinkled pro-
fusely with white sheep. A trodden path crossed it diago-
nally. After she had gone more than half way she turned
her head for the first time. Keeping five feet or so
behind, Captain Anthony was following her with an air
of extreme interest. Interest or eagerness. At any rate
she caught an expression on his face which frightened
her. But not enough to make her run. And indeed, it
would have had to be something incredibly awful to scare
into a run a girl who had come to the end of her courage
to live.

"As if encouraged by this glance over the shoulder
Captain Anthony came up boldly, and now that he was
by her side, she felt his nearness intimately, like a touch.
She tried to disregard this sensation. But she was not
angry with him now. It wasn't worth while. She was
thankful that he had the sense not to ask questions as to
this crying. Of course he didn't ask because he didn't
care. No one in the world cared for her, neither those
who pretended nor yet those who did not pretend. She
preferred the latter.

"Captain Anthony opened for her a gate into another
field; when they got through he kept walking abreast,
elbow to elbow almost. His voice growled pleasantly in
her very ear. Staying in this dull place was enough to
give any one the blues. His sister scribbled all day. It
was positively unkind. He alluded to his nieces as rude,
selfish monkeys, without either feelings or manners. And
he went on to talk about his ship being laid up for a
month and dismantled for repairs. The worst was that on
arriving in London he found he couldn't get the rooms
he was used to, where they made him as comfortable as
such a confirmed seadog as himself could be anywhere
on shore.

"In the effort to subdue by dint of talking and to keep
in check the mysterious, the profound attraction he felt
already for that delicate being of flesh and blood, with
pale cheeks, with darkened eyelids and eyes scalded with
hot tears, he went on speaking of himself as a confirmed
enemy of life on shore—a perfect terror to a simple man,
what with the fads and proprieties and the ceremonies
and affectations. He hated all that. He wasn't fit for it.
There was no rest and peace and security but on the sea.

"This gave one a view of Captain Anthony as a hermit withdrawn from a wicked world. It was amusingly unexpected to me and nothing more. But it must have appealed straight to that bruised and battered young soul. Still shrinking from his nearness she had ended by listening to him with avidity. His deep murmuring voice soothed her. And she thought suddenly that there was peace and rest in the grave too.

"She heard him say: 'Look at my sister. She isn't a bad woman by any means. She asks me here because it's right and proper, I suppose, but she has no use for me. There you have your shore people. I quite understand anybody crying. I would have been gone already, only, truth to say, I haven't any friends to go to.' He added brusquely: 'And you?'

"She made a slight negative sign. He must have been observing her, putting two and two together. After a pause he said simply: 'When I first came here I thought you were governess to these girls. My sister didn't say a word about you to me.'

"Then Flora spoke for the first time.

" 'Mrs. Fyne is my best friend.'

" 'So she is mine,' he said without the slightest irony or bitterness, but added with conviction: 'That shows you what life ashore is. Much better be out of it.'

"As they were approaching the cottage he was heard again as though a long silent walk had not intervened: 'But anyhow I shan't ask her anything about you.'

"He stopped short and she went on alone. His last words had impressed her. Everything he had said seemed somehow to have a special meaning under its obvious conversational sense. Till she went in at the door of the cottage she felt his eyes resting on her.

"That is it. He had made himself felt. That girl was, one may say, washing about with slack limbs in the ugly surf of life with no opportunity to strike out for herself, when suddenly she had been made to feel that there was somebody beside her in the bitter water. A most considerable moral event for her; whether she was aware of it or not. They met again at the one o'clock dinner. I am inclined to think that, being a healthy girl under her frail appearance, and fast walking and what I may call relief-crying (there are many kinds of crying) making one hungry, she made a good meal. It was Captain Anthony who had no appetite. His sister commented on it in a curt, businesslike manner, and the eldest of his delightful nieces said mockingly: 'You have been taking too much exercise this morning, Uncle Roderick.' The mild Uncle Roderick turned upon her with a 'What do you know about it, young lady?' so charged with suppressed savagery that the whole round table gave one gasp and went dumb for the rest of the meal. He took no notice whatever of Flora de Barral. I don't think it was from prudence or any calculated motive. I believe he was so full of her aspects that he did not want to look in her direction when there were other people to hamper his imagination.

"You understand I am piecing here bits of disconnected statements. Next day Flora saw him leaning over the field-gate. When she told me this, I didn't of course ask her how it was she was there. Probably she could not have told me how it was she was there. The difficulty here is to keep steadily in view the then conditions of her existence, a combination of dreariness and horror.

"That hermit-like but not exactly misanthropic sailor was leaning over the gate moodily. When he saw the white-faced restless Flora drifting like a lost thing along the road he put his pipe in his pocket and called out 'Good morning, Miss Smith' in a tone of amazing happiness. She, with one foot in life and the other in a nightmare, was at the same time inert and unstable, and very much at the mercy of sudden impulses. She swerved, came distractedly right up to the gate and looking straight into his eyes: 'I am not Miss Smith. That's not my name. Don't call me by it.'

"She was shaking as if in a passion. His eyes expressed nothing; he only unlatched the gate in silence, grasped her arm and drew her in. Then closing it with a kick—

" 'Not your name? That's all one to me. Your name's the least thing about you I care for.' He was leading her firmly away from the gate though she resisted slightly. There was a sort of joy in his eyes which frightened her. 'You are not a princess in disguise,' he said with an unexpected laugh she found bloodcurdling. 'And that's all I care for. You had better understand that I am not blind and not a fool. And then it's plain for even a fool to see that things have been going hard with you. You are on a lee shore and eating your heart out with worry.'

"What seemed most awful to her was the elated light in his eyes, the rapacious smile that would come and go on his lips as if he were gloating over her misery. But her misery was his opportunity and he rejoiced while the tenderest pity seemed to flood his whole being. He pointed out to her that she knew who he was. He was Mrs. Fyne's brother. And, well, if his sister was the best friend she had in the world, then, by Jove, it was about time somebody came along to look after her a little.

"Flora had tried more than once to free herself, but he tightened his grasp on her arm each time and even shook it a little without ceasing to speak. The nearness of his face intimidated her. He seemed striving to look her through. It was obvious the world had been using her ill. And even as he spoke with indignation the very marks and stamp of this ill-usage of which he was so certain seemed to add to the inexplicable attraction he felt for her person. It was not pity alone, I take it. It was something more spontaneous, perverse and exciting. It gave him the feeling that if only he could get hold of her, no woman would belong to him so completely as this woman.

" 'Whatever your troubles,' he said, 'I am the man to take you away from them; that is, if you are not afraid. You told me you had no friends. Neither have I. Nobody ever cared for me as far as I can remember. Perhaps you could. Yes, I live on the sea. But who would you be parting from? No one. You have no one belonging to you.'

"At this point she broke away from him and ran. He did not pursue her. The tall hedges tossing in the wind, the wide fields, the clouds driving over the sky and the sky itself wheeled about her in masses of green and white and blue as if the world were breaking up silently in a whirl, and her foot at the next step were bound to find the void. She reached the gate all right, got out, and, once on the road, discovered that she had not the courage to look back. The rest of that day she spent with the Fyne girls who gave her to understand that she was a slow and unprofitable person. Long after tea, nearly at dusk, Captain Anthony (the son of the poet) appeared suddenly before her in the little garden in front of the cottage. They were alone for the moment. The wind had dropped. In the calm evening air the voices of Mrs. Fyne and the girls strolling aimlessly on the road could be heard. He said to her severely:

" 'You have understood?'

"She looked at him in silence.

" 'That I love you,' he finished.

"She shook her head the least bit.

" 'Don't you believe me?' he asked in a low, infuriated voice.

" 'Nobody would love me,' she answered in a very quiet tone, 'Nobody could.'

"He was dumb for a time, astonished beyond measure as he well might have been. He doubted his ears. He was outraged.

" 'Eh? What? Couldn't love you? What do you know about it? It's my affair, isn't it? You dare say *that* to a man who has just told you! You must be mad!'

" 'Very nearly,' she said with the accent of pent-up sincerity, and even relieved because she was able to say something which she felt was true. For the last few days she had felt herself several times near that madness which is but an intolerable lucidity of apprehension.

"The clear voices of Mrs. Fyne and the girls were coming nearer, sounding affected in the peace of the passion-laden earth. He began storming at her hastily.

" 'Nonsense! Nobody could . . . Indeed! Pah! You'll have to be shown that somebody can. I can. Nobody . . .' He made a contemptuous hissing noise. 'More likely *you* can't. They have done something to you. Something's crushed your pluck. You can't face a man—that's what it is. What made you like this? Where do you come from? You have been put upon. The scoundrels—whoever they are, men or women, seem to have robbed you of your very name. You say you are not Miss Smith. Who are you, then?'

"She did not answer. He muttered, 'Not that I care,' and fell silent, because the famous self-confident chatter of the Fyne girls could be heard at the very gate. But they were not going to bed yet. They passed on. He waited a little in silence and immobility, then stamped his foot and lost control of himself. He growled at her in a savage passion. She felt certain that he was threatening her and calling her names. She was no stranger to abuse, as we know, but there seemed to be a particular kind of ferocity in this which was new to her. She began to tremble. The especially terrifying thing was that she could not make out the nature of these awful menaces and names. Not a word. Yet it was not the shrinking anguish of her other experiences of angry scenes. She made a mighty effort, though her knees were knocking together, and in an expiring voice demanded that he should let her go indoors. 'Don't stop me. It's no use. It's no use,' she repeated faintly, feeling an invincible obstinacy rising within her, yet without anger against that raging man.

"He became articulate suddenly, and, without raising his voice, perfectly audible.

" 'No use! No use! You dare stand here and tell me that—you white-faced wisp, you wreath of mist, you little ghost of all the sorrow in the world. You dare! Haven't I been looking at you? You are all eyes. What makes your cheeks always so white as if you had seen something . . Don't speak. I love it . . . No use! And you really think that I can now go to sea for a year or more, to the other side of the world somewhere, leaving you behind! Why! You would vanish . . . what little there is of you. Some rough wind will blow you away altogether. You have no holding ground on earth. Well, then, trust yourself to me—to the sea—which is deep like your eyes.'

"She said: 'Impossible.' He kept quiet for a while, then asked in a totally changed tone, a tone of gloomy curiosity:

" 'You can't stand me then? Is that it?'

" 'No,' she said, more steady herself. 'I am not thinking of you at all.'

"The inane voices of the Fyne girls were heard over the sombre fields calling to each other, thin and clear. He muttered: 'You could try to. Unless you are thinking of somebody else.'

" 'Yes. I am thinking of somebody else, of someone who has nobody to think of him but me.'

"His shadowy form stepped out of her way, and suddenly leaned sideways against the wooden support of the porch. And as she stood still, surprised by this staggering movement, his voice spoke up in a tone quite strange to her:

" 'Go in then. Go out of my sight—I thought you said nobody could love you.'

"She was passing him when suddenly he struck her as so forlorn that she was inspired to say: 'No one has ever loved me—not in that way—if that's what you mean. Nobody would.'

"He detached himself brusquely from the post, and she did not shrink; but Mrs. Fyne and the girls were already at the gate.

"All he understood was that everything was not over yet. There was no time to lose; Mrs. Fyne and the girls had come in at the gate. He whispered 'Wait' with such authority (he was the son of Carleon Anthony, the domestic autocrat) that it did arrest her for a moment long enough to hear him say that he could not be left like this to puzzle over her nonsense all night. She was to slip down again into the garden later on, as soon as she could do so without being heard. He would be there waiting for her till—till daylight. She didn't think he could go to sleep, did she? And she had better come, or—— He broke off on an unfinished threat.

"She vanished into the unlighted cottage just as Mrs. Fyne came up to the porch. Nervous, holding her breath in the darkness of the living-room, she heard her best friend say: 'You ought to have joined us, Roderick.' And then: 'Have you seen Miss Smith anywhere?'

"Flora shuddered, expecting Anthony to break out into betraying imprecations on Miss Smith's head, and cause a painful and humiliating explanation. She imagined him full of his mysterious ferocity. To her great surprise, Anthony's voice sounded very much as usual, with perhaps a slight tinge of grimness: 'Miss Smith! No I've seen no Miss Smith.'

"Mrs. Fyne seemed satisfied—and not much concerned really.

"Flora, relieved, got clear away to her room upstairs and shutting her door quietly, dropped into a chair. She was used to reproaches, abuse, to all sorts of wicked ill usage—short of actual beating on her body. Otherwise inexplicable angers had cut and slashed and trampled down her youth without mercy—and mainly, it appeared because she was the financier de Barral's daughter and also condemned to a degrading sort of poverty through the action of treacherous men who had turned upon her father in his hour of need. And she thought with the tenderest possible affection of that upright figure buttoned up in a long frock-coat, soft-voiced and having but little to say to his girl. She seemed to feel his hand closed round hers. On his flying visits to Brighton he would always walk hand in hand with her. People stared covertly at them; the band was playing; and there was the sea—the blue gaiety of the sea. They were quietly happy together. . . . It was all over!

"An immense anguish of the present wrung her heart, and she nearly cried aloud. That dread of what was before her which had been eating up her courage slowly in the course of odious years, flamed up into an access of panic, that sort of headlong panic which had already driven her out twice to the top of the cliff-like quarry. She jumped up, saying to herself: 'Why not now? At once! Yes. I'll do it now—in the dark!' The very horror of it seemed to give her additional resolution.

"She came down the staircase quietly, and only on the point of opening the door and because of the discovery that it was unfastened, she remembered Captain Anthony's threat to stay in the garden all night. She hesitated. She did not understand the mood of that man clearly. He was violent. But she had gone beyond the point where things matter. What would he think of her coming down to him—as he would naturally suppose? And even that didn't matter. He could not despise her more than she despised herself. She must have been light-headed because the thought came into her mind that should he get into ungovernable fury from disappointment, and perchance strangle her, it would be as good a way to be done with it as any.

" 'You had that thought!' I exclaimed in wonder.

"With downcast eyes and speaking with a most painstaking precision (her very lips, her red lips, seemed to move just enough to be heard and no more), she said that, yes, the thought came into her head. This makes one shudder at the mysterious ways girls acquire knowledge. For this was a thought, wild enough, I admit, but which could only have come from the depths of that sort of experience which she had not had, and went far beyond a young girl's possible conception of the strongest and most veiled of human emotions.

" 'He was there, of course?' I said.

" 'Yes, he was there.' She saw him on the path directly she stepped outside the porch. He was very still. It was as though he had been standing there with his face to the door for hours.

"Shaken up by the changing moods of passion and tenderness, he must have been ready for any extravagance of conduct. Knowing the profound silence each night brought to that nook of the country, I could imagine them having the feeling of being the only two people on the wide earth. A row of six or seven lofty elms just across the road opposite the cottage made the night more obscure in that little garden. If these two could just make out each other that was all.

" 'Well! And were you very much terrified?' I asked.

"She made me wait a little before she said, raising her eyes: 'He was gentleness itself.'

"I noticed three abominable, drink-sodden loafers, sallow and dirty, who had come to range themselves in a row within ten feet of us against the front of the public-house. They stared at Flora de Barral's back with unseeing, mournful fixity.

" 'Let's move this way a little,' I proposed.

"She turned at once and we made a few paces; not too far to take us out of sight of the hotel door, but very nearly. I could just keep my eyes on it. After all, I had not been so very long with the girl. If you were to disentangle the words we actually exchanged from my comments you would see that they were not so very many, including everything she had so unexpectedly told me of her story. No, not so very many. And now it seemed as though there would be no more. No! I could expect no more. The confidence was wonderful enough in its nature as far as it went, and perhaps not to have been expected from any other girl under the sun. And I felt a little ashamed. The origin of our intimacy was too gruesome. It was as if listening to her I had taken advantage of having seen her poor, bewildered, scared soul without its veils. But I was curious, too; or, to render myself justice without false modesty—I was anxious; anxious to know a little more.

"I felt like a blackmailer all the same when I made my attempt with a light-hearted remark.

" 'And so you gave up that walk you proposed to take?'

" 'Yes, I gave up the walk,' she said slowly before raising her downcast eyes. When she did so it was with an extraordinary effect. It was like catching sight of a piece of blue sky, of a stretch of open water. And for a moment I understood the desire of that man to whom the sea and sky of his solitary life had appeared suddenly incomplete without that glance which seemed to belong to them both. He was not for nothing the son of a poet. I looked into those unabashed eyes while the girl went on, her demure appearance and precise tone changed to a very earnest expression. Woman is various indeed.

" 'But I want you to understand, Mr. . . .' she had actually to think of my name . . . 'Mr. Marlow, that I have written to Mrs. Fyne that I haven't been—that I have done nothing to make Captain Anthony behave to me as he has behaved. I haven't. I haven't. It isn't my doing. It isn't my fault—if she likes to put it in that way. But she, with her ideas, ought to understand that I couldn't, that I couldn't . . . I know she hates me now: I think she never liked me. I think nobody ever cared for me. I was told once nobody could care for me; and I think it is true. At any rate I can't forget it.'

"Her abominable experience with the governess had implanted in her unlucky breast a lasting doubt, an ineradicable suspicion of herself and of others. I said:

" 'Remember, Miss de Barral, that to be fair you must trust a man altogether—or not at all.'

"She dropped her eyes. suddenly. I thought I heard a faint sigh. I tried to take a light tone again, and yet it seemed impossible to get off the ground which gave me my standing with her.

" 'Mrs. Fyne is absurd. She's an excellent woman, but really you could not be expected to throw away your chance of life simply that she might cherish a good opinion of your memory. That would be excessive.'

" 'It was not of my life that I was thinking while Cap-

tain Anthony was—was speaking to me,' said Flora de
Barral with an effort.

"I told her that she was wrong then. She ought to have
been thinking of her life, and not only of her life, but of
the life of the man who was speaking to her too. She let
me finish, then shook her head impatiently.

" 'I mean—death.'

" 'Well,' I said, 'when he stood before you there, outside the cottage, he really stood between you and that.
I have it out of your own mouth. You can't deny it.'

" 'If you will have it that he saved my life, then he
has got it. It was not for me. Oh no! It was not for me
that I—— It was not fear! There!' She finished petu-
lantly: 'And you may just as well know it.'

"She hung her head and swung the parasol slightly to
and fro. I thought a little.

" 'Do you know French, Miss de Barral?' I asked.

"She made a sign with her head that she did, but without showing any surprise at the question and without
ceasing to swing her parasol.

" 'Well then, somehow or other I have the notion that
Captain Anthony is what the French call *un galant
homme*. I should like to think he is being treated as he
deserves.'

"The form of her lips (I could see them under the brim
of her hat) was suddenly altered into a line of seriousness. The parasol stopped swinging.

" 'I have given him what he wanted—that's myself,'
she said without a tremor and with a striking dignity of
tone.

"Impressed by the manner and the directness of the
words, I hesitated for a moment what to say. Then made
up my mind to clear up the point.

" 'And you have got what you wanted? Is that it?'

"The daughter of the egregious financier de Barral did
not answer at once this question going to the heart of
things. Then raising her head and gazing wistfully across
the street noisy with the endless transit of innumerable
bargains, she said with intense gravity:

" 'He has been most generous.'

"I was pleased to hear these words. Not that I doubted
the infatuation of Roderick Anthony, but I was pleased
to hear something which proved that she was sensible

and open to the sentiment of gratitude which in this case was significant. In the face of man's desire a girl is excusable if she thinks herself priceless. I mean a girl of our civilization which has established a dithyrambic phraseology for the expression of love. A man in love will accept any convention exalting the object of his passion and in this indirect way his passion itself. In what the captain of the ship *Ferndale* gave proofs of lover-like lavishness I could not guess very well. But I was glad she was appreciative. It is lucky that small things please women. And it is not silly of them to be thus pleased. It is in small things that the deepest loyalty, that which they need most, the loyalty of the passing moment, is best expressed.

"She had remained thoughtful, letting her deep motionless eyes rest on the streaming jumble of traffic. Suddenly she said:

" 'And I wanted to ask you . . . I was really glad when I saw you actually here. Who would have expected you here, at this spot, before this hotel! I certainly never . . . You see it meant a lot to me. You are the only person who knows . . . who knows for certain . . .'

" 'Knows what?' I said, not discovering at first what she had in her mind. Then I saw it. 'Why can't you leave that alone?' I remonstrated, rather annoyed at the invidious position she was forcing on me in a sense. 'It's true that I was the only person to see,' I added. 'But, as it happens, after your mysterious disappearance I told the Fynes the story of our meeting.'

"Her eyes raised to mine had an expression of dreamy, unfathomable candour, if I dare say so. And if you wonder what I mean I can only say that I have seen the sea wear such an expression on one or two occasions shortly before sunrise on a calm, fresh day. She said as if meditating aloud that she supposed the Fynes were not likely to talk about that. She couldn't imagine any connection in which. . . . Why should she?

"As her tone became interrogatory I assented. 'To be sure. There's no reason whatever—' thinking to myself that they would be more likely to keep quiet about it. They had other things to talk of. And then remembering little Fyne stuck upstairs for an unconscionable time, enough to blurt out everything he ever knew in his life, I reflected that he would assume naturally that Captain

Anthony had nothing to learn from him about Flora de Barral. It had been up to now my assumption too. I saw my mistake. The sincerest of women will make no unnecessary confidences to a man. And this is as it should be.

" 'No—no!' I said reassuringly. 'It's most unlikely. Are you much concerned?'

" 'Well, you see, when I came down,' she said again in that precise demure tone, 'when I came down—into the garden Captain Anthony misunderstood——'

" 'Of course he would. Men are so conceited,' I said.

"I saw it well enough that he must have thought she had come down to him. What else could he have thought? And then he had been 'gentleness itself.' A new experience for that poor, delicate, and yet so resisting creature. Gentleness in passion! What could have been more seductive to the scared, starved heart of that girl? Perhaps had he been violent, she might have told him that what she came down to keep was the tryst of death— not of love. It occurred to me as I looked at her, young, fragile in aspect, and intensely alive in her quietness, that perhaps she did not know herself then what sort of tryst she was coming down to keep.

"She smiled faintly, almost awkwardly as if she were totally unused to smiling, at my cheap jocularity. Then she said with that forced precision, a sort of conscious primness:

" 'I didn't want him to know.'

"I approved heartily. Quite right. Much better. Let him ever remain under his misapprehension which was so much more flattering for him.

"I tried to keep it in the tone of comedy; but she was, I believe, too simple to understand my intention. She went on, looking down.

" 'Oh! You think so? When I saw you I didn't know why you were here. I was glad when you spoke to me because this is exactly what I wanted to ask you for. I wanted to ask you if you ever meet Captain Anthony— by any chance—anywhere—you are a sailor too, are you not?—that you would never mention—never—that—that you had seen me over there.'

" 'My dear young lady,' I cried, horror-struck at the

supposition. 'Why should I? What makes you think I should dream of . . .'

"She had raised her head at my vehemence. She did not understand it. The world had treated her so dishonourably that she had no notion even of what mere decency of feeling is like. It was not her fault. Indeed, I don't know why she should have put her trust in anybody's promises. But I thought it would be better to promise. So I assured her that she could depend on my absolute silence.

" 'I am not likely to ever set eyes on Captain Anthony,' I added with conviction—as a further guarantee.

"She accepted my assurance in silence, without a sign. Her gravity had in it something acute, perhaps because of that chin. While we were still looking at each other she declared:

" 'There's no deception in it really. I want you to believe that if I am here, like this, to-day, it is not from fear. It is not!'

" 'I quite understand,' I said. But her firm yet self-conscious gaze became doubtful. 'I do,' I insisted. 'I understand perfectly that it was not of death that you were afraid.'

"She lowered her eyes slowly, and I went on:

" 'As to life, that's another thing. And I don't know that one ought to blame you very much—though it seemed rather an excessive step. I wonder now if it isn't the ugliness rather than the pain of the struggle which . . .'

"She shuddered visibly: 'But I do blame myself,' she exclaimed with feeling. 'I am ashamed.' And, dropping her head, she looked in a moment the very picture of remorse and shame.

" 'Well, you will be going away from all its horrors,' I said. 'And surely you are not afraid of the sea. You are a sailor's granddaughter, I understand.'

"She sighed deeply. She remembered her grandfather only a little. He was a clean-shaven man with a ruddy complexion and long, perfectly white hair. He used to take her on his knee, and putting his face near hers, talk to her in loving whispers. If only he were alive now . . . !

"She remained silent for a while.

" 'Aren't you anxious to see the ship?' I asked.

"She lowered her head still more so that I could not see anything of her face.

" 'I don't know,' she murmured.

"I had already the suspicion that she did not know her own feelings. All this work of the merest chance had been so unexpected, so sudden. And she had nothing to fall back upon, no experience but such as to shake her belief in every human being. She was dreadfully and pitifully forlorn. It was almost in order to comfort my own depression that I remarked cheerfully:

" 'Well, I know of somebody who must be growing extremely anxious to see you.'

" 'I am before my time,' she confessed simply, rousing herself. 'I had nothing to do. So I came out.'

"I had the sudden vision of a shabby, lonely little room at the other end of the town. It had grown intolerable to her restlessness. The mere thought of it oppressed her. Flora de Barral was looking frankly at her chance confidant.

" 'And I came this way,' she went on. 'I appointed the time myself yesterday, but Captain Anthony would not have minded. He told me he was going to look over some business papers till I came.'

"The idea of the son of the poet, the rescuer of the most forlorn damsel of modern times, the man of violence, gentleness and generosity, plunged up to his neck in ship's accounts amused me. 'I am sure he would not have minded,' I said, smiling. But the girl's stare was sombre, her thin white face seemed pathetically careworn.

" 'I can hardly believe yet,' she murmured anxiously.

" 'It's quite real. Never fear,' I said encouragingly, but had to change my tone at once. 'You had better go down that way a little,' I directed her abruptly.

"I had seen Fyne come striding out of the hotel door. The intelligent girl, without staying to ask questions, walked away from me quietly down one street while I hurried on to meet Fyne coming up the other at his efficient pedestrian gait. My object was to stop him getting as far as the corner. He must have been thinking too hard to be aware of his surroundings. I put myself in his way, and he nearly walked into me.

" 'Hallo!' I said.

"His surprise was extreme. 'You here! You don't mean to say you have been waiting for me?'

"I said negligently that I had been detained by unexpected business in the neighbourhood, and thus happened to catch sight of him coming out.

"He stared at me with solemn distraction, obviously thinking of something else. I suggested that he had better take the next city-ward tramcar. He was inattentive, and I perceived that he was profoundly perturbed. As Miss de Barral (she had moved out of sight) could not possibly approach the hotel door as long as we remained where we were, I proposed that we should wait for the car on the other side of the street. He obeyed rather the slight touch on his arm than my words, and while we were crossing the wide roadway in the midst of the lumbering wheeled traffic, he exclaimed in his deep tone, 'I don't know which of these two is more mad than the other!'

" 'Really!' I said, pulling him forward from under the noses of two enormous sleepy-headed cart-horses. He skipped wildly out of the way and up on the curbstone with a purely instinctive precision; his mind had nothing to do with his movements. In the middle of his leap, and while in the act of sailing gravely through the air, he continued to relieve his outraged feelings.

" 'You would never believe! They *are* mad!'

I took care to place myself in such a position that to face me he had to turn his back on the hotel across the road. I thought there was some misapprehension in the first statement he shot out at me without loss of time, that Captain Anthony had been glad to see him. It was indeed difficult to believe that, directly he opened the door, his wife's 'sailor-brother' had positively shouted: 'Oh, it's you! The very man I wanted to see.'

" 'I found him sitting there,' went on Fyne impressively in his grave chest voice, 'drafting his will.'

"This was unexpected, but I preserved a noncommittal attitude, knowing full well that our actions in themselves are neither mad nor sane. But I did not see what there was to be excited about. And Fyne was distinctly excited. I understood it better when I learned that the captain of the *Ferndale* wanted little Fyne to be one of the trustees. He was leaving everything to his wife. Naturally, a request which involved him into sanctioning in a way a proceeding which he had been sent by his wife to oppose must have appeared sufficiently mad to Fyne.

" 'Me! Me, of all people in the world!' he repeated portentously. But I could see that he was frightened. Such want of tact!

" 'He knew I came from his sister. You don't put a man into such an awkward position,' complained Fyne. 'It made me speak much more strongly against all this very painful business than I would have had the heart to do otherwise.'

"I pointed out to him concisely, and keeping my eyes on the door of the hotel, that he and his wife were the only bond with the land Captain Anthony had. Who else could he have asked?

" 'I explained to him that he was breaking this bond,' declared Fyne solemnly. 'Breaking it once for all. And for what—for what?'

"He glared at me. I could perhaps have given him an inkling for what, but I said nothing. He started again:

" 'My wife assures me that the girl does not love him a bit. She goes by that letter she received from her. There is a passage in it where she practically admits that she was quite unscrupulous in accepting this offer of marriage, but says to my wife that she supposes she, my wife, will not blame her—as it was in self-defence. My wife has her own ideas, but this is an outrageous misapprehension of her views. Outrageous.'

"The good little man paused and then added weightily:

" 'I didn't tell that to my brother-in-law—I mean, my wife's views.'

" 'No,' I said. 'What would have been the good?'

" 'It's positive infatuation,' agreed little Fyne, in the tone as though he had made an awful discovery. 'I have never seen anything so hopeless and inexplicable in my life. I—I felt quite frightened and sorry,' he added, while I looked at him curiously asking myself whether this excellent civil servant and notable pedestrian had felt the breath of a great and fatal love-spell passing him by in the room of that East-End hotel. He did look for a moment as though he had seen a ghost, an other-world thing. But that look vanished instantaneously, and he nodded at me with mere exasperation at something quite of this world—whatever it was. 'It's a bad business. My brother-in-law knows nothing of women,' he cried with an air of profound, experienced wisdom.

"What he imagined he knew of women himself I can't tell. I did not know anything of the opportunities he might have had. But this is a subject which, if approached with undue solemnity, is apt to elude one's grasp entirely. No doubt Fyne knew something of a woman who was Captain Anthony's sister. But that, admittedly, had been a very solemn study. I smiled at him gently, and as if encouraged or provoked, he completed his thought rather explosively.

" 'And that girl understands nothing. . . . It's sheer lunacy.'

" 'I don't know,' I said, 'whether the circumstances of isolation at sea would be any alleviation to the danger. But it's certain that they will have the opportunity to learn everything about each other in a lonely *tête-à-tête*.'

" 'But dash it all,' he cried in hollow accents which at the same time had the tone of bitter irony—I had never before heard a sound so quaintly ugly and almost horrible—'You forget Mr. Smith.'

" 'What Mr. Smith?' I asked innocently.

"Fyne made an extraordinary simiesque grimace. I believe it was quite involuntary, but you know that a grave, much-lined, shaven countenance when distorted in an unusual way is extremely apelike. It was a surprising sight, and rendered me not only speechless but stopped the progress of my thought completely. I must have presented a remarkably imbecile appearance.

" 'My brother-in-law considered it amusing to chaff me about us introducing the girl as Miss Smith,' said Fyne, going surly in a moment. 'He said that perhaps if he had heard her real name from the first it might have restrained him. As it was, he made the discovery too late. Asked me to tell Zoe this together with a lot more nonsense.'

"Fyne gave me the impression of having escaped from a man inspired by a grimly playful ebullition of high spirits. It must have been most distasteful to him; and his solemnity got damaged somehow in the process, I perceived. There were holes in it through which I could see a new, an unknown Fyne.

" 'You wouldn't believe it,' he went on, 'but that girl looks upon her father exclusively as a victim. I don't know,' he burst out suddenly through an enormous rent in his solemnity, 'if she thinks him absolutely a saint, but she certainly imagines him to be a martyr.'

"It is one of the advantages of that magnificent invention, the prison, that you may forget people who are put there as though they were dead. One needn't worry about them. Nothing can happen to them that you can help. They can do nothing which might possibly matter to anybody. They come out of it, though, but that seems hardly an advantage to themselves or any one else. I had completely forgotten the financier de Barral. The girl for me was an orphan, but now I perceived suddenly the force of Fyne's qualifying statement, 'to a certain extent.' It would have been infinitely more kind all round for the law to have shot, beheaded, strangled, or otherwise destroyed this absurd de Barral, who was a danger to a moral world inhabited by a credulous multitude not fit to take care of itself. But I observed to Fyne that, however insane was the view she held, one could not declare the girl mad on that account.

" 'So she thinks of her father—does she? I suppose she would appear to us saner if she thought only of herself.'

" 'I am positive,' Fyne said earnestly, 'that she went and made desperate eyes at Anthony . . .'

" 'Oh come!' I interrupted. 'You haven't seen her make eyes. You don't know the colour of her eyes.'

" 'Very well! It don't matter. But it could hardly have come to that if she hadn't. . . . It's all one, though. I tell you she has led him on, or accepted him, if you like, simply because she was thinking of her father. She doesn't care a bit about Anthony, I believe. She cares for no one. Never cared for any one. Ask Zoe. For myself I don't blame her,' added Fyne, giving me another view of unsuspected things through the rags and tatters of his damaged solemnity. 'No! by heavens, I don't blame her—the poor devil.'

"I agreed with him silently. I suppose affections are, in a sense, to be learned. If there exists a native spark of love in all of us, it must be fanned while we are young. Hers, if she ever had it, had been drenched in as ugly a lot of corrosive liquid as could be imagined. But I was surprised at Fyne obscurely feeling this.

" 'She loves no one except that preposterous advertising shark,' he pursued venomously, but in a more deliberate manner. 'And Anthony knows it.'

" 'Does he?' I said doubtfully.

" 'She's quite capable of having told him herself,' affirmed Fyne, with amazing insight. 'But whether or no, *I've* told him.'

" 'You did? From Mrs. Fyne, of course.'

"Fyne only blinked owlishly at this piece of my insight.

" 'And how did Captain Anthony receive this interesting information?' I asked further.

" 'Most improperly,' said Fyne, who really was in a state in which he didn't mind what he blurted out. 'He isn't himself. He begged me to tell his sister that he offered no remarks on her conduct. Very improper and inconsequent. He said . . . I was tired of this wrangling. I told him I made allowances for the state of excitement he was in.'

" 'You know, Fyne,' I said, 'a man in jail seems to me such an incredible, cruel, nightmarish sort of thing that I can hardly believe in his existence. Certainly not in relation to any other existences.'

" 'But dash it all,' cried Fyne, 'he isn't shut up for life. They are going to let him out. He's coming out! That's the whole trouble. What is he coming out to, I want to know? It seems a more cruel business than the shutting him up was. This has been the worry for weeks. Do you see now?'

"I saw, all sorts of things! Immediately before me I saw the excitement of little Fyne—mere food for wonder. Further off, in a sort of gloom and beyond the light of day and the movement of the street, I saw the figure of a man, stiff like a ramrod, moving with small steps, a slight girlish figure by his side. And the gloom was like the gloom of villainous slums, of misery, of wretchedness, of a starved and degraded existence. It was a relief that I could see only their shabby hopeless backs. He was an awful ghost. But indeed to call him a ghost was only a refinement of polite speech, and a manner of concealing one's terror of such things. Prisons are wonderful contrivances. Open—shut. Very neat. Shut—open. And out

comes some sort of corpse, to wander awfully in a world
in which it has no possible connections and carrying with
it the appalling tainted atmosphere of its silent abode.
Marvellous arrangement. It works automatically, and,
when you look at it, the perfection makes you sick; which
for a mere mechanism is no mean triumph. Sick and
scared. It had nearly scared that poor girl to her death.
Fancy having to take such a thing by the hand! Now I
understood the remorseful strain I had detected in her
speeches.

" 'By Jove!' I said. 'They are about to let him out! I
never thought of that.'

"Fyne was contemptuous either of me or of things at
large.

" 'You didn't suppose he was to be kept in jail for
life?'

"At that moment I caught sight of Flora de Barral at
the junction of the two streets. Then some vehicles following each other in quick succession hid from my sight
the black slight figure with just a touch of colour in her
hat. She was walking slowly; and it might have been caution or reluctance. While listening to Fyne I stared hard
past his shoulder, trying to catch sight of her again. He
was going on with positive heat, the rags of his solemnity
dropping off him at every second sentence.

"That was just it. His wife and he had been perfectly
aware of it. Of course the girl never talked of her father
with Mrs. Fyne. I suppose with her theory of innocence
she found it difficult. But she must have been thinking
of it day and night. What to do with him? Where to go?
How to keep body and soul together? He had never
made any friends. The only relations were the atrocious
East-End cousins. We know what they were. Nothing but
wretchedness, whichever way she turned in an unjust and
prejudiced world. And to look at him helplessly she felt
would be too much for her.

"I won't say I was thinking these thoughts. It was not
necessary. This complete knowledge was in my head
while I stared hard across the wide road, so hard that I
failed to hear little Fyne till he raised his deep voice
indignantly.

" 'I don't blame the girl,' he was saying. 'He is infatuated with her. Anybody can see that. Why she got such

a hold on him I can't understand. She said "Yes" to him only for the sake of that fatuous, swindling father of hers. It's perfectly plain if one thinks it over a moment. One needn't even think of it. We have it under her own hand. In that letter to my wife she says she has acted unscrupulously. She has owned up, then, for what else can it mean, I should like to know. And so they are to be married before that old idiot comes out. . . . He will be surprised,' commented Fyne suddenly in a strangely malignant tone. 'He will be met at the jail door by a Mrs. Anthony, a Mrs. Captain Anthony. Very pleasant for Zoe. And for all I know, my brother-in-law means to turn up dutifully too. A little family event. It's extremely pleasant to think of. Delightful. A charming family party. We three against the world—and all that sort of thing. And what for? For a girl that doesn't care twopence for him.'

"The demon of bitterness had entered into little Fyne. He amazed me as though he had changed his skin from white to black. It was quite as wonderful. And he kept it up, too.

" 'Luckily there are some advantages in the—the profession of a sailor. As long as they defy the world away at sea somewhere eighteen thousand miles from here, I don't mind so much. I wonder what that interesting old party will say. He will have another surprise. They mean to drag him along with them on board the ship straight away. Rescue work. Just think of Roderick Anthony, the son of a gentleman, after all. . . .'

"He gave me a little shock. I thought he was going to say the 'son of the poet,' as usual; but his mind was not running on such vanities now. His unspoken thought must have gone on 'and uncle of my girls.' I suspect that he had been roughly handled by Captain Anthony up there, and the resentment gave a tremendous fillip to the slow play of his wits. Those men of sober fancy, when anything rouses their imaginative faculty, are very thorough. 'Just think!' he cried. 'The three of them crowded into a four-wheeler, and Anthony sitting deferentially opposite that astonished old jail-bird!'

"The good little man laughed. An improper sound it was to come from his manly chest; and what made it worse was the thought that for the least thing, by a mere

hair's breadth, he might have taken this affair sentimentally. But clearly Anthony was no diplomatist. His
brother-in-law must have appeared to him, to use the
language of shore people, a perfect philistine with a heart
like a flint. What Fyne precisely meant by 'wrangling' I
don't know but I had no doubt that these two had 'wran-
gled' to a profoundly disturbing extent. How much the
other was affected I could not even imagine; but the man
before me was quite amazingly upset.

" 'In a four-wheeler! Take him on board!' I muttered,
startled by the change in Fyne.

" 'That's the plan—nothing else. If I am to believe
what I have been told, his feet will scarcely touch the
ground between the prison-gates and the deck of that
ship.'

"The transformed Fyne spoke in a forcibly lowered
tone which I heard without difficulty. The rumbling,
composite noises of the street were hushed for a moment,
during one of these sudden breaks in the traffic as if the
stream of commerce had dried up at its source. Having
an unobstructed view past Fyne's shoulder, I was astonished to see that the girl was still there. I thought she
had gone up long before. But there was her black slender
figure, her white face under the roses of her hat. She
stood on the edge of the pavement as people stand on
the bank of a stream, very still, as if waiting—or as if
unconscious of where she was. The three dismal, sodden
loafers (I could see them too; they hadn't budged an
inch) seemed to me to be watching her. Which was
horrible.

"Meantime Fyne was telling me rather remarkable
things—for him. He declared first it was a mercy in a
sense. Then he asked me if it were not real madness, to
saddle one's existence with such a perpetual reminder.
The daily existence. The isolated sea-bound existence.
To bring such an additional strain into the solitude
already trying enough for two people was the craziest
thing. Undesirable relations were bad enough on shore.
One could cut them or at least forget their existence now
and then. He himself was preparing to forget his brother-
in-law's existence as much as possible.

"That was the general sense of his remarks, not his
exact words. I thought that his wife's brother's existence

had never been very embarrassing to him, but that now of course he would have to abstain from his allusions to the 'son of the poet—you know.' I said 'yes, yes' in the pauses because I did not want him to turn round; and all the time I was watching the girl intently. I thought I knew now what she meant with her 'He was most generous.' Yes. Generosity of character may carry a man through any situation. But why didn't she go then to her generous man? Why stand there as if clinging to this solid earth which she surely hated as one must hate the place where one has been tormented hopeless, unhappy? Suddenly she stirred. Was she going to cross over? No. She turned and began to walk slowly close to the curbstone, reminding me of the time when I discovered her walking near the edge of a ninety-foot sheer drop. It was the same impression, the same carriage, straight, slim, with rigid head and the two hands hanging lightly clasped in front—only now a small sunshade was dangling from them. I saw something fateful in that deliberate pacing towards the inconspicuous door with the words *Hotel Entrance* on the glass panels.

"She was abreast of it now and I thought that she would stop again; but no! She swerved rigidly—at the moment there was no one near her; she had that bit of pavement to herself—with inanimate slowness as if moved by something outside herself.

" 'A confounded convict,' Fyne burst out.

"With the sound of that word offending my ears I saw the girl extend her arm, push the door open a little way and glide in. I saw plainly that movement, the hand put out in advance with the gesture of a sleep-walker.

"She had vanished, her black figure had melted in the darkness of the open door. For some time Fyne said nothing; and I thought of the girl going upstairs, appearing before the man. Were they looking at each other in silence and feeling they were alone in the world as lovers should at the moment of meeting? But that fine forgetfulness was surely impossible to Anthony the seaman directly after the wrangling interview with Fyne the emissary of an order of things which stops at the edge of the sea. How much he was disturbed I couldn't tell because I did not know what that impetuous lover had had to listen to.

" 'Going to take the old fellow to sea with them,' I
said. 'Well I really don't see what else they could have
done with him. You told your brother-in-law what you
thought of it? I wonder how he took it.'

" 'Very improperly,' repeated Fyne. 'His manner was
offensive, derisive, from the first. I don't mean he was
actually rude in words. Hang it all, I am not a contemptible ass. But he was exulting at having got hold of a
miserable girl.'

" 'It is pretty certain that she will be much less poor
and miserable,' I murmured.

"It looked as if the exultation of Captain Anthony
had got on Fyne's nerves. 'I told the fellow very plainly
that he was abominably selfish in this,' he affirmed
unexpectedly.

" 'You did! Selfish!' I said, rather taken aback. 'But
what if the girl thought that, on the contrary, he was
most generous?'

" 'What do you know about it?' growled Fyne. The
rents and slashes of his solemnity were closing up gradually but it was going to be a surly solemnity. 'Generosity!
I am disposed to give it another name. No. Not folly,'
he shot out at me as though I had meant to interrupt
him. 'Still another. Something worse. I need not tell you
what it is,' he added with grim meaning.

" 'Certainly. You needn't—unless you like,' I said
blankly. Little Fyne had never interested me so much
since the beginning of the de Barral-Anthony affair when
I first perceived possibilities in him. The possibilities of
dull men are exciting because when they happen they
suggest legendary cases of 'possession' not exactly by the
devil but, anyhow, by a strange spirit.

" 'I told him it was a shame,' said Fyne. 'Even if the
girl did make eyes at him—but I think with you that
she did not. Yes! A shame to take advantage of a girl's
distress—a girl that does not love him in the least.'

" 'You think it's so bad as that?' I said. 'Because you
know I don't.'

" 'What can you think about it?' he retorted on me
with a solemn stare. 'I go by her letter to my wife.'

" 'Ah! that famous letter. But you haven't actually
read it,' I said.

" 'No, but my wife told me. Of course it was a most

improper sort of letter to write considering the circumstances. It pained Mrs. Fyne to discover how thoroughly she had been misunderstood. But what is written is not all. It's what my wife could read between the lines. She says that the girl is really terrified at heart.'

" 'She had not much in life to give her any very special courage for it, or any great confidence in mankind. That's very true. But this seems an exaggeration.'

" 'I should like to know what reasons you have to say that?' asked Fyne with offended solemnity. 'I really don't see any. But I had sufficient authority to tell my brother-in-law that if he thought he was going to do something chivalrous and fine he was mistaken. I can see very well that he will do everything she asks him to do—but, all the same, it is rather a pitiless transaction.'

"For a moment I felt it might be so. Fyne caught sight of an approaching tram-car and stepped out on the road to meet it. 'Have you a more compassionate scheme ready?' I called after him. He made no answer, clambered on to the rear platform, and only then looked back. We exchanged a perfunctory wave of the hand. We also looked at each other, he rather angrily, I fancy, and I with wonder. I may also mention that it was for the last time. From that day I never set eyes on the Fynes. As usual the unexpected happened to me. It had nothing to do with Flora de Barral. The fact is that I went away. My call was not like her call. Mine was not urged on me with passionate vehemence or tender gentleness made all the finer and more compelling by the allurements of generosity which is a virtue as mysterious as any other but having a glamour of its own. No, it was just a prosaic offer of employment on rather good terms which, with a sudden sense of having wasted my time on shore long enough, I accepted without misgivings. And once started out of my indolence I went, as my habit was, very, very far away and for a long, long time. Which is another proof of my indolence. How far Flora went I can't say. But I will tell you my idea: my idea is that she went as far as she was able—as far as she could bear it—as far as she had to. . . ."

Part II

THE KNIGHT

CHAPTER ONE

The Ferndale

I have said that the story of Flora de Barral was imparted to me in stages. At this stage I did not see Marlow for some time. At last, one evening rather early, very soon after dinner, he turned up in my rooms.

I had been waiting for his call primed with a remark which had not occurred to me till after he had gone away.

"I say," I tackled him at once, "how can you be certain that Flora de Barral ever went to sea? After all, the wife of the Captain of the *Ferndale*—'the lady that mustn't be disturbed' of the old ship-keeper—may not have been Flora."

"Well, I do know," he said, "if only because I have been keeping in touch with Mr. Powell."

"You have!" I cried. "This is the first I hear of it. And since when?"

"Why, since the first day. You went up to town leaving me in the inn. I slept ashore. In the morning Mr. Powell came in for breakfast; and after the first awkwardness of meeting a man you have been yarning with over-night had worn off, we discovered a liking for each other."

As I had discovered the fact of their mutual liking before either of them, I was not surprised.

"And so you kept in touch," I said.

"It was not so very difficult. As he was always knocking about the river, I hired Dingle's sloop-rigged three-tonner to be more on an equality. Powell was friendly but elusive. I don't think he ever wanted to avoid me. But it is a fact that he used to disappear out of the river in a very mysterious manner sometimes. A man may land anywhere and bolt inland—but what about his five-ton cutter? You can't carry that in your hand like a suit-case.

"Then as suddenly he would reappear in the river, after one had given him up. I did not like to be beaten. That's why I hired Dingle's decked boat. There was just the accommodation in her to sleep a man and a dog. But I had no dog-friend to invite. Fyne's dog who saved Flora de Barral's life is the last dog-friend I had. I was rather lonely cruising about; but that, too, on the river has its charm, sometimes. I chased the mystery of the vanishing Powell dreamily, looking about me at the ships, thinking of the girl Flora, of life's chances—and, do you know, it was very simple."

"What was very simple?" I asked innocently.

"The mystery."

"They are generally that," I said.

Marlow eyed me for a moment in a peculiar manner.

"Well, I have discovered the mystery of Powell's disappearances. The fellow used to run into one of these narrow tidal creeks on the Essex shore. These creeks are so inconspicuous that till I had studied the chart pretty carefully I did not know of their existence. One afternoon, I made out Powell's boat, heading into the shore. By the time I got close to the mud-flat his craft had disappeared inland. But I could see the mouth of the creek by then. The tide being on the turn I took the risk of getting stuck in the mud suddenly and headed in. All I had to guide me was the top of the roof of some sort of small building. I got in more by good luck than by good management. The sun had set some time before; my boat glided in a sort of winding ditch between two low grassy banks; on both sides of me was the flatness of the Essex marsh, perfectly still. All I saw moving was a heron; he was flying low, and disappeared in the murk. Before I had gone half a mile, I was up with the building the roof of which I had seen from the river. It looked like a small barn. A row of piles driven into the soft bank in front of it and supporting a few planks made a sort of wharf. All this was black in the falling dusk, and I could just distinguish the whitish ruts of a cart-track stretching over the marsh towards the higher land, far away. Not a sound was to be heard. Against the low streak of light in the sky I could see the mast of Powell's cutter moored to the bank some twenty yards, no more, beyond that black barn or whatever it was. I hailed him with a loud shout. Got no answer. After making fast my boat just astern, I walked along the bank to have a look at Powell's. Being so much bigger than mine she was aground already. Her sails were furled; the slide of her scuttle hatch was closed and padlocked. Powell was gone. He had walked off into that dark, still marsh somewhere. I had not seen a single house anywhere near; there did not seem to be any human habitation for miles; and now as darkness fell denser over the land I couldn't see the glimmer of a single light. However, I supposed that there must be some village or hamlet not very far away; or only one of these mysterious little inns one comes upon sometimes in most unexpected and lonely places.

"The stillness was oppressive. I went back to my boat, made some coffee over a spirit-lamp, devoured a few biscuits, and stretched myself aft, to smoke and gaze at the stars. The earth was a mere shadow, formless and silent, and empty, till a bullock turned up from somewhere, quite shadowy too. He came smartly to the very edge of the bank as though he meant to step on board, stretched his muzzle right over my boat, blew heavily once, and walked off contemptuously into the darkness from which he had come. I had not expected a call from a bullock, though a moment's thought would have shown me that there must be lots of cattle and sheep on that marsh. Then everything became still as before. I might have imagined myself arrived on a desert island. In fact, as I reclined smoking, a sense of absolute loneliness grew on me. And just as it had become intense, very abruptly and without any preliminary sound I heard firm, quick footsteps on the little wharf. Somebody coming along the cart-track had just stepped at a swinging gait on to the planks. That somebody could only have been Mr. Powell. Suddenly he stopped short, having made out that there

were two masts alongside the bank where he had left
only one. Then he came on silent on the grass. When I
spoke to him he was astonished.

" 'Who would have thought of seeing you here!' he
exclaimed, after returning my good evening.

"I told him I had run in for company. It was rigorously
true.

" 'You knew I was here?' he exclaimed.

" 'Of course,' I said. 'I tell you I came in for company.'

"He is really a good fellow," went on Marlow. "And
his capacity for astonishment is quickly exhausted, it
seems. It was in the most matter-of-fact manner that he
said, 'Come on board of me, then; I have here enough
supper for two.' He was holding a bulky parcel in the
crook of his arm. I did not wait to be asked twice, as
you may guess. His cutter has a very neat little cabin,
quite big enough for two men not only to sleep but to
sit and smoke in. We left the scuttle wide open, of
course. As to his provisions for supper, they were not of
a luxurious kind. He complained that the shops in the
village were miserable. There was a big village within a
mile and a half. It struck me he had been very long doing
his shopping; but naturally I made no remark. I didn't
want to talk at all except for the purpose of setting him
going."

"And did you set him going?" I asked.

"I did," said Marlow, composing his features into an
impenetrable expression which somehow assured me of
his success better than an air of triumph could have done.

"You made him talk?" I said after a silence.

"Yes, I made him . . . about himself."

"And to the point?"

"If you mean by this," said Marlow, "that it was about
the voyage of the *Ferndale*, then again, yes. I brought
him to talk about that voyage, which, by the by, was not
the first voyage of Flora de Barral. The man himself, as
I told you, is simple, and his faculty of wonder not very
great. He's one of those people who form no theories
about facts. Straightforward people seldom do. Neither
have they much penetration. But in this case it did not
matter. I—we—have already the inner knowledge. We
know the history of Flora de Barral. We know something

of Captain Anthony. We have the secret of the situation.
The man was intoxicated with the pity and tenderness of
his part. Oh, yes! Intoxicated is not too strong a word;
for you know that love and desire take many disguises.
I believe that the girl had been frank with him, with
the frankness of women to whom perfect frankness is
impossible, because so much of their safety depends on
judicious reticences. I am not indulging in cheap sneers.
There is necessity in these things. And moreover she
could not have spoken with a certain voice in the face of
his impetuosity, because she did not have time to understand either the state of her feelings, or the precise
nature of what she was doing.

"Had she spoken ever so clearly he was, I take it, too
elated to hear her distinctly. I don't mean to imply that
he was a fool. Oh, dear no! But he had no training in
the usual conventions, and we must remember that he
had no experience whatever of women. He could only
have an ideal conception of his position. An ideal is often
but a flaming vision of reality.

"To him enters Fyne, wound up, if I may express
myself so irreverently, wound up to a high pitch by his
wife's interpretation of the girl's letter. He enters with
his talk of meanness and cruelty, like a bucket of water
on the flame. Clearly a shock. But the effects of a bucket
of water are diverse. They depend on the kind of flame.
A mere blaze of dry straw, of course . . . but there can
be no question of straw there. Anthony of the *Ferndale*
was not, could not have been, a straw-stuffed specimen
of a man. There are flames a bucket of water sends leaping sky-high.

"We may well wonder what happened when, after
Fyne had left him, the hesitating girl went up at last and
opened the door of that room where our man, I am certain, was not extinguished. Oh, no! Nor cold; whatever
else he might have been.

"It is conceivable he might have cried at her in the
first moment of humiliation, of exasperation, 'Oh, it's you!
Why are you here? If I am so odious to you that you
must write to my sister to say so, I give you back your
word.' But then, don't you see, it could not have been
that. I have the practical certitude that soon afterwards
they went together in a hansom to see the ship—as

agreed. That was my reason for saying that Flora de Bar
ral did go to sea. . . ."

"Yes. It seems conclusive," I agreed. "But even with
out that—if, as you seem to think, the very desolation
of that girlish figure had a sort of perversely seductive
charm, making its way through his compassion to his
senses (and everything is possible)—then such words
could not have been spoken."

"They might have escaped him involuntarily," observ
ed Marlow. "However, a plain fact settles it. They went
off together to see the ship."

"Do you conclude from this that nothing whatever was
said?" I inquired.

"I should have liked to see the first meeting of their
glances stairs there," mused Marlow. "And perhaps
nothing was said. But no man comes out of such a 'wran-
gle' (as Fyne called it) without showing some traces of
it. And you may be sure that a girl so bruised all over
would feel the slightest touch of anything resembling
coldness. She was mistrustful; she could not be otherwise; for the energy of evil is so much more forcible than
the energy of good that she could not help looking still
upon her abominable governess as an authority. How
could one have expected her to throw off the unholy
prestige of that long domination? She could not help
believing what she had been told; that she was in some
mysterious way odious and unlovable It was cruelly
true—*to her*. The oracle of so many years had spoken
finally. Only other people did not find her out at
once. . . . I would not go so far as to say she believed it
altogether. That would be hardly possible. But then
haven't the most flattered, the most conceited of us their
moments of doubt? Haven't they? Well, I don't know.
There may be lucky beings in this world unable to believe
any evil of themselves. For my own part I'll tell you that
once, many years ago now, it came to my knowledge
that a fellow I had been mixed up with in a certain transaction—a clever fellow whom I really despised—was going
around telling people that I was a consummate hypocrite.
He could know nothing of it. It suited his humour to say
so. I had given him no ground for that particular calumny.
Yet to this day there are moments when it comes into my
mind, and involuntarily I ask myself, 'What if it were

true?' It's absurd, but it has on one or two occasions
nearly affected my conduct. And yet I was not an impressionable, ignorant young girl. I had taken the exact measure of the fellow's utter worthlessness long before. He
had never been for me a person of prestige and power,
like that awful governess to Flora de Barral. See the
might of suggestion? We live at the mercy of a malevolent word. A sound, a mere disturbance of the air, sinks
into our very soul sometimes. Flora de Barral had been
more astounded than convinced by the first impetuosity
of Roderick Anthony. She let herself be carried along by
a mysterious force which her person had called into
being, as her father had been carried away out of his
depth by the unexpected power of successful advertising.

"They went on board that morning. The *Ferndale* had
just come to her loading berth. The only living creature
on board was the ship-keeper—whether the same who
had been described to us by Mr. Powell, or another, I
don't know. Possibly some other man. He, looking over
the side, saw, in his own words, 'the captain come sailing
round the corner of the nearest cargo-shed, in company
with a girl.' He lowered the accommodation ladder down
on to the jetty . . ."

"How do you know all this?" I interrupted.

Marlow interjected an impatient—"You shall see by
and by. . . . Flora went up first, got down on deck and
stood stock-still till the captain took her by the arm and
led her aft. The ship-keeper let them into the saloon. He
had the keys of all the cabins, and stumped in after them.
The captain ordered him to open all the doors, every
blessed door; state-rooms, passages, pantry, fore-cabin—
and then sent him away.

"The *Ferndale* had magnificent accommodation. At
the end of a passage leading from the quarter-deck there
was a long saloon, its sumptuosity slightly tarnished perhaps, but having a grand air of roominess and comfort.
The harbour carpets were down, the swinging lamps
hung, and everything in its place, even to the silver on
the sideboard. Two large stern cabins opened out of it,
one on each side of the rudder casing. These two cabins
communicated through a small bathroom between them,
and one was fitted up as the captain's state-room. The
other was vacant, and furnished with arm-chairs and a

round table, more like a room on shore, except for the long curved settee following the shape of the ship's stern. In a dim inclined mirror, Flora caught sight down to the waist of a pale-faced girl in a white straw hat trimmed with roses, distant, shadowy, as if immersed in water, and was surprised to recognize herself in those surroundings. They seemed to her arbitrary, bizarre, strange. Captain Anthony moved on, and she followed him. He showed her the other cabins. He talked all the time loudly in a voice she seemed to have known extremely well for a long time; and yet, she reflected, she had not heard it often in her life. What he was saying she did not quite follow. He was speaking of comparatively indifferent things in a rather moody tone, but she felt it round her like a caress. And when he stopped she could hear, alarming in the sudden silence, the precipitated beating of her heart.

"The ship-keeper dodged about the quarter-deck, out of hearing, and trying to keep out of sight. At the same time, taking advantage of the open doors with skill and prudence, he could see the captain and 'that girl' the captain had brought aboard. The captain was showing her round very thoroughly. Through the whole length of the passage, far away aft in the perspective of the saloon the ship-keeper had interesting glimpses of them as they went in and out of the various cabins, crossing from side to side, remaining invisible for a time in one or another of the state-rooms, and then reappearing again in the distance. The girl, always following the captain, had her sun-shade in her hands. Mostly she would hang her head, but now and then she would look up. They had a lot to say to each other and seemed to forget they weren't alone in the ship. He saw the captain put his hand on her shoulder, and was preparing himself with a certain zest for what might follow, when the 'old man' seemed to recollect himself, and came striding down all the length of the saloon. At this move the ship-keeper promptly dodged out of sight, as you may believe, and heard the captain slam the inner door of the passage. After that disappointment the ship-keeper waited resentfully for them to clear out of the ship. It happened much sooner than he had expected. The girl walked out on deck first. As before she did not look round. She didn't look at anything; and she seemed to be in such a hurry to get ashore that she made for the gangway and started down the ladder without waiting for the captain.

"What struck the ship-keeper most was the absent, unseeing expression of the captain, striding after the girl. He passed him, the ship-keeper, without notice, without an order, without so much as a look. The captain had never done so before. Always had a nod and a pleasant word for a man. From this slight the ship-keeper drew a conclusion unfavourable to the strange girl. He gave them time to get down on the wharf before crossing the deck to steal one more look at the pair over the rail. The captain took hold of the girl's arm just before a couple of railway trucks drawn by a horse came rolling along and hid them from the ship-keeper's sight for good.

"Next day, when the chief mate joined the ship, he told him the tale of the visit, and expressed himself about the girl 'who had got hold of the captain' disparagingly. She didn't look healthy, he explained. 'Shabby clothes, too,' he added spitefully.

"The mate was very much interested. He had been with Anthony for several years, and had won for himself in the course of many long voyages, a footing of familiarity, which was to be expected with a man of Anthony's character. But in that slowly grown intimacy of the sea, which in its duration and solitude had its unguarded moments, no words had passed, even of the most casual, to prepare him for the vision of his captain associated with any kind of girl. His impression had been that women did not exist for Captain Anthony. Exhibiting himself with a girl! A girl! What did he want with a girl? Bringing her on board and showing her round the cabin! That was really a little bit too much. Captain Anthony ought to have known better.

"Franklin (the chief mate's name was Franklin) felt disappointed; almost disillusioned. Silly thing to do! Here was a confounded old ship-keeper set talking. He snubbed the ship-keeper, and tried to think of that insignificant bit of foolishness no more; for it diminished Captain Anthony in his eyes of a jealously devoted subordinate.

"Franklin was over forty; his mother was still alive. She stood in the forefront of all women for him, just as Captain Anthony stood in the forefront of all men. We may suppose that these groups were not very large. He had gone to sea at a very early age. The feelings which caused these two people to partly eclipse the rest of mankind were of course not similar; though in time he had acquired the conviction that he was 'taking care' of them both. The 'old lady' of course had to be looked after as long as she lived. In regard to Captain Anthony, he used to say that: why should he leave him? It wasn't likely that he would come across a better sailor or a better man or a more comfortable ship. As to trying to better himself in the way of promotion, commands were not the sort of thing one picked up in the streets, and when it came to that, Captain Anthony was as likely to give him a lift on occasion as any one in the world.

"From Mr. Powell's description Franklin was a short, thick, black-haired man, bald on the top. His head sunk between the shoulders, his staring prominent eyes and a florid colour gave him a rather apoplectic appearance. In repose, his congested face had a humorously melancholy expression.

"The ship-keeper having given him up all the keys and having been chased forward with the admonition to mind his own business and not to chatter about what did not concern him, Mr. Franklin went under the poop. He opened one door after another; and, in the saloon, in the captain's state-room and everywhere, he stared anxiously as if expecting to see on the bulkheads, on the deck, in the air, something unusual—sign, mark, emanation, shadow—he hardly knew what—some subtle change wrought by the passage of a girl. But there was nothing. He entered the unoccupied stern cabin and spent some time there unscrewing the two stem ports. In the absence of all material evidences his uneasiness was passing away. With a last glance round he came out and found himself in the presence of his captain advancing from the other end of the saloon.

"Franklin, at once, looked for the girl. She wasn't to be seen. The captain came up quickly. 'Oh! you are here, Mr. Franklin.' And the mate said, 'I was giving a little air to the place, sir.' Then the captain, his hat pulled down over his eyes, laid his stick on the table and asked in his kind way: 'How did you find your mother, Franklin?'—'The old lady's first-rate, sir, thank you.' And then they had nothing to say to each other. It was a strange and disturbing feeling for Franklin. He, just back from leave, the ship just come to her loading berth, the captain just come on board, and apparently nothing to say! The several questions he had been anxious to ask as to various things which had to be done had slipped out of his mind. He, too, felt as though he had nothing to say.

"The captain, picking up his stick off the table, marched into his state-room and shut the door after him. Franklin remained still for a moment and then started slowly to go on deck. But before he had time to reach the other end of the saloon he heard himself called by name. He turned round. The captain was staring from the doorway of his state-room. Franklin said, 'Yes, sir.' But the captain, silent, leaned a little forward grasping the door handle. So he, Franklin, walked aft keeping his eyes on him. When he had come up quite close he said again, 'Yes, sir?' interrogatively. Still silence. The mate didn't like to be stared at in that manner, a manner quite new in his captain, with a defiant and self-conscious stare, like a man who feels ill and dares you to notice it. Franklin gazed at his captain, felt that there was something wrong, and in his simplicity voiced his feelings by asking point-blank—

" 'What's wrong, sir?'

"The captain gave a slight start, and the character of his stare changed to a sort of sinister surprise. Franklin grew very uncomfortable, but the captain asked negligently—

" 'What makes you think that there's something wrong?'

" 'I can't say exactly. You don't look quite yourself, sir,' Franklin owned up.

" 'You seem to have a confoundedly piercing eye,' said the captain in such an aggressive tone that Franklin was moved to defend himself.

" 'We have been together now over six years, sir, so I suppose I know you a bit by this time. I could see there was something wrong directly you came on board.'

" 'Mr. Franklin,' said the captain, 'we have been more than six years together, it is true, but I didn't know you for a reader of faces. You are not a correct reader

though. It's very far from being wrong. You understand?
As far from being wrong as it can very well be. It ought
to teach you not to make rash surmises. You should leave
that to the shore people. They are great hands at spying
out something wrong. I dare say they know what they
have made of the world. A dam' poor job they make of
it, and that's plain. The world is a confoundedly ugly
place, Mr. Franklin. You don't know anything of it?
Well—no, we sailors don't. Only now and then one of
us runs against something cruel or underhand, enough to
make your hair stand on end. And when you do see a
piece of their wickedness you find that to set it right is
not so easy as it looks. . . . Oh! I called you back to tell
you that there will be a lot of workmen, joiners and all
that, sent down on board first thing to-morrow morning
to start making alterations in the cabin. You will see to
it that they don't loaf. There isn't much time.'

"Franklin was impressed by this unexpected lecture
upon the wickedness of the solid world surrounded by
the salt, uncorruptible waters on which he and his captain
had dwelt all their lives in happy innocence. What he
could not understand was why it should have been delivered, and what connection it could have with such a matter as the alterations to be carried out in the cabin. The
work did not seem to him to be called for in such a
hurry. What was the use of altering anything? It was a
very good accommodation, spacious, well-distributed, on
a rather old-fashioned plan, and with its decorations
somewhat tarnished. But a dab of varnish, a touch of
gilding here and there, was all that was necessary. As to
comfort, it could not be improved by any alterations. He
resented the notion of change; but he said dutifully that
he would keep his eye on the workmen if the captain
would only let him know what was the nature of the
work he had ordered to be done.

" 'You'll find a note of it on this table. I'll leave it for
you as I go ashore,' said Captain Anthony hastily. Franklin thought there was no more to hear, and made a movement to leave the saloon. But the captain continued after
a slight pause, 'You will be surprised, no doubt, when
you look at it. There'll be a good many alterations. It's
on account of a lady coming with us. I am going to get
married, Mr. Franklin!'

CHAPTER TWO

Young Powell Sees and Hears

"You remember," went on Marlow, "how I feared that Mr. Powell's want of experience would stand in his way of appreciating the unusual. The unusual I had in my mind was something of a very subtle sort: the unusual in marital relations. I may well have doubted the capacity of a young man too much concerned with the creditable performance of his professional duties to observe what in the nature of things is not easily observable in itself, and still less so under the special circumstances. In the majority of ships a second officer has not many points of contact with the captain's wife. He sits at the same table with her at meals, generally speaking; he may now and then be addressed more or less kindly on insignificant matters, and have the opportunity to show her some small attentions on deck. And that is all. Under such conditions, signs can be seen only by a sharp and practised eye. I am alluding now to troubles which are subtle often to the extent of not being understood by the very hearts they devastate or uplift.

"Yes, Mr. Powell, whom the chance of his name had thrown upon the floating stage of that tragi-comedy, would have been perfectly useless for my purpose if the unusual of an obvious kind had not aroused his attention from the first.

"We know how he joined that ship so suddenly offered to his anxious desire to make a real start in his profession. He had come on board breathless with the hurried winding up of his shore affairs, accompanied by two horrible night-birds, escorted by a dock policeman on the make, received by an asthmatic shadow of a ship-keeper, warned not to make a noise in the darkness of the passage because the captain and his wife were already on board. That in itself was already somewhat unusual. Captains and their wives do not, as a rule, join a moment sooner than is necessary. They prefer to spend the last moments with their friends and relations. A ship in one of London's older docks with their restrictions as to lights and so on is not the place for a happy evening. Still as the tide served at six in the morning, one could understand them coming on board the evening before.

"Just then young Powell felt as if anybody ought to be glad enough to be quit of the shore. We know he was an orphan from a very early age, without brothers or sisters—no near relations of any kind, I believe, except that aunt who had quarrelled with his father. No affections stood in the way of the quiet satisfaction with which he thought that now all the worries were over, that there was nothing before him but duties, that he knew what he would have to do as soon as the dawn broke and for a long succession of days. A most soothing certitude. He enjoyed it in the dark, stretched out in his bunk with his new blankets pulled over him. Some clock ashore beyond the dock-gates struck two. And then he heard nothing more, because he went off into a light sleep from which he woke up with a start. He had not taken his clothes off, it was hardly worth while. He jumped up and went on deck.

"The morning was clear, colourless, grey overhead; the dock like a sheet of darkling glass crowded with upside-down reflections of warehouses, of hulls and masts of silent ships. Rare figures moved here and there on the distant quays. A knot of men stood alongside with clothes-bags and wooden chests at their feet. Others were coming down the lane between tall, blind walls, surrounding a hand-cart loaded with more bags and boxes.

It was the crew of the *Ferndale*. They began to come on board. He scanned their faces as they passed forward filling the roomy deck with the shuffle of their footsteps and the murmur of voices, like the awakening to life of a world about to be launched into space.

"Far away down the clear glassy stretch in the middle of the long dock, Mr. Powell watched the tugs coming in quietly through the open gates. A subdued firm voice behind him interrupted this contemplation. It was Franklin, the thick chief mate, who was addressing him with a watchful appraising stare of his prominent black eyes: 'You'd better take a couple of these chaps with you and look out for her aft. We are going to cast off.'

" 'Yes, sir,' Powell said with proper alacrity; but for a moment they remained looking at each other fixedly. Something like a faint smile altered the set of the chief mate's lips just before he moved off forward with his brisk step.

"Mr. Powell, getting up on the poop, touched his cap to Captain Anthony, who was there alone. He tells me that it was only then that he saw his captain for the first time. The day before, in the shipping office, what with the bad light and his excitement at this berth obtained as if by a brusque and unscrupulous miracle, did not count. He had then seemed to him much older and heavier. He was surprised at the lithe figure, broad of shoulder, narrow at the hips, the fire of the deep-set eyes, the springiness of the walk. The captain gave him a steady stare, nodded slightly, and went on pacing the poop with an air of not being aware of what was going on, his head rigid, his movements rapid.

"Powell stole several glances at him with a curiosity very natural under the circumstances. He wore a short grey jacket and a grey cap. In the light of the dawn, growing more limpid rather than brighter, Powell noticed the slightly sunken cheeks under the trimmed beard, the perpendicular fold on the forehead, something hard and set about the mouth.

"It was too early yet for the work to have begun in the dock. The water gleamed placidly, no movement anywhere on the long straight lines of the quays, no one about to be seen except the few dock hands busy alongside the *Ferndale*, knowing their work, mostly silent or

exchanging a few words in low tones as if they, too, had
been aware of that lady 'who mustn't be disturbed.' The
Ferndale was the only ship to leave that tide. The others
seemed still asleep, without a sound, and only here and
there a figure, coming up on the forecastle, leaned on
the rail to watch the proceedings idly. Without trouble
and fuss and almost without a sound was the *Ferndale*
leaving the land, as if stealing away. Even the tugs, now
with their engines stopped, were approaching her without
a ripple, the burly-looking paddle-boat sheering forward,
while the other, a screw, smaller and of slender shape,
made for her quarter so gently that she did not divide
the smooth water, but seemed to glide on its surface as
if on a sheet of plate-glass, a man in her bow, the master
at the wheel visible only from the waist upwards above
the white screen of the bridge, both of them so still-eyed
as to fascinate young Powell into curious self-forgetfulness
and immobility. He was steeped, sunk in the general
quietness, remembering the statement 'she's a lady that
mustn't be disturbed,' and repeating to himself idly: 'No.
She won't be disturbed. She won't be disturbed.' Then
the first loud words of that morning breaking that strange
hush of departure with a sharp hail: 'Look out for that
line there,' made him start. The line whizzed past his
head, one of the sailors aft caught it, and there was an
end to the fascination, to the quietness of spirit which
had stolen on him at the very moment of departure.
From that moment till two hours afterwards, when the
ship was brought up in one of the lower reaches of the
Thames of an apparently uninhabited shore, near some
sort of inlet where nothing but two anchored barges flying a red flag could be seen, Powell was too busy to
think of the lady 'that mustn't be disturbed,' or of his
captain—or of anything else unconnected with his immediate duties. In fact, he had no occasion to go on the
poop or even look that way much; but while the ship was
about to anchor, casting his eyes in that direction, he
received an absurd impression that his captain (he was
up there, of course) was sitting on both sides of the
aftermost skylight at once. He was too occupied to reflect
on this curious delusion, this phenomenon of seeing double as though he had had a drop too much. He only
smiled at himself.

"As often happens after a grey daybreak the sun had risen in a warm and glorious splendour above the smooth immense gleam of the enlarged estuary. Wisps of mist floated like trails of luminous dust, and in the dazzling reflections of water and vapour, the shores had the murky, semi-transparent darkness of shadows cast mysteriously from below. Powell, who had sailed out of London all his young seaman's life, told me that it was then, in a moment of entranced vision an hour or so after sunrise, that the river was revealed to him for all time, like a fair face often seen before, which is suddenly perceived to be the expression of an inner and unsuspected beauty, of that something unique and only its own which rouses a passion of wonder and fidelity and an unappeasable memory of its charm. The hull of the *Ferndale,* swung head to the eastward, caught the light, her tall spars and rigging steeped in a bath of red-gold, from the water-line full of glitter to the trucks slight and gleaming against the delicate expanse of the blue.

" 'Time we had a mouthful to eat,' said a voice at his side. It was Mr. Franklin, the chief mate, with his head sunk between his shoulders, and melancholy eyes. 'Let the men have their breakfast, bo'sun,' he went on, 'and have the fire out in the galley in half an hour at the latest, so that we can call these barges of explosives alongside. Come along, young man. I don't know your name. Haven't seen the captain, to speak to, since yesterday afternoon when he rushed off to pick up a second mate somewhere. How did he get you?'

"Young Powell, a little shy notwithstanding the friendly disposition of the other, answered him smilingly, aware somehow that there was something marked in this inquisitiveness, natural, after all—something anxious. His name was Powell, and he was put in the way of this berth by Mr. Powell, the shipping master. He blushed.

" 'Ah, I see. Well, you have been smart in getting ready. The ship-keeper, before he went away, told me you joined at one o'clock. I didn't sleep on board last night. Not I. There was a time when I never cared to leave this ship for more than a couple of hours in the evening, even while in London, but now, since——'

"He checked himself with a roll of his prominent eyes towards that youngster, that stranger. Meantime, he was leading the way across the quarter-deck under the poop into the long passage with the door of the saloon at the far end. It was shut. But Mr. Franklin did not go so far. After passing the pantry he opened suddenly a door on the left of the passage, to Powell's great surprise.

" 'Our mess-room,' he said, entering a small cabin painted white, bare, lighted from part of the foremost skylight, and furnished only with a table and two settees with movable backs. 'That surprises you? Well, it isn't usual. And it wasn't so in this ship either, before. It's only since——'

"He checked himself again. 'Yes. Here we shall feed, you and I, facing each other for the next twelve months or more—God knows how much more! The bo'sun keeps the deck at meal-times in fine weather.'

"He talked not exactly wheezing, but like a man whose breath is somewhat short, and the spirit (young Powell could not help thinking) embittered by some mysterious grievance.

"There was enough of the unusual there to be recognized even by Powell's inexperience. The officers kept out of the cabin against the custom of the service, and then this sort of accent in the mate's talk. Franklin did not seem to expect conversational ease from the new second mate. He made several remarks about the old, deploring the accident. Awkward. Very awkward this thing to happen on the very eve of sailing.

" 'Collar-bone and arm broken,' he sighed. 'Sad, very sad. Did you notice if the captain was at all affected? Eh? Must have been.'

"Before this congested face, these globular eyes turned yearningly upon him, young Powell (one must keep in mind he was but a youngster then) who could not remember any signs of visible grief, confessed with an embarrassed laugh that, owing to the suddenness of this lucky chance coming to him, he was not in a condition to notice the state of other people.

" 'I was so pleased to get a ship at last,' he murmured, further disconcerted by the sort of pent-up gravity in Mr. Franklin's aspect.

" 'One man's food another man's poison,' the mate remarked. 'That holds true beyond mere victuals. I sup-

pose it didn't occur to you that it was a dam' poor way
for a good man to be knocked out.'

"Mr. Powell admitted openly that he had not thought
of that. He was ready to admit that it was very reprehensible of him. But Franklin had no intention apparently
to moralize. He did not fall silent either. His further
remarks were to the effect that there had been a time
when Captain Anthony would have showed more than
enough concern for the least thing happening to one of
his officers. Yes, there had been a time!

" 'And mind,' he went on, laying down suddenly a
half-consumed piece of bread and butter and raising his
voice, 'poor Mathews was the second man the longest on
board. I was the first. He joined a month later—about
the same time as the steward by a few days. The bo'sun
and the carpenter came the voyage after. Steady men.
Still here. No good man need ever have thought of leaving the *Ferndale* unless he were a fool. Some good men
are fools. Don't know when they are well off. I mean
the best of good men; men that you would do anything
for. They go on for years, then all of a sudden——'

"Our young friend listened to the mate with a queer
sense of discomfort growing on him. For it was as though
Mr. Franklin were thinking aloud, and putting him into
the delicate position of an unwilling eavesdropper. But
there was in the mess-room another listener. It was the
steward, who had come in carrying a tin coffee-pot with
a long handle, and stood quietly by: a man with a middle-
aged, sallow face, long features, heavy eyelids, a soldierly
grey moustache. His body encased in a short black jacket
with narrow sleeves, his long legs in very tight trousers,
made up an agile, youthful, slender figure. He moved forward suddenly, and interrupted the mate's monologue.

" 'More coffee, Mr. Franklin? Nice fresh lot. Piping
hot. I am going to give breakfast to the saloon directly,
and the cook is raking his fire out. Now's your chance.'

"The mate who, on account of his peculiar build, could
not turn his head freely, twisted his thick trunk slightly,
and ran his black eyes in the corners towards the steward.

" 'And is the precious pair of them out?' he growled.

"The steward, pouring out the coffee into the mate's
cup, muttered moodily but distinctly: 'The lady wasn't
when I was laying the table.'

"Powell's ears were fine enough to detect something hostile in this reference to the captain's wife. For of what other person could they be speaking? The steward added with a gloomy sort of fairness: 'But she will be before I bring the dishes in. She never gives that sort of trouble. That she doesn't.'

" 'No. Not in that way,' Mr. Franklin agreed, and then both he and the steward, after glancing at Powell—the stranger to the ship—said nothing more.

"But this had been enough to rouse his curiosity. Curiosity is natural to man. Of course it was not a malevolent curiosity which, if not exactly natural, is to be met fairly frequently in men and perhaps more frequently in women—especially if a woman be in question; and that woman under a cloud, in a manner of speaking. For under a cloud Flora de Barral was fated to be even at sea. Yes. That sort of darkness which attends a woman for whom there is no clear place in the world hung over her. Yes. Even at sea!

"And this is the pathos of being a woman. A man can struggle to get a place for himself or perish. But a woman's part is passive, say what you like, and shuffle the facts of the world as you may, hinting at lack of energy, of wisdom, of courage. As a matter of fact, almost all women have all that—of their own kind. But they are not made for attack. Wait they must. I am speaking here of women who are really women. And it's no use talking of opportunities, either. I know that some of them do talk of it. But not the genuine women. Those know better. Nothing can beat a true woman for a clear vision of reality; I would say a cynical vision if I were not afraid of wounding your chivalrous feelings—for which, by the by, women are not so grateful as you may think, to fellows of your kind. . . ."

"Upon my word, Marlow," I cried, "what are you flying out at me for like this? I wouldn't use an ill-sounding word about women, but what right have you to imagine that I am looking for gratitude?"

Marlow raised a soothing hand.

"There! There! I take back the ill-sounding word, with the remark, though, that cynicism seems to me a word invented by hypocrites. But let that pass. As to women, they know that the clamour for opportunities for them to become something which they cannot be is as reasonable as if mankind at large started asking for opportunities of winning immortality in this world, in which death is the very condition of life. You must understand that I am not talking here of material existence. That naturally is implied; but you won't maintain that a woman who, say, enlisted for instance (there have been cases) has conquered her place in the world. She has only got her living in it—which is quite meritorious, but not quite the same thing.

"All these reflections which arise from my picking up the thread of Flora de Barral's existence did not, I am certain, present themselves to Mr. Powell—not the Mr. Powell we know, taking solitary week-end cruises in the estuary of the Thames (with mysterious dashes into lonely creeks), but to the young Mr. Powell, the chance second officer of the ship *Ferndale,* commanded (and for the most part owned) by Roderick Anthony, the son of the poet—you know. A Mr. Powell, much slenderer than our robust friend is now, with the bloom of innocence not quite rubbed off his smooth cheeks, and apt not only to be interested but also to be surprised by the experience life was holding in store for him. This would account for his remembering so much of it with considerable vividness. For instance, the impressions attending his first breakfast on board the *Ferndale,* both visual and mental, were as fresh to him as if received yesterday.

"The surprise, it is easy to understand, would arise from the inability to interpret aright the signs which experience (a thing mysterious in itself) makes to our understanding and emotions. For it is never more than that. Our experience never gets into our blood and bones. It always remains outside of us. That's why we look with wonder at the past. And this persists even when from practice and through growing callousness of fibre we come to the point when nothing that we meet in that rapid blinking stumble across a flick of sunshine—which our life is—nothing, I say which we run against surprises us any more. Not at the time, I mean. If, later on, we recover the faculty with some such exclamation: 'Well! Well! I'll be hanged if I ever, ...' it is probably because this very thing that there should be a past to look back upon, other people's, is very astounding in itself when one has the time, a fleeting and immense instant to think of it . . ."

I was on the point of interrupting Marlow when he stopped of himself, his eyes fixed on vacancy, or—perhaps—(I wouldn't be too hard on him) on a vision. He has the habit, or, say, the fault, of defective mantel-piece clocks, of suddenly stopping in the very fullness of the tick. If you have ever lived with a clock afflicted with that perversity, you know how vexing it is—such a stoppage. I was vexed with Marlow. He was smiling faintly while I waited. He even laughed a little. And then I said acidly— "Am I to understand that you have ferreted out something comic in the history of Flora de Barral?"

"Comic!" he exclaimed. "No! What makes you say? Oh, I laughed—did I? But don't you know that people laugh at absurdities that are very far from being comic? Didn't you read the latest books about laughter written by philosophers, psychologists? There is a lot of them . . ."

"I dare say there has been a lot of nonsense written about laughter—and tears, too, for that matter," I said impatiently.

"They say," pursued the unabashed Marlow, "that we laugh from a sense of superiority. Therefore, observe, simplicity, honesty, warmth of feeling, delicacy of heart and of conduct, self-confidence, magnanimity are laughed at, because the presence of these traits in a man's character often puts him into difficult, cruel or absurd situations, and makes us, the majority who are fairly free as a rule from these peculiarities, feel pleasantly superior."

"Speak for yourself," I said. "But have you discovered all these fine things in the story; or has Mr. Powell discovered them to you in his artless talk? Have you two been having good healthy laughs together? Come! Are your sides aching yet, Marlow?"

Marlow took no offence at my banter. He was quite serious.

"I should not like to say off-hand how much of that there was," he pursued with amusing caution. "But there was a situation, tense enough for the signs of it to give many surprises to Mr. Powell—neither of them shocking in itself, but with a cumulative effect which made the whole unforgettable in the detail of its progress. And the first surprise came very soon, when the explosives (to which he owed his sudden chance of engagement)—dynamite in cases and blasting powder in barrels—taken on board, main hatch battened for sea, cook restored to his functions in the galley, anchor fished and the tug ahead, rounding the South Foreland, and with the sun sinking clear and red down the purple vista of the channel, he went on the poop, on duty, it is true, but with time to take the first freer breath in the busy day of departure. The pilot was still on board, who gave him first a silent glance, and then passed an insignificant remark before resuming his lounging to and fro between the steering wheel and the binnacle. Powell took his station modestly at the break of the poop. He had noticed across the skylight a head in a grey cap. But when, after a time, he crossed over to the other side of the deck he discovered that it was not the captain's head at all. He became aware of grey hairs curling over the nape of the neck. How could he have made that mistake? But on board ship away from the land one does not expect to come upon a stranger.

"Powell walked past the man. A thin, somewhat sunken face, with a tightly closed mouth, stared at the distant French coast, vague like a suggestion of solid darkness, lying abeam beyond the evening light reflected from the level waters, themselves growing more sombre than the sky; a stare, across which Powell had to pass and did pass with a quick side glarce, noting its immovable stillness. His passage disturbed those eyes no more than if he had been as immaterial as a ghost. And this failure of his person in producing an impression affected him strangely. Who could that old man be?

"He was so curious that he even ventured to ask the pilot in a low voice. The pilot turned out to be a good-natured specimen of his kind, condescending, sententious. He had been down to his meals in the main cabin, and had something to impart.

" 'That? Queer fish—eh? Mrs. Anthony's father. I've been introduced to him in the cabin at breakfast-time. Name of Smith. Wonder if he has all his wits about him. They take him about with them it seems. Don't look very happy—eh?'

"Then, changing his tone abruptly, he desired Powell to get all hands on deck and make sail on the ship. 'I shall be leaving you in half an hour. You'll have plenty of time to find out all about the old gent,' he added with a thick laugh.

"In the secret emotion of giving his first order as a fully responsible officer, young Powell forgot the very existence of that old man in a moment. The following days, in the interest of getting in touch with the ship, with the men in her, with his duties, in the rather anxious period of settling down, his curiosity slumbered; for of course the pilot's few words had not extinguished it.

"This settling down was made easy for him by the friendly character of his immediate superior—the chief mate. Powell could not defend himself from some sympathy for that thick, bald man, comically shaped, with his crimson complexion and something pathetic in the rolling of his very movable black eyes in an apparently immovable head, who was so tactfully ready to take his competency for granted.

"There can be nothing more reassuring to a young man tackling his life's work for the first time. Mr. Powell, his mind at ease about himself, had time to observe the people around with friendly interest. Very early in the beginning of the passage, he had discovered with some amusement that the marriage of Captain Anthony was resented by those to whom Powell (conscious of being looked upon as something of an outsider) referred in his mind as 'the old lot.'

"They had the funny, regretful glances, intonations, nods of men who had seen other, better times. What difference it could have made to the bo'sun and the carpenter Powell could not very well understand. Yet these two pulled long faces and even gave hostile glances to the poop. The cook and the steward might have been more directly concerned. But the steward used to remark on occasion, 'Oh, she gives no extra trouble,' with a scrupulous fairness of the most gloomy kind. He was rather a silent man with a great sense of his personal worth which made his speeches guarded. The cook, a neat man with fair side whiskers, who had been only three years in the ship, seemed the least concerned. He was even known to have inquired once or twice as to the success of some of his dishes with the captain's wife. This was considered a sort of disloyal falling away from the ruling feeling.

"The mate's annoyance was yet the easiest to understand. As he let it out to Powell before the first week of the passage was over: 'You can't expect me to be pleased at being chucked out of the saloon as if I weren't good enough to sit down to meat with that woman.' But he hastened to add: 'Don't you think I'm blaming the captain. He isn't a man to be found fault with. You, Mr. Powell, are too young yet to understand such matters.'

"Some considerable time afterwards, at the end of a conversation of that aggrieved sort, he enlarged a little more by repeating: 'Yes! You are too young to understand these things. I don't say you haven't plenty of sense. You are doing very well here. Jolly sight better than I expected, though I liked your looks from the first.'

"It was in the trade-winds, at night, under a velvety, bespangled sky, a great multitude of stars watching the shadows of the sea gleaming mysteriously in the wake of the ship; while the leisurely swishing of the water to leeward was like a drowsy comment on her progress. Mr. Powell expressed his satisfaction by a half-bashful laugh. The mate mused on: 'And of course you haven't known the ship as she used to be. She was more than a home to a man. She was not like any other ship; and Captain Anthony was not like any other master to sail with. Neither is she now. But before one never had a care in the world as to her—and as to him, too. No, indeed, there was never anything to worry about.'

"Young Powell couldn't see what there was to worry about even then. The serenity of the peaceful night seemed as vast as all space and as enduring as eternity itself. It's true the sea is an uncertain element, but no sailor remembers this in the presence of its bewitching power any more than a lover ever thinks of the proverbial inconstancy of women. And Mr. Powell, being young, thought naïvely that the captain being married, there could be no occasion for anxiety as to his condition. I suppose that to him life, perhaps not so much his own as that of others, was something still in the nature of a fairy-tale with a 'they lived happy ever after' termination.

We are the creatures of our light literature much more than is generally suspected in a world which prides itself on being scientific and practical, and in possession of incontrovertible theories. Powell felt in that way the more because the captain of a ship at sea is a remote, inaccessible creature something like a prince of a fairy-tale, alone of his kind, depending on nobody, not to be called to account except by powers practically invisible and so distant, that they might well be looked upon as supernatural for all that the rest of the crew knows of them, as a rule.

"So he did not understand the aggrieved attitude of the mate—or rather he understood it obscurely as a result of simple causes which did not seem to him adequate. He would have dismissed all this out of his mind with a contemptuous: 'What the devil do I care?' if the captain's wife herself had not been so young. To see her the first time had been something of a shock to him. He had some preconceived ideas as to captains' wives which, while he did not believe the testimony of his eyes, made him open them very wide. He had stared till the captain's wife noticed it plainly and turned her face away. Captain's wife! That girl covered with rugs in a long chair. Captain's . . . ! He gasped mentally. It had never occurred to him that a captain's wife could be anything but a woman to be described as stout or thin, as jolly or crabbed, but always mature, and even, in comparison with his own years, frankly old. But this! It was a sort of moral upset as though he had discovered a case of abduction or something as surprising as that. You understand that nothing is more disturbing than the upsetting of a preconceived idea. Each of us arranges the world according to his own notion of the fitness of things. To behold a girl where your average mediocre imagination had placed a comparatively old woman may easily become one of the strongest shocks . . ."

Marlow paused, smiling to himself.

"Powell remained impressed after all these years by the very recollection," he continued in a voice, amused perhaps but not mocking. "He said to me only the other day with something like the first awe of that discovery lingering in his tone—he said to me: 'Why, she seemed so young, so girlish, that I looked round for some woman who would be the captain's wife, though of course I knew there was no other woman on board that voyage.' The voyage before, it seems, there had been the steward's wife to act as maid to Mrs. Anthony; but she was not taken that time for some reason he didn't know. Mrs. Anthony . . . ! If it hadn't been the captain's wife he would have referred to her mentally as a kid, he said. I suppose there must be a sort of divinity hedging in a captain's wife (however incredible) which prevented him applying to her that contemptuous definition in the secret of his thoughts.

"I asked him when this had happened; and he told me that it was three days after parting from the tug, just outside the channel—to be precise. A head wind had set in with unpleasant damp weather. He had come up to leeward of the poop, still feeling very much of a stranger, and an untried officer, at six in the evening to take his watch. To see her was quite as unexpected as seeing a vision. When she turned away her head he recollected himself and dropped his eyes. What he could see then was only, close to the long chair on which she reclined, a pair of long thin legs ending in black cloth boots tucked in close to the skylight seat. Whence he concluded that the 'old gentleman,' who wore a grey cap like the captain's, was sitting by her—his daughter. In his first astonishment he had stopped dead short, with the consequence that now he felt very much abashed at having betrayed his surprise. But he couldn't very well turn tail and bolt off the poop. He had come here on duty. So, still with downcast eyes, he made his way past them. Only when he got as far as the wheel-grating did he look up. She was hidden from him by the back of her deck-chair; but he had the view of the owner of the thin, aged legs seated on the skylight, his clean-shaved cheek, his thin compressed mouth with a hollow in each corner, the sparse grey locks escaping from under the tweed cap, and curling slightly on the collar of the coat. He leaned forward a little over Mrs. Anthony, but they were not talking. Captain Anthony, walking with a springy hurried gait on the other side of the poop from end to end, gazed straight before him. Young Powell might have thought that his captain was not aware of his presence either. However, he knew better, and for that reason spent a

most uncomfortable hour motionless by the compass
before his captain stopped in his swift pacing and with
an almost visible effort made some remark to him about
the weather in a low voice. Before Powell, who was startled, could find a word of answer, the captain swung off
again on his endless tramp with a fixed gaze. And till the
supper bell rang silence dwelt over that poop like an evil
spell. The captain walked up and down looking straight
before him, the helmsman steered, looking upwards at
the sails, the old gent on the skylight looked down on
his daughter—and Mr. Powell confessed to me that he
didn't know where to look, feeling as though he had
blundered in where he had no business—which was
absurd. At last he fastened his eyes on the compass card,
took refuge, in spirit, inside the binnacle. He felt chilled
more than he should have been by the chilly dusk falling
on the muddy green sea of the soundings from a
smoothly clouded sky. A fitful wind swept the cheerless
waste, and the ship, hauled up so close as to check her
way, seemed to progress by languid fits and starts against
the short seas which swept along her sides with a snarling
sound.

"Young Powell thought that this was the dreariest evening aspect of the sea he had ever seen. He was glad
when the other occupants of the poop left it at the sound
of the bell. The captain first, with a sudden swerve in his
walk towards the companion and not even looking once
towards his wife and his wife's father. Those two got up
and moved towards the companion, the old gent very
erect, his thin locks stirring gently about the nape of his
neck, and carrying the rugs over his arm. The girl who
was Mrs. Anthony went down first. The murky twilight
had settled in deep shadow on her face. She looked at
Mr. Powell in passing. He thought that she was very
pale. Cold perhaps. The old gent stopped a moment, thin
and stiff, before the young man, and in a voice which
was low but distinct enough, and without any particular
accent—not even of inquiry—he said—

" 'You are the new second officer, I believe.'

"Mr. Powell answered in the affirmative, wondering if
this was a friendly overture. He had noticed that Mr.
Smith's eyes had a sort of inward look as though he had
disliked or disdained his surroundings. The captain's wife

had disappeared then down the companion stairs. Mr. Smith said 'Ah!' and waited a little longer to put another question in his incurious voice.

" 'And did you know the man who was here before you?'

" 'No,' said young Powell, 'I didn't know anybody belonging to this ship before I joined.'

" 'He was much older than you. Twice your age. Perhaps more. His hair was iron grey. Yes. Certainly more.'

The low, repressed voice paused, but the old man did not move away. He added: 'Isn't it unusual?'

"Mr. Powell was surprised not only by being engaged in conversation, but also by its character. It might have been the suggestion of the word uttered by this old man, but it was distinctly at that moment that he became aware of something unusual not only in this encounter but generally around him, about everybody, in the atmosphere. The very sea, with short flashes of foam bursting out here and there in the gloomy distances, the unchangeable, safe sea sheltering a man from all passions, except its own anger, seemed queer to the quick glance he threw to windward where the already effaced horizon traced no reassuring limit to the eye. In the expiring, diffused twilight, and before the clouded night dropped its mysterious veil, it was the immensity of space made visible— almost palpable. Young Powell felt it. He felt it in the sudden sense of his isolation; the trustworthy, powerful ship of his first acquaintance reduced to a speck, to something almost undistinguishable, the mere support for the soles of his two feet before that unexpected old man becoming so suddenly articulate in a darkening universe.

"It took him a moment or so to seize the drift of the question. He repeated slowly: 'Unusual. . . . Oh, you mean for an elderly man to be the second of a ship. I don't know. There are a good many of us who don't get on. He didn't get on, I suppose.'

"The other, his head bowed a little, had the air of listening with acute attention.

" 'And now he has been taken to the hospital,' he said.

" 'I believe so. Yes. I remember Captain Anthony saying so in the shipping office.'

" 'Possibly about to die,' went on the old man, in his

careful deliberate tone. 'And perhaps glad enough to die.'

"Mr. Powell was young enough to be startled at the suggestion, which sounded confidential and blood-curdling in the dusk. He said sharply that it was not very likely, as if defending the absent victim of the accident from an unkind aspersion. He felt, in fact, indignant. The other emitted a short stifled laugh of a conciliatory nature. The second bell rang under the poop. He made a movement at the sound, but lingered.

" 'What I said was not meant seriously,' he murmured with that strange air of fearing to be overheard. 'Not in this case. I know the man.'

"The occasion, or rather the want of occasion, for this conversation, had sharpened the perceptions of the unsophisticated second officer of the *Ferndale*. He was alive to the slightest shade of tone, and felt as if this 'I know the man' should have been followed by a 'he was no friend of mine.' But after the shortest possible break the old gentleman continued to murmur distinctly and evenly—

" 'Whereas you have never seen him. Nevertheless when you have gone through as many years as I have, you will understand how an event putting an end to one's existence may not be altogether unwelcome. Of course there are stupid accidents. And even then one needn't be very angry. What is it to be deprived of life? It's soon done. But what would you think of the feelings of a man who should have had his life stolen from him? Cheated out of it, I say!'

"He ceased abruptly, and remained still long enough for the astonished Powell to stammer out an indistinct: 'What do you mean? I don't understand.' Then, with a low 'Good-night' glided a few steps, and sank through the shadow of the companion into the lamplight below which did not reach higher than the turn of the staircase.

"The strange words, the cautious tone, the whole person left a strong uneasiness in the mind of Mr. Powell. He started walking the poop in great mental confusion. He felt all adrift. This was funny talk and no mistake. And this cautious low tone as though he were watched by someone was more than funny. The young second officer hesitated to break the established rule of every ship's discipline; but at last could not resist the temptation of getting hold of some other human being, and spoke to the man at the wheel.

" 'Did you hear what this gentleman was saying to me?'

" 'No, sir,' answered the sailor quietly. Then, encouraged by this evidence of laxity in his officer, made bold to add, 'A queer fish, sir.' This was tentative, and Mr. Powell, busy with his own view, not saying anything, he ventured further. 'They are more like passengers. One sees some queer passengers.'

" 'Who are like passengers?' asked Powell gruffly.

" 'Why, these two, sir.'

CHAPTER THREE

Devoted Servants—and the Light of a Flare

"Young Powell thought to himself: 'The men, too, are noticing it.' Indeed, the captain's behaviour to his wife and to his wife's father was noticeable enough. It was as if they had been a pair of not very congenial passengers. But perhaps it was not always like that. The captain might have been put out by something.

"When the aggrieved Franklin came on deck Mr. Powell made a remark to that effect. For his curiosity was aroused.

"The mate grumbled 'Seems to you? . . . Put out? . . . eh?' He buttoned his thick jacket up to the throat, and only then added a gloomy 'Aye, likely enough,' which discouraged further conversation. But no encouragement would have induced the newly joined second mate to enter the way of confidences. His was an instinctive prudence. Powell did not know why it was he had resolved to keep his own counsel as to his colloquy with Mr. Smith. But his curiosity did not slumber. Some time afterwards again at the relief of watches in the course of a little talk he mentioned Mrs. Anthony's father quite casually, and tried to find out from the mate who he was.

" 'It would take a clever man to find that out as things

are on board now,' Mr. Franklin said, unexpectedly communicative. 'The first I saw of him was when she brought him alongside in a four-wheeler one morning about half-past eleven. The captain had come on board early, and was down in the cabin that had been fitted out for him. Did I tell you that if you want the captain for any thing you must stamp on the port side of the deck? That's so. This ship is not only unlike what she used to be, but she is like no other ship, anyhow. Did you ever hear of the captain's room being on the port side? Both of them stern cabins have been fitted up afresh like a blessed palace. A gang of people from some tip-top West-End house were fussing here on board with hangings and furniture for a fortnight, as if the Queen were coming with us. Of course the starboard cabin is the bedroom one, but the poor captain hangs out to port on a couch, so that in case we want him on deck at night, Mrs. Anthony should not be startled. Nervous! Phoo! A woman who marries a sailor and makes up her mind to come to sea should have no blamed jumpiness about her, I say. But never mind. Directly the old cab pointed round the corner of the warehouse I called out to the captain that his lady was coming aboard. He answered me, but as I didn't see him coming, I went down the gangway myself to help her alight. She jumps out excitedly without touching my arm, or as much as saying "thank you" or "good morning" or anything, turns back to the cab, and then that old joker comes out slowly. I hadn't noticed him inside. I hadn't expected to see anybody. It gave me a start. She says: "My father—Mr. Franklin." He was staring at me like an owl. "How do you do, sir?" says I. Both of them looked funny. It was as if something had happened to them on the way. Neither of them moved, and I stood by waiting. The captain showed himself on the poop; and I saw him at the side looking over, and then he disappeared; on the way to meet them on shore, I expected. But he just went down below again. So, not seeing him, I said: "Let me help you on board, sir." "On board!" says he in a silly fashion. "On board!" "It's not a very good ladder, but it's quite firm," says I, as he seemed to be afraid of it. And he didn't look a broken-down old man, either. You can see yourself what he is. Straight as a poker, and life enough in him yet. But he made no move, and I began to feel foolish. Then she comes forward. "Oh! Thank you, Mr. Franklin. I'll help my father up." Flabbergasted me—to be choked off like this. Pushed in between him and me without as much as a look my way. So of course I dropped it. What do you think? I fell back. I would have gone up on board at once and left them on the quay to come up or stay there till next week, only they were blocking the way. I couldn't very well shove them on one side. Devil only knows what was up between them. There she was, pale as death, talking to him very fast. He got as red as a turkeycock—dash me if he didn't. A bad-tempered old bloke, I can tell you. And a bad lot, too. Never mind. I couldn't hear what she was saying to him, but she put force enough into it to shake her. It seemed—it seemed, mind!—that he didn't want to go on board. Of course it couldn't have been that. I know better. Well, she took him by the arm above the elbow, as if to lead him or push him rather. I was standing not quite ten feet off. Why should I have gone away? I was anxious to get back on board as soon as they would let me. I didn't want to overhear her blamed whispering either. But I couldn't stay there for ever, so I made a move to get past them if I could. And that's how I heard a few words. It was the old chap—something nasty about being "under the heel" of somebody or other. Then he says, "I don't want this sacrifice." What it meant I can't tell. It was a quarrel—of that I am certain. She looks over her shoulder, and sees me pretty close to them. I don't know what she found to say into his ear, but he gave way suddenly. He looked round at me too, and they went up together so quickly then that when I got on the quarter-deck I was only in time to see the inner door of the passage close after them. Queer—eh? But if it were only queerness one wouldn't mind. Some luggage in new trunks came on board in the afternoon. We undocked at midnight. And may I be hanged if I know who or what he was or is. I haven't been able to find out. No, I don't know. He may have been anything. All I know is that once, years ago when I went to see the Derby with a friend, I saw a pea-and-thimble chap who looked just like that old mystery father out of a cab.'

"All this the goggle-eyed mate had said in a resentful

and melancholy voice, with pauses, to the gentle murmur
of the sea. It was for him a bitter sort of pleasure to
have a fresh pair of ears, a new-comer, to whom he could
repeat all these matters of grief and suspicion talked over
endlessly by the band of Captain Anthony's faithful sub-
ordinates. It was evidently so refreshing to his worried
spirit that it made him forget the advisability of a little
caution with a complete stranger. But really with Mr.
Powell there was no danger. Amused, at first, at these
plaints, he provoked them for fun. Afterwards, turning
them over in his mind, he became impressed; and as the
impression grew stronger with the days his resolution to
keep it to himself grew stronger too.

"What made it all the easier to keep—I mean the resolution—was that Powell's sentiment of amused surprise
at what struck him at first as mere absurdity was not
unmingled with indignation. And his years were too few,
his position too novel, his reliance on his own opinion
not yet firm enough to allow him to express it with any
effect. And then—what would have been the use, anyhow—and where was the necessity?

"But this thing, familiar and mysterious at the same
time, occupied his imagination. The solitude of the sea
intensifies the thoughts and the facts of one's experience
which seems to lie at the very centre of the world, as the
ship which carries one always remains the centre figure
of the round horizon. He viewed the apoplectic, goggle-
eyed mate and the saturnine, heavy-eyed steward as the
victims of a peculiar and secret form of lunacy which
poisoned their lives. But he did not give them his sympathy on that account. No. That strange affliction awakened in him a sort of suspicious wonder.

"Once—and it was at night again; for the officers of
the *Ferndale* keeping watch and watch as was customary
in those days, had but few occasions for intercourse—
once, I say, the thick Mr. Franklin, a quaintly bulky figure under the stars, the usual witnesses of his out-
pourings, asked him with an abruptness which was not
callous, but in his simple way—

" 'I believe you have no parents living?'

"Mr. Powell said that he had lost his father and mother
at a very early age.

" 'My mother is still alive,' declared Mr. Franklin in a tone which suggested that he was gratified by the fact. 'The old lady is lasting well. Of course she's got to be made comfortable. A woman must be looked after, and, if it comes to that, I say, give me a mother. I dare say if she had not lasted it out so well I might have gone and got married. I don't know, though. We sailors haven't got much time to look about us to any purpose. Anyhow, as the old lady was there I haven't, I may say, looked at a girl in all my life. Not that I wasn't partial to female society in my time,' he added with a pathetic intonation, while the whites of his goggle eyes gleamed amorously under the clear night sky. 'Very partial, I may say.'

"Mr. Powell was amused; and as these communications took place only when the mate was relieved off duty he had no serious objection to them. The mate's presence made the first half-hour and sometimes even more of his watch on deck pass away. If his senior did not mind losing some of his rest it was not Mr. Powell's affair. Franklin was a decent fellow. His intention was not to boast of his filial piety.

" 'Of course I mean respectable female society,' he explained. 'The other sort is neither here nor there. I blame no man's conduct, but a well-brought-up young fellow like you knows that there's precious little fun to be got out of it.' He fetched a deep sigh. 'I wish Captain Anthony's mother had been a lasting sort like my old lady. He would have had to look after her and he would have done it well. Captain Anthony is a proper man. And it would have saved him from the most foolish——'

He did not finish the phrase which certainly was turning bitter in his mouth. Mr. Powell thought to himself: 'There he goes again.' He laughed a little.

" 'I don't understand why you are so hard on the captain, Mr. Franklin. I thought you were a great friend of his.'

"Mr. Franklin exclaimed at this. He was not hard on the captain. Nothing was farther from his thoughts. Friend! Of course he was a good friend and a faithful servant. He begged Powell to understand that if Captain Anthony chose to strike a bargain with Old Nick tomorrow, and Old Nick were good to the captain, he (Franklin) would find it in his heart to love Old Nick for the captain's sake. That was so. On the other hand, if a saint, an angel with white wings came along and——

"He broke off short again as if his own vehemence had frightened him. Then in his strained pathetic voice (which he had never raised) he observed that it was no use talking. Anybody could see that the man was changed.

" 'As to that,' said young Powell, 'it is impossible for me to judge.'

" 'Good Lord!' whispered the mate. 'An educated, clever young fellow like you with a pair of eyes on him and some sense too! Is that how a happy man looks? Eh? Young you may be, but you aren't a kid; and I dare you to say "Yes!" '

"Mr. Powell did not take up the challenge. He did not know what to think of the mate's view. Still, it seemed as if it had opened his understanding in a measure. He conceded that the captain did not look very well.

" 'Not very well,' repeated the mate mournfully. 'Do you think a man with a face like that can hope to live his life out? You haven't knocked about long in this world yet, but you are a sailor, you have been in three or four ships, you say. Well, have you ever seen a shipmaster walking his own deck as if he did not know what he had underfoot? Have you? Dam'me if I don't think that he forgets where he is. Of course he can be no other than a prime seaman; but it's lucky, all the same, he has me on board. I know by this time what he wants done without being told. Do you know that I have had no order given me since we left port? Do you know that he has never once opened his lips to me unless I spoke to him first? I! His chief officer; his shipmate for full six years, with whom he had no cross word—not once in all that time. Aye. Not a cross look even. True that when I do make him speak to me, there is his dear old self, the quick eye, the kind voice. Could hardly be other to his old Franklin. But what's the good? Eyes, voice, everything's miles away. And for all that I take good care never to address him when the poop isn't clear. Yes! Only we two and nothing but the sea with us. You think it would be all right; the only chief mate he ever had—Mr. Franklin here and Mr. Franklin there—when anything went wrong the first word you would hear about the decks was "Franklin!"—I am thirteen years older than he is—you would think it would be all right, wouldn't you? Only we two on this poop on which we saw each other first—he a young master—told me that he thought I would suit him very well—we two, and thirty-one days out at sea, and it's no good! It's like talking to a man standing on shore. I can't get him back. I can't get at him. I feel sometimes as if I must shake him by the arm: "Wake up! Wake up! You are wanted, sir . . . !" '

"Young Powell recognized the expression of a true sentiment, a thing so rare in this world where there are so many mutes and so many excellent reasons even at sea for an articulate man not to give himself away, that he felt something like respect for this outburst. It was not loud. The grotesque squat shape, with the knob of the head as if rammed down between the square shoulders by a blow from a club, moved vaguely in a circumscribed space limited by the two harness-casks lashed to the front rail of the poop, without gestures, hands in the pockets of the jacket, elbows pressed closely to its side; and the voice without resonance, passed from anger to dismay and back again without a single louder word in the hurried delivery, interrupted only by slight gasps for air as if the speaker were being choked by the suppressed passion of his grief.

"Mr. Powell, though moved to a certain extent, was by no means carried away. And just as he thought that it was all over, the other, fidgeting in the darkness, was heard again explosive, bewildered but not very loud in the silence of the ship and the great empty peace of the sea.

" 'They have done something to him! What is it? What can it be? Can't you guess? Don't you know?'

" 'Good heavens!' Young Powell was astounded on discovering that this was an appeal addressed to him. 'How on earth can I know?'

" 'You do talk to that white-faced, black-eyed . . . I've seen you talking to her more than a dozen times.'

"Young Powell, his sympathy suddenly chilled, remarked in a disdainful tone that Mrs. Anthony's eyes were not black.

" 'I wish to God she had never set them on the captain, whatever colour they are,' retorted Franklin. 'She and that old chap with the scraped jaws who sits over her and stares down at her dead-white face with his yellow eyes—confound them! Perhaps you will tell us that his eyes are not yellow?'

"Powell, not interested in the colour of Mr. Smith's eyes, made a vague gesture. Yellow or not yellow, it was all one to him.

"The mate murmured to himself: 'No. He can't know. No! No more than a baby. It would take an older head.'

" 'I don't even understand what you mean,' observed Mr. Powell coldly.

" 'And even the best head would be puzzled by such devil-work,' the mate continued, muttering. 'Well, I have heard tell of women doing for a man in one way or another when they got him fairly ashore. But to bring their devilry to sea and fasten on such a man! . . . It's something I can't understand. But I can watch. Let them look out—I say!'

"His short figure, unable to stoop, without flexibility, could not express dejection. He was very tired suddenly; he dragged his feet going off the poop. Before he left it with nearly an hour of his watch below sacrificed, he addressed himself once more to our young man who stood abreast of the mizzen rigging in an unreceptive mood expressed by silence and immobility. He did not regret, he said, having spoken openly on this very serious matter.

" 'I don't know about its seriousness, sir,' was Mr. Powell's frank answer. 'But if you think you have been telling me something very new you are mistaken. You can't keep that matter out of your speeches. It's the sort of thing I've been hearing more or less ever since I came on board.'

"Mr. Powell, speaking truthfully, did not mean to speak offensively. He had instincts of wisdom; he felt that this was a serious affair, for it had nothing to do with reason. He did not want to raise an enemy for himself in the mate. And Mr. Franklin did not take offence. To Mr. Powell's truthful statement he answered with equal truth and simplicity that it was very likely, very likely. With a thing like that (next door to witchcraft almost) weighing on his mind, the wonder was that he could think of anything else. The poor man must have found in the

restlessness of his thoughts the illusion of being engaged
in an active contest with some power of evil; for his last
words as he went lingeringly down the poop ladder
expressed the quaint hope that he would get him, Powell,
'on our side yet.'

"Mr. Powell—just imagine a straightforward youngster
assailed in this fashion on the high seas—answered
merely by an embarrassed and uneasy laugh which
reflected exactly the state of his innocent soul. The apoplectic mate, already half-way down, went up again three
steps of the poop ladder. Why, yes. A proper young
fellow, the mate expected, wouldn't stand by and see a
man, a good sailor and his own skipper, in trouble without taking his part against a couple of shore people
who—Mr. Powell interrupted him impatiently, asking
what was the trouble?

" 'What is it you are hinting at?' he cried with an inexplicable irritation.

" 'I don't like to think of him all alone down there
with these two,' Franklin whispered impressively. 'Upon
my word I don't. God only knows what may be going on
there. . . . Don't laugh. . . . It was bad enough last voyage when Mrs. Brown had a cabin aft; but now it's worse.
It frightens me. I can't sleep sometimes for thinking of
him all alone there, shut off from us all.'

"Mrs. Brown was the steward's wife. You must understand that shortly after his visit to the Fyne cottage (with
all its consequences), Anthony had got an offer to go to
the Western Islands, and bring home the cargo of some
ship which, damaged in a collision or a stranding, took
refuge in St. Michael, and was condemned there. Roderick Anthony had connections which would put such pay-
ing jobs in his way. So Flora de Barral had but a five
months' voyage, a mere excursion, for her first trial of
sea-life. And Anthony, clearly trying to be most attentive, had induced this Mrs. Brown, the wife of his faithful
steward, to come along as maid to his bride. But for
some reason or other this arrangement was not continued. And the mate, tormented by indefinite alarms and
forebodings, regretted it. He regretted that Jane Brown
was no longer on board—as a sort of representative of
Captain Anthony's faithful servants, to watch quietly
what went on in that part of the ship this fatal marriage

had closed to their vigilance. That had been excellent. For she was a dependable woman.

"Powell did not detect any particular excellence in what seemed a spying employment. But in his simplicity he said that he should have thought Mrs. Anthony would have been glad anyhow to have another woman on board. He was thinking of the white-faced girlish personality which it seemed to him ought to have been cared for. The innocent young man always looked upon the girl as immature; something of a child yet.

" 'She! glad! Why it was she who had her fired out. She didn't want anybody around the cabin. Mrs. Brown is certain of it. She told her husband so. You ask the steward and hear what he has to say about it. That's why I don't like it. A capable woman who knew her place. But no. Out she must go. For no fault, mind you. The captain was ashamed to send her away. But that wife of his—aye, the precious pair of them have got hold of him. I can't speak to him for a minute on the poop without that thimble-rigging coon coming gliding up. I'll tell you what. I overheard once—God knows I didn't try to—only he forgot I was on the other side of the skylight with my sextant—I overheard him—you know how he sits hanging over her chair and talking away without properly opening his mouth—yes I caught the word right enough. He was alluding to the captain as "the jailer." The jail . . . !'

"Franklin broke off with a profane execration. A silence reigned for a long time and the slight, very gentle rolling of the ship slipping before the N.E. trade-wind seemed to be a soothing device for lulling to sleep the suspicions of men who trust themselves to the sea.

"A deep sigh was heard followed by the mate's voice asking dismally if that was the way one would speak of a man to whom one wished well? No better proof of something wrong was needed. Therefore he hoped, as he vanished at last, that Mr. Powell would be on their side. And this time Mr. Powell did not answer this hope with an embarrassed laugh.

"That young officer was more and more surprised at the nature of the incongruous revelations coming to him in the surroundings and in the atmosphere of the open sea. It is difficult for us to understand the extent, the completeness, the comprehensiveness of his inexperience, for us who didn't go to sea out of a small private school at the age of fourteen years and nine months. Leaning on his elbow in the mizzen rigging and so still that the helmsman over there at the other end of the poop might have (and he probably did) suspect him of being criminally asleep on duty, he tried to 'get hold of that thing' by some side which would fit in with his simple notions of psychology. 'What the deuce are they worrying about?' he asked himself in a dazed and contemptuous impatience. But all the same, 'jailer' was a funny name to give a man; unkind, unfriendly, nasty. He was sorry that Mr. Smith was guilty in that matter because, the truth must be told, he had been to a certain extent sensible of having been noticed in a quiet manner by the father of Mrs. Anthony. Youth appreciates that sort of recognition which is the subtlest form of flattery age can offer. Mr. Smith seized opportunities to approach him on deck. His remarks were sometimes weird and enigmatical. He was doubtless an eccentric old gent. But from that to calling his son-in-law (whom he never approached on deck) nasty names behind his back was a long step.

"And Mr. Powell marvelled. . . .

"While he was telling me all this"—Marlow changed his tone—"I marvelled even more. It was as if misfortune marked its victims on the forehead for the dislike of the crowd. I am not thinking here of numbers. Two men may behave like a crowd, three certainly will when their emotions are engaged. It was as if the forehead of Flora de Barral were marked. Was the girl born to be a victim; to be always disliked and crushed as if she were too fine for this world? Or too luckless—since that also is often counted as sin.

"Yes, I marvelled more since I knew more of the girl than Mr. Powell—if only her true name; and more of Captain Anthony—if only the fact that he was the son of a delicate erotic poet of a markedly refined and autocratic temperament. Yes, I know their joint stories which Mr. Powell did not know. The chapter in it he was opening to me, the sea-chapter, with such new personages as the sentimental and apoplectic chief-mate and the morose steward, however astounding to him in its detached condition was much more so to me as a member of a series, following the chapter outside the Eastern Hotel in which I myself had played my part. In view of her declarations and my sage remarks it was very unexpected. She had meant well, and I had certainly meant well too. Captain Anthony—as far as I could gather from little Fyne—had meant well. As far as such lofty words may be applied to the obscure personages of this story, we were all filled with the noblest sentiments and intentions. The sea was there to give them the shelter of its solitude free from the earth's petty suggestions. I could well marvel in myself, as to what had happened.

"I hope that if he saw it, Mr. Powell forgave me the smile of which I was guilty at that moment. The light in the cabin of his little cutter was dim. And the smile was dim too. Dim and fleeting. The girl's life had presented itself to me as a tragicomical adventure, the saddest thing on earth, slipping between frank laughter and unabashed tears. Yes, the saddest facts and the most common, and, being common, perhaps the most worthy of our unreserved pity.

"The purely human reality is capable of lyrism but not of abstraction. Nothing will serve for its understanding but the evidence of rational linking up of characters and facts. And beginning with Flora de Barral, in the light of my memories I was certain that she at least must have been passive; for that is of necessity the part of women, this waiting on fate which some of them, and not the most intelligent, cover up by the vain appearances of agitation. Flora de Barral was not exceptionally intelligent but she was thoroughly feminine. She would be passive (and that does not mean inanimate) in the circumstances, where the mere fact of being a woman was enough to give her an occult and supreme significance. And she would be enduring, which is the essence of woman's visible, tangible power. Of that I was certain. Had she not endured already? Yet it is so true that the germ of destruction lies in wait for us mortals, even at the very source of our strength, that one may die of too much endurance as well as of too little of it.

"Such was my train of thought. And I was mindful also of my first view of her—toying or perhaps communing in earnest with the possibilities of a precipice. But I did not ask Mr. Powell anxiously what had happened to Mrs. Anthony in the end. I let him go on in his own way, feeling that no matter what strange facts he would have to disclose, I was certain to know much more of them than he ever did know or could possibly guess. . . ."

Marlow paused for quite a long time. He seemed uncertain as though he had advanced something beyond my grasp. Purposely I made no sign. "You understand?" he asked.

"Perfectly," I said. "You are the expert in the psychological wilderness. This is like one of those Redskin stories where the noble savages carry off a girl and the honest backwoodsman with his incomparable knowledge follows the track and reads the signs of her fate in a footprint here, a broken twig there, a trinket dropped by the way. I have always liked such stories. Go on."

Marlow smiled indulgently at my jesting. "It is not exactly a story for boys," he said. "I go on then. The sign, as you call it, was not very plentiful but very much to the purpose, and when Mr. Powell heard (at a certain moment I felt bound to tell him), when he heard that I had known Mrs. Anthony before her marriage, that, to a certain extent, I was her confidant . . . For you can't deny that to a certain extent . . . Well, let us say that I had a look in. . . . A young girl, you know, is something like a temple. You pass by and wonder what mysterious rites are going on in there, what prayers, what visions? The privileged man, the lover, the husband, who are given the key of the sanctuary do not always know how to use it. For myself, without claim, without merit, simply by chance I had been allowed to look through the half-opened door and I had seen the saddest possible desecration, the withered brightness of youth, a spirit neither made cringing nor yet dulled but as if bewildered in quivering hopelessness by gratuitous cruelty; self-confidence destroyed and, instead, a resigned recklessness, a mournful callousness (and all this simple, almost naïve)—before the material and moral difficulties of the situation. The passive anguish of the luckless!

"I asked myself: wasn't that ill-luck exhausted yet? Ill-luck which is like the hate of invisible powers interpreted, made sensible and injurious by the actions of men?

"Mr. Powell as you may well imagine had opened his

eyes at my statement. But he was full of his recalled experiences on board the *Ferndale,* and the strangeness of being mixed up in what went on aboard simply because his name was also the name of a shipping master, kept him in a state of wonder which made other coincidences, however unlikely, not so very surprising after all.

"This astonishing occurrence was so present to his mind that he always felt as though he were there under false pretences. And this feeling was so uncomfortable that it nerved him to break through the awe-inspiring aloofness of his captain. He wanted to make a clean breast of it. I imagine that his youth stood in good stead to Mr. Powell. Oh, yes. Youth is a power. Even Captain Anthony had to take some notice of it, as if it refreshed him to see something untouched, unscarred, unhardened by suffering. Or perhaps the very novelty of that face, on board a ship where he had seen the same faces for years, attracted his attention.

"Whether one day he dropped a word to his new second officer or only looked at him I don't know; but Mr. Powell seized the opportunity whatever it was. The captain who had started and stopped in his everlasting rapid walk smoothed his brow very soon, heard him to the end and then laughed a little.

" 'Ah! That's the story. And you felt you must put me right as to this.'

" 'Yes, sir.'

" 'It doesn't matter how you came on board,' said Anthony. And then showing that perhaps he was not so utterly absent from his ship as Franklin supposed: 'That's all right. You seem to be getting on very well with everybody,' he said in his curt hurried tone, as if talking hurt him, and his eyes already straying over the sea as usual.

" 'Yes, sir.'

"Powell tells me that looking then at the strong face to which that haggard expression was returning, he had the impulse, from some confused friendly feeling, to add: 'I am very happy on board here, sir.'

"The quickly returning glance, its steadiness, abashed Mr. Powell and made him even step back a little. The captain looked as though he had forgotten the meaning of the word.

" 'You—what? Oh yes . . . You . . . of course . . . Happy. Why not?'

"This was merely muttered; and next moment Anthony was off on his headlong tramp, his eyes turned to the sea away from his ship.

"A sailor indeed looks generally into the great distances, but in Captain Anthony's case there was—as Powell expressed it—something particular, something purposeful like the avoidance of pain or temptation. It was very marked once one had become aware of it. Before, one felt only a pronounced strangeness. Not that the captain—Powell was careful to explain—didn't see things as a ship-master should. The proof of it was that on that very occasion he desired him suddenly, after a period of silent pacing, to have all the staysails sheets eased off, and he was going on with some other remarks on the subject of these staysails when Mrs. Anthony followed by her father emerged from the companion. She established herself in her chair to leeward of the skylight as usual. Thereupon the captain cut short whatever he was going to say, and in a little while went down below.

"I asked Mr. Powell whether the captain and his wife never conversed on deck. He said no—or at any rate they never exchanged more than a couple of words. There was some constraint between them. For instance, on that very occasion, when Mrs. Anthony came out they did look at each other; the captain's eyes indeed followed her till she sat down; but he did not speak to her; he did not approach her; and afterwards left the deck without turning his head her way after this first silent exchange of glances.

"I asked Mr. Powell what did he do then, the captain being out of the way. 'I went over and talked to Mrs. Anthony. I was thinking that it must be very dull for her. She seemed to be such a stranger to the ship.'

" 'The father was there of course?'

" 'Always,' said Powell. 'He was always there sitting on the skylight, as if he were keeping watch over her. And I think,' he added, 'that he was worrying her. Not that she showed it in any way. Mrs. Anthony was always very quiet and always ready to look one straight in the face.'

" 'You talked together a lot?' I pursued my inquiries.

" 'She mostly let me talk to her,' confessed Mr. Powell. 'I don't know that she was very much interested—but still she let me. She never cut me short.'

"All the sympathies of Mr. Powell were for Flora Anthony, *née* de Barral. She was the only human being younger than himself on board that ship, since the *Ferndale* carried no boys and was manned by a full crew of able seamen. Yes! their youth had created a sort of bond between them. Mr. Powell's open countenance must have appeared to her distinctly pleasing amongst the mature, rough, crabbed or even inimical faces she saw around her. With the warm generosity of his age young Powell was on her side, as it were, even before he knew that there were sides to be taken on board that ship, and what this taking sides was about. There was a girl. A nice girl. He asked himself no questions. Flora de Barral was not so much younger in years than himself, but for some reason, perhaps by contrast with the accepted idea of a captain's wife, he could not regard her otherwise but as an extremely youthful creature. At the same time, apart from her exalted position, she exercised over him the supremacy a woman's earlier maturity gives her over a young man of her own age. As a matter of fact we can see that, without ever having more than half an hour's consecutive conversation together, and the distances duly preserved, these two were becoming friends—under the eye of the old man, I suppose.

"How he first got in touch with his captain's wife Powell relates in this way. It was long before his memorable conversation with the mate and shortly after getting clear of the channel. It was gloomy weather; dead head wind, blowing quite half a gale; the *Ferndale* under reduced sail was stretching close-hauled across the track of the homeward-bound ships, just moving through the water and no more, since there was no object in pressing her and the weather looked threatening. About ten o'clock at night he was alone on the poop, in charge, keeping well aft by the weather rail and staring to windward, when amongst the white, breaking seas, under the black sky, he made out the lights of a ship. He watched them for some time. She was running dead before the wind, of course. She will pass jolly close—he said to himself; and then suddenly he felt a great mistrust of that

approaching ship. She's heading straight for us—he
thought. It was not his business to get out of the way.
On the contrary. And his uneasiness grew by the recollection of the forty tons of dynamite in the body of the
Ferndale; not the sort of cargo one thinks of with equanimity in connexion with a threatened collision. He gazed
at the two small lights in the dark immensity filled with
the angry noise of the seas. They fascinated him till their
plainness to his sight gave him a conviction that there
was danger there. He knew in his mind what to do in
emergency but very properly he felt that he must call the
captain at once.

"He crossed the deck in one bound. By the immemo-
rial custom and usage of the sea the captain's room is on
the star-board side. You would just as soon expect your
captain to have his nose at the back of his head as to
have his stateroom on the port side of the ship. Powell
forgot all about the direction on that point given him by
the chief. He flew over as I said, stamped with his foot
and then putting his face to the cowl of the big ventilator
shouted down there: 'Please come on deck, sir,' in a
voice which was not trembling or scared but which we
may call fairly expressive. There could not be a mistake
as to the urgence of the call. But instead of the expected
alert 'All right!' and the sound of a rush down there, he
heard only a faint exclamation—then silence.

"Think of his astonishment! He remained there, his
ear in the cowl of the ventilator, his eyes fastened on
those menacing sidelights dancing on the gusts of wind
which swept the angry darkness of the sea. It was as
though he had waited an hour but it was something much
less than a minute before he fairly bellowed into the wide
tube 'Captain Anthony!' An agitated 'What is it?' was
what he heard down there in Mrs. Anthony's voice, light
rapid footsteps. . . . Why didn't she try to wake him up?
'I want the captain,' he shouted, then gave it up, making
a dash at the companion where a blue light was kept,
resolved to act for himself.

"On the way he glanced at the helmsman whose face
lighted up by the binnacle lamps was calm. He said rapidly to him: 'Stand by to spin that helm up at the first
word.' The answer 'Aye, aye, sir,' was delivered in a
steady voice. Then Mr. Powell, after a shout for the

watch on deck to 'lay aft,' ran to the ship's side and struck the blue light on the rail.

"A sort of nasty little spitting of sparks was all that came. The light (perhaps affected by damp) had failed to ignite. The time of all these various acts must be counted in seconds. Powell confessed to me that at this failure he experienced a paralysis of thought, of voice, of limbs. The unexpectedness of this misfire positively overcame his faculties. It was the only thing for which his imagination was not prepared. It was knocked clean over. When it got up it was with the suggestion that he must do something at once or there would be a broadside smash accompanied by the explosion of dynamite, in which both ships would be blown up and every soul on board of them would vanish off the earth in an enormous flame and uproar.

"He saw the catastrophe happening and at the same moment, before he could open his mouth or stir a limb to ward off the vision, a voice very near his ear, the measured voice of Captain Anthony, said: 'Wouldn't light—eh? Throw it down! Jump for the flare-up.'

"The spring of activity in Mr. Powell was released with great force. He jumped. The flare-up was kept inside the companion with a box of matches ready to hand. Almost before he knew he had moved he was diving under the companion slide. He got hold of the can in the dark and tried to strike a light. But he had to press the flareholder to his breast with one arm, his fingers were damp and stiff, his hands trembled a little. One match broke. Another went out. In its flame he saw the colourless face of Mrs. Anthony a little below him, standing on the cabin stairs. Her eyes which were very close to his (he was in a crouching posture on the top step) seemed to burn darkly in the vanishing light. On deck the captain's voice was heard sudden and unexpectedly sardonic: 'You had better look sharp, if you want to be in time.'

" 'Let me have the box,' said Mrs. Anthony in a hurried and familiar whisper which sounded amused as if they had been a couple of children up to some lark behind a wall. He was glad of the offer which seemed to him very natural, and without ceremony—

" 'Here you are. Catch hold.'

"Their hands touched in the dark and she took the

box while he held the paraffin-soaked torch in its iron holder. He thought of warning her: 'Look out for yourself.' But before he had the time to finish the sentence the flare blazed up violently between them and he saw her throw herself back with an arm across her face. 'Hallo,' he exclaimed; only he could not stop a moment to ask if she was hurt. He bolted out of the companion straight into his captain who took the flare from him and held it high above his head.

"The fierce flame fluttered like a silk flag, throwing an angry swaying glare mingled with moving shadows over the poop, lighting up the concave surfaces of the sails, gleaming on the wet paint of the white rails. And young Powell turned his eyes to windward with a catch in his breath.

"The strange ship, a darker shape in the night, did not seem to be moving onwards but only to grow more distinct right abeam, staring at the *Ferndale* with one green and one red eye which swayed and tossed as if they belonged to the restless head of some invisible monster ambushed in the night amongst the waves. A moment, long like eternity, elapsed, and, suddenly, the monster which seemed to take to itself the shape of a mountain shut its green eye without as much as a preparatory wink.

"Mr. Powell drew a free breath. 'All right now,' said Captain Anthony in a quiet undertone. He gave the blazing flare to Powell and walked aft to watch the passing of that menace of destraction coming blindly with its particoloured stare out of a blind night on the wings of a sweeping wind. Her very form could be distinguished now black and elongated amongst the hissing patches of foam bursting along her path.

"As is always the case with a ship running before wind and sea she did not seem to an onlooker to move very fast; but to be progressing indolently in long, leisurely bounds and pauses in the midst of the overtaking waves. It was only when actually passing the stern within easy hail of the *Ferndale* that her headlong speed became apparent to the eye. With the red light shut off and soaring like an immense shadow on the crest of a wave she was lost to view in one great, forward swing, melting into the lightless space.

" 'Close shave,' said Captain Anthony in an indifferent

voice just raised enough to be heard in the wind. 'A blind lot on board that ship. Put out the flare now.'

"Silently Mr. Powell inverted the holder, smothering the flame in the can, bringing about by the mere turn of his wrist the fall of darkness upon the poop. And at the same time vanished out of his mind's eye the vision of another flame enormous and fierce shooting violently from a white churned patch of the sea, lighting up the very clouds and carrying upwards in its volcanic rush flying spars, corpses, the fragments of two destroyed ships. It vanished and there was an immense relief. He told me he did not know how scared he had been, not generally but of that very thing his imagination had conjured, till it was all over. He measured it (for fear is a great tension) by the feeling of slack weariness which came over him all at once.

"He walked to the companion and stooping low to put the flare in its usual place saw in the darkness the motionless pale oval of Mrs. Anthony's face. She whispered quietly—

" 'Is anything going to happen? What is it?'

" 'It's all over now,' he whispered back.

"He remained bent low, his head inside the cover staring at that white ghostly oval. He wondered she had not rushed out on deck. She had remained quietly there. This was pluck. Wonderful self-restraint. And it was not stupidity on her part. She knew there was imminent danger and probably had some notion of its nature.

" 'You stayed here waiting for what would come,' he murmured admiringly.

" 'Wasn't that the best thing to do?' she asked.

"He didn't know. Perhaps. He confessed he could not have done it. Not he. His flesh and blood could not have stood it. He would have felt he must see what was coming. Then he remembered that the flare might have scorched her face, and expressed his concern.

" 'A bit. Nothing to hurt. Smell the singed hair?'

"There was a sort of gaiety in her tone. She might have been frightened but she certainly was not overcome and suffered from no reaction. This confirmed and augmented if possible Mr. Powell's good opinion of her as a 'jolly girl,' though it seemed to him positively monstrous to refer in such terms to one's captain's wife. 'But she doesn't look it,' he thought in extenuation and was going to say something more to her about the lighting of that flare when another voice was heard in the companion, saying some indistinct words. Its tone was contemptuous; it came from below, from the bottom of the stairs. It was a voice in the cabin. And the only other voice which could be heard in the main cabin at this time of the evening was the voice of Mrs. Anthony's father. The indistinct white oval sank from Mr. Powell's sight so swiftly as to take him by surprise. For a moment he hung at the opening of the companion, and now that her slight form was no longer obstructing the narrow and winding staircase the voices came up louder but the words were still indistinct. The old gentleman was excited about something and Mrs. Anthony was 'managing him' as Powell expressed it. They moved away from the bottom of the stairs and Powell went away from the companion. Yet he fancied he had heard the words 'Lost to me' before he withdrew his head. They had been uttered by Mr. Smith.

"Captain Anthony had not moved away from the taffrail. He remained in the very position he took up to watch the other ship go by rolling and swinging all shadowy in the uproar of the following seas. He stirred not; and Powell keeping near by did not dare speak to him, so enigmatical in its contemplation of the night did his figure appear to his young eyes: indistinct—and in its immobility staring into gloom, the prey of some incomprehensible grief, longing or regret.

"Why is it that the stillness of a human being is often so impressive, so suggestive of evil—as if our proper fate were a ceaseless agitation? The stillness of Captain Anthony became almost intolerable to his second officer. Mr. Powell loitering about the skylight wanted his captain off the deck now. 'Why doesn't he go below?' he asked himself impatiently. He ventured a cough.

"Whether the effect of the cough or not Captain Anthony spoke. He did not move the least bit. With his back remaining turned to the whole length of the ship he asked Mr. Powell with some brusqueness if the chief mate had neglected to instruct him that the captain was to be found on the port side.

" 'Yes, sir,' said Mr. Powell approaching his back.

'The mate told me to stamp on the port side when I wanted you; but I didn't remember at the moment.'

" 'You should remember,' the captain uttered with an effort. Then added mumbling, 'I don't want Mrs. Anthony frightened. Don't you see? . . .'

" 'She wasn't this time,' Powell said innocently: 'She lighted the flare-up for me, sir.'

" 'This time,' Captain Anthony exclaimed and turned round. 'Mrs. Anthony lighted the flare? Mrs. Anthony! . . .' Powell explained that she was in the companion all the time.

" 'All the time,' repeated the captain. It seemed queer to Powell that instead of going himself to see, the captain should ask him—

" 'Is she there now?'

"Powell said that she had gone below after the ship had passed clear of the *Ferndale*. Captain Anthony made a movement towards the companion himself, when Powell added the information: 'Mr. Smith called to Mrs. Anthony from the saloon, sir. I believe they are talking there now.'

"He was surprised to see the captain give up the idea of going below after all.

"He began to walk the poop instead regardless of the cold, of the damp wind and of the sprays. And yet he had nothing on but his sleeping suit and slippers. Powell placing himself on the break of the poop kept a look-out. When after some time he turned his head to steal a glance at his eccentric captain he could not see his active and shadowy figure swinging to and fro. The second mate of the *Ferndale* walked aft peering about and addressed the seaman who steered.

" 'Captain gone below?'

" 'Yes, sir,' said the fellow who with a quid of tobacco bulging out of his left cheek kept his eyes on the compass card. 'This minute. He laughed.'

" 'Laughed,' repeated Powell incredulously. 'Do you mean the captain did? You must be mistaken. What would he want to laugh for?'

" 'Don't know, sir.'

"The elderly sailor displayed a profound indifference towards human emotions. However, after a longish pause he conceded a few words more to the second officer's weakness. 'Yes. He was walking the deck as usual when suddenly he laughed a little and made for the companion. Thought of something funny all at once.'

"Something funny! That Mr. Powell could not believe. He did not ask himself why, at the time. Funny thoughts come to men, though, in all sorts of situations; they come to all sorts of men. Nevertheless Mr. Powell was shocked to learn that Captain Anthony had laughed without visible cause on a certain night. The impression for some reason was disagreeable. And it was then, while finishing his watch, with the chilly gusts of wind sweeping at him out of the darkness where the short sea of the soundings growled spitefully all round the ship, that it occurred to his unsophisticated mind that perhaps things are not what they are confidently expected to be; that it was possible that Captain Anthony was not a happy man. . . . In so far you will perceive he was to a certain extent prepared for the apoplectic and sensitive Franklin's lamentations about his captain. And though he treated them with a contempt which was in a great measure sincere, yet he admitted to me that deep down within him an inexplicable and uneasy suspicion that all was not well in that cabin, so unusually cut off from the rest of the ship, came into being and grew against his will. . . ."

CHAPTER FOUR

Anthony and Flora

Marlow emerged out of the shadow of the bookcase to get himself a cigar from a box which stood on a little table by my side. In the full light of the room I saw in his eyes that slightly mocking expression with which he habitually covers up his sympathetic impulses of mirth and pity before the unreasonable complications the idealism of mankind puts into the simple but poignant problem of conduct on this earth.

He selected and lit the cigar with affected care, then turned upon me. I had been looking at him silently.

"I suppose," he said, the mockery of his eyes giving a pellucid quality to his tone, "that you think it's high time I told you something definite. I mean something about that psychological cabin mystery of discomfort (for it's obvious that it must be psychological) which affected so profoundly Mr. Franklin the chief mate, and had even disturbed the serene innocence of Mr. Powell, the second of the ship *Ferndale,* commanded by Roderick Anthony—the son of the poet, you know."

"You are going to confess now that you have failed to find it out," I said in pretended indignation.

"It would serve you right if I told you that I have. But

I won't. I haven't failed. I own though that for a time I was puzzled. However, I have now seen our Powell many times under the most favourable conditions—and besides I came upon a most unexpected source of information. . . . But never mind that. The means don't concern you except in so far as they belong to the story. I'll admit that for some time the old-maiden-lady-like occupation of putting two and two together failed to procure a coherent theory. I am speaking now as an investigator—a man of deductions. With what we know of Roderick Anthony and Flora de Barral I could not deduct an ordinary marital quarrel beautifully matured in less than a year—could I? If you ask me what is an ordinary marital quarrel I will tell you that it is a difference about nothing; I mean, these nothings which, as Mr. Powell told us when we first met him, shore people are so prone to start a row about, and nurse into hatred from an idle sense of wrong, from perverted ambition, for spectacular reasons too. There are on earth no actors too humble and obscure not to have a gallery, that gallery which envenoms the play by stealthy jeers, counsels of anger, amused comments or words of perfidious compassion. However, the Anthonys were free from all demoralizing influences. At sea, you know, there is no gallery. You hear no tormenting echoes of your own littleness there, where either a great elemental voice roars defiantly under the sky or else an elemental silence seems to be part of the infinite stillness of the universe.

"Remembering Flora de Barral in the depths of moral misery, and Roderick Anthony carried away by a gust of tempestuous tenderness, I asked myself, Is it all forgotten already? What could they have found to estrange them from each other with this rapidity and this thoroughness so far from all temptations, in the peace of the sea and in an isolation so complete that if it had not been for the jealous devotion of the sentimental Franklin stimulating the attention of Powell, there would have been no record, no evidence of it at all.

"I must confess at once that it was Flora de Barral whom I suspected. In this world as at present organized women are the suspected half of the population. There are good reasons for that. These reasons are so discoverable with a little reflection that it is not worth my while to set them out for you. I will only mention this: that the part falling to women's share being all 'influence' has an air of occult and mysterious action, something not altogether trustworthy, like all natural forces which, for us, work in the dark because of our imperfect comprehension.

"If women were not a force of nature, blind in its strength and capricious in its power, they would not be mistrusted. As it is one can't help it. You will say that this force having been in the person of Flora de Barral captured by Anthony . . . Why yes. He had dealt with her masterfully. But man has captured electricity too. It lights him on his way, it warms his home, it will even cook his dinner for him—very much like a woman. But what sort of conquest would you call it? He knows nothing of it. He has got to be mighty careful what he is about with his captive. And the greater the demand he makes on it in the exultation of his pride the more likely it is to turn on him and burn him to a cinder. . . ."

"A far-fetched enough parallel," I observed coldly to Marlow. He had returned to the arm-chair in the shadow of the bookcase. "But accepting the meaning you have in your mind it reduces itself to the knowledge of how to use it. And if you mean that this ravenous Anthony——"

"Ravenous is good," interrupted Marlow. "He was a-hungering and a-thirsting for femininity to enter his life in a way no mere feminist could have the slightest conception of. I reckon that this accounts for much of Fyne's disgust with him. Good little Fyne. You have no idea what infernal mischief he had worked during his call at the hotel. But then who could have suspected Anthony of being a heroic creature. There are several kinds of heroism and one of them at least is idiotic. It is the one which wears the aspect of sublime delicacy. It is apparently the one of which the son of the delicate poet was capable.

"He certainly resembled his father, who, by the way, wore out two women without any satisfaction to himself, because they did not come up to his supra-refined standard of the delicacy which is so perceptible in his verses. That's your poet. He demands too much from others. The inarticulate son had set up a standard for himself with that need for embodying in his conduct the dreams,

the passion, the impulses the poet puts into arrangements
of verses, which are dearer to him than his own self—
and may make his own self appear sublime in the eyes
of other people, and even in his own eyes.

"Did Anthony wish to appear sublime in his own eyes?
I should not like to make that charge; though indeed
there are other, less noble, ambitions at which the world
does not dare to smile. But I don't think so; I do not
even think that there was in what he did a conscious and
lofty confidence in himself, a particularly pronounced
sense of power which leads men so often into impossible
or equivocal situations. Looked at abstractedly (the way
in which truth is often seen in its real shape) his life had
been a life of solitude and silence—and desire.

"Chance had thrown that girl in his way; and if we
may smile at his violent conquest of Flora de Barral we
must admit also that this eager appropriation was truly
the act of a man of solitude and desire; a man also, who,
unless a complete imbecile, must have been a man of
long and ardent reveries wherein the faculty of sincere
passion matures slowly in the unexplored recesses of the
heart. And I know also that a passion, dominating or
tyrannical, invading the whole man and subjugating all
his faculties to its own unique end, may conduct him
whom it spurs and drives, into all sorts of adventures, to
the brink of unfathomable dangers, to the limits of folly,
and madness, and death.

"To the man then of a silence made only more impressive by the inarticulate thunders and mutters of the great
seas, an utter stranger to the clatter of tongues, there
comes the muscular little Fyne, the most marked representative of that mankind whose voice is so strange to
him, the husband of his sister, a personality standing out
from the misty and remote multitude. He comes and
throws at him more talk than he had ever heard boomed
out in an hour, and certainly touching the deepest things
Anthony had ever discovered in himself, and flings words
like 'unfair' whose very sound is abhorrent to him.
Unfair! Undue advantage! He! Unfair to that girl? Cruel
to her!

"No scorn could stand against the impression of such
charges advanced with heat and conviction. They shook
him. They were yet vibrating in the air of that stuffy

hotel-room, terrific, disturbing, impossible to get rid of, when the door opened and Flora de Barral entered.

"He did not even notice that she was late. He was sitting on a sofa plunged in gloom. Was it true? Having himself always said exactly what he meant he imagined that people (unless they were liars, which of course his brother-in-law could not be) never said more than they meant. The deep chest voice of little Fyne was still in his ear. 'He knows,' Anthony said to himself. He thought he had better go away and never see her again. But she stood there before him accusing and appealing. How could he abandon her? That was out of the question. She had no one. Or rather she had some one. That father. Anthony was willing to take him at her valuation. This father may have been the victim of the most atrocious injustice. But what could a man coming out of jail do? An old man too. And then—what sort of man? What would become of them both? Anthony shuddered slightly and the faint smile with which Flora had entered the room faded on her lips. She was used to his impetuous tenderness. She was no longer afraid of it. But she had never seen him look like this before, and she suspected at once some new cruelty of life. He got up with his usual ardour but as if sobered by a momentous resolve and said—

" 'No. I can't let you out of my sight. I have seen you. You have told me your story. You are honest. You have never told me you loved me.'

"She waited, saying to herself that he had never given her time, that he had never asked her! And that, in truth, she did not know!

"I am inclined to believe that she did not. As abundance of experience is not precisely her lot in life, a woman is seldom an expert in matters of sentiment. It is the man who can and generally does 'see himself' pretty well inside and out. Women's self-possession is an outward thing; inwardly they flutter, perhaps because they are, or they feel themselves to be, encaged. All this speaking generally. In Flora de Barral's particular case ever since Anthony had suddenly broken his way into her hopeless and cruel existence she lived like a person liberated from a condemned cell by a natural cataclysm, a tempest, an earthquake; not absolutely terrified, because

nothing can be worse than the eve of execution, but
stunned, bewildered—abandoning herself passively. She
did not want to make a sound, to move a limb. She
hadn't the strength. What was the good? And deep
down, almost unconsciously she was seduced by the feeling of being supported by this violence. A sensation she
had never experienced before in her life.

"She felt as if this whirlwind were calming down somehow! As if this feeling of support, which was tempting
her to close her eyes deliciously and let herself be carried
on and on into the unknown, undefiled by vile experiences, were less certain, had wavered threateningly. She
tried to read something in his face, in that energetic
kindly face to which she had become accustomed so
soon. But she was not yet capable of understanding its
expression. Scared, discouraged on the threshold of ado-
lescence, plunged in moral misery of the bitterest kind,
she had not learned to read—not that sort of language.

"If Anthony's love had been as egoistic as love generally is, it would have been greater than the egoism of his
vanity—or of his generosity, if you like—and all this
could not have happened. He would not have hit upon
that renunciation at which one does not know whether
to grin or shudder. It is true too that then his love would
not have fastened itself upon the unhappy daughter of
de Barral. But it was a love born of that rare pity which
is not akin to contempt because rooted in an overwhelmingly strong capacity for tenderness—the tenderness of
the fiery predatory kind—the tenderness of silent solitary
men, the voluntary, passionate outcasts of their kind. At
the same time I am forced to think that his vanity must
have been enormous.

" 'What big eyes she has,' he said to himself, amazed.

"No wonder. She was staring at him with all the might
of her soul awakening slowly from a poisoned sleep, in
which it could only quiver with pain but could neither
expand nor move. He plunged into them breathless and
tense, deep, deep, like a mad sailor taking a desperate
dive from the masthead into the blue unfathomable sea
so many men have execrated and loved at the same time.
And his vanity was immense. It had been touched to the
quick by that muscular little feminist, Fyne. 'I! I! Take
advantage of her helplessness. I! Unfair to that crea-

ture—that wisp of mist, that white shadow homeless in an ugly dirty world. I could blow her away with a breath,' he was saying to himself with horror. 'Never!' All the supremely refined delicacy of tenderness, expressed in so many fine lines of verse by Carleon Anthony, grew to the size of a passion filling with inward sobs the big frame of the man who had never in his life read a single one of those famous sonnets singing of the most highly civilized, chivalrous love, of those sonnets which'. . . You know there's a volume of them. My edition has the portrait of the author at thirty, and when I showed it to Mr. Powell the other day he exclaimed: 'Wonderful! One would think this the portrait of Captain Anthony himself if . . .' I wanted to know what that if was. But Powell could not say. There was something—a difference. No doubt there was—in fineness perhaps. The father, fastidious, cerebral, morbidly shrinking from all contacts, could only sing in harmonious numbers of what the son felt with a dumb and reckless sincerity.

"Possessed by most men's touching illusion as to the frailness of women and their spiritual fragility, it seemed to Anthony that he would be destroying, breaking something very precious inside that being. In fact nothing less than partly murdering her. This seems a very extreme effect to flow from Fyne's words. But Anthony, unaccustomed to the chatter of the firm earth, never stayed to ask himself what value these words could have in Fyne's mouth. And indeed the mere dark sound of them was utterly abhorrent to his native rectitude, sea-salted, hardened in the winds of wide horizons, open as the day.

"He wished to blurt out his indignation, but she regarded him with an expectant air which checked him. His visible discomfort made her uneasy. He could only repeat, 'Oh, yes. You are perfectly honest. You might have, but I daresay you are right. At any rate you have never said anything to me which you didn't mean.'

" 'Never,' she whispered after a pause.

"He seemed distracted, choking with an emotion she could not understand because it resembled embarrassment, a state of mind inconceivable in that man.

"She wondered what it was she had said; remembering that in very truth she had hardly spoken to him except

when giving him the bare outline of her story which he
seemed to have hardly had the patience to hear, waving
it perpetually aside with exclamations of horror and
anger, with fiercely sombre mutters 'Enough! Enough!'
and with alarming starts from a forced stillness, as though
he meant to rush out at once and take vengeance on
somebody. She was saying to herself that he caught her
words in the air, never letting her finish her thought.
Honest. Honest. Yes, certainly she had been that. Her
letter to Mrs. Fyne had been prompted by honesty. But
she reflected sadly that she had never known what to say
to him. That perhaps she had nothing to say.

" 'But you'll find out that I can be honest too,' he
burst out in a menacing tone she had learned to appreciate with an amused thrill.

"She waited for what was coming. But he hung in the
wind. He looked round the room with disgust as if he
could see traces on the walls of all the casual tenants
that had ever passed through it. People had quarrelled
in that room; they had been ill in it, there had been
misery in that room, wickedness, crime perhaps—death
most likely. This was not a fit place. He snatched up his
hat. He had made up his mind. The ship—the ship he
had known ever since she came off the stocks, his
home—her shelter—the uncontaminated, honest ship,
was the place.

" 'Let us go on board. We'll talk there,' he said. 'And
you will have to listen to me. For whatever happens, no
matter what they say, I cannot let you go.'

"You can't say that (misgivings or no misgivings) she
could have done anything else but go on board. It was
the appointed business of that morning. During the drive
he was silent. Anthony was the last man to condemn
conventionally any human being, to scorn and despise
even deserved misfortune. He was ready to take old de
Barral—the convict—on his daughter's valuation without
the slightest reserve. But love like this, though it may
drive one into risky folly by the proud consciousness of
its own strength, has a sagacity of its own. And now, as
if lifted up into a higher and serene region by its purpose
of renunciation, it gave him leisure to reflect for the first
time in these last few days. He said to himself: 'I don't
know that man. She does not know him either. She was

barely sixteen when they locked him up. She was a child. What will he say? What will he do? No,' he concluded, 'I cannot leave her behind with that man who would come into the world as if out of a grave.'

"They went on board in silence, and it was after showing her round and when they had returned to the saloon that he assailed her in his fiery, masterful fashion. At first she did not understand. Then when she understood that he was giving her her liberty she went stiff all over, her hand resting on the edge of the table, her face set like a carving of white marble. It was all over. It was as that abominable governess had said. She was insignificant, contemptible. Nobody could love her. Humiliation clung to her like a cold shroud—never to be shaken off, unwarmed by this madness of generosity.

" 'Yes. Here. Your home. I can't give it to you and go away, but it is big enough for us two. You need not be afraid. If you say so I shall not even look at you. Remember that grey head of which you have been thinking night and day. Where is it going to rest? Where else if not here, where nothing evil can touch it. Don't you understand that I won't let you buy shelter from me at the cost of your very soul? I won't. You are too much part of me. I have found myself since I came upon you and I would rather sell my own soul to the devil than let you go out of my keeping. But I must have the right.'

"He went away brusquely to shut the door leading on deck and came back the whole length of the cabin repeating—

" 'I must have the legal right. Are you ashamed of letting people think you are my wife?'

"He opened his arms as if to clasp her to his breast but mastered the impulse and shook his clenched hands at her, repeating: 'I must have the right if only for your father's sake. I must have the right. Where would you take him? To that infernal cardboard-box maker? I don't know what keeps me from hunting him up in his virtuous home and bashing his head in. I can't bear the thought. Listen to me, Flora! Do you hear what I am saying to you? You are not so proud that you can't understand that I as a man have my pride too?'

"He saw a tear glide down her white cheek from under each lowered eyelid. Then, abruptly, she walked out of the cabin. He stood for a moment, concentrated, reckoning his own strength, interrogating his heart, before he followed her hastily. Already she had reached the wharf.

"At the sound of his pursuing footsteps her strength failed her. Where could she escape from this? From this new perfidy of life taking upon itself the form of magnanimity. His very voice was changed. The sustaining whirlwind had let her down, to stumble on again, weakened by the fresh stab, bereft of moral support which is wanted in life more than all the charities of material help. She had never had it. Never. Not from the Fynes. But where to go? Oh yes, this dock—a placid sheet of water close at hand. But there was that old man with whom she had walked hand in hand on the parade by the sea. She seemed to see him coming to meet her, pitiful, a little greyer, with an appealing look and an extended, tremulous arm. It was for her now to take the hand of that wronged man more helpless than a child. But where could she lead him? Where? And what was she to say to him? What words of cheer, of courage and of hope? There were none. Heaven and earth were mute, unconcerned at their meeting. But this other man was coming up behind her. He was very close now. His fiery person seemed to radiate heat, a tingling vibration into the atmosphere. She was exhausted, careless, afraid to stumble, ready to fall. She fancied she could hear his breathing. A wave of languid warmth overtook her, she seemed to lose touch with the ground under her feet; and when she felt him slip his hand under her arm she made no attempt to disengage herself from that grasp which closed upon her limb, insinuating and firm.

"He conducted her through the dangers of the quayside. Her sight was dim. A moving truck was like a mountain gliding by. Men passed by as if in a mist; and the buildings, the sheds, the unexpected open spaces, the ships, had strange, distorted, dangerous shapes. She said to herself that it was good not to be bothered with what all these things meant in the scheme of creation (if indeed anything had a meaning), or were just piled-up matter without any sense. She felt how she had always been unrelated to this world. She was hanging on to it merely by that one arm grasped firmly just above the elbow. It was a captivity. So be it. Till they got out into the street and saw the hansom waiting outside the gates Anthony spoke only once, beginning brusquely but in a much gentler tone than she had ever heard from his lips.

" 'Of course I ought to have known that you could not care for a man like me, a stranger. Silence gives consent. Yes? Eh? I don't want any of that sort of consent. And unless some day you find you can speak . . . No! No! I shall never ask you. For all the sign I will give you you may go to your grave with sealed lips. But what I have said you must do!'

"He bent his head over her with tender care. At the same time she felt her arm pressed and shaken inconspicuously, but in an undeniable manner. 'You must do it.' A little shake that no passer-by could notice; and this was going on in a deserted part of the dock. 'It must be done. You are listening to me—eh? or would you go again to my sister?'

"His ironic tone, perhaps from want of use, had an awful grating ferocity.

" 'Would you go to her?' he pursued in the same strange voice. 'Your best friend! And say nicely—I am sorry. Would you? No! You couldn't. There are things that even you, poor dear lost girl, couldn't stand. Eh? Die rather. That's it. Of course. Or can you be thinking of taking your father to that infernal cousin's house? No! Don't speak. I can't bear to think of it. I would follow you there and smash the door!'

"The catch in his voice astonished her by its resemblance to a sob. It frightened her too. The thought that came to her head was: 'He mustn't.' He was putting her into the hansom. 'Oh! He mustn't, he mustn't.' She was still more frightened by the discovery that he was shaking all over. Bewildered, shrinking into the far-off corner, avoiding his eyes, she yet saw the quivering of his mouth and made a wild attempt at a smile, which broke the rigidity of her lips and set her teeth chattering suddenly.

" 'I am not coming with you,' he was saying. 'I'll tell the man . . . I can't. Better not. What is it? Are you cold? Come! What is it? Only to go to a confounded stuffy room, a hole of an office. Not a quarter of an hour. I'll come for you—in ten days. Don't think of it too much. Think of no man, woman, or child of all that silly crowd cumbering the ground. Don't think of me either. Think of yourself. Ha! Nothing will be able to touch you then—at last. Say nothing. Don't move. I'll have everything arranged; and as long as you don't hate the sight of me—and you don't—there's nothing to be frightened about. One of their silly offices with a couple of ink-slingers of no consequence; poor, scribbling devils.'

"The hansom drove away with Flora de Barral inside, without movement, without thought, only too glad to rest, to be alone and still moving away without effort in solitude and silence.

"Anthony roamed the streets for hours without being able to remember in the evening where he had been—in the manner of a happy and exulting lover. But nobody could have thought so from his face, which bore no signs of blissful anticipation. Exulting indeed he was, but it was a special sort of exultation which seemed to take him by the throat like an enemy.

"Anthony's last words to Flora referred to the Registry Office where they were married ten days later. During that time Anthony saw no one or anything, though he went about restlessly here and there, amongst men and things. This special state is peculiar to common lovers, who are known to have no eyes for anything except for the contemplation, actual or inward, of one human form which for them contains the soul of the whole world in all its beauty, perfection, variety and infinity. It must be extremely pleasant. But felicity was denied to Roderick Anthony's contemplation. He was not a common sort of lover; and he was punished for it as if Nature (which it is said abhors a vacuum) were so very conventional as to abhor every sort of exceptional conduct. Roderick Anthony had begun already to suffer. That is why perhaps he was so industrious in going about amongst his fellow-men who would have been surprised and humiliated had they known how little solidity and even existence they had in his eyes. But they could not suspect anything so queer. They saw nothing extraordinary in him during that fortnight. The proof of this is that they were willing to transact business with him. Obviously they were; since it is then that the offer of chartering his ship for the special purpose of proceeding to the Western Islands was put in his way by a firm of shipbrokers who had no doubt of his sanity.

"He probably looked sane enough for all the practical purposes of commercial life. But I am not so certain that he really was quite sane at that time.

"However, he jumped at the offer. Providence itself was offering him this opportunity to accustom the girl to sea-life by a comparatively short trip. This was the time when everything that happened, everything he heard, casual words, unrelated phrases, seemed a provocation or an encouragement, confirmed him in his resolution. And indeed to be busy with material affairs is the best preservative against reflection, fears, doubts—all these things which stand in the way of achievement. I suppose a fellow proposing to cut his throat would experience a sort of relief while occupied in stropping his razor carefully.

"And Anthony was extremely careful in preparing for himself and for the luckless Flora an impossible existence. He went about it with no more tremors than if he had been stuffed with rags or made of iron instead of flesh and blood, an existence, mind you, which, on shore, in the thick of mankind, of varied interests, of distractions, of infinite opportunities to preserve your distance from each other, is hardly conceivable; but on board ship, at sea, *en tête-à-tête* for days and weeks and months together, could mean nothing but mental torture, an exquisite absurdity of torment. He was a simple soul. His hopelessly masculine ingenuousness is displayed in a tuuching way by his care to procure some woman to attend on Flora. The condition of guaranteed perfect respectability gave him moments of anxious thought. When he remembered suddenly his steward's wife he must have exclaimed *eureka* with particular exultation. One does not like to call Anthony an ass. But really to put any woman within scenting distance of such a secret and suppose that she would not track it out!

"No woman, however simple, could be as ingenuous as that. I don't know how Flora de Barral qualified him in her thoughts when he told her of having done this amongst other things intended to make her comfortable. I should think that, for all *her* simplicity, she must have been appalled. He stood before her on the appointed day outwardly calmer than she had ever seen him before. And this very calmness, that scrupulous attitude which

he felt bound in honour to assume then and for ever,
unless she would condescend to make a sign at some
future time, added to the heaviness of her heart innocent
of the most pardonable guile.

"The night before she had slept better than she had
done for the past ten nights. Both youth and weariness
will assert themselves in the end against the tyranny of
nerve-racking stress. She had slept, but she woke up with
her eyes full of tears. There were no traces of them when
she met him in the shabby little parlour downstairs. She
had swallowed them up. She was not going to let him
see. She felt bound in honour to accept the situation for
ever and ever unless . . . Ah, unless . . . She dissembled
all her sentiments, but it was not duplicity on her part.
All she wanted was to get at the truth; to see what would
come of it.

"She beat him at his own honourable game and the
thoroughness of her serenity disconcerted Anthony a bit.
It was he who stammered when it came to talking. The
suppressed fierceness of his character carried him on
after the first word or two masterfully enough. But it was
as if they both had taken a bite of the same bitter fruit.
He was thinking with mournful regret not unmixed with
surprise: 'That fellow Fyne has been telling me the truth.
She does not care for me a bit.' It humiliated him and
also increased his compassion for the girl who in this
darkness of life, buffeted and despairing, had fallen into
the grip of his stronger will, abandoning herself to his
arms as on a night of shipwreck. Flora on her side with
partial insight (for women are never blind with the complete masculine blindness) looked on him with some pity;
and she felt pity for herself too. It was a rejection, a
casting out; nothing new to her. But she who supposed
all her sensibility dead by this time, discovered in herself
a resentment of this ultimate betrayal. She had no resignation for this one. With a sort of mental sullenness she
said to herself: 'Well, I am here. I am here without any
nonsense. It is not my fault that I am a mere worthless
object of pity.'

"And these things which she could tell herself with a
clear conscience served her better than the passionate
obstinacy of purpose could serve Roderick Anthony. She
was much more sure of herself than he was. Such are

the advantages of mere rectitude over the most exalted
generosity.

"And so they went out to get married, the people of
the house where she lodged having no suspicion of anything of the sort. They were only excited at a 'gentleman
friend' (a very fine man too) calling on Miss Smith for
the first time since she had come to live in the house.
When she returned, for she did come back alone, there
were allusions made to that outing. She had to take her
meals with these rather vulgar people. The woman of the
house, a scraggy, genteel person, tried even to provoke
confidences. Flora's white face with the deep blue eyes
did not strike their hearts as it did the heart of Captain
Anthony as the very face of the suffering world. Her
pained reserve had no power to awe them into decency.

"Well, she returned alone—as in fact might have been
expected. After leaving the Registry Office Flora de Barral and Roderick Anthony had gone for a walk in a park.
It must have been an East-End park, but I am not sure.
Anyway that's what they did. It was a sunny day. He
said to her: 'Everything I have in the world belongs to
you. I have seen to that without troubling my brother-
in-law. They have no call to interfere.'

"She walked with her hand resting lightly on his arm.
He had offered it to her on coming out of the Registry
Office, and she had accepted it silently. Her head
drooped, she seemed to be turning matters over in her
mind. She said, alluding to the Fynes: 'They have been
very good to me.' At that he exclaimed—

" 'They have never understood you. Well, not properly. My sister is not a bad woman, but . . .'

"Flora didn't protest; asking herself whether he imagined that he himself understood her so much better.
Anthony dismissing his family out of his thoughts went
on: 'Yes. Everything is yours. I have kept nothing back.
As to the piece of paper we have just got from that
miserable quill-driver if it wasn't for the law, I wouldn't
mind if you tore it up here, now, on this spot. But don't
you do it. Unless you should some day feel that——'

"He choked, unexpectedly. She, reflective, hesitated a
moment then making up her mind bravely:

" 'Neither am I keeping anything back from you.'

"She had said it! But he in his blind generosity

assumed that she was alluding to her deplorable history and hastened to mutter—

" 'Of course! Of course! Say no more. I have been lying awake thinking of it all no end of times.'

"He made a movement with his other arm as if restraining himself from shaking an indignant fist at the universe; and she never even attempted to look at him. His voice sounded strangely, incredibly lifeless in comparison with these tempestuous accents that in the broad fields, in the dark garden had seemed to shake the very earth under her weary and hopeless feet.

"She regretted them. Hearing the sigh which escaped her Anthony instead of shaking his fist at the universe began to pat her hand resting on his arm and then desisted, suddenly, as though he had burnt himself. Then after a silence—

" 'You will have to go by yourself to-morrow. I . . . No, I think I mustn't come. Better not. What you two will have to say to each other——'

"She interrupted him quickly—

" 'Father is an innocent man. He was cruelly wronged.'

" 'Yes. That's why,' Anthony insisted earnestly. 'And you are the only human being that can make it up to him. You alone must reconcile him with the world if anything can. But of course you shall. You'll have to find words. Oh you'll know. And then the sight of you, alone, would soothe——'

" 'He's the gentlest of men,' she interrupted again.

"Anthony shook his head. 'It would take no end of generosity, no end of gentleness, to forgive such a dead set. For my part I would have liked better to have been killed and done with at once. It could not have been worse for you—and I suppose it was of you that he was thinking most while those infernal lawyers were badgering him in court. Of you. And now I think of it perhaps the sight of you may bring it all back to him. All these years, all these years—and you his child left alone in the world. I would have gone crazy. For even if he had done wrong——'

" 'But he hasn't,' insisted Flora de Barral with a quite unexpected fierceness. 'You mustn't even suppose it. Haven't you read the accounts of the trial?'

" 'I am not supposing anything,' Anthony defended

himself. He just remembered hearing of the trial. He assured her that he was away from England, the second voyage of the *Ferndale*. He was crossing the Pacific from Australia at the time and didn't see any papers for weeks and weeks. He interrupted himself to suggest—

" 'You had better tell him at once that you are happy.'

"He had stammered a little, and Flora de Barral uttered a deliberate and concise 'Yes.'

"A short silence ensued. She withdrew her hand from his arm. They stopped. Anthony looked as if a totally unexpected catastrophe had happened.

" 'Ah,' he said. 'You mind . . .'

" 'No! I think I had better,' she murmured.

" 'I dare say. I dare say. Bring him along straight on board to-morrow. Stop nowhere.'

"She had a moment of vague gratitude, a momentary feeling of peace which she referred to the man before her. She looked up at Anthony. His face was sombre. He was miles away and muttered as if to himself—

" 'Where could he want to stop though?'

" 'There's not a single being on earth that I would want to look at his dear face now, to whom I would willingly take him,' she said, extending her hand frankly and with a slight break in her voice, 'but you—Roderick.'

"He took that hand, felt it very small and delicate in his broad palm.

" 'That's right. That's right,' he said with a conscious and hasty heartiness and, as if suddenly ashamed of the sound of his voice, turned half round and absolutely walked away from the motionless girl. He even resisted the temptation to look back till it was too late. The gravel path lay empty to the very gate of the park. She was gone—vanished. He had an impression that he had missed some sort of chance. He felt sad. That excited sense of his own conduct which had kept him up for the last ten days buoyed him no more. He had succeeded!

"He strolled on aimlessly, a prey to gentle melancholy. He walked and walked. There were but few people about in this breathing space of a poor neighbourhood. Under certain conditions of life there is precious little time left for mere breathing. But still a few here and there were indulging in that luxury; yet few as they were Captain Anthony, though the least exclusive of men, resented their presence. Solitude had been his best friend. He wanted some place where he could sit down and be alone. And in his need his thoughts turned to the sea which had given him so much of that congenial solitude. There, if always with his ship (but that was an integral part of him), he could always be as solitary as he chose. Yes. Get out to sea!

"The night of the town with its strings of lights, rigid, and crossed like a net of flames thrown over the sombre immensity of walls, closed round him, with its artificial brilliance overhung by an emphatic blackness, its unnatural animation of a restless, overdriven humanity. His thoughts which somehow were inclined to pity every passing figure, every single person glimpsed under a street lamp, fixed themselves at last upon a figure which certainly could not have been seen under the lamps on that particular night. A figure unknown to him. A figure shut up within high unscalable walls of stone or bricks till next morning . . . The figure of Flora de Barral's father. De Barral the financier—the convict.

"There is something in that word with its suggestions of guilt and retribution which arrests the thought. We feel ourselves in the presence of the power of organized society—a thing mysterious in itself and still more mysterious in its effect. Whether guilty or innocent, it was as if old de Barral had been down to the Nether Regions. Impossible to imagine what he would bring out from there to the light of this world of uncondemned men. What would he think? What would he have to say? And what was one to say to him?

"Anthony, a little awed, as one is by a range of feelings stretching beyond one's grasp, comforted himself by the thought that probably the old fellow would have little to say. He wouldn't want to talk about it. No man would. It must have been a real hell to him.

"And then Anthony, at the end of the day in which he had gone through a marriage ceremony with Flora de Barral, ceased to think of Flora's father except, as in some sort, the captive of his triumph. He turned to the mental contemplation of the white, delicate and appealing face with great blue eyes which he had seen weep and wonder and look profoundly at him, sometimes with incredulity, sometimes with doubt and pain, but always irresistible in the power to find their way right into his breast, to stir there a deep response which was something more than love—he said to himself—as men understand it. More? Or was it only something other? Yes. It was something other. More or less. Something as incredible as the fulfilment of an amazing and startling dream in which he could take the world in his arms—all the suffering world—not to possess its pathetic fairness but to console and cherish its sorrow.

"Anthony walked slowly to the ship and that night slept without dreams.

CHAPTER FIVE

The Great de Barral

"Renovated certainly the saloon of the *Ferndale* was to receive the 'strange woman.' The mellowness of its old-fashioned, tarnished decoration was gone. And Anthony looking round saw the glitter, the gleams, the colour of new things, untried, unused, very bright—too bright. The workmen had gone only last night; and the last piece of work they did was the hanging of the heavy curtains which looped midway the length of the saloon— divided it in two if released, cutting off the after end with its companionway leading direct on the poop, from the forepart with its outlet on the deck; making a privacy within a privacy, as though Captain Anthony could not place obstacles enough between his new happiness and the men who shared his life at sea. He inspected that arrangement with an approving eye then made a particular visitation of the whole, ending by opening a door which led into a large state-room made of two knocked into one. It was very well furnished and had, instead of the usual bedplace of such cabins, an elaborate swinging cot of the latest pattern. Anthony tilted it a little by way of trial. 'The old man will be very comfortable in here,' he said to himself, and stepped back into the saloon closing the door gently. Then another thought occurred to him obvious under the circumstances but strangely enough presenting itself for the first time. 'Jove! Won't he get a shock,' thought Roderick Anthony.

"He went hastily on deck. 'Mr. Franklin, Mr. Franklin.' The mate was not very far. 'Oh! Here you are. Miss . . . Mrs. Anthony'll be coming on board presently. Just give me a call when you see the cab.'

"Then, without noticing the gloominess of the mate's countenance, he went in again. Not a friendly word, not a professional remark, or a small joke, not as much as a simple and inane 'fine day.' Nothing. Just turned about and went in.

"We know that, when the moment came, he thought better of it and decided to meet Flora's father in that privacy of the main cabin which he had been so careful to arrange. Why Anthony appeared to shrink from the contact, he who was sufficiently self-confident not only to face but to absolutely create a situation almost insane in its audacious generosity, is difficult to explain. Perhaps when he came on the poop for a glance he found that man so different outwardly from what he expected that he decided to meet him for the first time out of everybody's sight. Possibly the general secrecy of his relation to the girl might have influenced him. Truly he may well have been dismayed. That man's coming brought him face to face with the necessity to speak and act a lie; to appear what he was not and what he could never be, unless, unless—

"In short, we'll say if you like that for various reasons all having to do with the delicate rectitude of his nature, Roderick Anthony (a man of whom his chief mate used to say: he doesn't know what fear is) was frightened. There is a Nemesis which overtakes generosity too, like all the other imprudences of men who dare to be lawless and proud . . ."

"Why do you say this?" I inquired, for Marlow had stopped abruptly and kept silent in the shadow of the bookcase.

"I say this because that man whom chance had thrown in Flora's way was both: lawless and proud. Whether he knew anything about it or not it does not matter. Very likely not. One may fling a glove in the face of nature

and in the face of one's own moral endurance quite innocently, with a simplicity which wears the aspect of perfectly Satanic conceit. However, as I have said, it does
not matter. It's a transgression all the same and has got
to be paid for in the usual way. But never mind that. I
paused because, like Anthony, I find a difficulty, a sort
of dread in coming to grips with old de Barral.

"You remember I had a glimpse of him once. He was
not an imposing personality: tall, thin, straight, stiff,
faded, moving with short steps and with a gliding motion,
speaking in an even low voice. When the sea was rough
he wasn't much seen on deck—at least not walking. He
caught hold of things then and dragged himself along as
far as the after skylight where he would sit for hours.
Our, then young, friend offered once to assist him, and
this service was the first beginning of a sort of friendship.
He clung hard to one—Powell says, with no figurative
intention. Powell was always on the lookout to assist,
and to assist mainly Mrs. Anthony, because he clung so
jolly hard to her that Powell was afraid of her being
dragged down notwithstanding that she soon became very
sure-footed in all sorts of weather. And Powell was the
only one ready to assist at hand because Anthony (by
that time) seemed to be afraid to come near them; the
unforgiving Franklin always looked wrathfully the other
way; the boatswain, if up there, acted likewise but sheep-
ishly; and any hands that happened to be on the poop
(a feeling spreads mysteriously all over a ship) shunned
him as though he had been the devil.

"We know how he arrived on board. For my part I
know so little of prisons that I haven't the faintest notion
how one leaves them. It seems as abominable an opera-
tion as the other, the shutting up with its mental suggestions of bang, snap, crash and the empty silence outside—
where an instant before you were—you *were*—and now
no longer are. Perfectly devilish. And the release! I don't
know which is worse. How do they do it? Pull the string,
door flies open, man flies through: Out you go! *Adios!*
And in the space where a second before you were not,
in the silent space there is a figure going away, limping.
Why limping? I don't know. That's how I see it. One
has a notion of a maiming, crippling process; of the individual coming back damaged in some subtle way. I admit

it is a fantastic hallucination, but I can't help it. Of course I know that the proceedings of the best machine-made humanity are employed with judicious care and so on. I am absurd, no doubt, but still . . . Oh, yes, it's idiotic. When I pass one of these places . . . did you notice that there is something infernal about the aspect of every individual stone or brick of them, something malicious as if matter were enjoying its revenge of the contemptuous spirit of man. Did you notice? You didn't? Eh? Well, I am perhaps a little mad on that point. When I pass one of these places I must avert my eyes. I couldn't have gone to meet de Barral. I should have shrunk from the ordeal. You'll notice that it looks as if Anthony (a brave man indubitably) had shirked it too. Little Fyne's flight of fancy picturing three people in the fatal four-wheeler—you remember?—went wide of the truth. There were only two people in the four-wheeler. Flora did not shrink. Women can stand anything. The dear creatures have no imagination when it comes to solid facts of life. In sentimental regions—I won't say. It's another thing altogether. There they shrink from or rush to embrace ghosts of their own creation just the same as any fool-man would.

"No. I suppose the girl Flora went on that errand reasonably. And then, why! This was the moment for which she had lived. It was her only point of contact with existence. Oh, yes. She had been assisted by the Fynes. And kindly. Certainly. Kindly. But that's not enough. There is a kind way of assisting our fellow-creatures which is enough to break their hearts while it saves their outer envelope. How cold, how infernally cold she must have felt—unless when she was made to burn with indignation or shame. Man, we know, cannot live by bread alone, but hang me if I don't believe that some women could live by love alone. If there be a flame in human beings fed by varied ingredients earthly and spiritual which tinge it in different hues, then I seem to see the colour of theirs. It is azure . . . What the devil are you laughing at? . . ."

Marlow jumped up and strode out of the shadow as if lifted by indignation, but there was the flicker of a smile on his lips. "You say I don't know women. Maybe. It's just as well not to come too close to the shrine. But I have a clear notion of *woman*. In all of them, termagant, flirt, crank, washerwoman, blue-stocking, outcast and even in the ordinary fool of the ordinary commerce there is something left, if only a spark. And when there is a spark there can always be a flame . . ."

He went back into the shadow and sat down again.

"I don't mean to say that Flora de Barral was one of the sort that could live by love alone. In fact she had managed to live without. But still, in the distrust of herself and of others she looked for love, any kind of love, as women will. And that confounded jail was the only spot where she could see it—for she had no reason to distrust her father.

"She was there in good time. I see her gazing across the road at these walls which are, properly speaking, awful. You do indeed seem to feel along the very lines and angles of the unholy bulk, the fall of time, drop by drop, hour by hour, leaf by leaf, with a gentle and implacable slowness. And a voiceless melancholy comes over one, invading, overpowering like a dream, penetrating and mortal like poison.

"When de Barral came out she experienced a sort of shock to see that he was exactly as she remembered him. Perhaps a little smaller. Otherwise unchanged. You come out in the same clothes, you know. I can't tell whether he was looking for her. No doubt he was. Whether he recognized her? Very likely. She crossed the road and at once there was reproduced at a distance of years, as if by some mocking witchcraft, the sight so familiar on the Parade at Brighton of the financier de Barral walking with his only daughter. One comes out of prison in the same clothes one wore on the day of condemnation, no matter how long one has been put away there. Oh, they last! They last! But there is something which is preserved by prison life even better than one's discarded clothing. It is the force, the vividness of one's sentiments. A monastery will do that too; but in the unholy claustration of a jail you are thrown back wholly upon yourself—for God and Faith are not there. The people outside disperse their affections, you hoard yours, you nurse them into intensity. What they let slip, what they forget in the movement and changes of free life, you hold on to, amplify, exaggerate into a rank growth of memories.

They can look with a smile at the troubles and pains of the past; but you can't. Old pains keep on gnawing at your heart, old desires, old deceptions, old dreams, assailing you in the dead stillness of your present where nothing moves except the irrecoverable minutes of your life.

"De Barral was out and, for a time speechless, being led away almost before he had taken possession of the free world, by his daughter. Flora controlled herself well. They walked along quickly for some distance. The cab had been left round the corner—round several corners for all I know. He was flustered, out of breath, when she helped him in and followed herself. Inside that rolling box, turning towards that recovered presence with her heart too full for words she felt the desire of tears she had managed to keep down abandon her suddenly, her half-mournful, half-triumphant exultation subside, every fibre of her body, relaxed in tenderness, go stiff in the close look she took at his face. He *was* different. There was something. Yes, there was something between them, something hard and impalpable, the ghost of these high walls.

"How old he was, how unlike!

"She shook off this impression, amazed and frightened by it of course. And remorseful too. Naturally. She threw her arms round his neck. He returned that hug awkwardly as if not in perfect control of his arms, with a fumbling and uncertain pressure. She hid her face on his breast. It was as though she were pressing it against a stone. They released each other and presently the cab was rolling along at a jog-trot to the docks with those two people as far apart as they could get from each other, in opposite corners.

"After a silence given up to mutual examination he uttered his first coherent sentence outside the walls of the prison.

" 'What has done for me was envy. Envy. There was a lot of them just bursting with it every time they looked my way. I was doing too well. So they went to the Public Prosecutor—'

"She said hastily: 'Yes! Yes! I know,' and he glared as if resentful that the child had turned into a young woman without waiting for him to come out. 'What do

you know about it?' he asked. 'You were too young.'
His speech was soft. The old voice, the old voice! It gave
her a thrill. She recognized its pointless gentleness always
the same no matter what he had to say. And she remembered that he never had much to say when he came down
to see her. It was she who chattered, chattered, on their
walks, while stiff and with a rigidly carried head, he
dropped a gentle word now and then.

"Moved by these recollections waking up within her,
she explained to him that within the last year she had
read and studied the report of the trial.

" 'I went through the files of several papers, papa.'

"He looked at her suspiciously. The reports were probably very incomplete. No doubt the reporters had gar-
bled his evidence. They were determined to give him no
chance either in court or before the public opinion. It
was a conspiracy. . . . 'My counsel was a fool too,' he
added. 'Did you notice? A perfect fool.'

"She laid her hand on his arm soothingly. 'Is it worth
while talking about that awful time? It is so far away
now.' She shuddered slightly at the thought of all the
horrible years which had passed over her young head;
never guessing that for him the time was but yesterday.
He folded his arms on his breast, leaned back in his
corner and bowed his head. But in a little while he made
her jump by asking suddenly:

" 'Who has got hold of the Lone Valley Railway?
That's what they were after mainly. Somebody has got
it. Parfitts and Co. grabbed it—eh? Or was it that fellow
Warner. . . .'

" 'I—I don't know,' she said, quite scared by the
twitching of his lips.

" 'Don't know!' he exclaimed softly. Hadn't her cousin
told her? Oh, yes. She had left them—of course. Why
did she? It was his first question about herself but she
did not answer it. She did not want to talk of these horrors. They were impossible to describe. She perceived
though that he had not expected an answer, because she
heard him muttering to himself that 'There was half a
million's worth of work done and material accumulated
there.'

" 'You mustn't think of these things, papa,' she said
firmly. And he asked her with that invariable gentleness,

in which she seemed now to detect some rather ugly shades, what else had he to think about? Another year or two, if they had only left him alone, he and everybody else would have been all right, rolling in money; and she, his daughter, could have married anybody—anybody. A lord.

"All this was to him like yesterday, a long yesterday, a yesterday gone over innumerable times, analyzed, meditated upon for years. It had a vividness and force for that old man of which his daughter who had not been shut out of the world could have no idea. She was to him the only living figure out of that past, and it was perhaps in perfect good faith that he added, coldly, inexpressive and thin-lipped: 'I lived only for you, I may say. I suppose you understand that. There were only you and me.'

"Moved by this declaration, wondering that it did not warm her heart more, she murmured a few endearing words while the uppermost thought in her mind was that she must tell him now of the situation. She had expected to be questioned anxiously about herself—and while she desired it she shrank from the answers she would have to make. But her father seemed strangely, unnaturally incurious. It looked as if there would be no questions. Still this was an opening. This seemed to be the time for her to begin. And she began. She began by saying that she had always felt like that. There were two of them, to live for each other. And if he only knew what she had gone through!

"Ensconced in his corner, with his arms folded, he stared out of the cab window at the street. How little he was changed after all. It was the unmovable expression, the faded stare she used to see on the Esplanade whenever walking by his side hand in hand she raised her eyes to his face—while she chattered, chattered. It was the same stiff, silent figure which at a word from her would turn rigidly into a shop and buy her anything it occurred to her that she would like to have. Flora de Barral's voice faltered. He bent on her that well-remembered glance in which she had never read anything as a child, except the consciousness of her existence. And that was enough for a child who had never known demonstrative affection. But she had lived a life so starved of all feeling that this was no longer enough for her. What was the good of telling him the story of all these miseries now past and gone, of all those bewildering difficulties and humiliations? What she *must* tell him was difficult enough to say. She approached it by remarking cheerfully—

" 'You haven't even asked me where I am taking you.'

"He started like a somnambulist awakened suddenly, and there was now some meaning in his stare; a sort of alarmed speculation. He opened his mouth slowly. Flora struck in with forced gaiety: 'You would never guess.'

"He waited, still more startled and suspicious. 'Guess! Why don't you tell me?'

"He uncrossed his arms and leaned forward towards her. She got hold of one of his hands. 'You must know first . . .' She paused, made an effort: 'I am married, papa.'

"For a moment they kept perfectly still in that cab rolling on at a steady jog-trot through a narrow city street full of bustle. Whatever she expected she did not expect to feel his hand snatched away from her grasp as if from a burn or a contamination. De Barral fresh from the stagnant torment of the prison (where nothing happens) had not expected that sort of news. It seemed to stick in his throat. In strangled low tones he cried out, 'You—married? You, Flora! When? Married! What for? Who to? Married!'

"His eyes which were blue like hers, only faded, without depth, seemed to start out of their orbits. He did really look as if he were choking. He even put his hand to his collar . . .

"You know," continued Marlow out of the shadow of the bookcase and nearly invisible in the depths of the arm-chair, "the only time I saw him he had given me the impression of absolute rigidity, as though he had swallowed a poker. But it seems that he could collapse. I can hardly picture this to myself. I understand that he did collapse to a certain extent in his corner of the cab. The unexpected had crumpled him up. She regarded him perplexed, pitying, a little disillusioned, and nodded at him gravely: Yes. Married. What she did not like was to see him smile in a manner far from encouraging to the devotion of a daughter. There was something unintentionally savage in it. Old de Barral could not quite command his muscles, as yet. But he had recovered command of his gentle voice.

" 'You were just saying that in this wide world there we were, only you and I, to stick to each other.'

"She was dimly aware of the scathing intention lurking in these soft low tones, in these words which appealed to her poignantly. She defended herself. Never, never for a single moment had she ceased to think of him. Neither did he cease to think of her, he said, with as much sinister emphasis as he was capable of.

" 'But, papa,' she cried, 'I haven't been shut up like you.' She didn't mind speaking of it because he was innocent. He hadn't been understood. It was a misfortune of the most cruel kind but no more disgraceful than an illness, a maiming accident or some other visitation of blind fate. 'I wish I had been too. But I was alone out in the world, the horrid world, that very world which had used you so badly.'

" 'And you couldn't go about in it without finding somebody to fall in love with?' he said. A jealous rage affected his brain like the fumes of wine, rising from some secret depths of his being so long deprived of all emotions. The hollows at the corners of his lips became more pronounced in the puffy roundness of his cheeks. Images, visions, obsess with particular force men withdrawn from the sights and sounds of active life. 'And I did nothing but think of you!' he exclaimed under his breath, contemptuously. 'Think of you! You haunted me, I tell you.'

"Flora said to herself that there was a being who loved her. 'Then we have been haunting each other,' she declared with a pang of remorse. For indeed he had haunted her nearly out of the world, into a final and irremediable desertion. 'Some day I shall tell you . . . No, I don't think I can ever tell you. There was a time when I was mad. But what's the good? It's all over now. We shall forget all this. There will be nothing to remind us.'

"De Barral moved his shoulders.

" 'I think you were mad to tie yourself to . . . How long is it since you are married?'

"She answered 'Not long,' that being the only answer

she dared to make. Everything was so different from what she imagined it would be. He wanted to know why she had said nothing of it in any of her letters; in her last letter. She said:

" 'It was after.'

" 'So recently!' he wondered. 'Couldn't you wait at least till I came out? You could have told me; asked me; consulted me! Let me see—'

"She shook her head negatively. And he was appalled. He thought to himself: Who can he be? Some miserable, silly youth without a penny. Or perhaps some scoundrel? Without making any expressive movement he wrung his loosely clasped hands till the joints cracked. He looked at her. She was pretty. Some low scoundrel who will cast her off. Some plausible vagabond. . . . 'You couldn't wait—eh?'

"Again she made a slight negative sign.

" 'Why not? What was the hurry?' She cast down her eyes. 'It had to be. Yes. It was sudden, but it had to be.'

"He leaned towards her, his mouth open, his eyes wild with virtuous anger, but meeting the absolute candour of her raised glance threw himself back into his corner again.

" 'So tremendously in love with each other—was that it? Couldn't let a father have his daughter all to himself even for a day after—after such a separation. And you know I never had any one, I had no friends. What did I want with those people one meets in the City? The best of them are ready to cut your throat. Yes! Business men, gentlemen, any sort of men and women—out of spite, or to get something. Oh, yes, they can talk fair enough if they think there's something to be got out of you. . . .' His voice was a mere breath yet every word came to Flora as distinctly as if charged with all the moving power of passion. . . . 'My girl, I looked at them making up to me and I would say to myself: What do I care for all that! I am a business man. I am the great Mr. de Barral (yes, yes, some of them twisted their mouths at it, but I was the great Mr. de Barral) and I have my little girl. I wanted nobody and I have never had anybody.'

"A true emotion had unsealed his lips but the words that came out of them were no louder than the murmur of a light wind. It died away.

" 'That's just it,' said Flora de Barral under her breath. Without removing his eyes from her he took off his hat. It was a tall hat. The hat of the trial. The hat of the thumb-nail sketches in the illustrated papers. One comes out in the same clothes, but seclusion counts! It is well known that lurid visions haunt secluded men, monks, hermits—then why not prisoners? De Barral the convict took off the silk hat of the financier de Barral and deposited it on the front seat of the cab. Then he blew out his cheeks. He was red in the face.

" 'And then what happens?' he began again in his contained voice. 'Here I am, overthrown, broken by envy, malice and all uncharitableness. I come out—and what do I find? I find that my girl Flora has gone and married some man or other, perhaps a fool, how do I know; or perhaps—anyway not good enough.'

" 'Stop, papa.'

" 'A silly love affair is likely as not,' he continued monotonously, his thin lips writhing between the ill-omened sunk corners. 'And a very suspicious thing it is too, on the part of a loving daughter.'

"She tried to interrupt him but he went on till she actually clapped her hand on his mouth. He rolled his eyes a bit, but when she took her hand away he remained silent.

" 'Wait. I must tell you. . . . And first of all, papa, understand this, for everything's in that: he is the most generous man in the world. He is . . .'

"De Barral very still in his corner uttered with an effort:

" 'You are in love with him.'

" 'Papa! He came to me. I was thinking of you. I had no eyes for anybody. I could no longer bear to think of you. It was then that he came. Only then. At that time when—when I was going to give up.'

"She gazed into his faded blue eyes as if yearning to be understood, to be given encouragement, peace—a word of sympathy. He declared without animation:

" 'I would like to break his neck.'

"She had the mental exclamation of the overburdened, 'Oh, my God!' and watched him with frightened eyes. But he did not appear insane or in any other way formidable. This comforted her. The silence lasted for some little time. Then suddenly he asked:

" 'What's your name then?'

"For a moment in the profound trouble of the task before her she did not understand what the question meant. Then, her face faintly flushing, she whispered: 'Anthony.'

"Her father, a red spot on each cheek, leaned his head back wearily in the corner of the cab.

" 'Anthony. What is he? Where did he spring from?'

" 'Papa, it was in the country, on a road——'

"He groaned, 'On a road,' and closed his eyes.

" 'It's too long to explain to you now. We shall have lots of time. There are things I could not tell you now. But some day. Some day. For now nothing can part us. Nothing. We are safe as long as we live—nothing can ever come between us.'

" 'You are infatuated with the fellow,' he remarked, without opening his eyes. And she said: 'I believe in him,' in a low voice. 'You and I must believe in him.'

" 'Who the devil is he?'

" 'He's the brother of the lady—you know Mrs. Fyne, she knew mother—who was so kind to me. I was staying in the country, in a cottage, with Mr. and Mrs. Fyne. It was there that we met. He came on a visit. He noticed me. I—well—we are married now.'

"She was thankful that his eyes were shut. It made it easier to talk of the future she had arranged, which now was an unalterable thing. She did not enter on the path of confidences. That was impossible. She felt he would not understand her. She felt also that he suffered. Now and then a great anxiety gripped her heart with a mysterious sense of guilt—as though she had betrayed him into the hands of an enemy. With his eyes shut he had an air of weary and pious meditation. She was a little afraid of it. Next moment a great pity for him filled her heart. And in the background there was remorse. His face twitched now and then just perceptibly. He managed to keep his eyelids down till he heard that the 'husband' was a sailor and that he, the father, was being taken straight on board ship ready to sail away from this abominable world of treacheries, and scorns and envies and lies, away, away over the blue sea, the sure, the inaccessible, the uncontaminated and spacious refuge for wounded souls.

"Something like that. Not the very words perhaps but such was the general sense of her overwhelming argument—the argument of refuge.

"I don't think she gave a thought to material conditions. But as part of that argument set forth breathlessly, as if she were afraid that if she stopped for a moment she could never go on again, she mentioned that generosity of a stormy type, which had come to her from the sea, had caught her up on the brink of unmentionable failure, had whirled her away in its first ardent gust and could be trusted now, implicitly trusted, to carry them both, side by side, into absolute safety.

"She believed it, she affirmed it. He understood thoroughly at last, and at once the interior of that cab, of an aspect so pacific in the eyes of the people on the pavements, became the scene of a great agitation. The generosity of Roderick Anthony—the son of the poet—affected the ex-financier de Barral in a manner which must have brought home to Flora de Barral the extreme arduousness of the business of being a woman. Being a woman is a terribly difficult trade since it consists principally of dealings with men. This man—the man inside the cab—cast off his stiff placidity and behaved like an animal. I don't mean it in an offensive sense. What he did was to give way to an instinctive panic. Like some wild creature scared by the first touch of a net falling on its back, old de Barral began to struggle, lank and angular, against the empty air—as much of it as there was in the cab—with staring eyes and gasping mouth from which his daughter shrank as far as she could in the confined space.

" 'Stop the cab. Stop him, I tell you. Let me get out!' were the strangled exclamations she heard. Why? What for? To do what? He would hear nothing. She cried to him 'Papa! Papa! What do you want to do?' And all she got from him was: 'Stop. I must get out. I want to think. I must get out to think.'

"It was a mercy that he didn't attempt to open the door at once. He only struck his head and shoulders out of the window, crying to the cabman. She saw the consequences, the cab stopping, a crowd collecting around a raving old gentleman. . . . In this terrible business of being a woman so full of fine shades, of delicate perplexities (and very small rewards) you can never know what rough work you may have to do, at any moment. Without hesitation Flora seized her father round the body and pulled back—being astonished at the ease with which she managed to make him drop into his seat again. She kept him there resolutely with one hand pressed against his breast, and leaning across him, she, in her turn, put her head and shoulders out of the window. By then the cab had drawn up to the curbstone and was stopped. 'No! I've changed my mind. Go on please where you were told first. To the docks.'

"She wondered at the steadiness of her own voice. She heard a grunt from the driver and the cab began to roll again. Only then she sank into her place keeping a watchful eye on her companion. He was hardly anything more by this time. Except for her childhood's impressions he was just—a man. Almost a stranger. How was one to deal with him? And there was the other too. Also almost a stranger. The trade of being a woman was very difficult. Too difficult. Flora closed her eyes saying to herself: 'If I think too much about it I shall go mad.' And then opening them she asked her father if the prospect of living always with his daughter and being taken care of by her affection away from the world, which had no honour to give to his grey hairs, was such an awful prospect.

" 'Tell me, is it so bad as that?'

"She put that question sadly, without bitterness. The famous—or notorious—de Barral had lost his rigidity now. He was bent. Nothing more deplorably futile than a bent poker. He said nothing. She added gently, suppressing an uneasy remorseful sigh:

" 'And it might have been worse. You might have found no one, no one in all this town, no one in all the world, not even me! Poor papa!'

"She made a conscience-stricken movement towards him thinking: 'Oh! I am horrible, I am horrible.' And old de Barral scared, tired, bewildered by the extraordinary shocks of his liberation, swayed over and actually leaned his head on her shoulder, as if sorrowing over his regained freedom.

"The movement by itself was touching. Flora, supporting him lightly, imagined that he was crying; and at the thought that had she smashed in a quarry that shoulder together with some other of her bones, this grey and pitiful head would have had nowhere to rest, she too gave way to tears. They flowed quietly, easing her over-strained nerves. Suddenly he pushed her away from him so that her head struck the side of the cab, pushing him-self away too from her as if something had stung him.

"All the warmth went out of her emotion. The very last tears turned cold on her cheek. But their work was done. She had found courage, resolution, as women do, in a good cry. With his hand covering the upper part of his face, whether to conceal his eyes or to shut out an unbearable sight, he was stiffening up in his corner to his usual poker-like consistency. She regarded him in silence. His thin obstinate lips moved. He uttered the name of the cousin—the man, you remember, who did not approve of the Fynes, and whom rightly or wrongly little Fyne suspected of interested motives, in view of de Barral having possibly put away some plunder, some-where before the smash.

"I may just as well tell you at once that I don't know anything more of him. But de Barral was of the opinion, speaking in his low voice from under his hand, that this relation would have been only too glad to have secured his guidance.

" 'Of course I could not come forward in my own name or person. But the advice of a man of my experi-ence is as good as a fortune to anybody wishing to ven-ture into finance. The same sort of thing can be done again.'

"He shuffled his feet a little, let fall his hand; and turning carefully towards his daughter his puffy round cheeks, his round chin resting on his collar, he bent on her the faded, resentful gaze of his pale eyes, which were wet.

" 'The start is really only a matter of judicious adver-tising. There's no difficulty. And here you go and . . .'

"He turned his face away. 'After all I am still de Bar-ral, *the* de Barral. Didn't you remember that?'

" 'Papa,' said Flora; 'listen. It's you who must remem-ber that there is no longer a de Barral . . .' He looked at her sideways anxiously. 'There is Mr. Smith, whom no harm, no trouble, no wicked lies of evil people can ever touch.'

" 'Mr. Smith,' he breathed out slowly. 'Where does he belong to? There's not even a Miss Smith.'

" 'There is your Flora.'

" 'My Flora! You went and . . . I can't bear to think of it. It's horrible.'

" 'Yes. It was horrible enough at times,' she said with feeling, because somehow, obscurely, what this man said appealed to her as if it were her own thought clothed in an enigmatic emotion. 'I think with shame sometimes how I . . . No not yet. I shall not tell you. At least not now.'

"The cab turned into the gateway of the dock. Flora handed the tall hat to her father. 'Here, papa. And please be good. I suppose you love me. If you don't, then I wonder who——'

"He put the hat on, and stiffened hard in his corner, kept a sidelong glance on his girl. 'Try to be nice for my sake. Think of the years I have been waiting for you. I do indeed want support—and peace. A little peace.'

"She clasped his arm suddenly with both hands pressing with all her might as if to crush the resistance she felt in him. 'I could not have peace if I did not have you with me. I won't let you go. Not after all I went through. I won't.' The nervous force of her grip frightened him a little. She laughed suddenly. 'It's absurd. It's as if I were asking you for a sacrifice. What am I afraid of? Where could you go? I mean now, to-day, to-night? You can't tell me. Have you thought of it? Well, I have been thinking of it for the last year. Longer. I nearly went mad trying to find out. I believe I was mad for a time or else I should never have thought . . .'

"This was as near as she came to a confession," remarked Marlow in a changed tone. "The confession I mean of that walk to the top of the quarry which she reproached herself with so bitterly. And he made of it what his fancy suggested. It could not possibly have been a just notion. The cab stopped alongside the ship and they got out in the manner described by the sensitive Franklin. I don't know if they suspected each other's sanity at the end of that drive. But that is possible. We all seem a little mad to each other; an excellent arrangement for the bulk of humanity which finds in it an easy motive of forgiveness. Flora crossed the quarterdeck with a rapidity born of apprehension. It had grown unbearable. She wanted this business over. She was thankful on looking back to see he was following her. 'If he bolts away,' she thought, 'then I shall know that I am of no account indeed! That no one loves me, that words and actions and protestations and everything in the world is false— and I shall jump into the dock. *That* at least won't lie.'

"Well, I don't know. If it had come to that she would have been most likely fished out, what with her natural want of luck and the good many people on the quay and on board. And just where the *Ferndale* was moored there hung on a wall (I know the berth) a coil of line, a pole, and a life-buoy kept there on purpose to save people who tumble into the dock. It's not so easy to get away from life's betrayals as she thought. However it did not come to that. .He followed her with his quick gliding walk. Mr. Smith! The liberated convict de Barral passed off the solid earth for the last time, vanished for ever, and there was Mr. Smith added to that world of waters which harbours so many queer fishes. An old gentleman in a silk hat, darting wary glances. He followed, because mere existence has its claims which are obeyed mechanically. I have no doubt he presented a respectable figure. Father-in-law. Nothing more respectable. But he carried in his heart the confused pain of dismay and affection, of involuntary repulsion and pity. Very much like his daughter. Only in addition he felt a furious jealousy of the man he was going to see.

"A residue of egoism remains in every affection—even paternal. And this man in the seclusion of his prison had thought himself into such a sense of ownership of that single human being he had to think about, as may well be inconceivable to us who have not had to serve a long (and wickedly unjust) sentence of penal servitude. She was positively the only thing, the one point where his thought found a resting-place, for years. She was the only outlet for his imagination. He had not much of that faculty to be sure, but there was in it the force of concentration. He felt outraged, and perhaps it was an absurdity on his part, but I venture to suggest rather in degree than in kind. I have a notion that no usual, normal father is pleased at parting with his daughter. No. Not even when he rationally appreciates 'Jane being taken off his hands' or perhaps is able to exult at an excellent match. At bottom, quite deep down, down in the dark (in some cases only by digging), there is to be found a certain repugnance. . . . With mothers of course it is different. Women are more loyal, not to each other, but to their common femininity which they behold triumphant with a secret and proud satisfaction.

"The circumstances of that match added to Mr. Smith's indignation. And if he followed his daughter into that ship's cabin it was as if into a house of disgrace and only because he was still bewildered by the suddenness of the thing. His will, so long lying fallow, was overborne by her determination and by a vague fear of that regained liberty.

"You will be glad to hear that Anthony, though he did shirk the welcome on the quay, behaved admirably, with the simplicity of a man who has no small meannesses and makes no mean reservations. His eyes did not flinch and his tongue did not falter. He was, I have it on the best authority, admirable in his earnestness, in his sincerity and also in his restraint. He was perfect. Nevertheless the vital force of his unknown individuality addressing him so familiarly was enough to fluster Mr. Smith. Flora saw her father trembling in all his exiguous length, though he held himself stiffer than ever if that was possible. He muttered a little and at last managed to utter, not loud of course but very distinctly: 'I am here under protest,' the corners of his mouth sunk disparagingly, his eyes stony. 'I am here under protest. I have been locked up by a conspiracy. I——'

"He raised his hands to his forehead—his silk hat was on the table rim upwards; he had put it there with a despairing gesture as he came in—he raised his hands to his forehead. 'It seems to me unfair. I——' He broke off again. Anthony looked at Flora who stood by the side of her father.—'Well, sir, you will soon get used to me. Surely you and she must have had enough of shore-people and their confounded half-and-half ways to last you both for a life-time. A particularly merciful lot they are too. You ask Flora. I am alluding to my own sister, her best friend, and not a bad woman either as they go.'

"The captain of the *Ferndale* checked himself. 'Lucky thing I was there to step in. I want you to make yourself at home, and before long——'

"The faded stare of the Great de Barral silenced Anthony by its inexpressive fixity. He signalled with his eyes to Flora towards the door of the state-room fitted specially to receive Mr. Smith, the free man. She seized the free man's hat off the table and took him caressingly under the arm. 'Yes! This is home, come and see your room, papa!'

"Anthony himself threw open the door and Flora took care to shut it carefully behind herself and her father. 'See,' she began but desisted because it was clear that he would look at none of the contrivances for his comfort. She herself had hardly seen them before. He was looking only at the new carpet and she waited till he should raise his eyes.

"He didn't do that but spoke in his usual voice. 'So this is your husband, that . . . And I locked up!'

" 'Papa, what's the good of harping on that?' she remonstrated no louder. 'He is kind.'

" 'And you went and . . . married him so that he should be kind to me. Is that it? How did you know that I wanted anybody to be kind to me?'

" 'How strange you are!' she said thoughtfully.

" 'It's hard for a man who has gone through what I have gone through to feel like other people. Has that occurred to you? . . .' He looked up at last. . . . 'Mrs. Anthony, I can't bear the sight of the fellow.' She met his eyes without flinching and he added, 'You want to go to him now.' His mild automatic manner seemed the effect of tremendous self-restraint—and yet she remembered him always like that. She felt cold all over.

" 'Why, of course, I must go to him,' she said with a slight start.

"He gnashed his teeth at her and she went out.

"Anthony had not moved from the spot. One of his hands was resting on the table. She went up to him, stopped, then deliberately moved still closer. 'Thank you, Roderick.'

" 'You needn't thank me,' he murmured. 'It's I who . . .'

" 'No, perhaps I needn't. You do what you like. But you are doing it well.'

"He sighed then hardly above a whisper because they were near the state-room door, 'Upset, eh?'

"She made no sign, no sound of any kind. The thorough falseness of the position weighed on them both. But he was the braver of the two. 'I dare say. At first. Did you think of telling him you were happy?'

" 'He never asked me,' she smiled faintly at him. She was disappointed by his quietness. 'I did not say more than I was absolutely obliged to say—of myself.' She was beginning to be irritated with this man a little. 'I told him I had been very lucky,' she said suddenly despondent, missing Anthony's masterful manner, that something arbitrary and tender which, after the first scare, she had accustomed herself to look forward to with pleasurable apprehension. He was contemplating her rather blankly. She had not taken off her outdoor things, hat, gloves. She was like a caller. And she had a movement suggesting the end of a not very satisfactory business call. 'Perhaps it would be just as well if we went ashore. Time yet.'

"He gave her a glimpse of his unconstrained self in the low vehement 'You dare!' which sprang to his lips and out of them with a most menacing inflection.

" 'You dare . . . What's the matter now?'

"These last words were shot out not at her but at some target behind her back. Looking over her shoulder she saw the bald head with black bunches of hair of the congested and devoted Franklin (he had his cap in his hand) gazing sentimentally from the saloon doorway with his lobster eyes. He was heard from the distance in a tone of injured innocence reporting that the berthing master was alongside and that he wanted to move the ship into the basin before the crew came on board.

"His captain growled 'Well, let him,' and waved away the ulcerated and pathetic soul behind these prominent eyes which lingered on the offensive woman while the mate backed out slowly. Anthony turned to Flora.

" 'You could not have meant it. You are as straight as they make them.'

" 'I am trying to be.'

" 'Then don't joke in that way. Think of what would become of—me.'

" 'Oh, yes. I forgot. No, I didn't mean it. It wasn't a joke. It was forgetfulness. You wouldn't have been wronged. I couldn't have gone. I—I am too tired.'

"He saw she was swaying where she stood and restrained himself violently from taking her into his arms, his frame trembling with fear as though he had been tempted to an act of unparalleled treachery. He stepped aside and lowering his eyes pointed to the door of the stern-cabin. It was only after she passed by him that he looked up and thus he did not see the angry glance she gave him before she moved on. He looked after her. She tottered slightly just before reaching the door and flung it to behind her nervously.

"Anthony—he had felt this crash as if the door had been slammed inside his very breast—stood for a moment without moving and then shouted for Mrs. Brown. This was the steward's wife, his lucky inspiration to make Flora comfortable. 'Mrs. Brown! Mrs. Brown!' At last she appeared from somewhere. 'Mrs. Anthony has come on board. Just gone into the cabin. Hadn't you better see if you can be of any assistance?'

" 'Yes, sir.'

"And again he was alone with the situation he had created in the hardihood and inexperience of his heart. He thought he had better go on deck. In fact he ought to have been there before. At any rate it would be the usual thing for him to be on deck. But a sound of muttering and of faint thuds somewhere near by arrested his attention. They proceeded from Mr. Smith's room, he perceived. It was very extraordinary. 'He's talking to himself,' he thought. 'He seems to be thumping the bulkhead with his fists—or his head.'

"Anthony's eyes grew big with wonder while he listened to these noises. He became so attentive that he did not notice Mrs. Brown till she actually stopped before him for a moment to say—

" 'Mrs. Anthony doesn't want any assistance, sir.'

"This was, you understand, the voyage before Mr. Powell—young Powell then—joined the *Ferndale;* chance having arranged that he should get his start in life in that

particular ship of all the ships then in the port of London.
The most unrestful ship that ever sailed out of any port
on earth. I am not alluding to her sea-going qualities.
Mr. Powell tells me she was as steady as a church. I mean
unrestful in the sense, for instance, which this planet of
ours is unrestful—a matter of an uneasy atmosphere disturbed by passions, jealousies, loves, hates and the troubles of transcendental good intentions, which, though
ethically valuable, I have no doubt cause often more
unhappiness than the plots of the most evil tendency. For
those who refuse to believe in chance he, I mean Mr.
Powell, must have been obviously predestined to add his
native ingenuousness to the sum of all the others carried
by the honest ship *Ferndale*. He was too ingenuous.
Everybody on board was, exception being made of Mr.
Smith who, however, was simple enough in his way, with
that terrible simplicity of the fixed idea, for which there
is also another name men pronounce with dread and
aversion. His fixed idea was to save his girl from the man
who had possessed himself of her (I use these words on
purpose because the image they suggest was clearly in
Mr. Smith's mind), possessed himself unfairly of her
while he, the father, was locked up.

" 'I won't rest till I have got you away from that man,'
he would murmur to her after long periods of contemplation. We know from Powell how he used to sit on the
skylight near the long deck-chair on which Flora was
reclining, gazing into her face from above with an air of
guardianship and investigation at the same time.

"It is almost impossible to say if he ever had considered the event rationally. The avatar of de Barral into
Mr. Smith had not been effected without a shock—that
much one must recognize. It may be that it drove all
practical considerations out of his mind, making room for
awful and precise visions which nothing could dislodge
afterwards. And it might have been the tenacity, the
unintelligent tenacity, of the man who had persisted in
throwing millions of other people's thrift into the Lone
Valley Railway, the Labrador Docks, the Spotted Leop-
ard Copper Mine, and other grotesque speculations
exposed during the famous de Barral trial, amongst mur-
murs of astonishment mingled with bursts of laughter.
For it is in the Courts of Law that Comedy finds its

last refuge in our deadly serious world. As to tears and lamentations these were not heard in the august precincts of Comedy, because they were indulged in privately in several thousand homes, where, with a fine dramatic effect, Hunger had taken the place of Thrift.

"But there was one at least who did not laugh in court. That person was the accused. The notorious de Barral did not laugh because he was indignant. He was impervious to words, to facts, to inferences. It would have been impossible to make him see his guilt or his folly—either by evidence or argument—if anybody had tried to argue.

"Neither did his daughter Flora try to argue with him. The cruelty of her position was so great, its complications so thorny if I may express myself so, that a passive attitude was yet her best refuge—as it had been before her of so many women.

"For that sort of inertia in woman is always enigmatic and therefore menacing. It makes one pause. A woman may be a fool, a sleepy fool, an agitated fool, a too awfully noxious fool, and she may even be simply stupid. But she is never dense. She's never made of wood through and through as some men are. There is in woman always, somewhere, a spring. Whatever men don't know about women (and it may be a lot or it may be very little) men and even fathers do know that much. And that is why so many men are afraid of them.

"Mr. Smith, I believe, was afraid of his daughter's quietness though of course he interpreted it in his own way.

"He would, as Mr. Powell depicts, sit on the skylight and bend over the reclining girl, wondering what there was behind the lost gaze under the darkened eyelids in the still eyes. He would look and look and then he would say, whisper rather, it didn't take much for his voice to drop to a mere breath—he would declare, transferring his faded stare to the horizon, that he would never rest till he had 'got her away from that man.'

" 'You don't know what you are saying, papa.'

"She would try not to show her weariness, the nervous strain of these two men's antagonism around her person which was the cause of her languid attitudes. For as a matter of fact the sea agreed with her.

"As likely as not Anthony would be walking on the

other side of the deck. The strain was making him restless. He couldn't sit still anywhere. He had tried shutting himself up in his cabin; but that was no good. He would jump up to rush on deck and tramp, tramp up and down that poop till he felt ready to drop, without being able to wear down the agitation of his soul, generous indeed, but weighted by its envelope of blood and muscle and bone; handicapped by the brain creating precise images and everlastingly speculating, speculating—looking out for signs, watching for symptoms.

"And Mr. Smith with a slight backward jerk of his small head at the footsteps on the other side of the skylight would insist in his awful, hopelessly gentle voice that he knew very well what he was saying. Hadn't she given herself to that man while he was locked up?

" 'Helpless, in jail, with no one to think of, nothing to look forward to, but my daughter. And then when they let me out at last I find her gone—for it amounts to this. Sold. Because you've sold yourself; you know you have.'

"With his round unmoved face, a lot of fine white hair waving in the wind-eddies of the spanker, his glance levelled over the sea, he seemed to be addressing the universe across her reclining form. She would protest sometimes.

" 'I wish you would not talk like this, papa. You are only tormenting me, and tormenting yourself.'

" 'Yes, I am tormented enough,' he admitted meaningly. But it was not talking about it that tormented him. It was thinking of it. And to sit and look at it was worse for him than it possibly could have been for her to go and give herself up, bad as that must have been.

" 'For of course you suffered. Don't tell me you didn't. You must have.'

"She had renounced very soon all attempts at protests. It was useless. It might have made things worse; and she did not want to quarrel with her father, the only human being that really cared for her, absolutely, evidently, completely—to the end. There was in him no pity, no generosity, nothing whatever of these fine things—it was for *her*, for her very own self, such as it was, that this human being cared. This certitude would have made her put up with worse torments. For, of course, she too was being tormented. She felt also helpless, as if the whole enterprise had been too much for her. This is the sort of conviction which makes for quietude. She was becoming a fatalist.

"What must have been rather appalling were the necessities of daily life, the intercourse of current trifles. That naturally had to go on. They wished good morning to each other, they sat down together to meals—and I believe there would be a game of cards now and then in the evening, especially at first. What frightened her most was the duplicity of her father, at least what looked like duplicity, when she remembered his persistent, insistent whispers on deck. However her father was a taciturn person as far back as she could remember him best—on the Parades. It was she who chattered, never troubling herself to discover whether he was pleased or displeased. And now she couldn't fathom his thoughts. Neither did she chatter to him. Anthony with a forced friendly smile as if frozen to his lips seemed only too thankful at not being made to speak. Mr. Smith sometimes forgot himself while studying his hand so long that Flora had to recall him to himself by a murmured 'Papa—your lead.' Then he apologized by a faint as if inward ejaculation. 'Beg your pardon, Captain.' Naturally she addressed Anthony as Roderick and he addressed her as Flora. This was all the acting that was necessary to judge from the wincing twitch of the old man's mouth at every uttered 'Flora.' On hearing the rare 'Rodericks' he had sometimes a scornful grimace as faint and faded and colourless as his whole stiff personality.

"He would be the first to retire. He was not infirm. With him too the life on board ship seemed to agree; but from a sense of duty, of affection, or to placate his hidden fury, his daughter always accompanied him to his stateroom 'to make him comfortable.' She lighted his lamp, helped him into his dressing-gown or got him a book from a bookcase fitted in there—but this last rarely, because Mr. Smith used to declare 'I am no reader' with something like pride in his low tones. Very often after kissing her good-night on the forehead he would treat her to some such fretful remark: 'It's like being in jail—'pon my word. I suppose that man is out there waiting for you. Head jailer! Ough!'

"She would smile vaguely; murmur a conciliatory 'How absurd.' But once, out of patience, she said quite sharply 'Leave off. It hurts me. One would think you hate me.'

" 'It isn't you I hate,' he went on monotonously breathing at her. 'No, it isn't you. But if I saw that you loved that man I think I could hate you too.'

"That word struck straight at her heart. 'You wouldn't be the first then,' she muttered bitterly. But he was busy with his fixed idea and uttered an awfully equable 'But you don't! Unfortunate girl!'

"She looked at him steadily for a time then said:

" 'Good-night, papa.'

"As a matter of fact Anthony very seldom waited for her alone at the table with the scattered cards, glasses, water-jug, bottles and so on. He took no more opportunities to be alone with her than was absolutely necessary for the edification of Mrs. Brown. Excellent, faithful woman; the wife of his still more excellent and faithful steward. And Flora wished all these excellent people, devoted to Anthony, she wished them all further; and especially the nice, pleasant-spoken Mrs. Brown with her beady, mobile eyes and her 'Yes, certainly, ma'am,' which seemed to her to have a mocking sound. And so this short trip—to the Western Islands only—came to an end. It was so short that when young Powell joined the *Ferndale* by a memorable stroke of chance, no more than seven months had elapsed since the—let us say liberation of the convict de Barral and his avatar into Mr. Smith.

"For the time the ship was loading in London Anthony took a cottage near a little country station in Essex, to house Mr. Smith and Mr. Smith's daughter. It was altogether his idea. How far it was necessary for Mr. Smith to seek rural retreat I don't know. Perhaps to some extent it was a judicious arrangement. There were some obligations incumbent on the liberated de Barral (in connection with reporting himself to the police I imagine) which Mr. Smith was not anxious to perform. De Barral had to vanish; the theory was that de Barral had vanished, and it had to be upheld. Poor Flora liked the country, even if the spot had nothing more to recommend it than its retired character.

"Now and then Captain Anthony ran down; but as the station was a real wayside one, with no early morning trains up, he could never stay for more than the afternoon. It appeared that he must sleep in town so as to be early on board his ship. The weather was magnificent and whenever the captain of the *Ferndale* was seen on a brilliant afternoon coming down the road Mr. Smith would seize his stick and toddle off for a solitary walk. But whether he would get tired or because it gave him some satisfaction to see 'that man' go away—or for some cunning reason of his own, he was always back before the hour of Anthony's departure. On approaching the cottage he would see generally 'that man' lying on the grass in the orchard at some distance from his daughter seated in a chair brought out of the cottage's living-room. Invariably Mr. Smith made straight for them and as invariably had the feeling that his approach was not disturbing a very intimate conversation. He sat with them, through a silent hour or so, and then it would be time for Anthony to go. Mr. Smith, perhaps from discretion, would casually vanish a minute or so before, and then watch through the diamond panes of an upstairs room 'that man' take a lingering look outside the gate at the invisible Flora, lift his hat, like a caller, and go off down the road. Then only Mr. Smith would join his daughter again.

"These were the bad moments for her. Not always, of course, but frequently. It was nothing extraordinary to hear Mr. Smith begin gently with some observation like this:

" 'That man is getting tired of you.'

"He would never pronounce Anthony's name. It was always 'that man.'

"Generally she would remain mute with wide-open eyes gazing at nothing between the gnarled fruit trees. Once, however, she got up and walked into the cottage. Mr. Smith followed her carrying the chair. He banged it down resolutely and in that smooth inexpressive tone so many ears used to bend eagerly to catch when it came from the Great de Barral he said:

" 'Let's get away.'

"She had the strength of mind not to spin round. On the contrary she went on to a shabby bit of a mirror on the wall. In the greenish glass her own face looked far off like the livid face of a drowned corpse at the bottom of a pool. She laughed faintly.

" 'I tell you that man's getting——'

" 'Papa,' she interrupted him. 'I have no illusions as to myself. It has happened to me before, but——'

"Her voice failing her suddenly her father struck in with quite an unwonted animation. 'Let's make a rush for it then.'

"Having mastered both her fright and her bitterness, she turned round, sat down and allowed her astonishment to be seen. Mr. Smith sat down too, his knees together and bent at right angles, his thin legs parallel to each other and his hands resting on the arms of the wooden arm-chair. His hair had grown long, his head was set stiffly, there was something fatuously venerable in his aspect.

" 'You can't care for him. Don't tell me. I understand your motive. And I have called you an unfortunate girl. You are that as much as if you had gone on the streets. Yes. Don't interrupt me, Flora. I was everlastingly being interrupted at the trial and I can't stand it any more. I won't be interrupted by my own child. And when I think that it is on the very day before they let me out that you . . .'

"He had wormed this fact out of her by that time because Flora had got tired of evading the question. He had been very much struck and distressed. Was that the trust she had in him? Was that a proof of confidence and love? The very day before! Never given him even half a chance. It was as at the trial. They never gave him a chance. They would not give him time. And there was his own daughter acting exactly as his bitterest enemies had done. Not giving him time!

"The monotony of that subdued voice nearly lulled her dismay to sleep. She listened to the unavoidable things he was saying.

" 'But what induced that man to marry you? Of course he's a gentleman. One can see that. And that makes it worse. Gentlemen don't understand anything about city affairs—finance. Why!—the people who started the cry after me were a firm of gentlemen. The counsel, the judge—all gentlemen—quite out of it! No notion of . . . And then he's a sailor too. Just a skipper——'

" 'My grandfather was nothing else,' she interrupted. And he made an angular gesture of impatience.

" 'Yes. But what does a silly sailor know of business? Nothing. No conception. He can have no idea of what it means to be the daughter of Mr. de Barral—even after his enemies had smashed him. What on earth induced him——'

"She made a movement because the level voice was getting on her nerves. And he paused, but only to go on again in the same tone with the remark:

" 'Of course you are pretty. And that's why you are lost—like many other poor girls. Unfortunate is the word for you.'

"She said: 'It may be. Perhaps it is the right word; but listen, papa. I mean to be honest.'

"He began to exhale more speeches.

" 'Just the sort of man to get tired and then leave you and go off with his beastly ship. And anyway you can never be happy with him. Look at his face. I want to save you. You see I was not perhaps a very good husband to your poor mother. She would have done better to have left me long before she died. I have been thinking it all over. I won't have you unhappy.'

"He ran his eyes over her with an attention which was surprisingly noticeable. Then said, 'H'm! Yes. Let's clear out before it is too late. Quietly, you and I.'

"She said as if inspired and with that calmness which despair often gives: 'There is no money to go away with, papa.'

"He rose up straightening himself as though he were a hinged figure. She said decisively:

" 'And of course you wouldn't think of deserting me, papa?'

" 'Of course not,' sounded his subdued tone. And he left her, gliding away with his walk which Mr. Powell described to me as being as level and wary as his voice. He walked as if he were carrying a glass full of water on his head.

"Flora naturally said nothing to Anthony of that edifying conversation. His generosity might have taken alarm at it and she did not want to be left behind to manage her father alone. And moreover she was too honest. She would be honest at whatever cost. She would not be the first to speak. Never. And the thought came into her head: 'I am indeed an unfortunate creature!'

"It was by the merest coincidence that Anthony coming for the afternoon two days later had a talk with Mr. Smith in the orchard. Flora for some reason or other had left them for a moment; and Anthony took that opportunity to be frank with Mr. Smith. He said: 'It seems to me, sir, that you think Flora has not done very well for herself. Well, as to that I can't say anything. All I want you to know is that I have tried to do the right thing.' And then he explained that he had willed everything he was possessed of to her. 'She didn't tell you, I suppose?'

"Mr. Smith shook his head slightly. And Anthony, trying to be friendly, was just saying that he proposed to keep the ship away from home for at least two years: 'I think, sir, that from every point of view it would be best,' when Flora came back and the conversation, cut short in that direction, languished and died. Later in the evening, after Anthony had been gone for hours, on the point of separating for the night, Mr. Smith remarked suddenly to his daughter after a long period of brooding:

" 'A will is nothing. One tears it up. One makes another.' Then after reflecting for a minute he added unemotionally:

" 'One tells lies about it.'

"Flora, patient, steeled against every hurt and every disgust to the point of wondering at herself, said: 'You push your dislike of—of—Roderick too far, papa. You have no regard for me. You hurt me.'

"He, as ever inexpressive to the point of terrifying her sometimes by the contrast of his placidity and his words, turned away from her a pair of faded eyes.

" 'I wonder how far *your* dislike goes,' he began. 'His very name sticks in your throat. I've noticed it. It hurts me. What do you think of that? You might remember that you are not the only person that's hurt by your folly, by your hastiness, by your recklessness.' He brought back his eyes to her face. 'And the very day before they were going to let me out.' His feeble voice failed him altogether, the narrow compressed lips only trembling for a time before he added with that extraordinary equanimity of tone, 'I call it sinful.'

"Flora made no answer. She judged it simpler, kinder and certainly safer to let him talk himself out. This, Mr. Smith, being naturally taciturn, never took very long to do. And we must not imagine that this sort of thing went on all the time. She had a few good days in that cottage. The absence of Anthony was a relief and his visits were pleasurable. She was quieter. He was quieter too. She was almost sorry when the time to join the ship arrived. It was a moment of anguish, of excitement; they arrived at the dock in the evening and Flora after 'making her father comfortable' according to established usage lingered in the state-room long enough to notice that he was surprised. She caught his pale eyes observing her quite stonily. Then she went out after a cheery good-night.

"Contrary to her hopes she found Anthony yet in the saloon. Sitting in his arm-chair at the head of the table he was picking up some business papers which he put hastily in his breast pocket and got up. He asked her if her day, travelling up to town and then doing some shopping, had tired her. She shook her head. Then he wanted to know in a half-jocular way how she felt about going away, and for a long voyage this time.

" 'Does it matter how I feel?' she asked in a tone that cast a gloom over his face. He answered with repressed violence which she did not expect:

" 'No, it does not matter, because I cannot go without you. I've told you. . . . You know it. You don't think I could.'

" 'I assure you I haven't the slightest wish to evade my obligations,' she said steadily. 'Even if I could. Even if I dared, even if I had to die for it!'

"He looked thunderstruck. They stood facing each other at the end of the saloon. Anthony stuttered. 'Oh, no. You won't die. You don't mean it. You have taken kindly to the sea.'

"She laughed, but she felt angry.

" 'No, I don't mean it. I tell you I don't mean to evade my obligations. I shall live on . . . feeling a little crushed, nevertheless.'

" 'Crushed!' he repeated. 'What's crushing you?'

" 'Your magnanimity,' she said sharply. But her voice was softened after a time. 'Yet I don't know. There is a perfection in it—do you understand me, Roderick?—which makes it almost possible to bear.'

"He sighed, looked away, and remarked that it was time to put out the lamp in the saloon. The permission was only till ten o'clock.

" 'But you needn't mind that so much in your cabin. Just see that the curtains of the ports are drawn close and that's all. The steward might have forgotten to do it. He lighted your reading-lamp in there before he went ashore for a last evening with his wife. I don't know if it was wise to get rid of Mrs. Brown. You will have to look after yourself, Flora.'

"He was quite anxious; but Flora as a matter of fact congratulated herself on the absence of Mrs. Brown. No sooner had she closed the door of her state-room than she murmured fervently 'Yes! Thank goodness, she is gone.' There would be no gentle knock, followed by her appearance with her equivocal stare and the intolerable: 'Can I do anything for you, ma'am?' which poor Flora had learned to fear and hate more than any voice or any words on board that ship—her only refuge from the world which had no use for her, for her imperfections and for her troubles.

"Mrs. Brown had been very much vexed at her dismissal. The Browns were a childless couple and the arrangement had suited them perfectly. Their resentment was very bitter. Mrs. Brown had to remain ashore alone with her rage, but the steward was nursing his on board. Poor Flora had no greater enemy, the aggrieved mate had no greater sympathizer. And Mrs. Brown, with a woman's quick power of observation and inference (the putting of two and two together), had come to a certain conclusion which she had imparted to her husband before leaving the ship. The morose steward permitted himself once to make an allusion to it in Powell's hearing. It was in the officers' messroom at the end of a meal while he lingered after putting a fruit pie on the table. He and the chief mate started a dialogue about the alarming change in the captain, the sallow steward looking down with a sinister frown, Franklin rolling upwards his eyes, sentimental in a red face. Young Powell had heard a lot of that sort of thing by that time. It was growing monotonous; it had always sounded to him a little absurd. He struck in impatiently with the remark that such lamentations over a man merely because he had taken a wife seemed to him like lunacy.

"Franklin muttered, 'Depends on what the wife is up to.' The steward leaning against the bulkhead near the door glowered at Powell, that new-comer, that ignoramus, that stranger without right or privileges. He snarled—

" 'Wife! Call her a wife, do you?'

" 'What the devil do you mean by this?' exclaimed young Powell.

" 'I know what I know. My old woman has not been six months on board for nothing. You had better ask her when we get back.'

"And meeting sullenly the withering stare of Mr. Powell the steward retreated backwards.

"Our young friend turned at once upon the mate. 'And you let that confounded bottle-washer talk like this before you, Mr. Franklin. Well, I am astonished.'

" 'Oh, it isn't what you think? It isn't what you think.' Mr. Franklin looked more apoplectic than ever. 'If it comes to that I *could* astonish you. But it's no use. I myself can hardly . . . You couldn't understand. I hope you won't try to make mischief. There was a time, young fellow, when I would have dared any man—any man, you hear?—to make mischief between me and Captain Anthony. But not now. Not now. There's a change! Not in me though . . .'

"Young Powell rejected with indignation any suggestion of making mischief. 'Who do you take me for?' he cried. 'Only you had better tell that steward to be careful what he says before me or I'll spoil his good looks for him for a month and will leave him to explain the why of it to the captain the best way he can.'

"This speech established Powell as a champion of Mrs. Anthony. Nothing more bearing on the question was ever said before him. He did not care for the steward's black looks; Franklin, never conversational even at the best of times and avoiding now the only topic near his heart, addressed him only on matters of duty. And for that, too, Powell cared very little. The woes of the apoplectic mate had begun to bore him long before. Yet he felt lonely a bit at times. Therefore the little intercourse with Mrs. Anthony either in one dog-watch or the other was something to be looked forward to. The captain did not mind it. That was evident from his manner. One night he inquired (they were then alone on the poop) what they had been talking about that evening? Powell had to confess that it was about the ship. Mrs. Anthony had been asking him questions.

" 'Takes interest—eh?' jerked out the captain, moving rapidly up and down the weather side of the poop.

" 'Yes, sir. Mrs. Anthony seems to get hold wonderfully of what one's telling her.'

" 'Sailor's granddaughter. One of the old school. Old sea-dog of the best kind, I believe,' ejaculated the captain, swinging past his motionless second officer and leaving the words behind him like a trail of sparks succeeded by a perfect conversational darkness, because, for the next two hours till he left the deck, he didn't open his lips again.

"On another occasion . . . we mustn't forget that the ship had crossed the line and was adding up south latitude every day by then . . . on another occasion, about seven in the evening, Powell on duty, heard his name uttered softly in the companion. The captain was on the stairs, thin-faced, his eyes sunk, on his arm a Shetland wool wrap.

" 'Mr. Powell—here.'

" 'Yes, sir.'

" 'Give this to Mrs. Anthony. Evenings are getting chilly.'

"And the haggard face sank out of sight. Mrs. Anthony was surprised on seeing the shawl.

" 'The captain wants you to put this on,' explained young Powell, and as she raised herself in her seat he dropped it on her shoulders. She wrapped herself up closely.

" 'Where was the captain?' she asked.

" 'He was in the companion. Called me on purpose,' said Powell, and then retreated discreetly, because she looked as though she didn't want to talk any more that evening. Mr. Smith—the old gentleman—was as usual sitting on the skylight near her head, brooding over the long chair but by no means inimical, as far as his unreadable face went, to those conversations of the two youngest people on board. In fact they seemed to give him some pleasure. Now and then he would raise his faded china eyes to the animated face of Mr. Powell thoughtfully. When the young sailor was by, the old man became less rigid, and when his daughter, on rare occasions, smiled at some artless tale of Mr. Powell, the inexpressive face of Mr. Smith reflected dimly that flash of evanescent mirth. For Mr. Powell had come now to entertain his captain's wife with anecdotes from the not very distant past when he was a boy, on board various ships— funny things do happen on board ship. Flora was quite surprised at times to find herself amused. She was even heard to laugh twice in the course of a month. It was not a loud sound but it was startling enough at the afterend of the *Ferndale* where low tones or silence was the rule. The second time this happened the captain himself must have been startled somewhere down below; because he emerged from the depths of his unobtrusive existence and began his tramping on the opposite side of the poop.

"Almost immediately he called his young second officer over to him. This was not done in displeasure. The glance he fastened on Mr. Powell conveyed a sort of approving wonder. He engaged him in desultory conversation as if for the only purpose of keeping a man who could provoke such a sound near his person. Mr. Powell felt himself liked. He felt it. Liked by that haggard, restless man who threw at him disconnected phrases to which his answers were, 'Yes, sir,' 'No, sir,' 'Oh, certainly,' 'I suppose so, sir,'—and might have been clearly anything else for all the other cared.

"It was then, Mr. Powell told me, that he discovered in himself an already old-established liking for Captain Anthony. He also felt sorry for him without being able to discover the origins of that sympathy of which he had become so suddenly aware.

"Meantime Mr. Smith, bending forward stiffly as though he had a hinged back, was speaking to his daughter.

"She was a child no longer. He wanted to know if she believed in—in hell. In eternal punishment?

"His peculiar voice, as if filtered through cotton-wool,

was inaudible on the other side of the deck. Poor Flora, taken very much unawares, made an inarticulate murmur, shook her head vaguely, and glanced in the direction of the pacing Anthony who was not looking her way. It was no use glancing in that direction. Of young Powell, leaning against the mizzen-mast and facing his captain, she could only see the shoulder and part of a blue serge back.

"And the unworried, unaccented voice of her father went on tormenting her.

" 'You see, you must understand. When I came out of jail it was with joy. That is, my soul was fairly torn in two—but anyway to see you happy—I had made up my mind to that. Once I could be sure that you were happy then of course I would have had no reason to care for life—strictly speaking—which is all right for an old man; though naturally . . . no reason to wish for death either. But this sort of life! What sense, what meaning, what value has it either for you or for me? It's just sitting down to look at the death that's coming, coming. What else is it? I don't know how you can put up with that. I don't think you can stand it for long. Some day you will jump overboard.'

"Captain Anthony had stopped for a moment staring ahead from the break of the poop, and poor Flora sent at his back a look of despairing appeal which would have moved a heart of stone. But as though she had done nothing he did not stir in the least. She got out of the long chair and went towards the companion. Her father followed carrying a few small objects, a handbag, her handkerchief, a book. They went down together.

"It was only then that Captain Anthony turned, looked at the place they had vacated and resumed his tramping, but not his desultory conversation with his second officer. His nervous exasperation had grown so much that now very often he used to lose control of his voice. If he did not watch himself it would suddenly die in his throat. He had to make sure before he ventured on the simplest saying, an order, a remark on the wind, a simple good morning. That's why his utterance was abrupt, his answers to people startlingly brusque and often not forthcoming at all.

"It happens to the most resolute of men to find himself

at grips not only with unknown forces, but with a well-known force the real might of which he had not understood. Anthony had discovered that he was not the proud master but the chafing captive of his generosity. It rose in front of him like a wall which his respect for himself forbade him to scale. He said to himself: 'Yes, I was a fool—but she has trusted me!' Trusted! A terrible word to any man somewhat exceptional in a world in which success has never been found in renunciation and good faith. And it must also be said, in order not to make Anthony more stupidly sublime than he was, that the behaviour of Flora kept him at a distance. The girl was afraid to add to the exasperation of her father. It was her unhappy lot to be made more wretched by the only affection which she could not suspect. She could not be angry with it, however, and out of deference for that exaggerated sentiment she hardly dared to look otherwise than by stealth at the man whose masterful compassion had carried her off. And quite unable to understand the extent of Anthony's delicacy, she said to herself that 'he didn't care.' He probably was beginning at bottom to detest her—like the governess, like the maiden lady, like the German woman, like Mrs. Fyne, like Mr. Fyne—only he was extraordinary, he was generous. At the same time she had moments of irritation. He was violent, headstrong—perhaps stupid. Well, he had had his way.

"A man who has had his way is seldom happy, for generally he finds that the way does not lead very far on this earth of desires which can never be fully satisfied. Anthony had entered with extreme precipitation the enchanted gardens of Armida saying to himself 'At last!' As to Armida herself, he was not going to offer her any violence. But now he had discovered that all the enchantment was in Armida herself, in Armida's smiles. This Armida did not smile. She existed, unapproachable, behind the blank wall of his renunciation. His force, fit for action, experienced the impatience, the indignation, almost the despair of his vitality arrested, bound, stilled, progressively worn down, frittered away by Time; by that force blind and insensible, which seems inert and yet uses one's life up by its imperceptible action, dropping minute after minute on one's living heart like drops of water wearing down a stone.

"He upbraided himself. What else could he have expected? He had rushed in like a ruffian; he had dragged the poor defenceless thing by the hair of her head, as it were, on board that ship. It was really atrocious. Nothing assured him that his person could be attractive to this or any other woman. And his proceedings were enough in themselves to make any one odious. He must have been bereft of his senses. She must fatally detest and fear him. Nothing could make up for such brutality. And yet somehow he resented this very attitude which seemed to him completely justifiable. Surely he was not too monstrous (morally) to be looked at frankly sometimes. But no! She wouldn't. Well, perhaps, some day . . . Only he was not going over to attempt to beg for forgiveness. With the repulsion she felt for his person she would certainly misunderstand the most guarded words, the most careful advances. Never! Never!

"It would occur to Anthony at the end of such meditations that death was not an unfriendly visitor after all. No wonder then that even young Powell, his faculties having been put on the alert, began to think that there was something unusual about the man who had given him his chance in life. Yes, decidedly, his captain was 'strange.' There was something wrong somewhere, he said to himself, never guessing that his young and candid eyes were in the presence of a passion profound, tyrannical and mortal, discovering its own existence, astounded at feeling itself helpless and dismayed at finding itself incurable.

"Powell had never before felt this mysterious uneasiness so strongly as on that evening when it had been his good fortune to make Mrs. Anthony laugh a little by his artless prattle. Standing out of the way, he had watched his captain walk the weather-side of the poop, he took full cognizance of his liking for that inexplicably strange man and saw him swerve towards the companion and go down below with sympathetic if utterly uncomprehending eyes.

"Shortly afterwards, Mr. Smith came up alone and manifested a desire for a little conversation. He, too, if not so mysterious as the captain, was not very comprehensible to Mr. Powell's uninformed candour. He often favoured thus the second officer. His talk alluded somewhat enigmatically and often without visible connection to Mr. Powell's friendliness towards himself and his daughter. 'For I am well aware that we have no friends on board this ship, my dear young man,' he would add, 'except yourself. Flora feels that too.'

"And Mr. Powell, flattered and embarrassed, could but emit a vague murmur of protest. For the statement was true in a sense, though the fact was in itself insignificant. The feelings of the ship's company could not possibly matter to the captain's wife and to Mr. Smith—her father. Why the latter should so often allude to it was what surprised our Mr. Powell. This was by no means the first occasion. More like the twentieth rather. And in his weak voice, with his monotonous intonation, leaning over the rail and looking at the water the other continued this conversation, or rather his remarks, remarks of such a monstrous nature that Mr. Powell had no option but to accept them for gruesome jesting.

" 'For instance,' said Mr. Smith, 'that mate, Franklin, I believe he would just as soon see us both overboard as not.'

" 'It's not so bad as that,' laughed Mr. Powell, feeling uncomfortable, because his mind did not accommodate itself easily to exaggeration of statement. 'He isn't a bad chap really,' he added, very conscious of Mr. Franklin's offensive manner of which instances were not far to seek. 'He's such a fool as to be jealous. He has been with the captain for years. It's not for me to say, perhaps, but I think the captain has spoiled all that gang of old servants. They are like a lot of pet old dogs. Wouldn't let anybody come near him if they could help it. I've never seen anything like it. And the second mate, I believe, was like that too.'

" 'Well, he isn't here, luckily. There would have been one more enemy,' said Mr. Smith. 'There's enough of them without him. And you being here instead of him makes it much more pleasant for my daughter and myself. One feels there may be a friend in need. For really, for a woman all alone on board ship amongst a lot of unfriendly men . . .'

" 'But Mrs. Anthony is not alone,' exclaimed Powell. 'There's you, and there's the . . .'

"Mr. Smith interrupted him.

" 'Nobody's immortal. And there are times when one feels ashamed to live. Such an evening as this for instance.'

"It was a lovely evening; the colours of a splendid sunset had died out and the breath of a warm breeze seemed to have smoothed out the sea. Away to the south the sheet lightning was like the flashing of an enormous lantern hidden under the horizon. In order to change the conversation Mr. Powell said—

" 'Anyway no one can charge you with being a Jonah, Mr. Smith. We have had a magnificent quick passage so far. The captain ought to be pleased. And I suppose you are not sorry either.'

"This diversion was not successful. Mr. Smith emitted a sort of bitter chuckle and said: 'Jonah! That's the fellow that was thrown overboard by some sailors. It seems to me it's very easy at sea to get rid of a person one does not like. The sea does not give up its dead as the earth does.'

" 'You forget the whale, sir,' said young Powell.

"Mr. Smith gave a start. 'Eh? What whale? Oh! Jonah. I wasn't thinking of Jonah. I was thinking of this passage which seems so quick to you. But only think what it is to me! It isn't a life, going about the sea like this. And, for instance, if one were to fall ill, there isn't a doctor to find out what's the matter with one. It's worrying. It makes me anxious at times.'

" 'Is Mrs. Anthony not feeling well?' asked Powell. But Mr. Smith's remark was not meant for Mrs. Anthony. She was well. He himself was well. It was the captain's health that did not seem quite satisfactory. Had Mr. Powell noticed his appearance?

"Mr. Powell didn't know enough of the captain to judge. He couldn't tell. But he observed thoughtfully that Mr. Franklin had been saying the same thing. And Franklin had known the captain for years. The mate was quite worried about it.

"This intelligence startled Mr. Smith considerably. 'Does he think he is in danger of dying?' he exclaimed with an animation quite extraordinary for him, which horrified Mr. Powell.

" 'Heavens! Die! No! Don't you alarm yourself, sir. I've never heard a word about danger from Mr. Franklin.'

" 'Well, well,' sighed Mr. Smith and left the poop for the saloon rather abruptly.

"As a matter of fact Mr. Franklin had been on deck for some considerable time. He had come to relieve young Powell; but seeing him engaged in talk with the 'enemy'—with one of the 'enemies' at least—had kept at a distance, which, the poop of the *Ferndale* being over seventy feet long, he had no difficulty in doing. Mr. Powell saw him at the head of the ladder leaning on his elbow, melancholy and silent. 'Oh! Here you are, sir.'

" 'Here I am. Here I've been ever since six o'clock. Didn't want to interrupt the pleasant conversation. If you like to put in half of your watch below jawing with a dear friend, that's not my affair. Funny taste though.'

" 'He isn't a bad chap,' said the impartial Powell.

"The mate snorted angrily, tapping the deck with his foot; then: 'Isn't he? Well, give him my love when you come together again for another nice long yarn.'

" 'I say, Mr. Franklin, I wonder the captain don't take offence at your manners.'

" 'The captain? I wish to goodness he would start a row with me. Then I should know at least I am somebody on board. I'd welcome it, Mr. Powell. I'd rejoice. And dam' me I would talk back too till I roused him. He's a shadow of himself. He walks about his ship like a ghost. He's fading away right before our eyes. But of course you don't see. You don't care a hang. Why should you?'

"Mr. Powell did not wait for more. He went down on the main deck. Without taking the mate's jeremiads seriously he put them beside the words of Mr. Smith. He had grown already attached to Captain Anthony. There was something not only attractive but compelling in the man. Only it is very difficult for youth to believe in the menace of death. Not in the fact itself, but in its proximity to a breathing, moving, talking, superior human being, showing no sign of disease. And Mr. Powell thought that this talk was all nonsense. But his curiosity was awakened. There was something, and at any time some circumstance might occur . . . No, he would never find out . . . There was nothing to find out, most likely. Mr. Powell went to his room where he tried to read a book he had already read a good many times. Presently a bell rang for the officers' supper.

CHAPTER SIX

"... A Moonless Night, Thick with Stars Above, Very Dark on the Water"

"In the mess-room Powell found Mr. Franklin hacking at a piece of cold salt beef with a table knife. The mate, fiery in the face and rolling his eyes over that task, explained that the carver belonging to the mess-room could not be found. The steward, present also, complained savagely of the cook. The fellow got things into his galley and then lost them. Mr. Franklin tried to pacify him with mournful firmness.

" 'There, there! That will do. We who have been all these years together in the ship have other things to think about than quarrelling among ourselves.'

"Mr. Powell thought with exasperation: 'Here he goes again,' for this utterance had nothing cryptic for him. The steward having withdrawn morosely, he was not surprised to hear the mate strike the usual note. That morning the mizzen topsail tie had carried away (probably a defective link) and something like forty feet of chain and wire-rope, mixed up with a few heavy iron blocks, had crashed down from aloft on the poop with a terrifying racket.

" 'Did you notice the captain then, Mr. Powell? Did you notice?'

"Powell confessed frankly that he was too scared himself when all that lot of gear came down on deck to notice anything.

" 'The gin-lock missed his head by an inch,' went on the mate impressively. 'I wasn't three feet from him. And what did he do? Did he shout, or jump, or even look aloft to see if the yard wasn't coming down too about our ears in a dozen pieces? It's a marvel it didn't. No, he just stopped short—no wonder; he must have felt the wind of that iron gin-lock on his face—looked down at it, there, lying close to his foot—and went on again. I believe he didn't even blink. It isn't natural. The man is stupefied.'

"He sighed ridiculously and Mr. Powell had suppressed a grin, when the mate added as if he couldn't contain himself:—

" 'He will be taking to drink next. Mark my words. That's the next thing.'

"Mr. Powell was disgusted.

" 'You are so fond of the captain and yet you don't seem to care what you say about him. I haven't been with him for seven years, but I know he isn't the sort of man that takes to drink. And then—why the devil should he?'

" 'Why the devil, you ask. Devil—eh? Well, no man is safe from the devil—and that's answer enough for you,' wheezed Mr. Franklin not unkindly. 'There was a time, a long time ago, when I nearly took to drink myself. What do you say to that?'

"Mr. Powell expressed a polite incredulity. The thick, congested mate seemed on the point of bursting with despondency. 'That was bad example though. I was young and fell into dangerous company, made a fool of myself—yes, as true as you see me sitting here. Drank to forget. Thought it a great dodge.'

"Powell looked at the grotesque Franklin with awakened interest and with that half-amused sympathy with which we receive unprovoked confidences from men with whom we have no sort of affinity. And at the same time he began to look upon him more seriously. Experience has its prestige. And the mate continued—

" 'If it hadn't been for the old lady, I would have gone to the devil. I remembered her in time. Nothing like having an old lady to look after to steady a chap and make him face things. But as bad luck would have it, Captain Anthony has no mother living, not a blessed soul belonging to him as far as I know. Oh, aye, I fancy he said once something to me of a sister. But she's married. She don't need him. Yes. In the old days he used to talk to me as if we had been brothers,' exaggerated the mate sentimentally. ' "Franklin"—he would say—"this ship is my nearest relation and she isn't likely to turn against me. And I suppose you are the man I've known the longest in the world." That's how he used to speak to me. Can I turn my back on him? He has turned his back on his ship; that's what it has come to. He has no one now but his old Franklin. But what's a fellow to do to put things back as they were and should be? Should be— I say!'

"His starting eyes had a terrible fixity. Mr. Powell's irresistible thought, 'he resembles a boiled lobster in distress,' was followed by annoyance. 'Good Lord,' he said, 'you don't mean to hint that Captain Anthony has fallen into bad company. What is it you want to save him from?'

" 'I do mean it,' affirmed the mate, and the very absurdity of the statement made it impressive—because it seemed so absolutely audacious. 'Well, you have a cheek,' said young Powell, feeling mentally helpless. 'I have a notion the captain would half kill you if he were to know how you carry on.'

" 'And welcome,' uttered the fervently devoted Franklin. 'I am willing, if he would only clear the ship afterwards of that . . . You are but a youngster and you may go and tell him what you like. Let him knock the stuffing out of his old Franklin first and think it over afterwards. Anything to pull him together. But of course you wouldn't. You are all right. Only you don't know that things are sometimes different from what they look. There are friendships that are no friendships, and marriages that are no marriages . . . Phoo! Likely to be right—wasn't it? Never a hint to me. I go off on leave and when I come back, there it is—all over, settled! Not a word beforehand. No warning. If only: "What do you think of it, Franklin?"—or anything of the sort. And that's a man who hardly ever did anything without asking

my advice. Why! He couldn't take over a new coat from
the tailor without . . . first thing, directly the fellow came
on board with some new clothes, whether in London or
in China, it would be: "Pass the word along there for
Mr. Franklin. Mr. Franklin wanted in the cabin." In I
would go. "Just look at my back, Franklin. Fits all right,
doesn't it?" And I would say: "First rate, sir," or whatever was the truth of it. That or anything else. Always
the truth of it. Always. And well he knew it; and that's
why he dare not speak right out. Talking about workmen, alterations, cabins. . . .Phoo! . . . instead of a
straightforward—"Wish me joy, Mr. Franklin!" Yes, that
was the way to let me know. God only knows what they
are—perhaps she isn't his daughter any more than she is
. . . She doesn't resemble that old fellow. Not a bit. Not
a bit. It's very awful. You may well open your mouth,
young man. But for goodness' sake, you who are mixed
up with that lot, keep your eyes and ears open too in
case—in case of . . . I don't know what. Anything. One
wonders what can happen here at sea! Nothing. Yet
when a man is called a jailer behind his back.'

"Mr. Franklin hid his face in his hands for a moment
and Powell shut his mouth, which indeed had been open.
He slipped out of the mess-room noiselessly. 'The mate's
crazy,' he thought. It was his firm conviction. Nevertheless, that evening, he felt his inner tranquillity disturbed
at last by the force and obstinacy of this craze. He
couldn't dismiss it with the contempt it deserved. Had
the word 'jailer' really been pronounced? A strange word
for the mate to even *imagine* he had heard. A senseless,
unlikely word. But this word being the only clear and
definite statement in these grotesque and dismal ravings
was comparatively restful to his mind. Powell's mind
rested on it still when he came up at eight o'clock to take
charge of the deck. It was a moonless-night, thick with
stars above, very dark on the water. A steady air from
the west kept the sails asleep. Franklin mustered both
watches in low tones as if for a funeral, then approaching
Powell—

" 'The course is east-south-east,' said the chief mate
distinctly.

" 'East-south-east, sir.'

" 'Everything's set, Mr. Powell.'

" 'All right, sir.'

"The other lingered, his sentimental eyes gleamed silvery in the shadowy face. 'A quiet night before us. I don't know that there are any special orders. A settled, quiet night. I dare say you won't see the captain. Once upon a time this was the watch he used to come up and start a chat with either of us then on deck. But now he sits in that infernal stern-cabin and mopes. Jailer—eh?'

"Mr. Powell walked away from the mate and when at some distance said, 'Damn!' quite heartily. It was a confounded nuisance. It had ceased to be funny; that hostile word 'jailer' had given the situation an air of reality.

"Franklin's grotesque mortal envelope had disappeared from the poop to seek its needful repose, if only the beworried soul would let it rest awhile. Mr. Powell, half sorry for the thick little man, wondered whether it would let him. For himself, he recognized that the charm of a quiet watch on deck when one may let one's thoughts roam in space and time had been spoiled without remedy. What shocked him most was the implied aspersion of complicity on Mrs. Anthony. It angered him. In his own words to me, he felt very 'enthusiastic' about Mrs. Anthony. 'Enthusiastic.' is good; especially as he couldn't exactly explain to me what he meant by it. But he felt enthusiastic, he says. That silly Franklin must have been dreaming. That was it. He had dreamed it all. Ass. Yet the injurious word stuck in Powell's mind with its associated ideas of prisoner, of escape. He became very uncomfortable. And just then (it might have been half an hour or more since he had relieved Franklin), just then Mr. Smith came up on the poop alone, like a gliding shadow, and leaned over the rail by his side. Young Powell was affected disagreeably by his presence. He made a movement to go away but the other began to talk—and Powell remained where he was as if retained by a mysterious compulsion. The conversation started by Mr. Smith had nothing peculiar. He began to talk of mailboats in general and in the end seemed anxious to discover what were the services from Port Elizabeth to London. Mr. Powell did not know for certain but imagined that there must be communication with England at least twice a month. 'Are you thinking of leaving us, sir; of going home by steam? Perhaps with Mrs. Anthony,' he asked anxiously.

" 'No! No! How can I?' Mr. Smith got quite agitated, for him, which did not amount to much. He was just asking for the sake of something to talk about. No idea at all of going home. One could not always do what one wanted and that's why there were moments when one felt ashamed to live. This did not mean that one did not want to live. Oh, no!

"He spoke with careless slowness, pausing frequently and in such a low voice that Powell had to strain his hearing to catch the phrases dropped overboard as it were. And indeed they seemed not worth the effort. It was like the aimless talk of a man pursuing a secret train of thought far removed from the idle words we so often utter only to keep in touch with our fellow beings. An hour passed. It seemed as though Mr. Smith could not make up his mind to go below. He repeated himself. Again he spoke of lives which one was ashamed of. It was necessary to put up with such lives as long as there was no way out, no possible issue. He even alluded once more to mail-boat services on the East coast of Africa and young Powell had to tell him once more that he knew nothing about them.

" 'Every fortnight, I thought you said,' insisted Mr. Smith. He stirred, seemed to detach himself from the rail with difficulty. His long, slender figure straightened into stiffness, as if hostile to the enveloping soft peace of air and sea and sky, emitted into the night a weak murmur which Mr. Powell fancied was the word 'Abominable' repeated three times, but which passed into the faintly louder declaration: 'The moment has come—to go to bed' followed by a just audible sigh.

" 'I sleep very well,' added Mr. Smith in his restrained tone. 'But it is the moment one opens one's eyes that is horrible at sea. These days! Oh, these days! I wonder how anybody can . . .'

" 'I like the life,' observed Mr. Powell.

" 'Oh, you. You have only yourself to think of. You have made your bed. Well, it's very pleasant to feel that you are friendly to us. My daughter has taken quite a liking to you, Mr. Powell.'

"He murmured, 'Good-night' and glided away rigidly. Young Powell asked himself with some distaste what was the meaning of these utterances. His mind had been worried at last into that questioning attitude by no other person than the grotesque Franklin. Suspicion was not natural to him. And he took good care to carefully separate in his thoughts Mrs. Anthony from this man of enigmatic words—her father. Presently he observed that the sheen of the two deck dead-lights of Mr. Smith's room had gone out. The old gentleman had been surprisingly quick in getting into bed. Shortly afterwards the lamp in the foremost skylight of the saloon was turned out; and this was the sign that the steward had taken in the tray and had retired for the night.

"Young Powell had settled down to the regular officer-of-the-watch tramp in the dense shadow of the world decorated with stars high above his head, and on earth only a few gleams of light about the ship. The lamp in the after skylight was kept burning through the night. There were also the dead-lights of the stern-cabins glimmering dully in the deck far aft, catching his eye when he turned to walk that way. The brasses of the wheel glittered too, with the dimly lit figure of the man detached, as if phosphorescent, against the black and spangled background of the horizon.

"Young Powell, in the silence of the ship, reinforced by the great silent stillness of the world, said to himself that there was something mysterious in such beings as the absurd Franklin, and even in such beings as himself. It was a strange and almost improper thought to occur to the officer of the watch of a ship on the high seas on no matter how quiet a night. Why on earth was he bothering his head? Why couldn't he dismiss all these people from his mind? It was as if the mate had infected him with his own diseased devotion. He would not have believed it possible that he should be so foolish. But he was—clearly. He was foolish in a way totally unforeseen by himself. Pushing this self-analysis further, he reflected that the springs of his conduct were just as obscure.

" 'I may be catching myself any time doing things of which I have no conception,' he thought. And as he was passing near the mizzen-mast he perceived a coil of rope left lying on the deck by the oversight of the sweepers.

By an impulse which had nothing mysterious in it, he stooped as he went by with the intention of picking it up and hanging it up on its proper pin. This movement brought his head down to the level of the glazed end of the after skylight—the lighted skylight of the most private part of the saloon, consecrated to the exclusiveness of Captain Anthony's married life; the part, let me remind you, cut off from the rest of that forbidden space by a pair of heavy curtains. I mention these curtains because at this point Mr. Powell himself recalled the existence of that unusual arrangement to my mind.

"He recalled them with simple-minded compunction at that distance of time. He said: 'You understand that directly I stooped to pick up that coil of running gear— the spanker foot-outhaul, it was—I perceived that I could see right into that part of the saloon the curtains were meant to make particularly private. Do you understand me?' he insisted.

"I told him that I understood; and he proceeded to call my attention to the wonderful linking up of small facts, with something of awe left yet, after all these years, at the precise workmanship of chance, fate, providence, call it what you will! 'For, observe, Marlow,' he said, making at me very round eyes which contrasted funnily with the austere touch of grey on his temples, 'observe, my dear fellow, that everything depended on the men who cleared up the poop in the evening leaving that coil of rope on the deck, and on the topsail-tie carrying away in a most incomprehensible and surprising manner earlier in the day, and the end of the chain whipping round the coaming and shivering to bits the coloured glass-pane at the end of the skylight. It had the arms of the city of Liverpool on it; I don't know why unless because the *Ferndale* was registered in Liverpool. It was very thick plate glass. Anyhow, the upper part got smashed, and directly we had attended to things aloft Mr. Franklin had set the carpenter to patch up the damage with some pieces of plain glass. I don't know where they got them; I think the people who fitted up new bookcases in the captain's room had left some spare panes. Chips was there the whole afternoon on his knees, messing with putty and red-lead. It wasn't a neat job when it was done, not by any means, but it would serve to keep the weather

out and let the light in. Clear glass. And of course I was
not thinking of it. I just stooped to pick up that rope and
found my head within three inches of that clear glass
and—dash it all! I found myself out. Not half an hour
before I was saying to myself that it was impossible to
tell what was in people's heads or at the back of their
talk, or what they were likely to be up to. And here I
found myself up to as low a trick as you can well think
of. For, after I had stooped, there I remained prying,
spying, anyway looking, where I had no business to look.
Not consciously at first, maybe. He who has eyes, you
know, nothing can stop him from seeing things as long
as there are things to see in front of him. What I saw at
first was the end of the table and the tray clamped on to
it, a patent tray for sea use, fitted with holders for a
couple of decanters, water-jug and glasses. The glitter of
these things caught my eye first; but what I saw next was
the captain down there, alone as far as I could see; and
I could see pretty well the whole of that part up to the
cottage piano, dark against the satin-wood panelling of
the bulkhead. And I remained looking. I did. And I
don't know that I was ashamed of myself either, then. It
was the fault of that Franklin, always talking of the man,
making free with him to that extent that really he seemed
to have become our property, his and mine, in a way.
It's funny, but one had that feeling about Captain
Anthony. To watch him was not so much worse than
listening to Franklin talking him over. Well, it's no use
making excuses for what's inexcusable. I watched; but I
dare say you know that there could have been nothing
inimical in this low behaviour of mine. On the contrary.
I'll tell you now what he was doing. He was helping
himself out of a decanter. I saw every movement, and I
said to myself mockingly as though jeering at Franklin in
my thoughts, "Hallo! Here's the captain taking to drink
at last." He poured a little brandy or whatever it was into
a long glass, filled it with water, drank about a fourth of
it and stood the glass back into the holder. Every sign
of a bad drinking bout, I was saying to myself, feeling
quite amused at the notions of that Franklin. He seemed
to me an enormous ass, with his jealousy and his fears.
At that rate a month would not have been enough for
anybody to get drunk. The captain sat down in one of

the swivel arm-chairs fixed around the table; I had him right under me and as he turned the chair slightly, I was looking, I may say, down his back. He took another little sip and then reached for a book which was lying on the table. I had not noticed it before. Altogether the proceedings of a desperate drunkard—weren't they? He opened the book and held it before his face. If this was the way he took to drink, then I needn't worry. He was in no danger from that, and as to any other, I assure you no human being could have looked safer than he did down there. I felt the greatest contempt for Franklin just then, while I looked at Captain Anthony sitting there with a glass of weak brandy-and-water at his elbow and reading in the cabin of his ship, on a quiet night—the quietest, perhaps the finest, of a prosperous passage. And if you wonder why I didn't leave off my ugly spying I will tell you how it was. Captain Anthony was a great reader just about that time; and I, too, I have a great liking for books. To this day I can't come near a book but I must know what it is about. It was a thickish volume he had there, small close print, double columns—I can see it now. What I wanted to make out was the title at the top of the page. I have very good eyes but he wasn't holding it conveniently—I mean for me up there. Well, it was a history of some kind, that much I read, and then suddenly he bangs the book face down on the table, jumps up as if something had bitten him and walks away aft.

" 'Funny thing shame is. I had been behaving badly and aware of it in a way, but I didn't feel really ashamed till the fright of being found out in my honourable occupation drove me from it. I slunk away to the forward end of the poop and lounged about there, my face and ears burning, and glad it was a dark night, expecting every moment to hear the captain's footsteps behind me. For I made sure he was coming on deck. Presently I thought I had rather meet him face to face and I walked slowly aft prepared to see him emerge from the companion before I got that far. I even thought of his having detected me by some means. But it was impossible, unless he had eyes in the top of his head. I had never had a view of his face down there. It was impossible; I was safe; and I felt very mean, yet, explain it as you may,

I seemed not to care. And the captain not appearing on
deck, I had the impulse to go on being mean. I wanted
another peep. I really don't know what was the beastly
influence except that Mr. Franklin's talk was enough to
demoralize any man by raising a sort of unhealthy curiosity which did away in my case with all the restraints of
common decency.

" 'I did not mean to run the risk of being caught squatting in a suspicious attitude by the captain. There was
also the helmsman to consider. So what I did—I am surprised at my low cunning—was to sit down naturally on
the skylight-seat and then by bending forward I found
that, as I expected, I could look down through the upper
part of the end-pane. The worst that could happen to me
then, if I remained too long in that position, was to be
suspected by the seaman aft at the wheel of having gone
to sleep there. For the rest my ears would give me sufficient warning of any movements in the companion.

" 'But in that way my angle of view was changed. The
field too was smaller. The end of the table, the tray and
the swivelchair I had right under my eyes. The captain
had not come back yet. The piano I could not see now;
but on the other hand I had a very oblique downward
view of the curtains drawn across the cabin and cutting
off the forward part of it just about the level of the sky-
light-end and only an inch or so from the end of the
table. They were heavy stuff, travelling on a thick brass
rod with some contrivance to keep the rings from sliding
to and fro when the ship rolled. But just then the ship
was as still almost as a model shut up in a glass case
while the curtains, joined closely, and, perhaps on purpose, made a little too long, moved no more than a solid
wall.' "

Marlow got up to get another cigar. The night was getting on to what I may call its deepest hour, the hour most
favourable to evil purposes of men's hate, despair or
greed—to whatever can whisper into their ears the unlawful
counsels of protest against things that are; the hour of ill-
omened silence and chill and stagnation, the hour when
the criminal plies his trade and the victim of sleeplessness
reaches the lowest depth of dreadful discouragement; the
hour before the first sign of dawn. I know it, because

while Marlow was crossing the room, I looked at the clock on the mantelpiece. He however never looked that way though it is possible that he, too, was aware of the passage of time. He sat down heavily.

"Our friend Powell," he began again, "was very anxious that I should understand the topography of that cabin. I was interested more by its moral atmosphere, that tension of falsehood, of desperate acting, which tainted the pure sea-atmosphere into which the magnanimous Anthony had carried off his conquest and—well— his self-conquest too, trying to act at the same time like a beast of prey, a pure spirit and the 'most generous of men.' Too big an order clearly because he was nothing of a monster but just a common mortal, a little more self-willed and self-confident than most, maybe, both in his roughness and in his delicacy.

"As to the delicacy of Mr. Powell's proceedings I'll say nothing. He found a sort of depraved excitement in watching an unconscious man—and such an attractive and mysterious man as Captain Anthony at that. He wanted another peep at him. He surmised that the captain must come back soon because of the glass two-thirds full and also of the book put down so brusquely. God knows what sudden pang had made Anthony jump up so. I am convinced he used reading as an opiate against the pain of his magnanimity which like all abnormal growths was gnawing at his healthy substance with cruel persistence. Perhaps he had rushed into his cabin simply to groan freely in absolute and delicate secrecy. At any rate he tarried there. And young Powell would have grown weary and compunctious at last if it had not become manifest to him that he had not been alone in the highly incorrect occupation of watching the movements of Captain Anthony.

"Powell explained to me that no sound did or perhaps could reach him from the saloon. The first sign—and we must remember that he was using his eyes for all they were worth—was an unaccountable movement of the curtain. It was wavy and very slight; just perceptible in fact to the sharpened faculties of a secret watcher; for it can't be denied that our wits are much more alert when engaged in wrong-doing (in which one mustn't be found out) than in a righteous occupation.

"He became suspicious, with no one and nothing definite in his mind. He was suspicious of the curtain itself and observed it. It looked very innocent. Then just as he was ready to put it down to a trick of imagination he saw trembling movements where the two curtains joined. Yes! Somebody else besides himself had been watching Captain Anthony. He owns artlessly that this roused his indignation. It was really too much of a good thing. In this state of intense antagonism he was startled to observe tips of fingers fumbling with the dark stuff. Then they grasped the edge of the further curtain and hung on there, just fingers and knuckles and nothing else. It made an abominable sight. He was looking at it with unaccountable repulsion when a hand came into view; a short, puffy, old freckled hand projecting into the lamplight, followed by a white wrist, an arm in a grey coat-sleeve, up to the elbow, beyond the elbow, extended tremblingly towards the tray. Its appearance was weird and nauseous, fantastic and silly. But instead of grabbing the bottle as Powell expected, this hand, tremulous with senile eagerness, swerved to the glass, rested on its edge for a moment (or so it looked from above) and went back with a jerk. The gripping fingers of the other hand vanished at the same time, and young Powell, staring at the motionless curtains, could indulge for a moment the notion that he had been dreaming.

"But that notion did not last long. Powell, after repressing his first impulse to spring for the companion and hammer at the captain's door, took steps to have himself relieved by the boatswain. He was in a state of distraction as to his feelings and yet lucid as to his mind. He remained on the skylight so as to keep his eye on the tray.

"Still the captain did not appear in the saloon. 'If he had,' said Mr. Powell, 'I knew what to do. I would have put my elbow through the pane instantly—crash.'

"I asked him why?

"'It was the quickest dodge for getting him away from that tray,' he explained. 'My throat was so dry that I didn't know if I could shout loud enough. And this was not a case for shouting, either.'

"The boatswain, sleepy and disgusted, arriving on the poop, found the second officer doubled up over the end of the skylight in a pose which might have been that of severe pain. And his voice was so changed that the man, though naturally vexed at being turned out, made no comment on the plea of sudden indisposition which young Powell put forward.

"The rapidity with which the sick man got off the poop must have astonished the boatswain. But Powell, at the moment he opened the door leading into the saloon from the quarter-deck, had managed to control his agitation. He entered swiftly, but without noise and found himself in the dark part of the saloon, the strong sheen of the lamp on the other side of the curtains visible only above the rod on which they ran. The door of Mr. Smith's cabin was in that dark part. He passed by it assuring himself by a quick side glance that it was imperfectly closed. 'Yes,' he said to me. 'The old man must have been watching through the crack. Of that I am certain; but it was not for me that he was watching and listening. Horrible! Surely he must have been startled to hear and see somebody he did not expect. He could not possibly guess why I was coming in but I suppose he must have been concerned.' Concerned indeed! He must have been thunderstruck, appalled.

"Powell's only distinct aim was to remove the suspected tumbler. He had no other plan, no other intention, no other thought. Do away with it in some manner. Snatch it up and run out with it.

"You know that complete mastery of one fixed idea, not a reasonable but an emotional mastery, a sort of concentrated exaltation. Under its empire men rush blindly through fire and water and opposing violence, and nothing can stop them—unless, sometimes, a grain of sand. For this blind purpose (and clearly the thought of Mrs. Anthony was at the bottom of it) Mr. Powell had plenty of time. What checked him at the crucial moment was the familiar, harmless aspect of common things, the steady light, the open book on the table, the solitude, the peace, the homelike effect of the place. He held the glass in his hand; all he had to do was to vanish back beyond the curtains, flee with it noiselessly into the night on deck, fling it unseen overboard. A minute or less. And then all that would have happened would have been the wonder at the utter disappearance of a glass

tumbler, a ridiculous riddle in pantry-affairs beyond the
wit of any one on board to solve. The grain of sand
against which Powell stumbled in his headlong career was
a moment of incredulity as to the truth of his own conviction because it had failed to affect the safe aspect of
familiar things. He doubted his eyes too. He must have
dreamt it all! 'I am dreaming now,' he said to himself.
And very likely for a few seconds he must have looked
like a man in a trance or profoundly asleep on his feet,
and with a glass of brandy-and-water in his hand.

"What woke him up and, at the same time, fixed his
feet immovably to the spot, was a voice asking him what
he was doing there in tones of thunder. Or so it sounded
to his ears. Anthony, opening the door of his stern-cabin,
had naturally exclaimed. What else could you expect?
And the exclamation must have been fairly loud if you
consider the nature of the sight which met his eye. There,
before him, stood his second officer, a seemingly decent,
well-bred young man, who, being on duty, had left the
deck and had sneaked into the saloon, apparently for the
inexpressibly mean purpose of drinking up what was left
of his captain's brandy-and-water. There he was, caught
absolutely with the glass in his hand.

"But the very monstrosity of appearances silenced
Anthony after the first exclamation; and young Powell
felt himself pierced through and through by the overshadowed glance of his captain. Anthony advanced quietly.
The first impulse of Mr. Powell, when discovered, had
been to dash the glass on the deck. He was in a sort of
panic. But deep down within him his wits were working,
and the idea that if he did that he could prove nothing
and that the story he had to tell was completely incredible, restrained him. The captain came forward slowly.
With his eyes now close to his, Powell, spell-bound,
numb all over, managed to lift one finger to the deck
above mumbling the explanatory words, 'Boatswain on
the poop.'

"The captain moved his head slightly as much as to
say, 'That's all right'—and this was all. Powell had no
voice, no strength. The air was unbreathable, thick,
sticky, odious, like hot jelly in which all movements
became difficult. He raised the glass a little with immense

difficulty and moved his trammelled lips sufficiently to
form the words—

" 'Doctored.'

"Anthony glanced at it for an instant, only for an
instant, and again fastened his eyes on the face of his
second mate. Powell added a fervent 'I believe' and put
the glass down on the tray. The captain's glance followed
the movement and returned sternly to his face. The
young man pointed a finger once more upwards and
squeezed out of his iron-bound throat six consecutive
words of further explanation: 'Through the skylight. The
white pane.'

"The captain raised his eyebrows very much at this,
while young Powell, ashamed but desperate, nodded
insistently several times. He meant to say that: Yes. Yes.
He had done that thing. He had been spying. . . . The
captain's gaze became thoughtful. And, now the confession was over, the iron-bound feeling of Powell's throat
passed away giving place to a general anxiety which from
his breast seemed to extend to all the limbs and organs
of his body. His legs trembled a little, his vision was
confused, his mind became blankly expectant. But he
was alert enough. At a movement of Anthony he
screamed in a strangled whisper.

" 'Don't, sir! Don't touch it.'

"The captain pushed aside Powell's extended arm,
took up the glass and raised it slowly against the lamplight. The liquid, of very pale amber colour, was clear,
and by a glance the captain seemed to call Powell's attention to the fact. Powell tried to pronounce the word 'dis-
solved,' but he only thought of it with great energy which
however failed to move his lips. Only when Anthony had
put down the glass and turned to him he recovered such
a complete command of his voice that he could keep it
down to a hurried, forcible whisper—a whisper that
shook him.

" 'Doctored! I swear it! I have seen. Doctored! I have
seen.'

"Not a feature of the captain's face moved. His was a
calm to take one's breath away. It did so to young Powell. Then for the first time Anthony made himself heard
to the point.

" 'You did! . . . Who was it?'

"And Powell gasped freely at last. 'A hand,' he whispered fearfully, 'a hand and the arm—only the arm—like that.'

"He advanced his own, slow, stealthy, tremulous in faithful reproduction, the tips of two fingers and the thumb pressed together and hovering above the glass for an instant—then the swift jerk back, after the deed.

" 'Like that,' he repeated, growing excited. 'From behind this.' He grasped the curtain and glaring at the silent Anthony flung it back disclosing the forepart of the saloon. There was no one to be seen.

"Powell had not expected to see anybody. 'But,' he said to me, 'I knew very well there was an ear listening and an eye glued to the crack of a cabin door. Awful thought. And that door was in that part of the saloon remaining in the shadow of the other half of the curtain. I pointed at it and I suppose that old man inside saw me pointing. The captain had a wonderful self-command. You couldn't have guessed anything from his face. Well, it was perhaps more thoughtful than usual. And indeed this was something to think about. But I couldn't think steadily. My brain would give a sort of jerk and then go dead again. I had lost all notion of time, and I might have been looking at the captain for days and months for all I knew before I heard him whisper to me fiercely: "Not a word!" This jerked me out of that trance I was in and I said, "No! No! I didn't mean even you."

" 'I wanted to explain my conduct, my intentions, but I read in his eyes that he understood me and I was only too glad to leave off. And there we were looking at each other, dumb, brought up short by the question "What next?"

" 'I thought Captain Anthony was a man of iron till I saw him suddenly fling his head to the right and to the left fiercely, like a wild animal at bay not knowing which way to break out. . . .'

"Truly," commented Marlow, "brought to bay was not a bad comparison; a better one than Mr. Powell was aware of. At that moment the appearance of Flora could not but bring the tension to the breaking point. She came out in all innocence but not without vague dread. Anthony's exclamation on first seeing Powell had reached her in her cabin, where, it seems, she was brushing her hair. She had heard the very words. 'What are you doing here?' And the unwonted loudness of the voice—his voice—breaking the habitual stillness of that hour would have startled a person having much less reason to be constantly apprehensive, than the captive of Anthony's masterful generosity. She had no means to guess to whom the question was addressed and it echoed in her heart, as Anthony's voice always did. Followed complete silence. She waited, anxious, expectant, till she could stand the strain no longer, and with the weary mental appeal of the overburdened, 'My God! What is it now?' she opened the door of her room and looked into the saloon. Her first glance fell on Powell. For a moment, seeing only the second officer with Anthony, she felt relieved and made as if to draw back; but her sharpened perception detected something suspicious in their attitudes, and she came forward slowly.

" 'I was the first to see Mrs. Anthony,' related Powell, 'because I was facing aft. The captain, noticing my eyes, looked quickly over his shoulder and at once put his finger to his lips to caution me. As if I were likely to let out anything before her! Mrs. Anthony had on a dressing-gown of some grey stuff with red facings and a thick red cord round her waist. Her hair was down. She looked a child; a pale-faced child with big blue eyes and a red mouth a little open showing a glimmer of white teeth. The light fell strongly on her as she came up to the end of the table. A strange child though; she hardly affected one like a child, I remember. Do you know,' exclaimed Mr. Powell, who clearly must have been, like many seamen, an industrious reader, 'do you know what she looked like to me with those big eyes and something appealing in her whole expression? She looked like a forsaken elf. Captain Anthony had moved towards her to keep her away from my end of the table, where the tray was. I had never seen them so near to each other before, and it made a great contrast. It was wonderful, for, with his beard cut to a point, his swarthy, sunburnt complexion, thin nose and his lean head there was something African, something Moorish in Captain Anthony. His neck was bare; he had taken off his coat and collar and had drawn on his sleeping-jacket in the time that he had been absent from the saloon. I seem to see him now. Mrs. Anthony too. She looked from him to me—I suppose I looked guilty or frightened—and from me to him, trying to guess what there was between us two. Then she burst out with a "What has happened?" which seemed addressed to me. I mumbled "Nothing! Nothing, ma'am," which she very likely did not hear.

" 'You must not think that all this had lasted a long time. She had taken fright at our behaviour and turned to the captain pitifully. "What is it you are concealing from me?" A straight question—eh? I don't know what answer the captain would have made. Before he could even raise his eyes to her she cried out: "Ah! Here's papa!" in a sharp tone of relief, but directly afterwards she looked to me as if she were holding her breath with apprehension. I was so interested in her that, how shall I say it, her exclamation made no connection in my brain at first. I also noticed that she had sidled up a little nearer to Captain Anthony, before it occurred to me to turn my head. I can tell you my neck stiffened in the twisted position from the shock of actually seeing that old man! He had dared! I suppose you think I ought to have looked upon him as mad. But I couldn't. It would have been certainly easier. But I could *not*. You should have seen him. First of all he was completely dressed with his very cap still on his head just as when he left me on deck two hours before, saying in his soft voice: "The moment has come to go to bed"—while he meant to go and do that thing and hide in his dark cabin, and watch the stuff do its work. A cold shudder ran down my back. He had his hands in the pockets of his jacket, his arms were pressed close to his thin, upright body, and he shuffled across the cabin with his short steps. There was a red patch on each of his old soft cheeks as if somebody had been pinching them. He drooped his head a little, and looked with a sort of underhand expectation at the captain and Mrs. Anthony standing close together at the other end of the saloon. The calculating horrible impudence of it! His daughter was there; and I am certain he had seen the captain putting his finger on his lips to warn me. And then he had coolly come out! He passed my imagination, I assure you. After that one shiver his pres-

ence killed every faculty in me—wonder, horror, indignation. I felt nothing in particular just as if he were still
the old gentleman who used to talk to me familiarly every
day on deck. Would you believe it?'

"Mr. Powell challenged my powers of wonder at this
internal phenomenon," went on Marlow after a slight
pause. "But even if they had not been fully engaged,
together with all my powers of attention in following the
facts of the case, I would not have been astonished by
his statements about himself. Taking into consideration
his youth they were by no means incredible; or, at any
rate, they were the least incredible part of the whole.
They were also the least interesting part. The interest
was elsewhere, and there of course all he could do was
to look at the surface. The inwardness of what was passing before his eyes was hidden from him, who had looked
on, more impenetrably than from me who at a distance
of years was listening to his words. What presently happened at this crisis in Flora de Barral's fate was beyond
his power of comment, seemed in a sense natural. And
his own presence on the scene was so strangely motivated
that it was left for me to marvel alone at this young man,
a completely chance-comer, having brought it about on
that night.

"Each situation created either by folly or wisdom has
its psychological moment. The behaviour of young Powell with its mixture of boyish impulses combined with
instinctive prudence had not created it—I can't say that—
but had discovered it to the very people involved. What
would have happened if he had made a noise about his
discovery? But he didn't. His head was full of Mrs.
Anthony and he behaved with a discretion beyond his
years. Some nice children often do; and surely it is not
from reflection. They have their own inspirations. Young
Powell's inspiration consisted in being 'enthusiastic' about
Mrs. Anthony. 'Enthusiastic' is really good. And he was
amongst them like a child, sensitive, impressionable,
plastic—but unable to find for himself any sort of
comment.

"I don't know how much mine may be worth; but I
believe that just then the tension of the false situation
was at its highest. Of all the forms offered to us by life
it is the one demanding a couple to realize it fully, which

is the most imperative. Pairing off is the fate of mankind. And if two beings thrown together, mutually attracted, resist the necessity, fail in understanding and voluntarily stop short of the—the embrace, in the noblest meaning of the word, then they are committing a sin against life, the call of which is simple. Perhaps sacred. And the punishment of it is an invasion of complexity, a tormenting, forcibly tortuous involution of feelings, the deepest form of suffering from which indeed something significant may come at last, which may be criminal or heroic, may be madness or wisdom—or even a straight if despairing decision.

"Powell on taking his eyes off the old gentleman noticed Captain Anthony, swarthy as an African, by the side of Flora whiter than the lilies, take his handkerchief out and wipe off his forehead the sweat of anguish—like a man who is overcome. 'And no wonder,' commented Mr. Powell here. Then the captain said, 'Hadn't you better go back to your room?' This was to Mrs. Anthony. He tried to smile at her. 'Why do you look startled? This night is like any other night.'

" 'Which,' Powell again commented to me earnestly 'was a lie. . . . No wonder he sweated.' You see from this the value of Powell's comments. Mrs. Anthony then said: 'Why are you sending me away?'

" 'Why! That you should go to sleep. That you should rest.' And Captain Anthony frowned. Then sharply, 'You stay here, Mr. Powell. I shall want you presently.' As a matter of fact Powell had not moved. Flora did not mind his presence. He himself had the feeling of being of no account to those three people. He was looking at Mrs. Anthony as unabashed as the proverbial cat looking at a king. Mrs. Anthony glanced at him. She did not move, gripped by an inexplicable premonition. She had arrived at the very limit of her endurance as the object of Anthony's magnanimity; she was the prey of an intuitive dread of she did not know what mysterious influence; she felt herself being pushed back into that solitude, that moral loneliness, which had made all her life intolerable. And then, in that close communion established again with Anthony, she felt—as on that night in the garden—the force of his personal fascination. The passive quietness with which she looked at him gave her the appearance of a person bewitched—or say, mesmerically put to sleep—beyond any notion of her surroundings.

"After telling Mr. Powell not to go away the captain remained silent. Suddenly Mrs. Anthony pushed back her loose hair with a decisive gesture of her arms and moved still nearer to him. 'Here's papa up yet,' she said, but she did not look towards Mr. Smith. 'Why is it? And you? I can't go on like this, Roderick—between you two. Don't.'

"Anthony interrupted her as if something had untied his tongue.

" 'Oh, yes. Here's your father. And . . . Why not? Perhaps it is just as well you came out. Between us two? Is that it? I won't pretend I don't understand. I am not blind. But I can't fight any longer for what I haven't got. I don't know what you imagine has happened. Something has though. Only you needn't be afraid. No shadow can touch you—because I give up. I can't say we had much talk about it, your father and I, but, the long and the short of it is that I must learn to live without you—which I have told you was impossible. I was speaking the truth. But I have done fighting, or waiting, or hoping. Yes. You shall go.'

"At this point Mr. Powell who (he confessed to me) was listening with uncomprehending awe, heard behind his back a triumphant chuckling sound. It gave him the shudders, he said, to mention it now; but at the time, except for another chill down the spine, it had not the power to destroy his absorption in the scene before his eyes, and before his ears too, because just then Captain Anthony raised his voice grimly. Perhaps he too had heard the chuckle of the old man.

" 'Your father has found an argument which makes me pause, if it does not convince me. No! I can't answer it. I—I don't want to answer it. I simply surrender. He shall have his way with you—and with me. Only,' he added in a gloomy lowered tone which struck Mr. Powell as if a pedal had been put down, 'only it will take a little time. I have never lied to you. Never. I renounce not only my chance but my life. In a few days, directly we get into port, the very moment we do, I, who have said I could never let you go, I shall let you go.'

"To the innocent beholder Anthony seemed at this point to become physically exhausted. My view is that the utter falseness of his, I may say, aspirations, the vanity of grasping the empty air, had come to him with an overwhelming force, leaving him disarmed before the other's mad and sinister sincerity. As he had said himself he could not fight for what he did not possess; he could not face such a thing as this for the sake of his mere magnanimity. The normal alone can overcome the abnormal. He could not even reproach that man over there. 'I own myself beaten,' he said in a firmer tone. 'You are free. I let you off since I .must.'

"Powell, the onlooker, affirms that at these incomprehensible words Mrs. Anthony stiffened into the very image of astonishment, with a frightened stare and frozen lips. But next minute a cry came out from her heart, not very loud but of a quality which made not only Captain Anthony (he was not looking at her), not only him but also the more distant (and equally unprepared) young man, catch their breath: 'But I don't want to be let off,' she cried.

"She was so still that one asked oneself whether the cry had come from her. The restless shuffle behind Powell's back stopped short, the intermittent shadowy chuckling ceased too. Young Powell, glancing round, saw Mr. Smith raise his head with his faded eyes very still, puckered at the corners, like a man perceiving something coming at him from a great distance. And Mrs. Anthony's voice reached Powell's ears, entreating and indignant.

" 'You can't cast me off like this, Roderick. I won't go away from you. I won't——'

"Powell turned about and discovered then that what Mr. Smith was puckering his eyes at, was the sight of his daughter clinging round Captain Anthony's neck—a sight not in itself improper, but which had the power to move young Powell with a bashfully profound emotion. It was different from his emotion while spying at the revelations of the skylight, but in this case too he felt the discomfort, if not the guilt, of an unseen beholder. Experience was being piled up on his young shoulders. Mrs. Anthony's hair hung back in a dark mass like the hair of a drowned woman. She looked as if she would let go and sink to the floor if the captain were to withhold his sustaining arm. But the captain obviously had no such intention. Standing firm and still he gazed with sombre eyes at Mr. Smith. For a time the low convulsive sobbing of Mr. Smith's daughter was the only sound to trouble the silence. The strength of Anthony's clasp pressing Flora to his breast could not be doubted even at that distance, and suddenly, awakening to his opportunity, he began to partly support her, partly carry her in the direction of her cabin. His head was bent over her solicitously, then recollecting himself, with a glance full of unwonted fire, his voice ringing in a note unknown to Mr. Powell, he cried to him, 'Don't you go on deck yet. I want you to stay down here till I come back. There are some instructions I want to give you.'

"And before the young man could answer, Anthony had disappeared in the stern-cabin, burdened and exulting.

" 'Instructions,' commented Mr. Powell. 'That was all right. Very likely; but they would be such instructions as, I thought to myself, no ship's officer perhaps had ever been given before. It made me feel a little sick to think what they would be dealing with, probably. But there! Everything that happens on board ship on the high seas has got to be dealt with somehow. There are no special people to fly to for assistance. And there I was with that old man left in my charge. When he noticed me looking at him he started to shuffle again athwart the saloon. He kept his hands rammed in his pockets, he was as stiff-backed as ever, only his head hung down. After a bit he says in his gentle soft tone: "Did you see it?" '

"There were in Powell's head no special words to fit the horror of his feelings. So he said—he had to say something, 'Good God! What were you thinking of, Mr. Smith, to try to . . .' And then he left off. He dared not utter the awful word poison. Mr. Smith stopped his prowl.

" 'Think! What do you know of thinking? I don't think. There is something in my head that thinks. The thoughts in men, it's like being drunk with liquor or—— You can't stop them. A man who thinks will think anything. No! But have you seen it? Have you?'

" 'I tell you I have! I am certain!' said Powell forcibly. 'I was looking at you all the time. You've done something to the drink in that glass.'

"Then Powell lost his breath somehow. Mr. Smith looked at him curiously, with mistrust.

" 'My good young man, I don't know what you are talking about. I ask you—have you seen? Who would have believed it? with her arms round his neck. When! Oh! Ha! Ha! You did see! Didn't you? It wasn't a delusion—was it? Her arms round . . . But I have never wholly trusted her.'

" 'Then I flew out at him,' said Mr. Powell. 'I told him he was jolly lucky to have fallen upon Captain Anthony. A man in a million. He started again shuffling to and fro. "You too," he said mournfully, keeping his eyes down. "Eh? Wonderful man? But have you a notion who I am? Listen! I have been the Great Mr. de Barral. So they printed it in the papers while they were getting up a conspiracy. And I have been doing time. And now I am brought low." His voice died down to a mere breath. "Brought low."

" 'He took his hands out of his pockets, dragged the cap down on his head and stuck them back into his pockets, exactly as if preparing himself to go out into a great wind. "But not so low as to put up with this disgrace, to see her, fast in this fellow's clutches, without doing something. She wouldn't listen to me. Frightened? Silly? I had to think of some way to get her out of this. Did *you* think she cared for him? No! Would anybody have thought so? No! She pretended it was for my sake. She couldn't understand that if I hadn't been an old man I would have flown at his throat months ago. As it was I was tempted every time he looked at her. My girl. Ough! Any man but this. And all the time the wicked little fool was lying to me. It was their plot, their conspiracy! These conspiracies are the devil. She has been leading me on, till she has fairly put my head under the heel of that jailer, of that scoundrel, of her husband. . . . Treachery! Bringing me low. Lower than herself. In the dirt. That's what it means. Doesn't it? Under his heel!" '

"He paused in his restless shuffle and again, seizing his cap with both hands, dragged it furiously right down on his ears. Powell had lost himself in listening to these broken ravings, in looking at that old feverish face when, suddenly, quick as lightning, Mr. Smith spun round, snatched up the captain's glass and with a stifled, hurried exclamation, 'Here's luck,' tossed the liquor down his throat.

" 'I know now the meaning of the word "Consternation," ' went on Mr. Powell. 'That was exactly my state of mind. I thought to myself directly: There's nothing in that drink. I have been dreaming. I have made the awfulest mistake! . . .'

"Mr. Smith put the glass down. He stood before Powell unharmed, quieted down, in a listening attitude, his head inclined on one side, chewing his thin lips. Suddenly he blinked queerly, grabbed Powell's shoulder and collapsed, subsiding all at once as though he had gone soft all over, as a piece of silk stuff collapses. Powell seized his arm instinctively and checked his fall; but as soon as Mr. Smith was fairly on the floor he jerked himself free and backed away. Almost as quickly he rushed forward again and tried to lift up the body. But directly he raised his shoulders he knew that the man was dead! Dead!

"He lowered him down gently. He stood over him without fear or any other feeling, almost indifferent, far away, as it were. And then he made another start and, if he had not kept Mrs. Anthony always in his mind, he would have let out a yell for help. He staggered to her cabin door, and, as it was, his call for 'Captain Anthony' burst out of him much too loud; but he made a great effort of self-control. 'I am waiting for my orders, sir,' he said outside that door distinctly, in a steady tone.

"It was very still in there; still as death. Then he heard a shuffle of feet and the captain's voice 'All right. Coming.' He leaned his back against the bulkhead as you see a drunken man sometimes propped up against a wall, half doubled up. In that attitude the captain found him, when he came out, pulling the door to after him quickly. At once Anthony let his eyes run all over the cabin. Powell, without a word, clutched his forearm, led him round the end of the table and began to justify himself. 'I couldn't stop him,' he whispered shakily. 'He was too quick for me. He drank it up and fell down.' But the captain was not listening. He was looking down at Mr. Smith, thinking perhaps that it was a mere chance his own body was not lying there. They did not want to speak. They made signs to each other with their eyes. The captain grasped Powell's shoulder as if in a vise and

glanced at Mrs. Anthony's cabin door, and it was
enough. He knew that the young man understood him.
Rather! Silence! Silence for ever about this. Their very
glances became stealthy. Powell looked from the body to
the door of the dead man's state-room. The captain nodded and let him go; and then Powell crept over, hooked
the door open and crept back with fearful glances
towards Mrs. Anthony's cabin. They stooped over the
corpse. Captain Anthony lifted up the shoulders.

"Mr. Powell shuddered. 'I'll never forget that interminable journey across the saloon, step by step, holding
our breath. For part of the way the drawn half of the
curtain concealed us from view had Mrs. Anthony
opened her door; but I didn't draw a free breath till after
we laid the body down on the swinging cot. The reflection of the saloon light left most of the cabin in the
shadow. Mr. Smith's rigid, extended body looked shadowy too, shadowy and alive. You know he always carried
himself as stiff as a poker. We stood by the cot as though
waiting for him to make us a sign that he wanted to be
left alone. The captain threw his arm over my shoulder
and said in my very ear: "The steward'll find him in the
morning."

" 'I made no answer. It was for him to say. It was
perhaps the best way. It's no use talking about my
thoughts. They were not concerned with myself, nor yet
with that old man who terrified me more now than when
he was alive. Him whom I pitied was the captain. He
whispered: "I am certain of you, Mr. Powell. You had
better go on deck now. As to me . . ." and I saw him
raise his hands to his head as if distracted. But his last
words before we stole out of that cabin stick to my mind
with the very tone of his mutter—to himself, not to me—

"No! No! I am not going to stumble now over that
corpse." '

"This is what our Mr. Powell had to tell me," said
Marlow, changing his tone. "I was glad to learn that
Flora de Barral had been saved from *that* sinister shadow
at least falling upon her path.

"We sat silent then, my mind running on the end of
de Barral, on the irresistible pressure of imaginary griefs,
crushing conscience, scruples, prudence, under their

ever-expanding volume, on the sombre and venomous irony in the obsession which had mastered that old man.

" 'Well,' I said.

" 'The steward found him,' Mr. Powell roused himself. 'He went in there with a cup of tea at five and of course dropped it. I was on watch again. He reeled up to me on deck, pale as death. I had been expecting it; and yet I could hardly speak. "Go and tell the captain quietly," I managed to say. He ran off muttering "My God! My God!" and I'm hanged if he didn't get hysterical while trying to tell the captain, and start screaming in the saloon, "Fully dressed! Dead! Fully dressed!" Mrs. Anthony ran out of course but she didn't get hysterical. Franklin, who was there too, told me that she hid her face on 'the captain's breast and then he went out and left them there. It was days before Mrs. Anthony was seen on deck. The first time I spoke to her she gave me her hand and said, "My poor father was quite fond of you, Mr. Powell." She started wiping her eyes and I fled to the other side of the deck. One would like to forget all this had ever come near me.'

"But clearly he could not, because after lighting his pipe he began musing aloud: 'Very strong stuff it must have been. I wonder where he got it. It could hardly be at a common chemist. Well, he had it from somewhere— a mere pinch it must have been, no more.'

"I have my theory,' observed Marlow, "which to a certain extent does away with the added horror of a coldly premeditated crime. Chance had stepped in there too. It was not Mr. Smith who obtained the poison. It was the Great de Barral. And it was not meant for the obscure, magnanimous conqueror of Flora de Barral; it was meant for the notorious financier whose enterprises had nothing to do with magnanimity. He had his physician in his days of greatness. I even seem to remember that the man was called at the trial on some small point or other. I can imagine that de Barral went to him when he saw, as he could hardly help seeing, the possibility of a 'triumph of envious rivals'—a heavy sentence.

"I doubt if for love or even for money, but I think possibly from pity that man provided him with what Mr. Powell called 'strong stuff.' From what Powell saw of the very act I am fairly certain it must have been contained

in a capsule and that he had it about him on the last day
of his trial, perhaps secured by a stitch in his waistcoat
pocket. He didn't use it. Why? Did he think of his child
at the last moment? Was it want of courage? We can't
tell. But he found it in his clothes when he came out of
jail. It had escaped investigation if there was any. Chance
had armed him. And chance alone, the chance of Mr.
Powell's life, forced him to turn the abominable weapon
against himself.

"I imparted my theory to Mr. Powell who accepted it
at once as, in a sense, favourable to the father of Mrs.
Anthony. Then he waved his hand. 'Don't let us think
of it.'

"I acquiesced and very soon he observed dreamily—

" 'I was with Captain and Mrs. Anthony sailing all
over the world for near on six years. Almost as long as
Franklin.'

" 'Oh, yes! What about Franklin?' I asked.

"Powell smiled. 'He left the *Ferndale* a year or so
afterwards, and I took his place. Captain Anthony recommended him for a command. You don't think Captain
Anthony would chuck a man aside like an old glove. But
of course Mrs. Anthony did not like him very much. I
don't think she ever let out a whisper against him but
Captain Anthony could read her thoughts.'

"And again Powell seemed to lose himself in the past.
I asked, for suddenly the vision of the Fynes passed
through my mind,

" 'Any children?'

"Powell gave a start. 'No! No! Never had any children,' and again subsided, puffing at his short briar pipe.

" 'Where are they now?' I inquired next as if anxious
to ascertain that all Fyne's fears had been misplaced and
vain as our fears often are; that there were no undesirable cousins for his dear girls, no danger of intrusion on
their spotless home. Powell looked round at me slowly,
his pipe smouldering in his hand.

" 'Don't you know?' he uttered in a deep voice.

" 'Know what?'

" 'That the *Ferndale* was lost this four years or more.
Sunk. Collision. And Captain Anthony went down with
her.'

" 'You don't say so!' I cried quite affected as if I had

known Captain Anthony personally. 'Was—was Mrs. Anthony lost too?'

" 'You might as well ask if I was lost,' Mr. Powell rejoined so testily as to surprise me. 'You see me here—don't you?'

"He was quite huffy, but noticing my wondering stare he smoothed his ruffled plumes. And in a musing tone:

" 'Yes. Good men go out as if there was no use for them in the world. It seems as if there were things that, as the Turks say, are written. Or else fate has a try and sometimes misses its mark. You remember that close shave we had of being run down at night, I told you of, my first voyage with them. This go it was just at dawn. A flat calm and a fog thick enough to slice with a knife. Only there were no explosives on board. I was on deck and I remember the cursed, murderous thing looming up alongside and Captain Anthony (we were both on deck) calling out, "Good God! What's this! Shout for all hands, Powell, to save themselves. There's no dynamite on board now. I am going to get the wife! . . ." I yelled, all the watch on deck yelled. Crash!'

"Mr. Powell gasped at the recollection. 'It was a Belgian Green Star liner, the *Westland*,' he went on, 'commanded by one of those stop-for-nothing skippers. Flaherty was his name and I hope he will die without absolution. She cut half through the old *Ferndale* and after the blow there was a silence like death. Next I heard the captain back on deck shouting, "Set your engines slow ahead," and a howl of "Yes, yes," answering him from her forecastle; and then a whole crowd of people up there began making a row in the fog. They were throwing ropes down to us in dozens, I must say. I and the captain fastened one of them under Mrs. Anthony's arms: I remember she had a sort of dim smile on her face.

" ' "Haul up carefully," I shouted to the people on the steamer's deck. "You've got a woman on that line."

" 'The captain saw her landed up there safe. And then we made a rush round our decks to see no one was left behind. As we got back the captain says: "Here she's gone at last, Powell; the dear old thing! Run down at sea."

" ' "Indeed she is gone," I said. "But it might have

been worse. Shin up this rope, sir, for God's sake. I will steady it for you."

" ' "What are you thinking about?" he says angrily. "It isn't my turn. Up with you."

" 'These were the last words he ever spoke on earth I suppose. I knew he meant to be the last to leave his ship, so I swarmed up as quick as I could, and those damned lunatics up there grab at me from above, lug me in, drag me along aft through the row and the riot of the silliest excitement I ever did see. Somebody hails from the bridge, "Have you got them all on board?" and a dozen silly asses start yelling all together, "All saved! All saved," and then that accursed Irishman on the bridge, with me roaring "No! No!" till I thought my head would burst, rings his engines astern. He rings the engines astern—I fighting like mad to make myself heard! And of course . . .'

"I saw tears, a shower of them, fall down Mr. Powell's face. His voice broke.

" 'The *Ferndale* went down like a stone and Captain Anthony went down with her, the finest man's soul that ever left a sailor's body. I raved like a maniac, like a devil, with a lot of fools crowding round me and asking: "Aren't you the captain?"

" ' "I wasn't fit to tie the shoe-strings of the man you have drowned," I screamed at them. . . . Well! Well! I could see for myself that it was no good lowering a boat. You couldn't have seen her alongside. No use. And only think, Marlow, it was I who had to go and tell Mrs. Anthony. They had taken her down below somewhere, first-class saloon. I had to go and tell her! That Flaherty, God forgive him, comes to me as white as a sheet, "I think you are the proper person." God forgive him. I wished to die a hundred times. A lot of kind ladies, passengers, were chattering excitedly around Mrs. Anthony— a real parrot house. The ship's doctor went before me. He whispers right and left and then there falls a sudden hush. Yes, I wished myself dead. But Mrs. Anthony was a brick.'

"Here Mr. Powell fairly burst into tears. 'No one could help loving Captain Anthony. I leave you to imagine what he was to her. Yet before the week was out it was she who was helping me to pull myself together.'

" 'Is Mrs. Anthony in England now?' I asked after a while.

"He wiped his eyes without any false shame. 'Oh, yes.' He began to look for matches, and while diving for the box under the table added: 'And not very far from here either. That little village up there—you know.'

" 'No! Really! Oh, I see!'

"Mr. Powell smoked austerely, very detached. But I could not let him off like this. The sly beggar. So this was the secret of his passion for sailing about the river, the reason of his fondness for that creek.

" 'And I suppose,' I said, 'that you are still as "enthusiastic" as ever. Eh? If I were you I would just mention my enthusiasm to Mrs. Anthony. Why not?'

"He caught his falling pipe neatly. But if what the French call *effarement* was ever expressed on a human countenance it was on this occasion, testifying to his modesty, his sensibility and his innocence. He looked afraid of somebody overhearing my audacious—almost sacrilegious hint—as if there had not been a mile and a half of lonely marshland and dykes between us and the nearest human habitation. And then perhaps he remembered the soothing fact, for he allowed a gleam to light up his eyes, like the reflection of some inward fire tended in the sanctuary of his heart by a devotion as pure as that of any vestal.

"It flashed and went out. He smiled a bashful smile, sighed—

" 'Pah! Foolishness. You ought to know better,' he said, more sad than annoyed. 'But I forgot that you never knew Captain Anthony,' he added indulgently.

"I reminded him that I knew Mrs. Anthony; even before he—an old friend now—had ever set eyes on her. And as he told me that Mrs. Anthony had heard of our meetings I wondered whether she would care to see me. Mr. Powell volunteered no opinion then; but next time we lay in the creek he said, 'She will be very pleased. You had better go to-day.'

"The afternoon was well advanced before I approached the cottage. The amenity of a fine day in its decline surrounded me with a beneficent, a calming influence; I felt it in the silence of the shady lane, in the pure air, in the blue sky. It is difficult to retain the memory of the conflicts, miseries, temptations and crimes of men's self-seeking existence when one is alone with the charming serenity of the unconscious nature. Breathing the dreamless peace around the picturesque cottage I was approaching, it seemed to me that it must reign everywhere, over all the globe of water and land and in the hearts of all the dwellers on this earth.

"Flora came down to the garden gate to meet me, no longer the perversely tempting, sorrowful wisp of white mist drifting in the complicated bad dream of existence. Neither did she look like a forsaken elf. I stammered out stupidly, 'Again in the country, Miss . . . Mrs. . . .' She was very good, returned the pressure of my hand, but we were slightly embarrassed. Then we laughed a little. Then we became grave.

"I am no lover of day-breaks. You know how thin, equivocal, is the light of the dawn. But she was now her true self, she was like a fine tranquil afternoon—and not so very far advanced either. A woman not much over thirty, with a dazzling complexion and a little colour, a lot of hair, a smooth brow, a fine chin, and only the eyes of the Flora of the old days, absolutely unchanged.

"In the room into which she led me we found a Miss Somebody—I didn't catch the name—an unobtrusive, even an indistinct, middle-aged person in black. A companion. All very proper. She came and went and even sat down at times in the room, but a little apart, with some sewing. By the time she had brought in a lighted lamp I had heard all the details which really matter in this story. Between me and her who was once Flora de Barral the conversation was not likely to keep strictly to the weather.

"The lamp had a rosy shade; and its glow wreathed her in perpetual blushes, made her appear wonderfully young as she sat before me in a deep, high-backed arm-chair. I asked:

" 'Tell me what was it you said in that famous letter which so upset Mrs. Fyne, and caused little Fyne to interfere in that offensive manner?'

" 'It was simply crude,' she said earnestly. 'I was feeling reckless and I wrote recklessly. I knew she would disapprove and I wrote foolishly. It was the echo of her own stupid talk. I said that I did not love her brother, but that I had no scruples whatever in marrying him.'

"She paused, hesitating, then with a shy half-laugh:

" 'I really believed I was selling myself, Mr. Marlow. And I was proud of it. What I suffered afterwards I couldn't tell you; because I only discovered my love for my poor Roderick through agonies of rage and humiliation. I came to suspect him of despising me; but I could not put it to the test because of my father. Oh! I would not have been too proud. But I had to spare poor papa's feelings. Roderick was perfect, but I felt as though I were on the rack and not allowed even to cry out. Papa's prejudice against Roderick was my greatest grief. It was distracting. It frightened me. Oh! I have been miserable! That night when my poor father died suddenly I am certain they had some sort of discussion about me. But I did not want to hold out any longer against my own heart! I could not.'

"She stopped short, then impulsively:

" 'Truth will out, Mr. Marlow.'

" 'Yes,' I said.

"She went on musingly:

" 'Sorrow and happiness were mingled at first like darkness and light. For months I lived in a dusk of feelings. But it was quiet. It was warm. . . .'

"Again she paused, then going back in her thoughts: 'No! There was no harm in that letter. It was simply foolish. What did I know of life then? Nothing. But Mrs. Fyne ought to have known better. She wrote a letter to her brother, a little later. Years afterwards Roderick allowed me to glance at it. I found in it this sentence: "For years I tried to make a friend of that girl, but I warn you once more that she has the nature of a heartless adventuress. . . ." Adventuress!' repeated Flora slowly. 'So be it. I have had a fine adventure.'

" 'It was fine, then,' I said, interested.

" 'The finest in the world! Only think! I loved and I was loved, untroubled, at peace, without remorse, without fear. All the world, all life were transformed for me. And how much I have seen! How good people were to me! Roderick was so much liked everywhere. Yes, I have known kindness and safety. The most familiar things appeared lighted up with a new light, clothed with a loveliness I had never suspected. The sea itself! . . . You are a sailor. You have lived your life on it. But do you know how beautiful it is, how strong, how charming, how friendly, how mighty? . . .'

"I listened amazed and touched. She was silent only a little while.

" 'It was too good to last. But nothing can rob me of it now. . . . Don't think that I repine. I am not even sad now. Yes, I have been happy. But I remember also the time when I was unhappy beyond endurance, beyond desperation. Yes. You remember that. And later on, too. There was a time on board the *Ferndale* when the only moments of relief I knew were when I made Mr. Powell talk to me a little on the poop. You like him?—don't you?'

" 'Excellent fellow,' I said warmly. 'You see him often?'

" 'Of course. I hardly know another soul in the world. I am alone. And he has plenty of time on his hands. His aunt died a few years ago. He's doing nothing, I believe.'

" 'He is fond of the sea,' I remarked. 'He loves it.'

" 'He seems to have given it up,' she murmured.

" 'I wonder why?'

"She remained silent. 'Perhaps it is because he loves something else better,' I went on. 'Come, Mrs. Anthony, don't let me carry away from here the idea that you are a selfish person, hugging the memory of your past happiness, like a rich man his treasure, forgetting the poor at the gate.'

"I rose to go, for it was getting late. She got up in some agitation and went out with me into the fragrant darkness of the garden. She detained my hand for a moment, and then in the very voice of the Flora of old days, with the exact intonation, showing the old mistrust, the old doubt of herself, the old scar of the blow received in childhood, pathetic and funny, she murmured, 'Do you think it possible that he should care for me?'

" 'Just ask him yourself. You are brave.'

" 'Oh, I am brave enough,' she said with a sigh.

" 'Then do. For if you don't you will be wronging that patient man cruelly.'

"I departed, leaving her dumb. Next day, seeing Powell making preparations to go ashore, I asked him to give my regards to Mrs. Anthony. He promised he would.

" 'Listen, Powell,' I said. 'We got to know each other by chance?'

" 'Oh, quite!' he admitted, adjusting his hat.

" 'And the science of life consists in seizing every chance that presents itself,' I pursued. 'Do you believe that?'

" 'Gospel truth,' he declared innocently.

" 'Well, don't forget it.'

" 'Oh, I! I don't expect now anything to present itself,' he said, jumping ashore.

"He didn't turn up at high water. I set my sail and just as I had cast off from the bank, round the black barn, in the dusk, two figures appeared and stood silent, indistinct.

" 'Is that you, Powell?' I hailed.

" 'And Mrs. Anthony,' his voice came impressively through the silence of the great marsh. 'I am not sailing to-night. I have to see Mrs. Anthony home.'

" 'Then I must even go alone,' I cried.

"Flora's voice wished me *'bon voyage'* in a most friendly but tremulous tone.

" 'You shall hear from me before long,' shouted Powell suddenly, just as my boat had cleared the mouth of the creek.

"This was yesterday," added Marlow, lolling in the armchair lazily. "I haven't heard yet; but I expect to hear any moment. . . . What on earth are you grinning at in this sarcastic manner? I am not afraid of going to church with a friend. Hang it all, for all my belief in Chance I am not exactly a pagan. . . ."

Selected Bibliography

WORKS BY JOSEPH CONRAD

Almayer's Folly, 1895 Novel
An Outcast of the Islands, 1896 Novel
The Nigger of the "Narcissus," 1897 Novel
Tales of Unrest, 1898 Stories
Lord Jim, 1900 Novel (Signet Classic 0451-511956)
The Inheritors, 1901, with Ford Madox Ford
Heart of Darkness, 1899, 1902 Short Novel (Signet Classic 0451-516680)
"Youth," 1898, 1902 Story (*Youth, a narrative, and Two Other Stories*, 1902)
Typhoon, 1902 Short Novel (Signet Classic 0451-515013)
Typhoon and Other Tales, 1903 Stories
Romance, 1903, with Ford Madox Ford
Nostromo, 1904 Novel (Signet Classic 0451-514556)
The Mirror of the Sea, 1906 Personal impressions
The Secret Agent, 1907 Novel
A Set of Six, 1908 Stories
The Secret Sharer, 1910 Short Novel (Signet Classic 0451-516680)
Under Western Eyes, 1911 Novel

'Twixt Land and Sea, 1912 Stories
A Personal Record, 1912 Autobiography
Chance, 1913 Novel
Victory, 1915 Novel
Within the Tides, 1915 Stories
The Shadow-Line, 1917 Short Novel
The Arrow of Gold, 1919 Novel
The Rescue, 1920 Novel
Notes on Life and Letters, 1921 Reminiscences
The Rover, 1923 Novel
The Nature of a Crime, 1924 (written in 1908), with Ford
   Madox Ford
Suspense, 1925 Novel (incomplete), posthumous
Tales of Hearsay, 1925 Stories
Last Essays, 1926 Essays
The Sisters, 1928 (written in 1896, incomplete)

BIOGRAPHY AND CRITICISM

Fleishman, Avrom. *Conrad's Politics: Community and Anarchy in the Fiction of Joseph Conrad* (1967).

Guerard, Albert. *Conrad the Novelist* (1958).

Hay, Eloise Knapp. *The Political Novels of Joseph Conrad* (1963)

Leon Higdon; ed. published at Texas Tech University.

Jean-Aubry, Gerard. *Joseph Conrad: Life and Letters* (1927).

Johnson, Bruce. *Conrad's Models of Mind* (1971).

The Collected Letters of Joseph Conrad, in 8 volumes; 4 volumes have appeared. Edited by Frederick R. Karl and Laurence Davies.

Karl, Frederick R. "Conrad's Literary Theory." *Criticism,* II, 317–36.

——*A Reader's Guide to Joseph Conrad* (1906, 1969, rev.).

——"*Victory:* Its Origin and Development." *Conradiana, XV,* 23–51.

Karl, Frederick R., ed. *Joseph Conrad: A Collection of Criticism* (1975).

Karl, Frederick R. *Joseph Conrad: The Three Lives* (1979).

Krzyzanowski, Ludwik, ed. *Joseph Conrad: Centennial Essays* (1960).

Meyer, Bernard. *Joseph Conrad: A Psychoanalytic Biography* (1967).

Moser, Thomas. *Joseph Conrad: Achievement and Decline* (1957).

Mudrick, Marvin, ed. *Conrad: A Collection of Critical Essays* (1966).

Conrad's Polish Background: Letters to and from Polish Friends. ed. Zdzislaw Najder (1964).

Conrad Under Familial Eyes, ed. Zdzislaw Najder (1983).

Najder, Zdzislaw. *Joseph Conrad: A Chronicle* (1983).

Sherry, Norman. *Conrad: The Critical Heritage* (1973).

——*Conrad's Eastern World* (1966).

——*Conrad's Western World* (1971).

Stallman, Robert Wooster, ed. *The Art of Joseph Conrad: A Critical Symposium* (1960).

Watt, Ian. *Conrad in the Nineteenth Century* (1979).

Zabel, Morton Dauwen, ed. (updated by Frederick R. Karl), *The Portable Conrad* (1947, 1969, rev.).